Helen

a novel

by
Anita Mishook

BERWICK COURT PUBLISHING
CHICAGO, IL

Although this novel was inspired by actual history, the characters and events depicted in this book are fictional and any resemblence to real people is purely coincidental.

Berwick Court Publishing Company
Chicago, Illinois
http://www.berwickcourt.com

Publisher's Cataloging-In- Publication Data
(Prepared by The Donohue Group, Inc.)

Names: Mishook, Anita.
Title: Helen : a novel / by Anita Mishook.
Description: Chicago, IL : Berwick Court Publishing, [2016]
Identifiers: LCCN 2016912633 | ISBN 978-1-944376-03-1
| ISBN 978-1-944376-04-8 (ebook)
Subjects: LCSH: Jewish women-- California-- History-- 20th century-- Fiction.
  | Silver Shirts of America (Organization)-- History-- 20th century--
  Fiction. | Nazis-- California-- History-- 20th century-- Fiction. | Anti-
  defamation League-- History-- 20th century-- Fiction. | Women spies--
  Fiction. | Jewish fiction. | LCGFT: Historical fiction.
Classification: LCC PS3613.I84 H45 2016 | DDC 813/.6-- dc23

1

A DEEP GOUGE OF DANK, WORM-INFESTED earth had been clawed into the ground in front of her, waiting like an open wolf's mouth to catch her if she fell. Moaning faceless figures, wrapped in black wool cloaks, jostled and bumped her ever closer to the pit. Then she was alone, her head whipping around and seeing nothing but sodden, grey sky.

Like a blind girl, Helen stabbed her hand out in every direction, finally feeling the feathery shock of real cloth. Heart pounding, she blinked her eyes open, bringing into focus curtains with a print of overly-bright carousel horses set against the sharp white of the wall.

The nightmare was her personal *dybbuk* carried out of Poland. The demon's icy fingers grabbed and twisted her sleep much less now than when she was six, but the lonely transcontinental train trip had revived it.

Pushing herself up onto her elbows, she breathed deeply, then rolled onto her back and stared up at the nubby stucco ceiling a yard above her head. Her nephew's bunk bed in Glendale—that's where she was. She sucked in another lung full of California air and let it out between pursed lips.

As she kicked the thin quilt off her legs, she said, "Los Angeles," careful to make the "g" soft, the way she had heard on the radio. Then she murmured, "Hollywood," the word tweaking her mouth into a smile.

Helen sat up, testing how much she could straighten her back before bumping her head. At least she'd learned that from the Pullman car. Swinging her long pajama-clad legs over the side, she half-slid, half-stepped onto the mattress of the bottom bunk and then onto the floor.

She fumbled through the dirty clothes in her suitcase, which lay on a twisted rag rug whose colors echoed the merry-go-round print of the curtains, sharp sapphire blue, the deep brownish-red of overripe apples, and a walked-on white. Wrinkling her nose against the stain and smell of other people's cigarettes that had crept into the fibers of her chenille robe, she put it on and opened the bedroom door.

Was Harry still home or had he gone to his liquor store already? She'd rather not start her first day listening to the Long Island nasality of his voice while trying to drink a cup of coffee.

Across the hall, she saw her sister, Sarah, standing at the kitchen stove. It was an O'Keefe and Merritt, one of its burners occupied with a black enamel saucepan, which Sarah stirred, balancing six-month-old Rachel on one hip. Sarah had written Helen the day the stove was delivered to show her how well Harry was taking care of his family. Helen had sighed and dropped the letter into the trash can.

Sarah wore a white cotton blouse, ironed creaseless, except where it was tucked into the calf-length black skirt or where Rachel clutched a fistful of fabric. Her fading titian hair with greying strands across her temples, like the feathers of a molting bird, was caught up in a bun at her neck. But, at thirty-three, mother of two, she still had the figure for a bathing suit on the beach at Coney Island.

Sarah could have had her pick of suitors. So why Harry? Helen had known that her sister would marry someone, sometime, and leave her to her own fate, but she didn't expect Sarah to marry a gnome with ties to Long Island crime.

Ben, the three-year-old, sat in a wooden high chair, with decals of circus animals plastered on its legs and the seat back, seals with multicolored balls, an all-white horse, with a bright red saddle, a single leg held high like a dancing girl. A yellow-maned lion leaped through a ring of tangerine and red fire just above Ben's head, giving him the aura of a center-ring angel.

"Good, you're up," Sarah said, as if the phrase was a single word and without turning around. "Take her."

Helen walked over and swung Rachel onto her own hip, feeling the baby's heft settling against her bone. Rachel looked stunned and began to suck in air through her nose with a whistling sound, preparing for a howl, throwing herself backwards against Helen's forearm.

Helen jiggled her at a fox trot pace, taking Rachel's clenched right fist into her left hand, and making "mmm" noises. After a snuffle, Rachel leaned forward, burying her face briefly in the musty chenille.

"Sleep?" Sarah asked.

Helen knew the cadence, abbreviations, elisions, and stammer of Sarah's American speech, which reduced verbal communication to its essence and then added on staccato, intonation, and anger to make its points. Still, Sarah never retreated to any other language she knew, Yiddish or Polish or German or Russian, unless she was desperate; never retreated to the world before she was fourteen unless dragged there by an undertow of illness or pennilessness or worse. It was only American radio, American newspapers, American food.

"Yes, fine."

"Cream of Wheat. You feed Ben. Bottles in the…" Sarah waved toward the refrigerator.

"Refrigerator?" Helen asked.

Sarah nodded. "For Rachel. Whole milk, extra cream. Warm them." She pointed to her wrist, "Not too hot."

"Yeah. Test it on my wrist. Sarah, I got to pee. Take a shower. I got to get dressed." Helen raised her left arm, sniffed under it, wrinkling her nose and making a "phew" sound.

She shook her head and winked at Ben, who smiled. "Phew," he said.

And, she thought, I need to know more than just where the milk is, which I could figure out on my own. Where am I? Where's the city?

"Go," Sarah nodded down the hall. Helen remembered the bathroom at 2:00 a.m., suitcase dropped on the hall carpet and slid into the bedroom, pulling down her underpants to sit on the cold seat, then changing into pajamas in the dark and clambering up to the top bunk, like an overgrown child, almost stepping on Ben's sleeping face. As Helen turned she saw Sarah slap a ladle full of Cream of Wheat into a Roy Rogers cereal bowl then set it down gentle as a kiss in front of her son.

After a quick, hot shower, Helen looked at herself in the oval mirror, with its filigreed frosty glass border, that hung over the sink. There were smudgy circles under her eyes, but otherwise her skin was like Rachel's milk with extra cream, cheeks a pale rose from the heat of the shower, her lips naturally bowed and so pink she hardly ever wore lipstick. She gathered her thick, butterscotch blonde hair with both hands at the nape of her neck, then worked it into a French twist. She jabbed in bobby pins strategically, but a lock of hair slid out, curving behind her ear.

While other women chopped their hair into fashionable, ear-length bobs, Helen enjoyed the length of her hair and the weight of it on her head. She loved its lack of fashion, much like a rag doll from childhood might be loved and given a place of honor on sateen bed sheets.

Dabbing Pepsodent on her index finger, she rubbed at her upper and lower front teeth, then her molars, just as her health and PE teachers had taught her. She had straight, white teeth, her smile as innocently seductive as those in the ads on the subway, teeth that should dazzle men in suits and ties, with futures stretching out before them like the highways they'd drive their Fords on, wife and children at their side.

Helen returned to the kitchen in gray slacks and a short-sleeved brown sweater, both urgently needing dry cleaning, so far as she was concerned, to find Sarah sitting, her right hand dabbing tepid cereal onto a small spoon and sweeping it into Rachel's open mouth. The baby was curlicued onto her mother's lap.

When she saw Helen, Sarah wiped Rachel's face with a dish towel and put her on the blanket that lay on the white-and-red-checkered linoleum floor. Ben was banging a spoon against the table's wooden leg and humming to himself.

"Diapers in the baby room, changing table." Sarah walked over to the kitchen counter, its space crowded with boxes and cans, and picked up a piece of paper.

"We are here." She pointed to the address on the paper. "You can walk around. Is safe. Take babies to the backyard if you don't want to go out there." Nodding vaguely in the direction of the front door to signify where "out there" was, Sarah put a set of house keys on top of the paper.

Then she turned and manacled her fingers around Helen's wrist as if imprisoning Helen's attention as well as her arm. Helen could almost feel the wind off the bow of the ship, the roll of the waves; she was eight again, Sarah, sixteen, her hand roping Helen to her.

Sarah's grip, like the rest of her, had hardened over that

journey. As the port of Amsterdam fell over the horizon, Helen had turned to Sarah and said, "Now I can't remember what Momma looked like."

And Sarah had replied, "I have a photograph." That was the last full exchange in Yiddish between them that Helen could remember.

"Phone number of store." Helen looked down at the paper again, where Sarah had written the store's full exchange name and number in the Europeanized fashion, hatching her sevens.

"Where's the phone?"

Sarah pointed into the hall, where Helen could see the narrow alcove, the squat, frog-like black Bell phone sitting on its small perch. Helen was reluctantly impressed at the extravagance. In Brooklyn, a telephone call was a boot-wearing, change-gathering journey to wherever you could find a public telephone, coins at the ready to fend off the terminal operator's voice saying, "Your time is up. Please insert another dime." The phone in the hall was a journey into the future, which was right here in her sister's bungalow.

"I don't understand why I don't go to work at Harry's liquor store and you stay here and take care of the children, Sarah. Wouldn't that be better for them? If it's the money," Helen paused, sucked in her lower lip and nibbled up and down before continuing, "I won't ask for much, really, and I'll pay you rent."

"No. This way is better." Sarah's voice was firm, but her fingers and palm cooled around Helen's wrist, then flew off and around her coffee cup.

"Okay for now. But I won't do this forever."

"Yeah, it's fine. Six months, like we said. You stay here then I find someone else and you go."

Sarah stared into the coffee cup as if there were tea leaves there and an answer was just about to appear. Even Ben's spoon percussion, which he had moved onto the floor close to Rachel's head, failed to rouse her.

Helen had never known Sarah to talk about being afraid, only to get cold and silent, like the statue of *The Old Woman* at the Met, with her bleak, marble stare.

"What is going on?" Helen touched her sister's hand.

Sarah looked up and shook her head. "Nothing. I am happy you are here."

After Sarah shut the front door, Helen stood fingering the house keys. At the breakfast table, Sarah had sat with that white-washing smile on her face, saying how happy she was that Helen was there at last. Then, tucking her blouse into her waistband, where Rachel had tugged it out, she kissed the children and abruptly left the house. She would need to work the problem out of her sister like a splinter deep in a thumb, with care and a sharp needle.

She walked Ben to the bathroom and counted out the sides of the hexagonal tiles on the floor and the subway tiles around the bath and shower combination to him while she washed his face and hands and helped him to balance on the short stool while he tried to aim into the toilet and not onto his pants. She returned to Rachel, still lying on the kitchen floor and waving her hands in the air.

"Rachel, little sweetie, let's change that diaper." She waltzed her niece down the hall and past Sarah and Harry's bedroom.

The pillows were fluffed, the red plaid wool blanket pulled up snugly over the double bed centered on the longest wall. In the next bedroom, a pale oak crib, side dropped to retrieve Rachel easily, was pressed against the outside wall, partly blocking a window with the shade drawn down. There was a matching changing table. Instead of brightening the room, the yellow shade dulled the morning light and sallowed Rachel's skin, making her look unwell.

Rachel was a baby who liked to have her diaper changed. That was clear from her smile and her patient, almost languourous sigh as Sarah cleaned her bottom and put the clean diaper and rubber panties on her. Then she grabbed a pair of what were clearly Ben's pants from "three months to six months" and a little t-shirt and dressed her. Ben wandered into the room and stared at her.

"How about a little walk?" she asked.

Helen wanted to walk a hundred miles after her train ride across the country. It had taken her from New York to Chicago to Los Angeles. Her fellow passengers had commented on the pleasant sway of the train cars, but Helen had steeled herself against the lurching, afraid of a roller-coaster effect like the ship on high, rough seas. Solid, stable ground was what she wanted.

Helen had faded out of her night school classes. Her bookkeeping job, the endless subway stairs up and down in a thin winter coat, and canned soup dinners all contributed to her ghostly demise as an NYCC part-time student. If she thought about it, which she tried not to do, she knew she had voluntarily given up on that specific ladder into the American world of Fifth Avenue department stores and lunches in restaurants climbed by almost every Jew who made it in the city.

When Sandor had given her a copy of Sinclair Lewis's *It Can't Happen Here*, she'd looked at the cover, thumbed through the first chapter, and placed it on her nightstand. It was his going away present to her, a single book plucked from the pyramid of books that dominated the window of the bookshop where he worked on a schedule so erratic it was hard to call it "part-time."

She knew the book was a best seller, but she didn't care. Something about an American fascist president, she'd heard.

It was almost too much—talk of Nazism in Germany, the Jewish Frenchman Blum whose beaten face had just adorned the front cover of *Time* magazine, problems in California, the acrid dust from the Midwest drought that had drifted all the way into New York, and the never ending Depression trapping her in a dead-end bookkeeping job. Like dirty dishwater into the drain, 1935 had slid into 1936.

"I'm telling you, Helen," Sandor's cigarette-breath in her ear, "I'm telling you not to go."

Three postcards from Sarah were pinned to the wall above the single bed, orange blossomed, blue-skied, and aromatic with promise. She and Sandy sat in her fifth-floor walk- up, with a tub in the kitchen, a view of the graying stones of the building next door, and the aroma of cooking cabbage in the hallways.

"I'll be okay, Sandy." She patted his arm and handed him the last bottle of beer.

"Look, at the ADL we know things."

"What could the Anti-Defamation League possibly see as a problem in California?" She puffed up each word as she said it. Sandy was inordinately secretive about whatever it was that he did for them.

"It's not so good in California."

"And it's so great here? Look at those postcards, Sandy, for crying out loud. And my sister and brother-in-law have a house with a backyard."

Sandy shrugged, his shoulders reaching up toward his

chiseled chin and topaz eyes. "Yeah, okay," he said in the perfectly unaccented American English he'd acquired as part of his actor's repertoire.

He kissed her on the cheek. Their kisses had reversed what she viewed as the natural order of passion.

When they'd first acted on the growing attraction between them three months before, in the alley in back of the cafeteria after the political discussion had heated everyone to a boil, they'd kissed ceaselessly for well over ten minutes. When they did separate, her lips were sore and her cheeks steamed in the frigid outdoor air.

They had three dates after that, followed by Sandy's disappearance and re-appearance in two and four day segments over the next six weeks. "Work," he'd said.

"What? Are you acting?" If he was, she wanted to see him doing Brecht, or Shakespeare, or anything at all. How would those honey-colored eyes seem from the audience? And his aquiline nose, noble, European, kingly even—how would that play?

"Mmmm," he said, reaching over her for another bottle of Budweiser. "Want to see a movie?"

Acting, and its many guises, Sandy told Helen, had captured him as an eight year old, when his father took him to the Grand Theater. Sandy couldn't remember the name of the play, but the audience's roars of delight, moans, and the tearfulness of the women around him tattooed the experience on his young mind.

For weeks after that he hopped onto a kitchen chair

to perform his own version of "The Tortoise and The Hare," complete with voice changes for the tedious turtle and his fleet, but distractible, racing foe.

He pestered his father to take him to another play. For his ninth birthday, he was rewarded with a trip to see the Yiddish version of *A Midsummer Night's Dream.* Thereafter, he'd focused on a career in acting the way a miner focuses on the exit out of the tunnel.

When Sarah sent the letter asking her to come to California, Helen began to worry. The perfect weather, the backyard, the children who needed someone to stay with them now that Rachel was five months old, how Harry needed Sarah back in the liquor store right now, how Helen could use the opportunity to "look around." All of this was written in Sarah's elegant middle-European cursive, so grammatically flawed and poorly spelled in English.

Sarah had worked from the day they got to New York, while Helen went to grade school, then junior high school and high school. The summer between Helen's eleventh and twelfth grade, Sarah had married Harry. And, in that senior year of high school, Helen had counted every day until her sister and her rat-spouse would scamper to California, as promised. It was impossible to explain this history to Sandy; it was like trying to explain the sky.

Helen and Sandy sat in the cafeteria where they'd met and she told him she had her train ticket. As he left, he'd leaned his six-foot-tall body over the table, his muscled arms taut against the wooden top, his eyes focused on hers, and kissed her lightly on the lips. After that, the kisses were sedate and brotherly, even if she moved her face to catch his lips on hers.

Helen worried that she would be considered a migrant, maybe even mistaken for an Okie, because she did not have a "real job" to go to and because she had the slightest accent, still, when she was stressed. Who knew what an Okie looked or sounded like, except for grainy photographs in the newspaper; she did not, nor did her friends.

So, she had worn her very best clothes on the train, a tweed pencil skirt, a brown cardigan sweater and matching short sleeved pull-over, or loose legged trousers, with cream, rose, and dark blue satiny blouses with cap sleeves and little rounded collars, folding each of the three blouses back into her suitcase as if for display at Gimble's, as she rotated them daily.

She sat in her seat, with her knees pressed together, straightening her back every time any man in a train uniform walked by her, even the Pullman porters. On her lap, like a baby, she held Sandy's only gift to her, as the train pulled out of Grand Central Station. Then she reached for her suitcase, shoved *It Can't Happen Here* deep inside, and grabbed *Silver Screen* and *Life* out of her valise.

Helen focused her voice to produce her cleanest American accent whenever spoken to, and whispered, "Yes, I am going to Los Angeles and then to Glendale," practicing the phrase to make the response automatic. When he asked how she was, she blurted it out to the young Bum Blockade cop, who looked at her, patted her hand, and said, "It's okay, Miss. We're after people sneaking in without, you know….what it takes to get by these days." Money, a job, an education, what it took to get by.

At the "Bum Blockade" stop at the railroad station in San Bernardino, the Los Angeles police, bulky and black-booted, opened up the baggage car and tossed luggage around. She felt as much as heard the deadened thumps in her passenger car, as the police scrambled on top of the train, like so many hungry cats, looking for "tramps and vagrants," as the blue-uniformed barely mustached officer had told her.

Back in New York, Helen's New York City College night school friends had discussed Frank Shaw, mayor of Los Angeles, with his plots to keep migrants out of the city. They bandied about words like *fascism*, *anti-proletariat*, *totalitarian*, and *un-American*, until at last everyone put down their coffee cups or dropped their empty beer bottles into the trash and went home.

Glad for the company and something to do on a winter night that did not cost much money, Helen went to the cafeteria and listened. But she was bored, which masked her irritation that she had never read Sinclair Lewis or heard of Upton Sinclair and could not keep Trotsky's positions separate from Lenin's in her head.

She shook as she left the train, grateful if only just this once for Harry, who pointed a porter toward her bag, took her arm, and escorted through the train station to the waiting car.

The baby stroller was by the front door, as was Ben's harness, draped over the front door handle. In one of Sarah's few letters before the request that she come to California, she'd described her son as running everywhere with such energy that she was afraid to hold his hand for fear he'd pull his arm right out of the socket, and yet was equally afraid he might leap into the street and be hit by a car.

So, Sarah wrote, she had searched around, asked the women who came into the liquor store—not those buying liquor, but those in for cigarettes or soda pop or the newspaper—for advice. One had recommended a leash, like for a dog. It seemed terrible, but it worked well. She'd sewn a sleeveless jacket out of denim, with a sturdy zipper in the front then grommeted the leash right onto the back.

Outside the air was warm and breezy, like a fan turned on low. A faint scent sweetened the air, as though a woman had passed by and vanished, leaving only her perfume. It seemed to come from a plant with emerald green leaves and just three tightly wrapped flowers, the color of fine white china, planted by the front step. The unclouded baby blue sky was all around, not crammed into pocket park spaces or sliced into vertical strips by high, dark, stone buildings. Even in her archive of childhood memories, taken out with the tenderness that their fragility warranted, she never saw a sky unchained from buildings.

Every house on the block, each painted a different muted tone of sage or gray, was just one story high, with a velvet green lawn, a deep front porch, and a door, always wood with a small geometrical glass inset for the peep-window, flanked by symmetrical windows.

Helen was astounded by the treasure of land and space. Glendale was the fastest growing city in the United States, or so its promotional ads said. Sunshine, homes, and the opportunities of California, those had been important to Harry and Sarah. More important than being with Helen for her last year of high school or giving her a home so she could go to college and not work full-time.

Helen had heard them argue about the move. She'd heard the thud of a fist on a door. She'd heard Harry shout. Then she heard Sarah tell her they were leaving.

Spying a stop sign at the intersection on her right about a half-dozen homes up the block, Helen turned the stroller in that direction and gave Ben a little tug. She began to walk.

Jewel City Dry Cleaning and Tailoring caught Helen's eye in the array of retail signage and she crossed the street, dancing the stroller wheels on tip toes off the curb and then up the other side. Ben, like a short-legged indoor dog eager to be walked at any opportunity, kept pace with her waltz.

She pushed open the door and started in, the heat and slight steam of pressed pants offering a perspiration-inducing greeting. On the customer side of the counter, a slim, dark-haired man stood, leaning on one navy blazer-clad elbow, and chatting with the much older woman on the other side. He stepped over to the door and held it for her with one hand, pushing slightly against the front wheels of the stroller with one shiny black leather shoe. With that, Helen entered the store, complete with entourage.

"Please," he said. Outside of the movies and Sandy's acting, Helen had never heard a voice so free of any accent. Even her friends born in New York were marked as New Yorkers by their sound.

"Go ahead and take care of her, Elsa," he said to the woman behind the counter. "Any mom out on her daily errands, well....." he trailed off, as if the importance of that was too obvious to mention, and his reasons for being in the cleaners too trivial to bear thought.

"Oh, no," Helen said, "I'm the aunt, just here for a visit." She looked at Elsa, "I have some clothes that need to be cleaned. Could you tell me how much?"

Elsa waved Helen over. "Here," she said, pointing down to a price list on the counter.

Helen heard a German accent.

"I don't mean to be forward," said the man. "I'm Joe Miller. Elsa has the best cleaning establishment in town." His gaze drifted to Helen's left hand then bounced back up to her face.

At that, Elsa chuckled. "Of course," she said, the words coming out guttural.

"Helen. Visiting family. I'm from New York." Her voice was crisp and clean.

Joe reached over, his hand out. His grip was solid, his palm warm against hers, his smile polite. He was, Helen thought, good looking in a not-movie-star way, in a good-enough way.

"Nice to meet you, Helen from New York. And these are?"

"My niece and nephew."

"So, Helen," Joe lowered and released her hand as if he were giving her a delicate flower to hold in her palm. He turned back to Elsa, "When will my suits and shirts be ready?"

"Tomorrow after noon."

"OK. I'll be back around noon. Unless you get them done sooner, Elsa, in which case call me."

Joe smiled more broadly than before as if charmed with the idea of again entering the Jewel City Dry Cleaning and Tailoring store.

He turned to Helen, adding, after half-a-heartbeat, "And I hope I'll see you around."

A warm flush seeped into Helen's cheeks and she was relieved when he turned, opened the door and walked out.

The waves at Coney Island had that same unsettling effect on her, lifting her without her permission, then setting her back down again on shifting sands and leaving her to walk back to shore against the water pulling out to sea. She hated the ocean, but would never want Sarah or, later, her friends, to know that.

The amusement park at Coney Island terrified her with its distorting mirrors and clowns raised to eight feet tall by stilts under their primary-colored legs. For a nine-year-old just off the boat, "real" was hard enough to deal with.

"You scream more from this than from dentist. I treat you to this and you cry." Sarah spat out the words, her nine hour work day and long commute like a weight around both their ankles.

Ben tugged at his leash. "Go walk," he said, pointing out the door.

"Thank you for the information," Helen said to Elsa, who nodded and turned away.

Helen fed the children, Ben at the table with leftover chicken she found in the refrigerator, sniffed at, and reheated, Rachel from the bottle with warmed, extra-rich milk. Before she put Ben down for his nap, she dragged her suitcase into the living room and, as both children slept, sorted through the pile of clothes, taking out the clothes to be dry-cleaned. She needed to settle in.

She filled the washer-ringer with warm water and a half-cup of Tide, into which she threw her underwear, stockings, three white cotton shirts, one beige linen skirt, and one pair of shorts. The two print cotton dresses, one purchased at Macy's Department Store with half her weekly bookkeeping salary went in too.

Secretly Helen hoped that the beige skirt would bleed onto at least one of the old shirts so she could justify buying a new one. She ran the washer. One at a time she put each piece through the wringer and into the laundry basket. She stepped outside into sunshine so bright and liquid it seemed to puddle around her feet. Then she consigned her clothes, pin by pin, to the line, where they hung, saluting her first day in California.

When Sarah and Harry walked in the door at seven, Helen had clean clothes on, Rachel and Ben were fed, Rachel was sleeping, Ben was eating a little ice cream at the table, and the stewing beef she'd found in the fridge was simmering on the stove with potatoes and carrots. As successful as she felt her day had been, Helen felt the half glass of milk she'd drunk at six begin to curdle in stomach acid as she stood to say hello to Harry.

Harry was a bulldog of a man: squared off, armored across the chest with muscles, arms and legs sausaged into shirts and slacks. He was an inch shorter than Sarah, and a resentment-filled two inches shorter than Helen. Whenever he stood close enough to Helen to have to raise his gaze to meet hers, even by the slightest fraction of an angle, he glowered for a second as if someone had placed his head in a vise and then twisted it up.

"Why Harry?" Helen had asked when Sarah told her she'd accepted his proposal.

"I love him," she'd replied, voice off-key, as if she'd meant to hit the note but hit its flat counterpart instead.

Helen had ground her teeth together, waiting.

"He's safe."

"For whom is he safe?"

"For me. He's safe for me."

"As long as you're on his side," Helen said.

Sarah nodded. "I'm on his side."

Harry offered Helen a tight smile. "We're so happy to have you here," he said. "I hope you've found the house to your liking." He walked up and air-kissed her on the cheek, touching her arm lightly as a fly wing with his hand.

He kissed Ben on the top of his head as Ben smiled up at him and uttered, "Daddy." Then Harry looked around. Helen pointed up the hall toward the closed door to Rachel's room. He nodded. The odor of cigarette smoke following him, he went down the hall, entered his bedroom, and closed the door.

Sarah busied herself in the kitchen putting out wine-colored earthenware plates for dinner. Helen knew her sister would be quiet until spoken to.

"How was the first day back at the store?"

"Good."

"Yeah?" Helen envisioned day after day of this rhythm of monosyllables and deadening thunks after each reply.

"I miss the babies," Sarah said, glancing up the hall toward her still closed bedroom door. "And Harry is mad when I do not speak so well to the customers. He needs...." She waved her hand as if shooing a cat away.

"So, tell him, Sarah, that I'll work there. And, I know bookkeeping."

Sarah heaped one plate with steaming stew, ladling white potatoes, carrots, and beef until the juices started to brim over, and Helen had to take it from her and put it at Harry's place.

"You are too stubborn," she whispered to Helen.

When Helen was five years old, she sat down in the middle of Moses Carnofsky's general store and would not move, digging her heels into the wooden planks of the floor when mother tried to drag her out, all other blandishments having failed. And why? Because she wanted a few inches of pink ribbon for her pigtails.

Sarah had been furious when mother relented. But Helen tried to fix it on Sarah's thirteenth birthday: a smile, the ribbons, squished in her hand and already worn to school, a birthday kiss, and a barely audible "I'll share."

Sarah sighed. "You don't like him."

"Harry brings problems like a mattress with bedbugs wherever he goes, but I'll manage."

"Things… go on…"

"Sarah, I'm not surprised. What worries you?" Uneasiness cocooned around her sister like a heavy coat and thick gloves.

Sarah shrugged. "No, it is maybe only my…"

"Imagination?"

Nodding, Sarah sighed, "Okay. I will talk to him."

By nine that night, Helen felt as if something was dragging her eyelids shut, like window shades. She said goodnight to Sarah and to Harry, who'd uttered scattered monosyllables at the table and then gone into the living room with a glass of scotch and turned on the radio.

"Ask him."

"Later. I know him. Later is better."

Harry's raised voice jarred Helen from her sleep like a slap across her face. She almost sat up until she remembered she was in the top bunk of Ben's bed.

"…useless, just useless to me."

She listened, not breathing in case the sound muffled Sarah's response. Still she heard nothing.

"Fine." A pause, then, "I don't care if I wake the children."

A very long pause, during which time Helen breathed quietly so as not to ruffle the air or wake Ben. Then, rhythmic thumps that traveled like the ripples of a stream through the walls.

Helen lay with her eyes closed until her thoughts became sloppy and unformed and she fell back to sleep.

2

"SO, I UNDERSTAND YOU'D RATHER work at the liquor store than take care of the house and children," Harry declared, his pale blue eyes fixed on the *Los Angeles Times*' front page.

Sarah stood at the stove, with her back to Harry, her head tilted toward the pot of oatmeal, her oven-mitted hand gripping the percolator. The dark, burnt aroma of coffee mixed with the smoke from Harry's Lucky Strike.

"Yes."

"You can start Monday."

Helen thought of her diminished, musty wardrobe. She'd need to walk the children back over to Jewel City Dry Cleaning today, this morning if possible. Maybe they could rush the job.

"Sure. Do you want me to help with the books, too?"

Sarah came over with the coffee, her hand trembling as if with the weight. When she reached Helen, she gave her sister a slight kick in the left shin, a "shut up" signal from Helen's abbreviated childhood on.

Helen recalibrated. "Never mind, Harry. You'll let me know what to do."

"Yeah. Fine. You almost ready, Sarah?" He glared over Helen's head at his wife, who removed her apron, hung it over the oven handle, smoothed her skirt, and nodded.

By mid-morning, Helen had dressed Ben and Rachel, given them a snack, and promised them a high adventure on the walk. She gathered her dry-cleanable wardrobe in a pillow case—three pullover sweaters, one cardigan, two pencil skirts, the trousers— and wore one of her two cotton dresses, starched and ironed.

When they emerged onto the sidewalk, she sighed and looked at the warm spring California sky. To walk bare armed in late March was heavenly.

She'd always thought of winter in shades of grays and whites and early spring as slush. But the walk today seemed like one through a landscaped park, with flowers whose names she did not know offering dense hot pink and tomato red petals. Against a wall, the one vine whose flowers she recognized as bougainvillea draped still-closed orange and yellow blooms against emerald green leaves.

She felt like Dorothy landing in Oz. That was one of the first books she had checked out of the library and read. Now she realized that she and Dorothy had much in common as displaced, orphaned immigrants.

She pushed open the door to the dry cleaners, shoved the stroller through the opening. Blocking the door's backward swing with her hip, she worked herself and Ben in as well. Putting the bag of dry cleaning on the counter, she tapped the bell. Elsa emerged from the rear of the store.

"Ah, you are back," she said.

"I need these cleaned, rush, if possible and if it doesn't cost too much." Surely Sarah wouldn't mind walking over to pick them up on Tuesday, she thought.

"Sure, sure."

Elsa began to tally up the items, her pencil moving down the small pad of paper, hatching sevens. Behind Helen, the door opened.

"Well, hello again."

Helen turned to see Joe Miller standing there, wearing gray slacks, and a white shirt rolled up to the elbows.

"Thanks for calling me about the clothes, Elsa. Tomorrow is…" He stopped and smiled, "you know, it's a big day. So it's a relief to have them done."

Elsa nodded and retreated to the rear of the building.

"Helen? That's right, isn't it? May I ask your whole name?" Joe said.

"Helen Rice." That surname had been good enough for Immigration when Sarah had offered it and it had stayed good enough for Helen.

"Helen, I don't mean to be forward. It just seems so lucky that I ran into you again. Would you like to go to the movies with me? Tonight?" He spoke in a hushed, rapid tone.

Elsa came back with an arm-load of silvery shirts. She hung them on a clothes bar at the counter and then retreated again.

"Do you wear all these shirts?" Helen asked, while she balanced Sarah, Harry, and whatever the night might hold against a possible late night movie with a strange man.

Joe shook his head and laughed. "They're for Metro-Goldwyn-Mayer, where I work. They're parts of costumes."

"Don't they have their own cleaners?" She smiled. Her second real day in California and she had already met someone with a job in the movie business. Slowly, still smiling, she lifted her right hand toward her hair and brushed a lock back from her face. His eyes followed her hand then settled on her lips.

"Sometimes that just doesn't happen." His lips continued to smile but his eyes did not.

"Oh." She paused. "Anyhow, about the movie. I need to see

what my sister and brother-in-law have in mind for tonight. So, could you call about seven?"

"What's the number?"

She recited the Dunkirk exchange and the digits from memory. She'd put the paper on which Sarah's phone number and address were written into her purse as a talisman against getting lost, but she didn't need it.

Joe scribbled the phone number on the back of his cleaning bill with a pencil he grabbed from Elsa's counter. When Elsa returned with two suits, and a slight frown on her face, he gathered all the clothes together, murmured that he'd call that night, and exited.

As she pushed Rachel's stroller and gently tugged at Ben to keep him walking along with her, she thought about Joe Miller of M-G-M. She and the children turned up the walk to the house, impeccable in its middle-classness, indistinguishable from any other house on the street, not even a mezuzah on the door.

Sarah raised an eyebrow and pursed her lips when Helen announced that she was going out on a date that night. In response, Helen felt a band of tense resentment creep up her neck and around her forehead, beginning to press on just the spot that would trigger a headache. Still, she was determined to sidestep any confrontation, any debate over her role, her position in the home, her right to make that kind of decision for herself, any echo of the old, stale argument that had never ended but simply gone to a different verse, the chorus for which was "You are not my mother. But I will do what you want."

"Let her have some fun." Harry's voice inserted itself between the two women from the living room, where he sat with his second shot of whiskey.

Tomorrow would be his only day off because of the blue laws. Otherwise, Helen was certain he would have been at the liquor store from eight to six just like today. He was getting a quick start on his Saturday night relaxation. The Zenith, perched on the side-table, was tuned to *Your Hit Parade*. Harry's feet were propped on the red upholstered ottoman, and the open bottle of Teacher's Highland Cream was on the fireplace mantel.

"Sure, sure." Sarah narrowed her eyes as if contemplating her options. Seeing none but agreement, she nodded, turned on her heel and walked toward Ben's bedroom door.

Helen pursed her lips. Even though Sarah walked away, Helen knew what she was thinking; she'd shared it so many times in letters. Thank heavens Sarah wouldn't put the words on a postcard for others to read, or Helen would never have pinned the California scenes to her wall.

"You should be married. You don't date a guy more than three or four times before dropping him. You've got looks, taste, and the intelligence to marry a doctor or a lawyer, but you hide in your apartment. And that actor, Sandor? His looks are no substitute for a steady job. What is wrong with you?"

Yes, that's what Sarah's steps and her stiff back said.

"Have fun," Sarah called out as she shut the door firmly behind her. Ben's squeal of pleasure at seeing his mother seeped into the hall. Helen knew she wouldn't see Sarah until the next morning.

"On Monday," Harry began, "you can walk with me to the store. It'll take about twenty minutes. No rain, no ice patches." His lips tipped up, trying to smile. "You can wear that. The customers will like it."

She'd put on the second of her cotton dresses, this one in tea-leaf brown, with a fitted bodice nipped by a belt at her waist and then falling to just below her knees.

"It's attractive," he continued in a neutral voice. "We have men."

"It's a liquor store, Harry, so I figured, yeah, men."

Harry raised his shoulders in the slightest hint of a shrug. "We can do that or not."

"Sorry." Helen stood between the dining room and the living room, leaning up against the wall. The entire interaction with Harry caught her by surprise, from his defense of her date to his refusal to engage with her sarcasm, her well-honed weapon in years past with him. "Sarcasm, from the Greek 'to tear the flesh,'" Sandy had said to her after their only fight.

The telephone rang, a bleating rasp that sent Helen scurrying to answer.

"Yes, Joe." He offered to pick her up in an hour. "That'll be fine."

At 7:45 exactly there was a quick, firm knock on the door.

Harry removed his feet from the ottoman, held his hand up to signal that he'd get the door, walked over, unlatched the lock, and acted the host.

Joe stood there, dangling car keys loosely from his finger. He switched them and held out his hand to Harry.

"Joe Miller."

"Harry Forester." Helen was surprised. Sarah had never written her that Harry was using a different last name. Is that what happened in California? You had no past you had to take with you and you could just pluck up a new present and move on?

"Of Forester Liquor?"

"Yes," Harry stood aside and waved Joe into the living room. "You know it?"

"I pass it every day. I hear from friends you have a wonderful selection of scotch and imported beers."

"We try."

"Great. I've been looking for a particular German ale."

"A little harder to get these days with all the…."

"Yes." Joe continued, "But I'd be willing to pay what it took." He turned toward Helen and said, "You look great. Enough talk about booze. Harry, good to meet you. I'll have her home by eleven."

Joe stood back from the door, waited for Helen to move onto the porch and then stepped out. "Your carriage, Madame," he said, pointing to the Ford coupe at the curb.

The car was cobalt blue, with white-walled tires as spotless as a new tablecloth. The seats were chestnut brown leather, undented by the human body. It was as if Joe had transported the car by magic from a showroom to this suburban street.

"What a nice car, Joe," she said.

"New. And I try to take really good care of it. I hope you haven't seen *Mutiny on the Bounty* yet. Gable is in it."

"No, not yet." Helen had seen it, with Sandy. But that was New York, the subway, and winter. This was a shiny California car that she longed to caress.

"I worked on the costumes for Clark," Joe added, his voice dropping low as if sharing a treasured secret with her and her alone.

Helen felt her cheeks flush. She bit down on her tongue to prevent a girlish "Oh wow" from slipping out. "How was that?"

"He's a great guy. Tells lots of jokes and plays them too, practical ones, on his friends, you know, the other actors. Easy going."

Joe drove, his left hand gripping the wheel, his right arm draped across the back of the seat, two fingers resting with the light weight of birds on her left shoulder. Those fingers generated a wave of heat that flowed to her neck.

"Anyhow, Clark is outstanding in this movie. He's a better actor than people give him credit for."

"I hear he ends up on an island." With her right hand, Helen stroked the seat and dashboard, smooth and cool, with only the glove box on her side, but heavily instrumented with stainless-steel-rimmed, round dials and knobs on the driver's side.

"I don't want to spoil it for you."

"Is it based on a true story?"

"So they say, but what does that matter?" Joe's voice had an edge to it.

"Yeah, no, it doesn't." Helen looked out the window at the landscape which was so foreign to her. A Texaco gas station gleamed white and red under its canopy of lights, gas pumps standing sentinel, taking space that in New York would have held at least two brownstones teeming with families.

To the right rear of an Oldsmobile parked by the first of the pumps, a reedy black man, wearing a white shirt and cap emblazoned with the sharp crimson Texaco logo held onto the nozzle, his head nodding up and down as the car's female driver leaned out the window to give some direction or another to him.

Joe was heading down Brand, a wide, busy boulevard. There were a dozen cars on the road, on each side of trolley tracks. She'd certainly seen this many cars on the street in Manhattan, but here it felt as if the cars possessed the road and the environment around it.

She'd heard Los Angeles was made for the car, that everyone had one. Here buildings had parking lots attached to them. A Safeway grocery store seemed unfriendly without an opening onto the sidewalk. But it invited its clients in through the doors that opened wide onto the white striped asphalt at its rear, an opening she glimpsed as Joe turned the corner onto Brand.

"What are you looking at?" Joe's voice was edgeless now, whatever tension gone or hidden.

"Cars. No subway entrances. It's different from New York."

His laugh was low and pleasant, brief enough to save her from embarrassment. "This is America, the new America. That's the old America."

She considered whether she had asked too much about Clark Gable and the movie and too little about Joe. Men didn't like that, having the attention bled away from them. Even with Sandy, she'd had to focus on what he was doing and what he thought and put away her own ideas.

> And, it wasn't just her, without a college education, because she saw how the CCNY girls did the same thing; when men were in the room, they got progressively more quiet. Except for Rose, who'd been Helen's one good friend at CCNY, and who'd announced in a sharp, clear tone that she was going to be a lawyer. Whispering in Helen's ear and grinning, she'd said, "I'm planning to master argumentation by verbally pounding men into submission."

"How did you get into your line of work?"

"I grabbed the first job I could get at MGM. That was loading equipment and making sure it got from one sound stage to the next intact. Klieg lights, mike booms, whatever. Just labor, manual labor was all it was. But I have real skills in here," he tapped his temple with his right forefinger, and she was more aware of the absence of his hand on her shoulder than she had been of its presence.

"Management, how to get things done, done right." He nodded, a quick, efficient tip of his chin, as if to demonstrate. "Organization and record keeping, that would be aces."

Helen recognized the signs of a man impressed with himself. To be fair, any man or woman able to find a job, keep it, and have it supply enough income for a car, decent clothes, and a date was doing more than just keeping afloat. The country was still sloughing through a depression and a drought. It felt to Helen like a great race to the bottom, a big pile up on a long slide, with the kids with the best grip either holding their place or clambering up on the shoulders, necks or knees of the ones below.

"And so?" she asked.

"I'm an assistant manager in the Wardrobe Department. These movies, well, like the one we're going to see or *The Good Earth*, which is going to come out—"

"Based on the Pearl Buck novel?"

Joe glanced at her, dropped his hand back on her shoulder, and pressed on. Helen gathered that he either had not read the book or didn't know it even existed. Here was a real depression and what did people read—a novel about a famine in China. She shrugged.

"So it requires organization?"

"Tons. Every scene, especially the ones with extras. Even if it's not filmed here in the studio, we have to know who wears what and make sure it's there, ready. I don't get involved in the creative stuff—if you can call dressing people in rags for that one creative—but I make sure we know what it is, where it is, and who'll use it. And, we're here." Joe pointed through the windshield.

"Alex Theater," Helen read aloud.

"It's a beauty and right here in Glendale, too. Look at this tower. It's got to be a hundred feet tall and all lit up with those neon lights. No need to go all the way into Hollywood if you don't want to. Look at those great Egyptian and Greek drawings on the columns." He nodded toward the theater as he drove by, looking for a parking space.

To park, Joe dropped the patina of a casual driver and edged the car into a spot on the street. He locked, then double checked, his door, strode around to open Helen's door, then locked and double checked it. "You can't be too careful."

"I guess not."

The movie had been out for several months and the theater was like a popcorn bag with just a few kernels left rolling around. Clark Gable ended up on a deserted island just as he had the first time Helen saw the film and she resented it about as much, since heroes should not, in her opinion, be abandoned in the middle of the Pacific Ocean.

"What's the point of having a screenwriter, if he has to follow the plot of the book, for heaven's sake," she said as she and Joe were drinking coffee at a local restaurant.

"No, it's Mayer's fault."

She paused, cup half way up to her mouth, the caffeinated aroma rich in her nostrils. "Who's Mayer?"

"Louis B. Louis B. Mayer, the Commie who owns the studio. He doesn't like American heroes, like Clark."

Helen took a careful swallow of coffee while keeping her gaze fixed on Joe's mouth from which those words had just slid into the world. A tiny burning sensation began in the back of her throat and so she swallowed again. "Commie" was the current code word for Jew, not that there weren't Jewish Communists and she could thank Karl Marx for that, but still no one ever yoked Jew and Republican like two oxen together in the same sentence.

> In New York she had paradoxically both thought and not thought about being a Jew. She'd never counted, but she knew that most of her CCNY friends were Jewish and some, like Sandy, vibrated like harps to every tap of events that seemed anti-Semitic in Europe and America. But she worked at a desk in a sea of desks occupied by women who wore dark skirts and white blouses every day to work, where no one asked who she was. And she liked that sense of being free of identities dumped on her without her agreement, immigrant, orphan, poor, Jew.

> She had submitted to a marathon lecture on California's current political situation just before she left, mostly because of how Sandy felt about why Upton Sinclair had lost the California governorship. So she

knew the Socialist lost because of Louie B. Mayer and his money.

"How's the coffee?" Joe asked.

"It's great, Joe," she said. She took two more sips, hoping the action would help unclench her jaw. "I heard that Mayer hated communists, though."

"You're new here, Helen. You'll see."

3

FORESTER LIQUOR SAT IN WHITE stucco splendor on the corner of East California Boulevard and Isabel, a residential side street. The entrance faced the corner, so that any pedestrian casually considering entering could do so from either road without extra effort. "Forester Liquor" was painted in art deco lettering on each side of the building.

A thin-trunked palm tree, leaves shimmering electrically in the early morning sun, cast a sharp, dark shadow on the building's side. The store's display windows had a sparkling transparency in which Helen recognized her sister's diligence.

The window dressing consisted of a dozen or so cardboard boxes labeled Pabst, Seagram, Martinis, and Johnnie Walker interspersed with display ads. Placed at strategic intervals, Pabst's ads touted that "Pabst gets the Call," but Gordon's Gin countered that it "has the Advantage."

The store had also been sent a Cinzano advertisement, although Helen could not imagine anyone in Glendale buying the Italian liquor. It was rare even in Manhattan. She'd had it only once, in a tony bar, Sandy's treat. Courtesy, he said, of the Anti-Defamation League.

Helen had dressed up, sat on a high stool with her legs crossed, one foot jiggling, drank a martini made with the Italian vermouth, and watched Sandy watch the room. He'd never said why he needed to be there or why the Anti-Defamation League would pay.

The zebras in the advertisement, one painted blue and white, one in shades of red, each with a bottle on its back, danced out of the poster at slight angles to each other. The people posed in restaurants and hotel lobbies in the other ads were no doubt made aware of the boredom of their lives by the animals waltzing by. Even the Highlander in one whisky advertisement, dressed in Scotch plaid and hoisting bagpipes, looked bemused.

"You like that ad?" Harry pointed at the Cinzano.

"Yeah, Harry, I do."

Harry nodded. "Good. I want people to see that and come in. I want them to think, here's something different. I'm cultivating a certain kind of customer."

Helen considered Harry's comment, while gazing at the ad. "Certain kinds of customers" pointed toward money, laughter that tinkled above the snick of cigarette lighters being flicked on, and the melting softness of sheared beaver jackets when winter nights were cold.

He slipped a key into the bolt lock at the top, then a second into the lock on the handle. Clicking both simultaneously, he pushed the door open with his left shoulder.

"Come on in." He turned on the lights, although the sun, streaming through the window, lit up the bottles on the shelves as if they were amber lanterns.

Standing in the center of the store, Helen turned slowly around, a spinning doll on the top of a music box. After three rotations, she was certain she knew the layout well enough to help a not-too-demanding customer find the beer instead of the whiskey. She recognized Sarah's hand in the orderliness of the stacks of booze categorized by type, the dustless shelves, and the soldiers-on-display linearity of the bottles.

On the dark wood counter stood a golden bronze and honey oak National cash register. With its heft, it was as solid and as heavy as a safe. She walked around the side of the counter and stood in front of the register, her fingers floating down onto the keys. Lightly ornamented with paisley swirls, the metal facing shone.

"You know how to use that?" Harry asked.

"I used something like it when I worked at Gimbel's before the bookkeeping job. So, I think I'll be okay on it."

Harry moved over, facing her across the counter. "So, here is what I need you to do. You speak your best American all the time. I don't care if a goddamn rabbi walks in, you don't say anything Jewish."

"Sure," she smiled her best all-American smile. Harry smiled back, slow and snake-like.

"Take a look at the books. They're under the register. Sara kept them up to date by dragging the babies in here to work on them. It'll be slow until lunch and then slow again until about four."

Helen slid a wooden stool over, pulled out the gray ledger labeled *January - June 1936* and opened it. She laid it on the counter and perched on the stool, leaning on one elbow as she turned the pages for January, February, and March. The entries were unmistakably Sarah's, the accounting system a straight-forward cash accumulation. Each day, Sarah entered every sale, splitting amounts, when needed, into the column for beer, or cigarettes, or scotch, or any of the other two dozen or so categories.

The numbers were summed across for the day, down for the category, and summed again for each week. It was painstaking. Accounts payable were less demanding. Forester Liquor ordered monthly or bi-monthly, except for cigarettes, which were ordered each week.

Dropping one foot, then the other onto the floor, Helen stood then squatted down behind the counter. Boxes labeled January 1936, February 1936, and March 1936 in Sarah's writing were tucked snuggly into cubby holes; each contained the month's receipts and invoices for what had been ordered.

Sarah might not have been trained in bookkeeping, but she was thorough, sharp, and driven by worries about authority that Helen knew well. Becoming a naturalized citizen did not diminish the flame of anxiety. Marrying a second-generation American Jew did nothing. And keeping records that would satisfy even the most indefatigable tax agent didn't either.

Helen pulled the ledger onto the floor next to her and paged more carefully through the final figures for January and February, her finger tapping on the final tally of accounts payable and accounts receivable. It all added up, but something was wrong. The problem was not in the figures, but in another place, which Helen could not quite bring into focus.

Helen was still crouched down, knees together, skirt circled in folds around her toes, book splayed open on the floor, when she heard the door open and the bell above it jingle.

"May I help...?" she began as she stood, her right leg tingly and half-asleep from crouching so long. A uniformed policeman, roughly the size of Sarah and Harry's front door, stood, staring at the Coors display immediately in front of Helen, his right hand resting lightly on the top of his holstered gun. He had a slight aroma of leather and Old Spice aftershave.

Harry came out from the rear of the store, the door just to Helen's right in back of the counter. He glanced at the officer, then at Helen, and shook his head in a sharply abbreviated "no." Then he looked down, toward where Helen had been, and she sank once again below the counter, feeling like a well-trained and abused pet dog.

"She's a new girl. My wife wants to be home with the babies," Harry said. "How are you, Pat?"

"Let's talk about that someplace private." Pat had a light tenor voice belonging to a man half his size and ten years younger.

"Sure. Come on back."

Helen watched as the legs of the men walked by, her gaze fixed on the floor. She would have closed her eyes but that seemed more worrisome than keeping them open. Closed eyes would signal that she knew something was wrong and she should not see it.

"Quite a looker." The light voice drifted away, carried by the stomp of leather boots.

Only when she heard the door to the storage area shut followed by a metallic click of a lock being turned did she stand up. Aware of a just-developed twitch in her left thumb, she rested both hands firmly on the counter, pressing down as if she planned to levitate her body. The spasm stopped.

The door's bell jingled again. A mid-sized woman in her early fifties, salt-and-pepper hair, wearing tan slacks, a turquoise short-sleeved blouse, and a light gray sweater over her arm, walked in. She had the aura of a person who fit into the neighborhood like a jigsaw piece into the right spot.

"A pack of Camels," she said.

Helen plucked the Camels from a shelf behind her, smiled at the woman, and busied herself with the cash register's buttons and readying the receipt pad.

"You're new here," the woman stated as if she would bear no argument.

"Oh, yes. I just started."

"The other woman, the one with the accent?"

"Family matters, I think," Helen did not allow the smile to leave her face. Behind her, the storage door lock clicked open and a slight breeze signaled that the door had been opened. But no one came out and the door was shut again.

"Where's Harry? He didn't leave you alone on your first day, did he?"

"No, no. He's in the storage room doing inventory."

"Can you get him for me?" The woman reached with her left hand into the brown leather shoulder bag that hung from her right shoulder. On her ring finger, she wore a large diamond, polished to send out light flares down the block. She pulled out an envelope and put it on the counter.

"Do you need a stamp for that?" Helen asked, wondering if Harry forgot to tell her that they sold stamps, too.

"No." The woman opened the pack of Camels, tapped a cigarette end on the counter, put the tapped end to her lips, and reached back into the bag for a gold-plated lighter. Nipping the end of the cigarette with the flame, she inhaled.

With her exhale, directed at Helen, she said, "Get Harry for me." There was a pause while the remainder of the smoke rolled out of her mouth. "Please."

"Sure." Helen turned to the storage room door and knocked twice. "Harry? There's a customer to see you."

The door handle moved and Helen stepped back and to the side. Harry emerged, closing the door firmly behind him. He looked exactly the same as he had when he walked into the storage room except for his left earlobe, which was several shades redder than the rest of his face and neck.

The woman at the counter nodded at him, then tapped the envelope with her ring finger and pushed it toward him. "Mail this for me."

Helen read "Two in the fifth, twelve in the seventh" on the envelope.

"Okay, Denise," Harry replied.

Denise glanced at Helen and then back at Harry. "She's fine, Denise. Don't worry."

"Tomorrow, then," Denise said, turned around, and walked out of the store.

"Harry, she didn't pay me for the Camels," Helen said.

"Not important." Harry picked up the envelope, opened it, and pulled out two fifty dollar bills, which he slipped into his left pant pocket.

Helen sucked in her lower lip and bit down on the tender tissue.

"You have a problem?" Harry asked.

"Nah, Harry. If you're running a bookmaking joint here, fine with me. Back east, there's numbers, too. Do you do that?"

Harry smiled his snake-smile. "You are a delightful surprise, Helen. I just do the horses. Numbers, hell, I'd have to hit up a hundred poor fuckers to get this much in."

"The liquor store?"

"It's absolutely legit and a money maker. Just not …."

"Not enough?"

"Exactly, Helen. Not enough."

Helen understood *nicht genug*, could hear her mother's voice and the feathery rustle of papers while fingers—were they her mother's?—fluttered through them like independent birds looking for crumbs.

> "There's not enough money for me to stay in school. That's how it is. I'll apprentice out." Her sister's voice tapered to a thin whisper in Helen's ear. Sarah could not have been older than thirteen. Had she spoken in Yiddish or German or Polish? Helen could not remember.

Not enough was what was odd about the bookkeeping figures. And not enough was sufficient to cause Sarah to look so distressed. Sarah would see the difference between what the store took in as profit and what their life style cost as clearly as she would see the new gray hairs on her head and the crow's feet around her eyes.

And Harry's bookmaking operation would be enough to make Sarah not want Helen to work at the store.

Suppressing a moan, Helen swallowed hard. That was Sarah protecting her again. But this time it wouldn't work. Sarah and the babies needed protection, and if she could provide that, maybe she would feel that her debt to her sister was paid.

When she and Sarah had first arrived in New York, Helen opened the apartment door just one time without checking with Sarah first. Sarah yanked her back from the opening by her arm and stood with the wooden rolling pin raised up. But the man who filled the opening was clean from the top of his hat to his shined shoes and he spoke Yinglish, that mashed version of two languages that marked the immigrant. He was selling numbers.

"Easy to win. Maybe you've had a dream with a number in it?" Just a nickel, or a dime, or a quarter for a chance to win five-hundred or even a thousand dollars. Helen longed to go to her closet and dig out the nickel she'd gotten for her birthday from the toe of her shoe.

"Go away," Sarah hissed, "and take your phony dream with you. That dream could get us kicked out of the country."

The man had tipped his hat, smiled, and turned away toward the Fidelman's apartment across the hall. Sarah slammed the door shut.

Sandy had laughed when Helen told him about her childhood adventure with the numbers man. "It's a real polyglot criminal activity here. The Jews, the Italians, the Negros, the Polacks, anyone who thinks they can squeeze a dime out of their poor landsman…yeah, their fellow immigrant's just a mark."

"But the Negros were here already."

"Sure, Helen, but they were in the South and now there's this great migration north, so they're immigrants too. And the Okies going to the west coast, same thing, just poor suckers every one."

I won't be another poor sucker, Helen thought, and smiled again at Harry. "I gather horse racing is different."

"Oh Helen, I'll take you out to this new track, Santa Anita. Or maybe down to Del Mar, when it opens. Movie stars. Limousines. You can smell the money like you can smell the orange blossoms in the spring."

"You're quite the poet, Harry."

The idea of asking Harry about the tank of a policeman who'd since left crossed Helen's mind. She forced it away. There was no need to be curious about danger. Danger would sense that and find you. Feigning an interest in the pricing of types of Scotch, she slid around the counter and over to the Scotch shelf. After a long minute, Harry returned to the storeroom.

With her head buried in the store's books, and the nine customers during the day, Helen realized late in the afternoon that she hadn't had lunch. She knocked lightly on the storeroom door.

"Harry? What do I do for lunch?"

Muffled through the door, Harry said, "Wait a minute." The door opened wide and Helen could see boxes of liquor stacked by size, a card table and two wooden kitchen chairs with peeling white paint, and a Philco radio, like the one at home, dark wood, with a cloverleaf pattern adorning the speakers, sitting on its own gateleg table. A dark green combination safe stood on the floor next to the gateleg table, its handle gleaming chrome like a well-kept car. On top of the safe a black telephone rested.

"Come in." Harry waved her across the threshold.

Stepping closer to the card table, Helen saw a *Daily Racing Form* tossed into a wastepaper basket just behind one of the chairs and three sheets of paper with dense pencil marks and indecipherable writing. An orange sat on top of the papers, and another orange's peel lay scattered, the aroma tickling the air. Helen was hungry enough to begin to salivate.

"Take the orange. Tomorrow, pack a lunch and you can eat it here." Harry didn't mention what he'd do.

The phone rang. Harry held up a finger, then pointed at the door Helen had just entered. He grabbed the orange and handed it to her. She backed up until she was in the store and Harry closed the door. No one was in the store, so Helen rested her ear against the door.

> Sarah had warned her about the demons of curiosity and danger. "Be curious about school. English, art, geometry, bookkeeping. Not about other stuff." *Other stuff* was unspecified but definitely included boys, sex, other peoples' religions, and anything else that would be a distraction to a job, money, a husband, and citizenship. But curiosity, Helen discovered, could not be contained that easily.

"…2 showed. Call me back after the 6th."

Helen moved back to the counter and reached onto the shelf just under the cash register where she'd put the two unsold copies of the *Daily Race Form*. Keeping an eye on the store entrance, she moved down the counter with one of the papers so that Harry, if he opened the door from the storage area, wouldn't see her immediately. She turned her back to the storage door and opened the paper, leaning against the counter to block the possible view Harry could have. In her stint as a salesclerk at Gimbel's, she'd followed what the other women had done if they wanted a quick snack or a quiet read on a customer-less afternoon, how they had quietly folded their bodies around their food or books as if around small treasures.

She quickly found the Santa Anita Racetrack listing for the fifth race and checked the time it went off against the time of the call. The six horse, Easy Breezy, won the race at four to one odds. Harry hadn't seemed upset for whatever that meant besides whatever share of the fifty he got to keep.

Scanning the information for the next race, the names of the horses read like half-done lyrics or puns but the colors of the jockeys were what she'd imagined knights' colors would be, crimson and gold, sapphire and silver, green and yellow. Re-folding the paper, she put it back on the shelf.

The image of the LA cop bulldozed his way back into her mind. She sighed and peeled the orange. Sunlight dazzled in through the bottles in the display window, in tones of amber, white, and blue.

Dinner was brisket, potatoes, carrots, and apple pie for dessert. Sarah kept a half-smile on her face while serving, as if the smile would keep tension at bay. It seemed to work. Harry ate without saying anything and Helen and Sarah talked about the children's day at home, Helen acting interested and avoiding Harry's occasional glance in her direction. When he was done with dinner, he went into the living room and turned on the radio.

Sarah cleared the table, put the dishes in the sink, and turned on the water. She motioned Helen over and leaned in to whisper, "How was it?"

"It'll be fine."

Sarah took a half step back and leaned against the counter looking at Helen with eyes slightly narrowed as if to sharpen the gaze into Helen's mind. Before Helen turned fourteen, Sarah's look would cause her to worriedly spill all her thoughts, laying them out for her sister to be examined for flaws and other unspecified problems. Now Helen carefully chose what to share behind her own fixed stare.

"Really, Sarah. It was okay."

"No problems?"

"What? No, I got the cash register right away, your bookkeeping is impeccable so far as I can see."

"Anything ... else?"

Helen did not want to share with Sarah that she knew Harry had an illegal bookie operation going. She did not know why, precisely, except that she somehow did not want to confirm that all three of them were engaged in illegal activity. If she didn't tell Sarah, she could imagine that Sarah did not know and Sarah could imagine that she did not know. Was that better than confirming Sarah's fears?

Helen sucked at her lower lip, then laughed, looked directly into Sarah's hazel eyes and said, "Some of the customers are kinda strange. Ask Harry. It's fine. There was this lady, Sarah, honest to God, she came in with a twenty dollar bill for a single pack of cigarettes. Money! Gee, it must be nice."

The ends of her mouth turned up, Sarah poised between belief and worry. "Okay, okay," she said.

"And Harry was fine to me. We're both...we're both older and we see each other differently."

At that, Sarah's smile slid into her eyes. "See. He is a good man."

Helen held an envelope in her hand and deciphered the smudged postmark. Sandy had sent it from New York two days after she'd left; what should she make of that?

Slitting it open with a kitchen knife, she shook out the single piece of lined yellow paper. He'd pulled it out of a notebook, that much was clear. And, he'd written it in pencil. She tossed her head and sniffed. After all, she hadn't been expecting a love letter from him after the cool way he'd handed her off at the train, with a hug and a peck on the cheek that could have come from an uncle. But those kisses early in their relationship had been like her first taste of chocolate ice cream, like the first time she'd ever touched a cashmere sweater. Eight dates, three months, that summed it up.

Dear Helen,

I hope the train trip out to California wasn't too bad and that you are enjoying the warmer climate. It is in the 50s here and rainy.

The weather! Maybe she should just put the note down and think about how to make contact with Joe of the cleaners again.

My agent knows someone in LA. That may bring me out to Southern California, but I'm not sure when. I will let you know when I find out and if you'd like to see an old friend from New York, you can tell me.

Your old friend from New York,

Sandy

Just like Sandy, mysterious and yet to the point. She stared at his return address, then refolded the note and put it back in the envelope and walked into her room.

Sarah had converted the baby's room into a bedroom for Helen, moving the crib back into the master bedroom. When she did it, Harry grunted and sat in the living room, radio on. There had been no argument.

In fact, Harry had been almost mellow for the last week. Helen had done everything he wanted at the store, from cashiering to dusting. But, she suspected, more than anything her ability to keep his bookmaking clientele in good spirits worked on him like a shot of Scotch. Helen had a sense for who they were.

"Harry," she'd call. "You have a special customer here to see you." Or, she'd give three rapid knocks on the storeroom door. Then she'd step away to the other side of the store, eyes lowered, face as stripped of emotion as a wall with only primer on it. "I have no opinion of you," her look said. The half dozen or so who were repeats for the week walked out, nodding to her. "So much better than that other salesgirl," said the lady with the fifty dollar bills and the free packs of cigarettes.

Helen went to the closet to check on what she could wear to work. She'd run through her stock of clean, ironed clothes but she could re-iron one of her dresses.

The days were a perpetual spring, with cloudless baby blue skies and the aroma of gardenias. *The cyclone had set the house down, very gently—for a cyclone—in the midst of a country of marvelous beauty.* The words floated into her head from her favorite childhood book, checked out so many times that the librarian had threatened to hide it "so other girls can read it, too, Helen." How grateful Dorothy had been for those "banks of gorgeous flowers" and "birds of rare and brilliant plumage." Except that Dorothy had Munchkins, and Helen had Harry. She sighed.

The cleaning was still out because she forgot to ask Sarah to pick it up for her, which put her in an evil mood. She'd have to walk over tomorrow on her lunch break to the cleaners and that meant asking Harry for some of her pay tonight. They'd come to an agreement at fifteen dollars a week, since she lived with them and ate with them. It should have been twenty-four by her calculations, without room and board. Was Harry being generous? It was hard to tell.

Maybe Joe would be there even though it was a work day. She

wouldn't mind going out again even to another movie she'd seen before with a guy who was a little iffy when it came to Jews.

The four o'clock sun beat into the display window. If the liquid in the Scotch bottles had been alcohol, not water, Harry would have lost hundreds of dollars in spoilage. As it was, hot water made the bottles painful to move when she dusted and she sucked on her fingers after touching each one.

The fan was on, throbbing to push the overheated air out the opened door. Helen stood in front of it, raising and lowering her arms like a trapped butterfly, her turquoise cotton skirt wrapped against the back of her legs, perspiration sliding from the back of her neck between her shoulder blades and down to her waist.

Her cleaning was hanging in the storage room, the wool garments an ironic testament to the sweat-filled walk to the cleaners in the heat of the day. No Joe. Not even a nod of recognition from Elsa, behind the counter.

Helen walked over to the cooler where Harry stocked Coca-Cola. She slid the top open and put both hands into the refrigerated unit, fondling the small bottle of soda as she lifted it up.

"You look like you want to dive in there."

Startled, she turned around. Joe stood in the entrance to the store, jacket-less, tanned arms emerging from a red-checked short-sleeved shirt, seemingly unfazed by the heat.

"I do." She smiled, then turned again to slide the top back in place.

"Let me treat you to that," Joe said, taking a dime from his pocket. "I'll have one, too."

"We've got cold beer."

"Nah, too early."

She got a second bottle. He walked over, took both from her, efficiently uncapped them with the bottle opener and handed her one.

"You'd think I'd be used to the heat, coming from New York."

"Different kind of heat," he said, his gaze focused on her eyes. She felt his look pinning her in place, her elbow lifting the bottle to her lips, her lips softening at its approach.

"Drink up." He raised his bottle, clinked it lightly against hers, and swallowed a good fourth of it in one gulp.

The icy, caramel-colored liquid was deliciously unlike any other drink; the bubbles tingly in her mouth the way she imagined Champagne might be. Enlivened by the first swallow, she took a second.

"The color's back in your cheeks, now," Joe said. She raised her empty hand to her cheek. "Funny how heat can make you pale," he added.

"Joe, what can I get for you? I almost forgot I work here," she laughed lightly.

"I didn't. And nothing, really. I came in to ask if you were busy this Friday night."

"No."

"I'll pick you up at seven then?"

"Okay. Sure. But what are we…"

"Dress for a party. A woman I know is having a little get together. You won't mind going with me?"

"Joe, I don't know anyone here except my sister and brother-in-law. So, you inviting me to meet your friends, that's a nice thing."

"We'll leave it at that, then." He smiled. "I'm giving you a chance to meet more people."

From the rear of the store, Harry's voice boomed out, as if he wanted to be heard across the street. "Our visitor from the other night. Joe, right?"

Helen heard the storage room door being shut firmly, as if to enforce the secrets in the room. But she knew, from going in there, that all anyone would see today was a gateleg table with a radio, a single folding chair, a large refrigerator unit to keep beer and other drinks cold, and boxes of liquor strategically stacked around the safe, hiding it from view in a cave of booze.

"Hello, Harry," Joe said. "I was just going by and thought I'd say hello to Helen."

Harry walked toward them. As he approached, Helen could see the customer-smile pasted on his face.

"Of course. Always nice to see you."

Harry was close enough now to Helen that she could feel heat off his skin. A half step back and she'd bump right into him. But she couldn't step forward because she'd be too close to Joe. Pressing her tongue up against her back molar as if she was going to push the tooth out her cheek, she took a deep breath and let it out quietly. She did not want either man to react to her. Harry's behavior was inexplicable on its face. That protective, possessive approach. Or was it? Did he just not want anyone in the store right now? And if that was so, why hadn't he just told her to put up the "Closed for Lunch" sign?

Joe put the now empty bottle of Coca-Cola onto the top of the cooler.

"That's fine," Harry said. "Helen will take care of it."

"See you Friday, then, Helen," Joe said. He took a step back, smiled at Harry, turned and left the store.

"Lock the door, Helen," Harry said, giving her a tap on the shoulder.

"Sure." She walked over, shut and locked the door. For good measure she pulled down the shades and flipped the store sign propped in the display window from Open to Closed.

"Okay. Go sit down someplace. Be quiet. Answer the phone if it rings, but that's it."

Helen grabbed a *Los Angeles Times* from the pile on the counter, perched on the stool near the register, and tried to narrow her senses down to whatever was on the printed page. Whatever or whoever Harry was waiting for, he wanted no questions. Helen figured it was either the over-sized cop coming for his bribe or a customer who didn't want to be seen. She worried that she'd be in the way, but Harry would have told her to leave if that's what he'd wanted.

A paper was always there on the counter, headlines glaring: *Times* in the morning, *Herald-Examiner* in the afternoon. Men would stop in and grab a copy with their evening beer. "Look at that," they'd say. "What do you know?"

She knew more now, driven out of boredom to read. The paper changed her boredom to anxiety. Soon she felt driven to finish all the stories, even the ones in the Sports Section on the Olympic contenders going to Berlin; no mention of Hitler there.

In New York, Sandy had coaxed her to a rally against US participation in the Olympics. She stood with hundreds of people waving placards, feeling tired, wishing she wasn't there, but smiling whenever Sandy looked over at her. It was useless. Maybe it was worse than useless because news photographers took pictures, shoving themselves in front of the protesters like lead dancers in front of a chorus line, black cameras pointed everywhere, spying.

Her hands trembling as if she were eighty, she had bought every New York paper for the next two days. She thumbed through them, washing the dark newsprint off her hands in the kitchen sink, and watching the dark water swirl into the drain. There were no pictures of her, nothing to trigger the government's interest in her, no smudge on her petition for naturalization.

Three weeks later, Helen received her citizenship papers. She walked out of the courtroom, out the courthouse doors, sank down on the top stair leading into the building, buried her head in her hands, and cried.

After Helen decided to move to California, the fluttering in her stomach whenever she walked by the Hudson River left her. Gone were the nightmares in which a wave taller than the Empire State Building swept her body back out into the Atlantic, past the Statue of Liberty, past Ellis Island. The length of the continent that would be between her and those roiling, cold waves would be an impenetrable barrier against that old orphaned world. In California she would no longer worry.

She read the weather, tapping her finger against the counter. There were unprecedented floods in the east, dust storms and tornadoes in the mid-west, and an over-heated spring in Los Angeles. Nature, she concluded, was not happy, as traumatized by the economy and the world's general bad situation as everyone else was. As for Helen, she would take a warm spring over a flood any day.

And there was the upcoming election and, more interesting, that divorcee, Wallis Simpson, seen all over with King Edward in England. Helen tapped her finger on the counter. What did Edward see in Wally, rail-thin, with a hard look that photographs couldn't disguise?

Behind her, the door to the storage room rattled like chattering teeth. Someone had entered from the alley letting the wind in as well. The chattering door quieted. Helen heard a raised voice, but whose she could not tell, followed by a slamming sound. The chattering started and stopped. Helen read the rest of the article on King Edward accompanied by silence.

The storage room door opened.

"Helen, come here," Harry whispered. She turned and stifled

a scream. Blood ran in thin, red rivulets from both nostrils and dripped off his chin even though he was pinching his nose shut at the bottom.

"Put your head back, Harry." She slid off the stool and flapped her hand at him as if he were a cat to be shooed out the door. He retreated into the storage room and sat down heavily on the chair as she entered. She walked past him to the tiny toilet area they shared and returned with a handful of toilet paper. He shoved wedges into each nostril and laid his head back.

"Your handkerchief," she said, holding out her hand.

He reached into a pocket and handed a white cloth over. She said nothing until she had cleaned the drying blood from the lower third of his face.

"So," she said and looked around. The cash box where Harry kept the betting money tucked away in the safe was open and a handful of small bills, mostly fives and tens, lay on the table, looking like abandoned children. Someone had forced a pay-off, but of a bet or protection money? It wasn't a robbery because all the money would be gone and the box, too. These were hard days; no one left a five dollar bill unless it was a message. Whoever had done this to Harry was too big to care about loose change.

Helen bit the inside of her cheek to trap the tension that was threatening to buckle her legs. She'd been in California less than two weeks, knew no one except Harry, Sarah, the kids, and that Joe fellow who didn't seem to like Jews much. Now this.

It was one thing for Harry to take a few horse bets on the side. That was like the deli owner in Brooklyn who did numbers. That guy wasn't ever slugged in the nose. Maybe she should make nice to Sandy when he came and go back to New York with him.

"Harry," she whispered.

Harry held the handkerchief with its beet-red stains against his nostrils, head back, and crimson wads of toilet paper on the table in front of him.

"What?"

"Was it the Al Capone gang?"

Harry laughed, then gripped the handkerchief tighter to his nose, pinching the bridge and wincing.

"Jesus, Helen, no. And it wasn't Little Caesar either. And," he leaned over toward her and grabbed her wrist, "you don't say anything to Sarah about this."

His grip loosened and, when he withdrew his hand, she rubbed her wrist.

"Sorry about that," he said. "This is no movie, Helen."

"Yeah, so what is it then, Harry?" She was satisfied that her voice didn't tremble. "This was one pissed off guy who came in. And I'm worried next time he will be even more pissed off."

Her humiliation at being laughed at by Harry flushed her cheeks. But she masked her emotions, pushing her tongue firmly against the roof of her mouth. The kids in grammar school had honed her coping skills the minute she was unceremoniously dumped in Miss Mitchell's third grade class with twenty-three English words to her name. The twenty-fourth one was "shaddup," fists cocked, behind the door of the girls' restroom.

"You don't know anything, Helen."

"Enlighten me then."

"It was a business misunderstanding. Speaking of which, go back in and open the store again. Go run *that* business." He got up and walked toward the closet where the toilet and sink were. "Go ahead unless you want to see me take a leak."

The evening air was cool and the sky had a gray tinge as the mountains seemed to tug the fog in from the coast. Joe had called to say he would pick her up later for the party. Helen sat at the kitchen table dressed in her interpretation of casual party attire, a calf-length dress in the color of vanilla ice-cream, the V-shaped neckline stopping just where the crevice between her breasts began. The matching belt hugged her twenty-three-inch waist, and the fabric of the skirt slid over her hips and flowed down her legs.

She was smiling at Sarah, half hearing what her sister was saying. Something about the children. Domestic talk all seemed the same, a rundown of what they had done during the day, the walk to the park, the neighbors who had children that age. It was dull, but in a way that made Sarah happy.

"Let me ask you something, Sarah."

"Sure."

"When customers at the store asked you about your accent, what did you tell them?"

"Why ask me this?"

"I don't know. It's been on my mind because Harry, you know…"

"I told them I was from Germany."

"Why not Poland?"

"Poland is not such a good place to be from."

"And Germany is better? Germany lost the war. Germany has Hitler."

"Germany has culture. That's what Harry said, so I said Germany. What do I care where I came from, Helen? I'm here now. You could say I came from the moon and it wouldn't matter to me."

"But …"

Sarah pushed the chair back and stood. She began to clean off the table, picking up the two coffee cups and clattering them into the sink.

"I have children now, so I feel how Mama worried." She clutched at her stomach, twisting the apron in a wet hand. "All she wanted was for us to be safe. Poland didn't care about her and she didn't care about Poland."

Mama had tried over and over to order them out of the bedroom, but Sarah would return with a basin of well water and clean rags, dipping one into the bowl and putting it on the fevered forehead, and using the other to wipe Mama's face. Helen grabbed a dripping cloth to help, but Sarah slapped her hand away. Mama's eyes were bloodshot and she smothered an exhausted moan as Sarah pressed the cool cloth onto her cheek

For a day it seemed she had miraculously gotten better, but then the fever and coughing returned.

"When I die, Sarah," Mama said, "you go with Helen to my brother. Ask him..." She hacked violently and spat bloody phlegm into the rag. "Ask him to find you a job and keep Helen."

Sarah nodded. But, when Helen went to the outhouse, she followed and said, "I won't leave you with Uncle Max forever. You're my sister."

Sarah was now stiff as the ironing board, leaning against the lip of the sink, her hands reddening under the hot water, soap suds building in the basin and steadily rising as if preparing to lap over onto the counter.

Helen rose and walked over, putting her hand on her sister's back with care, in part to be gentle, in part because her role as comforter to Sarah was strange, as if the egg were coddling the hen.

"Glendale seems like a very safe place," she said.

Sarah shook her head. "Not so safe. I know Harry didn't get his nose bloodied because he walked into a door." Sarah's harsh whisper and steaming breath slid into Helen's ear. "He runs a bookie joint."

Despite the heat of the dirty dish water and Sarah's anger, warmth fled from Helen's hands. Her fingers were cold and she longed to pull her hand away from the small of Sarah's back before it gave her away.

"Sarah, dear," Helen whispered back, glad that a whisper did not allow her voice to shake. "I just work there."

"Do not play me for a fool, sister. You of the big eyes and the Cadillac taste are not a fool either." Sarah reached up with a dripping hand and pulled Helen's hand away from her back. "This is my family. Dragna…"

The doorbell clang startled them both. Helen took a step back. "It must be Joe," she said. She would ask Sarah later just what or who Dragna was.

"If he asks, I'm from Germany. You, too," Sarah said.

"Just come and say 'hi' to him. Who cares where we were from?"

Joe drove the Ford with his right arm draped over the seat back, fingers dangling on her shoulder, tapping them lightly with each bump in the road. The randomness and lightness of the touch made her want to push them away, as if they were the spider in Little Miss Muffet's rhyme, but she didn't. The hand came down to the gear shift at each light, then drifted back up to the seat back when the car was again in third.

Glendale's streets were wide, the pavement like smooth, dark skin of the earth beneath the car's tires. Even with the spider-finger touches, Helen settled back against the seat, enjoying the breeze that came in through Joe's open widow. There was an expansiveness to driving like this that she had never experienced.

"*This* is what I thought the West Coast would be like," she said. "Although I hope to see the real Los Angeles and Hollywood soon."

"And I'd like to take you to see them, Helen," Joe replied. "Maybe this Sunday?"

Helen considered how non-committal she could be. Joe seemed to be giving her what her girlfriends would call a "rush job," but her sense of discomfort, she thought, came more from his edginess about Jews. She'd stick to Sarah's advice and tell him they were from Germany. Maybe that would be all he'd need to know. And she wasn't going to marry him, after all, just go to this party and maybe to Los Angeles and Hollywood.

"Sure, Joe. Maybe we can work that out."

He smiled and she was reminded of the male mannequins at Gimbel's, who were oddly handsome and garnered more attention from the women customers than the men. It was the precision and exactness of the male figure, taut, no body fat, fitting into clothes perfectly and always smiling that seemed so attractive.

"How is work?" she asked.

"I saw Clark again this week. And I put my name in to be an extra if they ever need me."

"Wow." It slipped out before she could catch it. Did stars like Clark Gable really just wander around the studio lot saying hello to people in wardrobe, like gods dropping from the firmament to play with mortals?

"Yes. I have to be a member of the union, which I'm not so happy about. But, I'm doing what I can to make sure I get the breaks I need."

"Do you think I could do that?"

"You have the looks, for sure." He turned his head, his gaze flickering over her face and down her neck. "But, you have a job and you're not a member of the union."

"Yes, well…" Helen considered how much to share about her commitment to the liquor store and to Sarah. "I don't plan to stay at the liquor store for a long time. I'll need another job."

Joe patted her shoulder. "Let me see what there is. And my friends have connections."

The car merged onto a wide boulevard, rimmed with stores, their display windows lit to entice the viewer back when the doors were again open for business. In one of the windows, Helen glimpsed a tall, faceless female mannequin, dressed in a sleek satin turquoise dress that skimmed the floor. That was not a depression dress; it was a party dress, fit for dinner and dancing.

"Where are we?" she asked.

"Pasadena. The host for the party has a nice house here." Joe's voice dropped on "nice" as if underlining the word.

"This was a great tourist town until the Depression hit," he added. "But people still have—"

"Money," Helen said. "I could see that from the dress in that window."

"That too. I was going to say they still have determination. You know, Helen, that's what makes this nation great. The individual joining with the State in something greater than just you or me."

"Yes, this is a great country," she replied.

"Are you interested in politics at all?" Joe asked.

"Not really."

"So what are you interested in, then?"

"Getting ahead a little, Joe. Not living with my brother-in-law, my sister, and my niece and nephew."

He smiled and rested the weight of his right hand on her shoulder, his fingers pressing into her upper arm. "I'll see what you need to do to become an extra."

"Now, that would be swell, Joe," she said and relaxed into his grip to emphasize her pleasure.

They were driving under a canopy of dark foliage, the kind of umbrella of leaves that mature trees planted for elegance produced. The air smelled of eucalyptus and evergreen. Joe turned right so sharply that she slid a few inches over on the seat. The car purred up a steeply sloping driveway. Without street lights and under the leafy branches, the night moved in more swiftly than it had on the Pasadena boulevard.

Abruptly, the canopy ended and a brightly lit house came into view. A mansion, really, Helen thought, considering its size. Three stories high, the building had a wide veranda festooned with a combination of tea candles in low white pottery bowls and small electric lights looped around columns that stretched the full height of the house.

On each side, wings of the house bookended the façade, like arms opened wide enough to invite a guest in. The house was painted bright white and green. Shutters adorned the windows that Helen could see. Outside of a twelfth grade American history book with dog-eared pages, four prior students' names written on the inside cover, and a picture of an antebellum Mississippi slaveholder's house, she'd never seen anything like it.

Guests stood on the veranda in clusters or posed on the stairs leading up to it. The women leaned sinuously against columns or sat on wicker chairs, wearing dresses that shimmered under the patio lights like liquid lacquer. The men wore slacks and shirts casually open at the neck. There wasn't a tie or a jacket in sight. Without exception that Helen could see, they looked young, rich, and drunk. She wondered if Gatsby had risen from his grave. And, she was relieved to see, she was not over-dressed.

Joe turned to her with a cat licking cream smile on his face. "This is it," he said, sweeping his left arm out of the window, as if presenting the house and all its festivities to her as a gift.

"Just in case I want to say thanks or something, Joe, who are the host and hostess?" Helen asked, keeping her voice light and dry. Inside she felt like she'd been dropped inside a movie without her lines and just the slightest hint of a plot to guide her. Her stomach began its ticklish preamble to fluttering and she could feel a tingling sensation, like ants in her veins, creeping down her left arm.

"Improvise," she heard Sandy say when describing what he'd do if he forgot his own lines. Improvise.

"Don't worry about that," Joe said, patting her hand. "If we have a chance, believe me I'll introduce you."

A man with dark-coffee skin, dressed in all white, circulated with a filigreed silver tray on which martini glasses and Champagne flutes stood, clinking together with every step. Not spilling a drop, the man slid around the guests and over to Helen and Joe.

Without asking, Joe grabbed one of each and handed the flute with the bubbly concoction to Helen. "You don't look like a martini girl to me," he said.

"I could be," she said. "But Champagne is fine."

"Your brother-in-law told me, when I asked, that you and your sister, Sarah, are immigrants from Germany. That would explain her accent," Joe said.

Helen nodded.

"Of course, there are not that many Germans in California and we like to make them feel very welcome in this country. I would love, at some point, to hear the whole story. All Harold told me was that you were orphaned."

"Yes." Helen wondered if there would ever be a point in her acquaintance with Joe where sharing that story would be appropriate. But she'd considered Sarah's insistence on stating they'd come from Germany. Really, she decided, it was not a lie or at least not by many miles.

Poland had burst back into being like a dormant seed watered after decades of drought. The end of the Great War was the downpour and Poland grew across lands conquered repeatedly by other countries, Germany included. They'd grown up a hundred kilometers inside land reclaimed by Poland and from which most Germans had fled. Just a little stretch to cover the distance, and she and Sarah could rightfully be said to be Germans.

Helen sipped the Champagne, cold bubbles sliding over her tongue. A hint of pear and apricot enveloped her nose. It was the opposite of Coca-Cola, with that heavy syrup smell. She smiled at

Joe, feeling much more relaxed as the alcohol began to quiet her stomach.

Joe took her by the elbow and led her across the porch and into the house. Although a few people nodded to Joe, he did not stop to introduce Helen, but only dipped his head each time in greeting.

The double doors were thrown wide open, their beveled glass frames held ajar by matching three-feet high dark green Chinese vases, each decorated with a gilt, fire-breathing dragon. In the entry, the dark mahogany floor was partially covered by a rug, which had a design of fuchsia and scarlet hibiscus atop an interlacing pattern of green leaves and light brown stems woven into it.

In the far right corner of the foyer, a scarlet and black parrot perched on a thick wrought iron stand. As Helen entered, the parrot gave a wolf-whistle.

To the left of the parrot, a wide staircase, carpeted in the same intense tropical hues as the foyer rug, reached up to a second floor balcony. The entry stretched upwards for a full three stories, ending in a domed skylight.

Midway down the stairs, a woman stood, as if waiting to be acknowledged. Her hair, swept up in a chignon, was ebony, and the style emphasized a slightly too long oval face, high cheekbones and gleaming eyes a shade lighter than the mahogany under her feet. Her skin was pale, as if the gold of the California sun had never touched it, and the sleeveless raspberry-red satin dress, lightly nipped at the waist and falling to mid-calf, covered a slender, long-legged form.

"Joe," the woman said in a raspy cigarette-whisper that carried down the stairs. "Who is that delightful young woman with you?"

"This is Helen Rice." Joe took half a step away from Helen, who felt like a fashion model on display, expected to make a full turn for the appraising eye of the buyer.

"Helen." The woman, now at the bottom of the stairs, said the name to weigh its worthiness, then nodded.

"You may call me Jessie," she said. The smile on her face stayed at her mouth. Her seal-brown eyes appraised Helen with a chill sweep. "Welcome to my home."

"Thank you. It's truly one of the most beautiful homes I've ever been in." In fact, other than the eighteenth century furniture gallery of the Metropolitan Museum of Art, Helen had never been in a setting as opulent. The pearls of culture she'd been able to grasp in New York seemed, in this setting, barely enough to make a baby's bracelet.

Jessie nodded her acknowledgment, then held out an open palm toward Joe. "Cigarette?"

Joe rapidly pulled a pack of Lucky Strikes from his trouser pocket and then lit the cigarette for Jessie, cupping his hand around the match flame against the slight breeze coming in through the door. He then offered one to Helen, who shook her head, before lighting one himself.

"Now let's all join the party outside, shall we?" Jessie asked. "Helen, where are you from, you delicious thing? Joe's very slow to bring his lady friends around."

"New York." Helen processed the information that Joe was well enough known to Jessie that she kept track of his comings and goings with women.

"And you met Joe how?"

"I picked her up at the cleaners along with my clothes," Joe said and smiled.

"Ha, ha." Jessie's laugh was percussive, beat then beat then full stop.

"Joe's been kind enough to show me around and wanted to introduce me to some of his friends since I'm new to the state."

"Well," Jessie took Helen's hand in a firm grasp and shook it like a man would, "do enjoy the party and meet people." She then turned and walked toward a cluster of men, who broke apart and then reassembled themselves with Jessie at the center of the group.

One of the men leaned over as Jessie whispered something in his ear, then looked over at Joe and Helen and waved. Then he scanned the clutter of people on the veranda before turning back to the hostess.

The waiter came around again, holding out his hand for Helen's now empty flute and handing her another one, the glass slick and cool in her hand. She began sipping immediately. The waiter then handed Joe a martini from the edge of the tray. Joe stubbed out his cigarette in a nearby ashtray.

"Tell me about your friends here, Joe."

"What would you like to know?" He had his new drink gripped by the stem and almost drained.

"Is Jessie in the movie business, too?" The wealth of the house seemed to seep into the air Helen breathed.

Sandy had said that only celebrities, thieves, and bottom-feeders still had money in the Great Depression. "Babe Ruth, John Dillinger, and Joe Kennedy," he had spat. "What a group."

"No, no." Joe shook his head a little too wildly. "Silver mines."

"In California?" She had never heard of silver mines in California, but she supposed that where there had been gold there could be silver.

"Nevada, mostly. Maybe one down in Julian, there," he pointed with a wavy finger in a south-easterly direction, "near, I don't know, San Diego."

"Ahh," Helen said. "Is there a Mr. Jessie?"

"He passed away. Mining accident, I think." Joe gave an exaggerated shrug.

Helen saw that tension and alcohol were making Joe's needle slide in its tracks and bobble from phrase to phrase. She decided to put down her second Champagne although reluctantly.

"Let's sit," she said. In the corner of the veranda, someone had hung a porch swing. She took Joe's hand and led him over to it. They both sank onto the wooden seat. She put the glasses on the deck. The seat swayed down, Joe tilting toward horizontal as it did.

"Sorry," he said, but he stayed limp as a deflated balloon, head between his knees.

"Hey, Joe." From over Helen's shoulder a man spoke, his voice smooth and sober, with a wisp of New Jersey in it. Simultaneously, Helen felt a firm grip on her upper arm. "I'll just help him inside where he can lie down for a while. Must be the unseasonable warmth."

Helen relaxed as the grip on her arm vanished and the man moved to the front of the swing. It was the same man who had waved from Jessie's pack of guys. Muscles bulged out of his shirt sleeves and he had a pink scar like a question mark on his left cheek that ran from just under the corner of his eye over to the bridge of his nose. The nose was slightly ajar, like a door handle that hadn't been properly closed. He crouched down in front of Joe, thick thighs straining the seams of his trousers. Then, he grabbed Joe under both arm pits and lifted him up, standing as he did so.

"You stay put, if you don't mind, Miss."

"Helen."

"Helen," he repeated. "I'm Ralph. I do think a nap will help." He draped Joe's left arm over his own shoulder, grabbed Joe around his upper torso and away they went toward the rear of the porch. "Guesthouse out by the pool," he called back.

Helen stood and smoothed out her dress. The air had cooled rapidly. Away from the heat generated by the crowd and the lights, it was almost chilly in the breeze. She brought her hands to her upper arms, rubbed them for warmth, and looked up at the array of stars splashed across the dark sky.

"My dear girl, I've just heard that Joe was taken ill and is resting. I am sure he'll be better." Jessie's tobacco-cured voice called out to Helen, who turned to see her hostess's half-faced smile.

"Now we have a chance to chat. Joe's tale of meeting you was so charming. But, really, I must know more about you."

In the New York that Helen knew, no one demanded personal information when they first met. It was as if the very nature of having so many people thronging about the streets, restaurants, and stores required that, if anything, people wanted to know less about each other. A stranger today would most likely be a stranger tomorrow, so why bother? But, possibly the rules in California were different, or the rules for this class were different.

"I'm from New York," Helen began.

"Originally?"

"No. I'm an immigrant from Germany."

"Ah," Jessie nodded. "A wonderful country. Quite the best of Europe, I think. But you must have been quite young because you have no accent, really, none at all that I can detect."

"I was eight."

"Did you come with your parents? Come, come, don't make me ask for each little morsel." Jessie walked over, took Helen's hand, and looked directly into her eyes. In the dark, the pupils had widened so there was just a hint of brown around the black.

Helen picked a smile out of her repertoire, one that she had used when Sarah was at her most mother-substitute demanding. A smile that was placating, submissive, and bright enough to hide behind.

"I came with my sister, who is eight years older than I am. We had been orphaned, once by the Great War, which killed our father, then again by influenza, which took our mother in 1919. For two years we stayed with other family…"

"In Germany?"

Helen nodded. "But once my sister, who was working for a dressmaker, had saved enough money, we came here. It took her two years to save. And six months to travel from where we were to Amsterdam to catch the ship."

"My dear, dear girl." Jessie patted the hand she held lightly. "Your father, what happened exactly?"

Their father had been grabbed and heaved onto a cart with other despairing young townsmen. In her memories she could feel his last kiss on her cheek, but she could not see his face. Weeping mothers and young wives held onto the wheel spokes until their fingers were pried off by the officer in charge of the conscription. Her mother stuck a reddened knuckle in her mouth and moaned. A child cried "Pappi, Pappi." Was it her voice, Sarah's, or just another soon-to-be orphan?

Whose army was it? Helen did not know. How did he die? She didn't know that either. Germany, Russia, and the Austro-Hungarian Empire all trampled through her parents' lives, grinding them into the ground like dry hay under their boots.

"He died in battle."

"Your father was a hero in the Fatherland." A single "ha" exited from Jessie's lips, then she squeezed them tightly together as if in penance. "I did not mean to laugh, not at all. I'm just so happy to meet the daughter of such a brave man. And look what happened to the country that gave us so much culture."

Germany was a mess, but Sarah and Helen had been too preoccupied with starving to care. And the Polish government didn't care either, holding Germany as responsible as every other country around for the demise of Poland. From the ashes of Germany, Poland had risen, stitched back together, yet not quite whole.

Sarah, stuffing paper into the bottom of Helen's shoes to cover the holes and then blackening the paper so no one could see them if Helen raised a foot, dressed them both in fashionable skirts and blouses she had sewn from cloth stolen from her employer, marched them to the train station, and handed forged documents to the border police with a wad of worthless *marka*.

The officer spit on the money. "German crap."

"We are going to America," Sarah told him. At sixteen, she was luminous, a heart-shaped face with porcelain skin and oxblood hair.

"Good for you. Can I come too?" He smiled at Sarah, then grabbed her around the waist, pulled her close, and kissed her on the lips. "Go with God."

Sarah fingered the small filigreed cross around her neck that she had bought at the flea market the day before. "Say thank you to the nice officer, Helen," she said.

"My father was one of many who died. Let us hope that the Great War was indeed the war to end all wars," Helen said.

"Walk with me, Helen," Jessie replied. They began a slow parade up the veranda, Jessie tucking Helen's hand through her arm. "I don't think it was that kind of war. It left too many problems," Jessie said.

"Maybe."

"Certainly. We are all patriots at this party," Jessie said. "And deeply concerned about the situation in Europe."

Helen looked around again. No one seemed the slightest bit concerned about anything except drinking more martinis and Champagne. Some guests held small plates on which Helen could see huge pink shrimp, small fragrant meatballs, and slices of white turkey breast heaped high, as if this were to be the last good meal. Helen wondered if they were playing the role to please their lavish hostess and if Jessie had held similar discussions with other guests in the past, while weaving with them up and down her long veranda.

"What are you doing now, Helen?" Jessie had stopped walking near a buffet table, whose platters were being refilled by a middle-aged woman uniformed as a maid.

"Pardon me?"

"Are you working?"

"Yes. In my brother-in-law's store."

"And then?"

"And then, if it suits me, I will stay here and find another job," Helen said.

"Maybe I can help with that. We'll see. Meantime, I need to talk to a few more people, Helen, so let me deposit you over here with Dodi and Mark. They're a lovely young couple. I'm sure Joe will be feeling better shortly."

Jessie walked Helen over to a man and woman who looked like figures on top of a wedding cake, although dressed not in a rococo white dress and black tux, but in the impeccably casual clothes of the wealthy.

"Dodi, Mark, this is Helen. Take good care of her for a while. Her date is Joe and he's a bit incapacitated."

"We'll protect her from mayhem," Dodi said in a low pitched tone. "Good for Joe that he finally showed up with a date and such a special one at that."

For the next hour, Helen nibbled on shrimp, turkey, and tender, sweet, tiny dinner rolls. She talked with Dodi and Mark and other guests, who wandered by, about Fred Astaire and Ginger Rogers, the weather, the Olympics starting that summer, and the elegant graciousness of their hostess.

Helen felt a hand on her shoulder and turned. Joe looked like a scolded puppy but he seemed put together, and his eyes were alert.

"I must apologize to you. That has never happened to me before," he said.

Helen was relieved that she did not have to find another ride home, but she felt no need to comfort Joe in his moment of chagrin.

"Joe, you naughty boy," Dodi said, slapping him playfully on an arm. "You should eat something next time before you come and drink."

Joe looked at her. "It just hit me suddenly," he said.

"Okay, Dodi," said Mark. "He's embarrassed enough. Look here, old sport, I'll just grab you a roll to settle your stomach." Mark took two steps back, snared some bread from a tray, and held it out to Joe on the palm of his hand.

Joe took it, tore off a piece the size of a quarter, and shoved it into the side of his mouth, where it found a pocket and remained unchewed, giving him the lopsided appearance of a man with a toothache. Helen felt her own stomach begin to churn as if in sympathy.

"I'm a little tired," she said. "Would it be all right to say our goodbyes now?"

Joe nodded, cheered by the idea of escape. "Of course."

Joe spent the ride home repeating his apology to Helen until she patted his arm and told him she could not bear to have him say "sorry" one more time. Because of the wealth she had seen, she steeled herself to try at least one more excursion with Joe, provided she could control what he drank and how much.

At the door, she smiled her billboard smile. Joe leaned in, directing his kiss toward her mouth like a bird on a trajectory. She turned her face so he landed wetly on her cheek instead. "It's only our second date," she said.

"I hope there'll be a third."

"Call me."

At that Joe took a step back, straightened up, and said, "Tomorrow."

She watched the new Ford coupe as he pulled it away from the curb. "Five hundred and ten dollars for that car," she whispered as she turned the key in the lock to go inside. "I wonder if he paid cash."

4

"HARRY, I'D LIKE TO ASK a question, but it might be too intrusive," Helen said as they walked to Forester Liquor to open for the Saturday trade. "On the other hand, if I know the score, I can be of more help than if I don't."

Harry continued to advance, head facing forward, torso leaning into each step and then jerking back as if the act of walking was new to him.

"What is it, Helen?" Harry's tone was that of a teacher bombarded with repeated requests to explain the algebra problem he'd just posted in detail on the blackboard.

"What's Dragna?"

"Dragna is a person. Okay, so I answered the question. That's enough. And don't," he turned to Helen with the mean stare she recalled from his days courting Sarah, "don't," he repeated, "talk to Sarah about this."

"Yes, sure. But, Harry, Sarah knows something about Dragna. I don't know what, but she does."

Harry quickened his pace. Helen lengthened her stride to keep up. "I don't know what I shouldn't talk to her about," she said.

Helen wondered how well Harry knew his wife, if he thought

Sarah had not already detected danger with her prickly sixth sense, nurtured in the ruins of post Great War Europe. Helen knew Sarah and Sarah's omniscient threat awareness.

Dragna had something to do with Harry, the store, probably the beating he had taken, and the small bookie operation that he was running. These were connected together like Ben's wooden train pieces, hook to eye, locomotive in front, caboose in back.

But if Harry told her more about this Dragna person, maybe she could keep from Sarah whatever Sarah did not yet know. She would practice misdirection and fudging, tricks that she had plied to keep her own life hidden from Sarah when they lived together.

"He's a gangster," Harry said.

"Not another bookie?"

"Yes, that too. He runs a huge gambling operation."

"And this has what to do with you?"

"He gets a cut of the profit and I get no competition in the area."

"So, Harry, is this serious, this protection money situation?"

Harry glanced at her, his features frozen in place, not an emotion to be seen, his tension seeping out cold from an open ice box door. "Not if I pay it. And I do."

"And the beating you took?"

Harry laughed, the ice box of tension heaving out a low, humorless chuckle. "That was not a beating, Helen. It was a gentle reminder that I was a day late. I'll tell you... it's hard to make a living in this Depression. Between the gangsters who get protection and the cops who collect it, I'm squeezed like a ripe California orange for juice every week." He plucked at his skin with thumb and forefinger. "Look at me. Just pith."

"Is that how you'll throw yourself on the mercy of the court? I couldn't make an illegal living because the other crooks were bigger."

Another snowball of laughter popped out. "You're good, Helen. You know that? So, you do not tell Sarah that I was a day late. You tell her everything is fine and that I just walked into the door, like I already told her I did."

"And if she asks me what I know?"

"What do you know? Nothing. You saw nothing, you heard nothing. And that's the truth."

"And if she asks what you told me?"

"I walked into a door. I give the beat cop free beers, which is why he comes into the storage room. I like the races, which is why I have the racing form. That's what I told her and it's what I'm telling you."

"But she knows about Dragna."

"Nah." Harry shook his head. "She heard the cop talking about him, is all. You know, just passing the time about stuff in LA. Nothing to put me and Dragna together."

Helen bit her lip and said nothing.

They reached the front door of the store. Harry lifted the stack of *Los Angeles Times* bundled together with twine. A second, smaller bundle sat next to the mail drop.

"Grab those, Helen."

She bent down. As she lifted the papers, the name *Variety* was clear.

Harry nodded at the papers she held. "We've got more people moving here who are in the movie industry. Like your friend, Joe. Maybe this'll be another draw."

A dozen customers wandered in and out of Forester Liquor during the day, buying liquor and cigarettes and holding the packages close to them as they exited, safety from the rest of the weekend that stretched before them unfilled. Helen sat behind the counter, finished the bookkeeping for the week, and thumbed through *Variety* when the store was empty.

The store, Harry, Sarah, all began to feel like a giant mouse trap into which she had wandered, tempted by free cheese. She could see herself repeating the pattern of home, store, home, one black tile, one white tile, one black tile, until her life was covered over by that monotonous pattern. Turning the pages of *Variety*, she pretended an interest she did not feel. She'd ask about the bus line into Hollywood and go there tomorrow just to see Grauman's Chinese Theater.

"Helen?" A deep voice called her from the open door.

She looked up but the figure was standing in the sunlight pouring into the entrance and bouncing off the windows. As the man stepped past the beer display, Helen recognized Ralph, who had hauled Joe like a large sack of potatoes to the cabana to sleep it off.

"Jessie wanted me to check on you and make sure you'd gotten home okay."

"But how...."

"I'd tell you Jessie has her ways, but that would be too mysterious. Fact is, I asked Joe last night where you lived because Jessie was worried about him taking you home in his condition. He couldn't remember the address but he said that between you and him, he'd get you home. Or maybe he just didn't want me to help." Ralph smiled wryly. "But he did say you worked at Forester's."

"Nice of Jessie. She could have just called." Helen felt alert, as if she'd just had a large cup of coffee and the caffeine was zipping through her.

"Jessie's a meticulous kind of person."

Harry came out of the storage room with a case of beer. He looked at Ralph and nodded. He replenished the Pabst in the cooler, the bottles clinking together rhythmically.

"My brother in law, the owner, Harry Forester," Helen said.

"Harry, this is Ralph…" She didn't know his last name. The party had not been full of genuine conversation, except the one she had with Jessie, just a lot of casual chat. And, in fact, she didn't even know Jessie's last name.

"Ralph Emory," Harry said, offering his hand after wiping the condensation off on his trouser. "Middle-weight boxer. Local clubs. I'm a boxing fan. You took quite a fall last time out."

"Thanks for reminding me," Ralph said, rubbing his cheek along the scar. "I don't do that anymore."

"Get knocked out?" Helen asked. Both men looked at her.

Ralph grinned. "I try not to. I'm pretty much out of the fight business."

Harry reached back into the cooler, pulled out a bottle with a cold sweat on it, and said, "Have one on me." He held it toward Ralph.

"If you're offering and you don't mind, I'll have a Coca-Cola instead."

Ralph and Harry hooked themselves over the corner of the counter, each with a Coca-Cola bottle. Harry made it a point never to drink the store wares on store time. Seven-Up and Coca-Cola were the exceptions. Helen drifted back to her *Variety* at the other end of the counter, near the register, which was where Harry always wanted her stationed.

She turned the pages of the newspaper, feigning interest. Her eyes fixed on the print she was not reading, she listened to the men talking. There was a loud laugh when they discovered they hailed from the same tough Hoboken neighborhood and had attended Hoboken High School, although five years apart.

Ralph, it appeared, had a solid and lucrative fighting career until he ended it after he was knocked out in the twelfth round and then given a sucker kick to the head by his frustrated opponent.

He'd spent three days in the hospital recovering and still had ringing in his ears.

"Bad enough I have a turnip ear," she heard him say. "My momma doesn't need a turnip brain for a son."

Harry laughed. "Those New Jersey mothers won't put up with nothin'." He laughed, then said something so quietly Helen could not hear.

"No. Jeez, I stay away from gangsters. They're the rot of society and the ruination of boxing. All you hear about is this guy took a fall, that guy took a fall. It's not right."

"Corruption."

"Thanks for the drink, Harry. Listen, I just want to ask Helen something and then I'll leave."

Ralph walked over to Helen and leaned in close enough to whisper. But, instead, he spoke in a normal voice, which startled her into turning her head toward him. Their eyes were inches apart and she could see his black pupils and her distorted reflection.

"If you and Joe aren't dating seriously, I'd like to take you out," he said. "I could pick you up tomorrow and show you Hollywood and Los Angeles. If you are serious with Joe, forget I asked."

"What time tomorrow?" He wrote down her address, grinned at Harry, and left.

Ralph spent ten minutes play-fighting with Ben and cooing at Rachel before he escorted Helen out to his car. By that time, five of the neighbor men had gathered around the Chrysler Imperial Roadster and were walking around it as if they were circling an exotic animal that had wandered into their backyard. The top was down, exposing the cream-colored seats and gleaming dashboard to the sky. The car was a caramel color, polished to a lacquered finish, and decorated with white striping down the sides.

"Can I ask how fast this will go?" said one of the younger men.

"It'll do eighty, but I won't," Ralph replied. The man laughed and shook his head.

"Did you know that some couple is trying to drive all the way from the tip of South Africa to Alaska?" another man asked.

"Never heard that," Ralph said, "but people will do anything for publicity I guess. Helen, shall we go?"

At that, the men pulled back from the car and stood on the sidewalk, parting for Helen to walk through. Ralph opened the door for her, she sat, and he walked to the other side. The men looked at her and then away almost in unison and she tried not to laugh. They'd been caught yearning for something they could not have, whether it was the car or her, she did not care.

After they'd gone a half-block, Ralph said, "I don't want you to get the wrong impression."

"Of what? This is a beautiful car and it's the perfect day to drive with the top down."

"I got this car from someone who was very down on his luck. Just bought it for cash from the prize money at one of my winning fights." He emphasized "winning" in a dry tone.

Helen laughed appreciatively. This was like the postcards, warm air almost blue like the sky brushing over her hair, her Pepsodent smile gleaming, pink lips turned up at the corners as if for a cover shoot. It was what she had come to California for.

"You said you weren't fighting anymore."

"I gave it up. But I'm working in the industry. I've gotten some bit parts, character roles really, and I moonlight as a bodyguard."

"What studio?"

"MGM, same as Joe. That's how I met him. How he recruited me."

"To do what?" she asked.

"He's close to Jessie. Beats me why, but he is. And Jessie always seems to need someone to stand guard over her. She's interesting that way. So I get to go places with her and I get to hover at her parties. Sometimes," he looked at her, "I even get to enjoy myself."

"What's her last name? And why does she need a watch dog?"

"Murphy. Money. Connections. Agendas."

Ralph's tone had cooled like a tendril of fog sliding into the sunshine sky. Like Sandy, like Joe, he seemed reluctant to talk when the topic wasn't him. Helen decided to heat up the conversation again and also take it in a direction of interest to her. Helen could wait to get more information about Jessie. And, if Jessie liked to hire people to serve her, Helen had no interest in being a maid.

"Other than as a way to meet you," she said loudly enough to be heard over the hum of the engine and the swooshing breeze, "I don't care."

Ralph had a number of bit parts in B movies, and some crowd appearances in A ones. He assured Helen that if she looked hard enough, she could see him in the crowd scene at the guillotine in *A Tale of Two Cities* and as a cab driver in *Werewolf of London*.

He had a small speaking role in *The Thin Man*, playing one of the comedic gangsters that populated that film. To his regret, he'd never met Myrna Loy. Not all the movies were MGM; rules were much more flexible for the lowest level of actor, that level of purgatory which he inhabited, than for the stable of actors and actresses under contract to MGM. That stellar assembly was a wholly owned subsidiary of Louis B. Mayer.

Gathering this information, which fell in a torrent from a surprisingly verbal Ralph, allowed Helen to relax into the car's smooth seat and watch Hollywood Boulevard come into focus. She asked how he got to be a bit player and mentally took notes as he explained.

Ralph parked and they walked a half-block to stand on the sidewalk across the street from Grauman's Chinese Theater. A scarlet-stippled pagoda with a gold triangular roof stretched into the sky, each corner guarded by an engraved black lion's head. Gilt Oriental letters a foot high decorated the columns.

Helen walked across the street, Ralph's hand at her elbow as if he thought she could not sightsee without tripping over her own feet. Turning to smile at him, she lengthened her stride to move away from his hand.

"I'm feeling like a movie star," she said, slipping under the portico and into the courtyard. Three other tourists were already there, huddled together and gazing down with Kodak Brownie cameras, lenses fixed on the concrete indented with the footprints and handprints of stars.

Helen slipped her foot into the impression left by Mary Pickford, like Cinderella sliding into the glass slipper. She had been America's sweetheart. And here, Shirley Temple had leaned into the wet sludge making hand- and footprints as if she were playing at the beach, forever a child, another of America's adored ones.

"Those'll be here forever," Ralph said, nodding at the small and scattered array of imprints and names now fossilized in stone.

"Or at least until they tear this place down," Helen said.

Next on Ralph's tour was the Egyptian Theater. The plaster temple columns formed a colonnade down which Helen walked. Ralph swung his hand once toward hers, but failing to catch it, he stayed half a step behind her.

"Home of the first movie premier," Ralph said, in true tourist guide fashion.

"Hmm. Very nice."

But Helen remembered the real Egyptian artifacts at the Metropolitan Museum of Art, ancient and preserved, gold, black and red hieroglyphics circling the coffins, the idea of the mummies inside making her shiver. Sandy put his arm around her, but teased her for being scared of the dead. "It's the not-quite-dead you need to worry about," he whispered in her ear.

Exhausting the draw of Hollywood, Ralph drove them into Beverly Hills by way of Wilshire Boulevard. The spacious street had been fully formed and fashioned for the automobile, and the stores that lined it, for the passengers.

Money was palpable in the newness of the architecture. One department store seemed to have been sent from the future, boldly rounded at the corner of Wilshire and Fairfax, the display window glass unblemished, the second story appearing to float on air. But a palpable stink hovered in the air, as if a giant had let out gas.

"Tar pits," Ralph said. "They get mastodon bones out of them. Can you believe dinosaurs roamed this once upon a time?" He nodded at the buildings that surrounded them and shook his head.

"Look up there." He pointed to the hills. She could see the Hollywoodland sign, white against the tan dirt.

By the time they reached the border of Beverly Hills, wealth assaulted the senses. Even the air seemed richer.

Up and down the residential streets they drove so slowly that a couple walking their fox terrier passed them by. The automobile did not so much run as hum, as if it was contentedly prowling its turf.

On these streets, shaded by trees with purple and yellow blossoms, the Packard seemed at home. Two- and three-story houses were set back at least fifty feet from the curb on grass so green Helen wondered if it had been painted. Each garden was a tropical feast of hues in mango, fuchsia, emerald green, royal purples and a pageantry of other colors. Ralph said that most of the houses had their own swimming pools, maids, butlers, and the occasional child of an occupant, accompanied by a nanny trained in England.

"Heaven," Helen said, closing her eyes and stretching out her arms.

"I'm glad to be your St. Peter," Ralph said. "We have enough time for me to show you where I live, if you'd like. All above board, I promise." He raised his right hand. "I was a Boy Scout."

"Scout to St. Peter via the boxing ring. An interesting journey."

Except for gently handing her into the car, Ralph had not touched her, his hands remaining on the wheel unless he needed to shift gears. Helen had always been attracted to handsome men, slim and lightly muscled, clean shaven, and unscarred. Ralph was thick, with arms roped with muscle, and a broken face. Maybe that accounted for his odd grace with her, a sort of holding back that she felt.

"Sure. If you can't trust a Boy Scout, really who can you trust?" she said.

He laughed.

They drove back to Wilshire Boulevard, then took a left so the low-slung Hollywood Hills faced them. The car easily handled the slight climb. Ralph only mentioned a few streets as they passed them. Hollywood Boulevard and Sunset Boulevard were the ones she recognized. Then they were on a narrow, graveled lane that rose at a sharper angle. The Packard moaned slightly and Ralph downshifted. Once out of its misery, the Packard quieted. A hundred yards up, Ralph slipped the car onto a parking apron that was cantilevered over the side of the hill.

Around them, the air smelled of pine and spruce. Birds called to one another. Looking around, Helen saw no signs of a house.

"We have to walk up a few steps," Ralph said. He pointed to a switchback of stone stairs embedded in the side of the hill to her left. An iron banister, flaking green paint and rust giving it the mottled look of a snake at the zoo, zigzagged along the side of the stairs.

"I'll bring up the rear," he added, "although I doubt you'll slip. You don't strike me as the type to make a false step."

"Cute," she replied.

At the top of the stairs, there was a leveled area just big enough to allow a large terra cotta pot containing an odd, twisted, prickly growth to coexist with a door. The house hovered at the edge of the hill, the rear wall keeping the barest toehold as the ground fell away behind it. Helen's impression was of windows and a reddish wood in a simple design.

"If you've never seen one, the plant there is a Yucca."

Helen started to giggle. "Yuck yuck."

"No, really. It's an agave plant that is called a Yucca." Ralph's voice had a professorial air, but he started to grin.

"Anyhow, moving on from the Yucca, we have my abode. It was the practice house of an architect friend of mine. He wanted to start really small and work his way up."

"And…"

"He's got his own firm now, and he's doing okay. But he doesn't get to do as much experimental stuff."

Ralph got out a key, moved to the front door, and opened it. Helen stepped in. Just twelve feet away the rear glass wall faced a canyon, dappled at this time of day with green light, and, further in the distance, city buildings, shadowy in the late afternoon sun. The living room had a small dark leather couch and a matching club chair, both facing the window. A low-slung coffee table gleamed metallically, with a chrome finish much like the hubcaps of the Packard outside.

To her left as she entered was a kitchen. Open to the living room, it had cabinets of the same type of wood she had seen on the façade of the house, a four-burner stove, refrigerator, counters fashioned out of a stone Helen did not recognize, and a sink.

"If you need the bathroom for any reason, it's that way." Ralph pointed to an archway through which Helen could see a double bed, trimly made with a gray spread and white pillows. She nodded and walked into the bedroom.

A small, polished black gun in black leather holster lay on top of the bureau. Underneath the gun there was a blood red pamphlet with a white swastika and a caricature of a hook-nosed Jew.

Helen's stomach turned and her mouth puckered even before she could begin to think. Stepping awkwardly toward the bathroom, she grabbed the corner of the bathroom sink, swung herself, still clothed, onto the toilet seat, and pulled the pocket door shut. The nausea billowed up, with the warm stench of acid in the back of her throat.

She breathed deeply, sitting up straight, as taught in her high school basic bookkeeping and office skills class by Miss Thworpe, a female martinet with a rigid sense of decorum to match her posture. "A young woman in a position of employment never allows any physical discomfort of whatever cause to affect her presentation." So the class gritted their way through menstrual cramps, clenched down on coughing spasms, and typed when the windows let in the numbingly cold New York winter air.

After a minute, her nerves calmed and the storm in her stomach eased. She completed the toileting she had come in for, carefully washed her hands and swallowed a gulp of cold water from the tap. Ralph, she told herself, clearly had no idea she was Jewish. He had not brought her up to his house to sew a yellow Star of David on her blouse. While sex was probably on his mind, he did not act like a rapist. And, if she stayed calm and played the part right, he would take her home. She would never have to see him again.

Helen tugged the door into its hole and turned back into the room, edging away from the bureau as if from a coiled snake. A few quick steps and she was in the living room, which was filled with an ambient pinkish glow from the sunset clouds just out the window.

"Helen," Ralph said, "I've poured you a little lemonade." He held a glass of light yellow liquid, with ice clinking against the rim, toward her.

She gazed at him, a slight smile hovering around her lips, and sighed. "I'm feeling a little off, I'm afraid." Her smile saddened around the corners. "Could you just run me home, please?"

She saw him hesitate, the hand holding the glass descending

as if it were the drooping tail of a friendly dog that had not been petted. "Of course," he said. "I'll just duck into the bedroom for a minute myself and we can go."

Helen positioned herself a few steps from the front door and stared out the window, willing herself to breathe steadily and to not bolt at the slightest sound from Ralph.

"Oh crap." Ralph's voice ricocheted off the front window from behind her.

Despite her efforts at calm, she turned, mouth dry, eyes wide open, heart pounding. She felt that if anyone really looked at her all they would see was a frozen scream.

"You saw this." Ralph held out the gun but not the Nazi pamphlet.

She nodded. The pamphlet's non-appearance rendered it ephemeral, just a little, nasty piece of Los Angeles business, except that it festered like a splinter in her mind.

"I didn't know I was going to ask you here. So I just left it there from my job last night. It must have frightened you." His voice was solicitous, apologetic, and so low it was gravelly. "You poor kid."

> When Helen was five, if she stood up straight and stared intently at uniformed legs and bellies, she always saw the gun in the holster. One time, she walked ever so slowly over to a uniformed man and reached up toward his gun. Her mother grabbed her by the back of her sweater and dragged her away. Everyone she knew stepped off the sidewalk to let the guns go by, watching these men walk into the pastry shop and get the sweetest treats without any money.

Helen nodded again, tilting her head slightly down, and sighing deeply. The sigh impacted Ralph as if she had fainted outright.

"Helen, Helen," he said, stepping toward her.

She backed up a step. "Please, Ralph, just take me home."

Ralph walked her out to the car in silence. Once they were in and he was backing out, he said, "The gun is for my work, Helen, really."

"You had the gun on you Friday night at Jessie's party?"

Ralph's jaw clenched and his eyes remained on the road's curves.

"Why does Jessie even need a bodyguard?" she asked.

Instead of answering, Ralph reached over, picked up her left hand from her lap and brought it to his mouth. He planted his lips on her palm, closed her fingers over and returned her hand to her lap.

Ralph walked her to the door. "I'll call you this week, Helen. And, I'll make sure the gun is put away. You'll never see it again," he said.

"Thanks for a lovely day," she replied, turning her cheek for his goodnight kiss.

5

O N TUESDAY, HELEN CLOSED FORESTER Liquor by herself. Harry left at three, saying he had a dentist appointment.
Helen suspected that the teeth being pulled were at the Santa Anita
race track. She could not decide if she wanted the experience to be
painful for Harry or not. She opted for not, for Sarah's sake. Losses
at the track would only compound Harry's after-dinner irritability,
soothed by a tumbler of scotch, two or three if he lost money on
horses or boxing or baseball, and *The Adventures of Gracie* on the
radio.

When she walked into the house, Sarah pointed to an envelope on the kitchen table and then returned to her silent vigil over
the stew simmering on the stove. The meaty, oniony aroma filled
the kitchen and spilled into the living room.

The envelope had Sandy's handwriting. Helen took it to her
room before opening it to postpone Sarah's staccato questions and
to prepare the best answers.

Hello Helen,

I will be in Los Angeles on April 22 or 23, depending
on the railroad schedule. If possible, and you would

be all right with it, I would like to see you. Your
friend, Sandy.

Possibly he was trying to save ink, she considered dryly. But,
she sank down onto the pink chenille bedspread, holding the letter
between her two clenched hands, the paper wrinkling in protest,
the ink smearing onto her perspiring palms. She put the paper
down and spread it out, her hand ironing out the twisted corners.

Thursday came and went without any contact from Sandy or
from Joe or Ralph. Relief at not hearing from Joe and Ralph felt
like the little Champagne bubbles from the party, tickly, frothy, and
freely rising.

Helen knew she could have used their knowledge of the film
industry to help her find a role as an extra or even a small walk-on.
She wanted to see the MGM lots, and either one of them would
have taken her. When she thought about what they could do for
her, and kept those thoughts removed from her physical reactions
to them and their distaste for Jews, it seemed that she could go
out with either of them again. But once her feelings engaged, spilling acid into her stomach, she sat straight up, breathed deeply, and
turned her thoughts to Forester Liquor, bookkeeping, or restocking
the beer in the cooler. She could not date either man again.

Numbers were quite calming as she inked them into their
proper cells on the page. She had quieted her feelings about being
on her own, back in New York, by intense focus on addition and
subtraction of columns and columns of numbers in her bookkeeping class and then in the spiritless job with its steady pay before she
came to California. It had been too bad about the job at Gimbel's,
but no one could work on commission during a depression.

Friday, customers came and went, pricking the boredom of the day with occasional chat about the weather, the cost of good vodka, or their plans for the weekend. Helen stifled yawns and thoughts that she could not possibly continue to work for Harry in his suburban liquor store for even one more week.

At 3:20 p.m., the liquor store phone rang. "For you," Harry said, holding the receiver out.

"Hello, Helen." The timbre was Sandy's, and the inflection was the flat, clipped, non-accent of a handful of customers who frequented the shop and shared with her that they were the most exotic of breeds, a true native Californian.

"Sandy?"

"Yes. I'll borrow a friend's car and come and get you around six. We'll have dinner. By then I'll be starving."

Before she left New York she would have pretended insult, eyes narrowing like shuttering blinds, lips pressed together like pounded pillows, at his assumption that she was free that night and would have dinner with him. But whatever his romantic intentions were or had been for her, she felt now as if the only friend she'd ever had in the world had just offered to climb eleven flights of stairs to see her.

"Sure. And...."

Sandy was no longer on the line.

Sandy made his usual good impression. He seemed to slide exactly into a space in Sarah and Harry's world that had not been visible until he walked through the door. Sarah chatted with him about his trip to Los Angeles with more gaiety than Helen had seen since her sister had gotten mildly tipsy on the wine in the Kiddush cup at her own wedding. Harry's affability came from a relaxed part of him that Helen had never encountered. But Sandy's interaction with Helen was blandly thoughtful and cheerily distant.

He escorted Helen to the small, older Ford coupe parked three houses down, opened the door for her, and she slid in.

"So, what have you been up to out here in California?" he asked.

"Working."

"And?"

"And what, Sandy?" His interactions with her up to that point were like being stuck in a tepid pool of water up to her waist and waiting for him to signal if he was reaching in for her or not. She resented the lack of physical contact. If he wanted to be just friends, she was certain she was not going to be the friendly type.

His eyebrow raised up in droll alarm, as if cued for a drawing room comedy. "Now, my dear," he said, his voice plummy and arch, "let's play nice. After all, I am not the one who moved twenty-five hundred miles away. Yet, here I am, borrowing a car, driving you around a strange city, and taking you out to dinner."

She smiled. "Here you are, indeed. And that's twenty-five hundred miles as the crow flies, not as the train runs."

"Indeed. Even further."

In the car, Sandy reached for Helen's hand just once, with a squeeze that felt platonic but left her feeling anything but that.

"So let's start with what else are you doing besides working in Forester Liquor, which is, I may say and with no disrespect to your brother-in-law, beneath your lovely skills."

"I am trying to meet people and develop connections."

"Hmm."

"I have met several people with connections to the studios," she said in a voice like a tart apple.

"All men?" Sandy retreated to his English farce voice.

"Oh my heavens, no." Her hand fluttered up to her face in her best imitation of a stage debutante. "But some."

"That's my Helen. Who could resist you?"

Harry had suggested a small Italian restaurant, with a dozen tables, ironed white tablecloths, and half-melted candles stuck in straw-wrapped Chianti bottles. Muffled Italian curses emanated from the kitchen and the slender, just-adolescent waiter had a slight Italian accent. Helen relaxed with a glass of house white and Sandy, with the red.

While they ate a green salad, lightly tossed with a glossy oil and vinegar dressing with a delicate sweet and sour taste, Helen listened as Sandy talked about the train trip out to Los Angeles and made brief comments about her own journey. She asked what brought him to California twice, but he waved her off each time, saying he'd talk about it later.

Gradually, over cheese and mushroom ravioli in a fresh tomato sauce, small chunks of which popped with tart flavor, just-cut basil, with its tangy vegetal smell and tongue-tickling, salty anchovies, Sandy turned the discussion back to what Helen was doing and who she was dating.

As if it was a shadow at the door, Helen could sense a purpose in his questions and felt flattered and piqued at the same time. This was a relationship he had closed down and what business was it of his? She decided to opt for honesty.

"Fine, Sandy. I have dated two men, one twice, one once. If I never see either of them again, I'll be happy."

He started to say something and she held up her hand. "I will say, though, that I met them both at the most interesting party."

She described the house, wings spread out to embrace the view from the hilltop, the food piled on trays that were filled from an overflowing kitchen, the liquor and Champagne in crystal glasses, and the people who were dressed as if they were models in magazines.

"Sounds like quite a party. Who's got money like that out here besides movie moguls?"

"Some woman named Jessie Murphy. I think it's her money. I heard she is a widow."

Sandy put down his fork and put one hand on hers, pressing her palm into the table.

"Jessie Murphy?"

"Why? Have you heard of her? Is she some kind of celebrity?"

"In Nazi circles maybe," he said, voice pitched low at her, hand firmly gripping hers as if to keep her from rising up.

"Nazi, like Hitler Nazi?" Helen tried to keep her voice steady, but it wobbled off pitch, ending just before a scream.

"Quietly, Helen. Yes. Jessie is quite the Nazi sympathizer. More than that, she supports the Silver Shirts with a lot of money."

"That American Nazi group?"

Helen had her voice corralled, matching Sandy's. He released her hand. She felt unmoored by the loss of pressure and pulled both her hands into her lap, where she squeezed them together, fingers interlaced, and held tight.

"Yes. I need to ask you more questions, Helen, but this isn't the place to do it. Finish your food and we'll talk in the car."

They ate in silence, as if they had quarreled and had only the food on the plate to console themselves with. Sandy handed the waiter a five-dollar bill and shook his head when asked if he wanted change. "Keep it as the tip."

"Thanks, sir," the boy said.

Sandy's chair scraped on the floor as he got up. Helen rose, too, leading the way to the door.

In response to Sandy's questions, Helen said that she had talked with Jessie Murphy for only about five minutes, that Jessie thought that Helen was a German émigré, and had offered to help her but in such a vague way that Helen felt it was just a hostess being nice.

"Can you get back in touch with her?"

"Why would I even want to, Sandy? I don't want anything to do with Nazis."

"I know. I'm just asking."

Helen might have kidded Sandy before about excessive suspicion, looking at the underbelly of America for so long that his eyes couldn't adjust to its upper side. This was different. She was tired, the kind of exhaustion that hits at the dead end of a long road. She'd have to start all over trying to make connections. And where would she do that, since Harry's liquor store attracted gamblers and those who fed off them?

Slumping against the back of the seat, she closed her eyes, the half-glass of wine she'd gulped down in an effort to get out of the restaurant adding to her stress. Her thoughts were like photographs spilled onto the floor and she tried to gather them, turn them right side up to recognize them, and put them in order.

Sandy was quiet, too, as if he'd run out of questions to ask her, even though he hadn't yet asked more about either Joe or Ralph. Helen turned her head to look at him. His brow was furrowed and his upper teeth gnawed at his lower lip before letting the lip go and retreating into his mouth. He shook his head once from left to right, then sighed.

"I'll get back in touch with you soon, Helen. For now, if any guests from the party or Jessie herself get in touch with you again, just act normal."

"You're kidding, right?" she said, not masking her distress. "Normal as in I'm not Jewish and they're not Nazis? That kind of normal?"

"Exactly," he said. "The best kind of normal. You'll be great if that happens." He smiled, but his eyes were tight and worried. "In the meantime, I'm going to run this by some people."

When Sandy walked her up to Sarah and Harry's door, he kissed her gently on her forehead, then on her cheek, before folding her into a hug. "I'll call you soon," he said.

"Helen," Sarah called from the kitchen, "did you have a nice time?"

Helen felt her body start to shiver as if she'd walked into a snow storm. "Yes. But I'm a not feeling too well, dear, so I'm going right to bed."

She went into the bathroom and closed the door. In the bathroom mirror, she was all eyes, the rest of her face a shadowy, pale outline in the dim light. She wondered how far away from Europe she would have to be to feel safe. California was not far enough.

In bed, she clenched her teeth, rolled into a fetal ball with her hands shoveled between her thighs, and waited for dawn.

At noon, the Forester Liquor phone rang. "It's for you again," Harry said.

Helen finished ringing up the Cinzano she'd convinced a blonde, turquoise-eyed thirty-year-old woman with a diamond the size of gumdrop to buy for her fifth anniversary celebration. "Your guests will love this," Helen said, sliding the bottle into a brown paper bag. "It's so sophisticated."

"It's Sandy," he said when she brought the receiver up to her ear. "People I know would like to meet you."

Helen said nothing. She'd had an almost sleepless night, falling into a drugged-like darkness around five a.m. During her wakeful watch, she had decided to return to New York when she'd saved enough money for the train fare and a small deposit on a fifth floor walk-up apartment, either in Brooklyn or Hell's Kitchen. She'd had enough of California.

"Helen, are you there?"

"What do they want to meet me about?"

"Just to ask you about Jessie Murphy."

"Sandy, I told you everything I could remember and you have to admit it was not much."

"Yes. Well, it's not my decision."

"It's my decision."

"Of course. Not what I meant. Please just say okay. It's not going to hurt you, promise."

She still hesitated. Jessie Murphy, Joe, Ralph, the party had taken on even more of a nightmare quality with almost no sleep. Her memories started to curl and fray at the edges, obscuring some details she previously thought she knew.

"Please, Helen," Sandy sighed in her ear.

"All right. Who with, though?"

"Concerned people."

She considered asking another question but it would just be more useless information to clutter her already stuffed head with.

"Fine."

"I'll pick you up tonight around seven."

6

SANDY DROVE DOWN WILSHIRE BOULEVARD then turned right, weaving though residential streets with a mix of Spanish style homes interspersed with fanciful cottages out of English and German fairy tales, all sitting on tight little lots. Helen was still unnerved by all the green grass and flowers that lived outside of city parks or pots on fire-escape stairs.

"Where are we?"

"Someplace."

She punched Sandy's arm lightly.

"Hey," he said.

"Let me rephrase. Where are we going?"

"To a meeting of a few well-placed people who are concerned about Nazi sympathizers in Hollywood and the West Coast in general."

"Not spies."

"No, you're with the only spy I know of." He smiled at her.

"Sandy, you are infuriating. I'm trying to be serious since you have dragged me to a meeting with people I don't know to talk about a party I went to and a woman I met just one time. You won't tell me who these people are and then you kid around about serious stuff."

Sandy made a left turn onto yet another residential street and parked in front of an English country bungalow, all peaked roof and green shutters.

"Those times when I was out of New York auditioning for parts, I was actually spying on behalf of the Anti-Defamation League. Really, Helen, I was."

Helen was tempted to roll her eyes and punch his arm again. But his voice was serious and there was no sign of a smile tweaking at the corners of his mouth.

"You, a spy?"

"Who better than an actor? Look, Stalin is nothing but trouble for the Jews. I don't care what my friends say. But Hitler is so very much worse."

With Sandy's eyes intent on hers, she considered the different reality of their New York relationship that he had just offered. One in which she was a young, flighty bauble of a woman bent on avoiding the seriousness of the world she was in and he was a man weighted with concern, maybe even despair, about that same world.

"I'm just a silly girl, Sandy. That's all. Why even bother with me?"

"You're not silly."

"Untested, raw, immature."

"Not with what you and Sarah went through. You've got steel in there, Helen." He pointed at her chest. "You just don't see it."

"Sarah made…"

"Sarah did a lot. You have made yourself. Who else? Sarah wasn't there."

"She was."

"She worked. She paid for things. She left."

He took her left hand, the heat of his palm calming the slight tremor in it. He'd always had that effect on her, easing her nerves as if his touch was a light, warm blanket wrapped around her. Then he leaned over and kissed her lightly on the lips and the tremor, motivated by a different feeling all together, returned.

"Are you coming in," he asked.

"Okay. But you have to promise me that you will be there. And that you will tell me more about your spying career."

He nodded and squeezed her hand. Helen sighed, shrugged, and removed her hand from his. Sandy was not reliable and he was obviously capable of lying to her. But if what was needed was for her to repeat her limited information, she could at least do that.

Sandy knocked twice on the oak door of a faux English cottage, with a window box planting in red geraniums, white shutters, a peaked roof of intricately laid shingles, and a neatly trimmed bright green lawn. He paused then knocked three times.

"Yes?" The peep hole opened and Helen could just see a blue eye of unknown gender gazing at her.

"It's Sandy."

"What, no special password?" Helen asked in a stage whisper. Sandy turned and glared at her.

The door opened inward to reveal a clean-shaven man with a bald head dressed in a rose-striped short-sleeved shirt tucked into cream linen pants. He was about five-and-a-half feet tall, compact, and in his mid-fifties, Helen guessed. He beckoned them in with a hand on which she glimpsed a ring set with a reddish stone the size of a grape. As she entered, the stone flashed with his movement.

The foyer of the house led into the living room where Helen could see three other people, two men and one woman, sitting. The men rose as she entered the room. Like the man she assumed was the host and owner of the home, the men were in their early fifties. One was over six feet tall, with black hair silvered at the temples, dressed much like the host, in a short-sleeved shirt and slacks. The other man was about Helen's height, but with a thin frame and pasty skin signaling illness. Based on the impeccable cut of his shirt and slacks, as well as the imperiousness of his gaze looking down a chiseled nose, Helen assumed he was very wealthy and powerful.

The woman remained seated. She was in her late fifties, with the careful grooming of someone who had been beautiful in her twenties and who retained a look not faded but handsome.

The woman said, "We'll dispense with introductions, Helen, if you don't mind. It is safer that way for now. Maybe later... ." Her voice was low and almost melodious. There was a slight hint of an accent, so smoothed away with time or with effort that its origin was impossible to determine. When she waved Helen over to an open chair, it was with a manicured hand, two fingers weighted with gold rings, another with a diamond that put the host's red stone to shame.

Helen took a seat without a word. She crossed one long leg over the other, folded her hands in her lap, and waited for the three men of the group and Sandy to take their places. Although she knew it was an important matter and time for serious thought, she acknowledged that she was happy she'd changed her clothes into something fresh after work. Then she considered that she had been right to tell Sandy she was immature and sighed.

"Are you all right, Helen?" the woman asked. "Let's get you a drink."

"Water, please."

The woman nodded and the host rose and walked through what Helen now saw was the adjoining dining room and then into the kitchen. The dining room was not furnished with a table, sideboard, and chairs, though. Instead there were two worn wooden desks, facing each other where the table would have been and, on the interior wall, a dusty, narrow table on which four telephones were placed.

Above the telephones, a blackboard took the place of a picture on one side and a cork board, loaded with newspaper clippings, on

the other. Just beside the narrow table, crammed into the space between it and the doorframe for the kitchen, were three four-drawer
file cabinets, the middle one with the top drawer open and tilting
perilously down.

As the host walked by, he stopped and jiggled the drawer up
and down. Then he tried shutting the drawer, but it resisted. Shrugging, he stepped by it and into the kitchen.

Helen looked around the group again. Except for Sandy, no
one was looking at her. Nor were they looking at each other. Only
when the host returned, a glass of water tinkling with ice cubes,
did everyone in the space resume engagement, as if someone had
pushed a button.

Taking the glass sweating with cold, Helen allowed herself a
small shiver and then composed herself. She focused on finding
that steel core Sandy swore she had.

"Helen, tell them what you told me," Sandy said.

She described again the house, the party, and her briefest of
brief encounters with Jessie Murphy. Was she certain that Jessie
Murphy had offered, even vaguely, to help her?

The woman asked for details of the party. The host held up a
hand, went to the dining room, and returned with a pad of paper
and a pencil. When he sat down, the woman motioned at Helen to
begin. The men said nothing, silent as sphinxes, motionless and
attentive, except for the scratch of pencil against paper.

"Is there anything else?" The woman put her empty glass on
the table.

Helen told them about the Nazi material in Ralph's bedroom.
Closing her eyes to see the pamphlet better, Helen found the details
leaping up as if she were still holding it in her hand.

"And Joe, is he still interested in seeing you?" the woman
asked. There was a hint of tension in the voice, as if the fine sand-
paper that had honed the tone so well had missed a small sliver of
emotion.

Helen glanced briefly at Sandy, but like everyone else in the room he had shuttered his emotions for the duration of the discussion.

"Yes."

"All right. Helen, Sandy will take you out now for about an hour. There's a coffee shop near here or, if you'd prefer, there's a nice bar, suitable for a young couple, not rough. You can decide. Sandy, be back at nine-thirty."

Sandy nodded, stood and held out his hand to help Helen up. She stood, smoothed down her dress, and sorted her feelings, her jaw tightening as she did. Unclenching her teeth, she took a deep breath.

"Wait a minute," she said. "I haven't agreed to this. Or to anything. I just told Sandy I would come and tell you in person what happened. I don't even know who you are. And I won't go out with Joe again. I just won't."

"Helen," the woman said. "We are just asking you to come back here in an hour so that we can talk freely among ourselves. That is all. Just an hour."

Sandy motioned with his head toward the door and smiled. "Come on. We deserve a drink after this," he said.

"Those people can help you far more than they would ever hurt you," Sandy said when they were back in his car.

"Who are they?"

"Well-placed people, with money and access. And a great deal of concern about the future of Jews in this country."

"But they don't have access to Jessie Murphy."

He paused then said, "Their access is limited. Jessie's crowd is the money for the American Bund as well as the Silver Shirts. Her crowd are the people behind the Aryan Bookstore downtown."

Helen expected him to continue with his drumbeat of worries

about the rise of Nazism in America, which would be just like the old times in New York.

Instead he said, "You are not prominent, not known, and apparently no one thinks you're Jewish."

"Yes, I owe it to my little upturned nose."

"No, I think that once they see those legs they don't think of anything else," he smiled and patted the top of her thigh. The touch was brief but she felt it for the eight minutes it took to drive to the coffee shop.

"No alcohol?"

"Not tonight. I want you to be able to think about what you may do with a clear head."

"Sandy, I don't want to do anything else for either set, the Jews in that house or the Nazis at that party."

Sandy got out of the car, went around to the passenger side and opened the door for her. He held out his hand to help her up from the seat and gently shut and locked the door once she was standing on the sidewalk. The front of the Sun Café was marked by a large sign that read "Coffee." In its fake brick façade and dusty display windows housing nothing but a slim view of the interior, it reminded Helen of New York.

Still saying nothing, Sandy and she walked to a booth for four at the end of the restaurant, which was almost empty. The table had been wiped smearily to a streaky off-white. Helen flicked a pie crust crumb off the seat before she sat down.

"Two Coca-Colas," he said when the waitress, a woman in her forties, graying hair pulled back in a bun, with a thumping, end-of-the-day walk, came to the table. Her name tag read "Joy."

Once the drinks, straws bobbing and ice cubes clinking, had been brought to the table, Sandy gulped half the glass at once, and then cleared his throat.

Helen was satisfied with the silence, since it meant that Sandy was not piling one word on top of another in an effort to get her to agree to something. A Jew born in America had no idea how much a Jew born elsewhere just wanted to be left alone, how much she just wanted to never feel that frightened and vulnerable again.

"The ADL needs someone in with Jessie Murphy and her crowd," Sandy said.

Helen slid to the aisle and stood. "And I need the ladies' room."

Sandy grabbed for her hand as she walked by him but she shook it off. Anger mixed with dread in her stomach and she wished she had sipped some of the soda since she had not eaten since noon.

In the tiny bathroom, the linoleum floor had been white once, but was now gray and a little sticky. The door had a hook and latch on the inside, the latch twisted at an odd angle, as if someone had pried the door open once and then tried to re-hang the latch in the wounded wood. Helen sagged against the sink, worried that if she locked the door she might not be able to get it open again.

She splashed tepid water from the cold tap on her wrists and stared at herself in the mirror. The naked light bulb overhead gave her a stark look. Hunger began to twist itself around the other writhing emotions.

Stepping out of the restroom, Helen almost tripped over Joy, now carrying two grilled cheese sandwiches, each cut on the diagonal, oozing yellow drops onto green pottery plates embellished with the coffee shop name.

"Excuse me." Helen maneuvered by her and walked over to the table. Sandy motioned to her to sit down.

"I've ordered something light for us," he said.

"Take me home right now." Helen leaned over and whispered in his ear.

He shook his head. Joy now stood directly in back of Helen, with the smell of the melted cheese drifting around like a cloud.

"I'm sorry," Helen turned to her. "I'm feeling quite under the weather. We won't be staying after all. Honey," she looked over at Sandy, "please pay the nice woman and take me home."

One of Sandy's eyebrows lifted slightly and a corner of his lip twitched up. As if she had said she'd just broken her leg, he grabbed immediately in his left rear pocket for his wallet, and slapped three one dollar bills on the table. As the Joy picked up the bills and stepped back, balancing the tray, he stood.

"Darling, what a shame. Another dinner spoiled," he murmured, just loud enough for Joy to smile sympathetically. "Let's go right now."

"Would you like me to wrap these to go?" Joy asked in a breathy accent Helen could only place as very south of New York.

Helen grabbed all four sandwich halves off the plates. "This'll do," she said, opening her mouth to the creamy glob of shiny yellow dripping from one end of the triangulated toasts.

As they stepped into the mild night, Helen took a deep breath. It and the mouthful of sandwich she had eaten calmed her stomach a bit.

"If you do not take me home, I will not get out of the car at that house. You must promise me now, Sandy, or I'll go back in that coffee shop and…"

"And…?" His face was all lines and shadows in the street lamp's light.

"I'll convince that nice waitress, Joy, that you are a horrible person and somehow I'll get her to call Harry and Harry will come and get me."

"Ahh. Very intrepid of you. Just what I'd expect."

During the car ride back to Harry and Sarah's the only sound was Helen chewing on smaller bites of the sandwich and Sandy breathing. Helen looked out the window in an effort to read landmarks that would convince her they were not returning to the spy house, as she now thought of it. Sandy kept his eyes on the road and his hands on the wheel.

When they reached the house, Helen got out and slammed the

door shut. She turned toward the house as Sandy drove away.

Harry was listening to the radio in the living room. Sarah was ironing clothes in the kitchen. The babies were asleep.

"I'm, you know… that time of month," Helen said to Sarah. She walked to her bedroom, crawled into bed, still dressed, and curled up.

"Do you need a hot water bottle?" Sarah asked from the doorway.

"No."

"Let me help with your dress, then." Sarah walked over to the bed and Helen let herself be undressed. Sarah smoothed the linen, hung it up, stepped out and closed the door.

> It was barely four years after they had gotten to the United States. Sarah returned from her shift at the Klein Garment Factory at a little after seven. Helen had laid in bed all afternoon, in her nightgown, gripping her stomach.
>
> As her sister opened the bedroom door, Helen said, "I'm dying." Her voice was husky with tears and pain.
>
> "Let me see."
>
> Sarah stood Helen up in the tub they shared in the co-op building and poured warm water from the kettle over her. She got a clean cotton rag from her drawer and showed Helen how to pin it into her underpants, how to rinse it in cold water until the blood came out, and how to be sure she always had an extra pair of underpants in her book bag "in case."
>
> Sarah brought Helen a cup of tea and a piece of toast, then crawled into bed, tucked her body next to Helen's, and held her. "If Mama was here, she would have helped you better," she said, smoothing Helen's hair back from her forehead.

Dusting the cheaper, smaller, vodka bottles on the lowest shelf, the ones that sold the fastest but to the clients Harry least wanted in the store, Helen said, "If anyone calls for me, just say I'm not here."

"Where should I say you are, then?" Harry's voice carried an edge of sarcasm.

"Yeah, Harry, so I don't care where you say I am, just like you don't care where I say you are if Sarah calls." Helen prepared for Harry's verbal assault, but he was quiet for a heartbeat.

"Okay. It was a bad night last night, I gather." Harry's back was to her, but she saw his shoulders drop an inch from his ears, a fighter withdrawing temporarily from the ring.

Helen wondered if Sarah had whispered in Harry's ear to leave her baby sister alone today. And if Sarah had, for what bargain? If she returned to New York, who would help Harry at the store for room and board and a few bucks a week? No one and then what would Sarah do?

Helen reminded herself that help was plentiful these days. Lots of people, good-looking women and well-dressed men among them, needed work.

The door opened and Helen looked briefly over her shoulder. It was Harry's LA cop-on-the-take, stomach pushing out against his dark blue shirt, tilting his LAPD belt buckle down toward the floor. He smirked at Helen, the ends of his mouth perking up in a gargoylish smile as she returned to the useless dusting.

But at least in New York she knew to stay away from the areas in the Bronx and Brooklyn where pro-Nazis stalked the sidewalks looking for Jews and no cop threatened a lowly office girl.

"Come on in," she heard Harry say to the cop. Harry took keys out of his pocket and unlocked the door to the back storage area. They both went in and the door slammed shut.

Helen stayed at the front of the store, hoping that no customer came in to force her back to the register near the storage door. She wanted no sound of thumping, crashing or raised voices today. If she had drunk any alcohol the night before, she would say she was hungover, since she had a pounding headache and her neck muscles ached whichever way she turned. She worried that she'd get a stiff neck, one where her muscles froze into place and nothing, not even being lifted by her head, relaxed them. Just time and maybe Sarah's hot water bottle.

Shiny specks floated in the beam of sun that entered the display window. On the street across from the store, a black Ford Model T with a bent front bumper pulled into a parking space. The man emerging from the driver's seat was the tallest person Helen had ever seen. His skin was translucently pale in the strong, yellow midday sun. Sunglasses perched on a nose that flared out slightly at the end, like a small shovel.

Leaning into the car, he emerged with a deep-brimmed straw hat, which he placed firmly on his head. He wore a long-sleeved blue checked shirt, buttoned to his neck, which reminded Helen of a goose's neck in its excessive length and slight forward curve. As he finished locking the car door, Helen saw that his right ring finger ended at the first knuckle, and that the rest of his fingers were thin and gnarled, like the stunted branches of a tree.

As he turned back to look directly at Forester Liquor, Helen considered flipping the Open sign to Closed. But then she would have to explain why to Harry, and she had no good reason other than that she was tired of dealing with men and no longer trusted her instincts with them. That was not an excuse she would offer to anyone.

He crossed the street in careful steps, like a daddy longlegs. He opened the door, the customer bell clattering cheerily in greeting, and said, "Are you open?" His baritone voice boomed out, seeming too deep for such a thin chest.

"Sure. Come on in."

"Do you have any cold soda?"

Helen nodded at the deep red refrigerator unit. "In there, you'll find Coca-Cola, Seven-Up, and Nehi Orange. Ten cents."

A single, long, shaky step and he was tugging the door open and reaching in. "Ahh," he said, wrapping his fingers like a spring around the coldly perspiring glass bottle of Seven-Up, whose transparency seemed to mimic his own lack of color.

"Not exactly what I wanted, but during a work day, it'll do for sure." He smiled at Helen, a splitting of his face into two parts separated by teeth and upturned white strips of lip. Reaching into the side pocket of his dark black cotton pants, pushing past the wrinkles that sitting in the car had produced, he pulled out a coin.

"One thin dime, I believe you said." He put it on the counter.

Helen nodded but didn't move. To get it she would have to move past him and over to the register, and neither was an action she wanted to take.

"Are you going to ring it up?"

"Sure. Just waiting to see if you want to buy something else," she said.

He nodded and stepped back into the middle of the store, his head slowly swiveling from right to left. He had not removed his sunglasses. Under the skin on his hands, elevated veins throbbed a dark blue. Helen had never seen anyone so much like an anatomy drawing in a biology book. She wondered if she could see his organs if he undressed, and shuddered.

"No, I don't see anything else right now."

Helen moved to the register, skirting around the display table and behind the counter she had dusted when she first arrived. Her fingers moved to the brass keys and she pushed firmly down. The cash drawer popped open, revealing small pockets of pennies, nickels, dimes, quarters, and half-dollars, and a short stack of ones, two fives, and a ten. Harry kept the bigger amounts in the safe in the storage room; those were mostly for his racetrack bettors.

She dropped the man's coin in and shut the drawer.

"Thanks for the business," she said.

Instead of walking toward the front door with his bottle of soda, as Helen had hoped he would do, the man stepped toward her.

Helen stepped back toward the storage room door, prepared to turn and pound on it to arouse Harry and his three-hundred-pound cop. She was not afraid, but she was leery, as if she was standing on a subway station platform with a strange man who could turn and grab her purse or just tip his hat and walk on by.

Removing his sunglasses, the man held them lightly in his raised left hand as if dropping his hand quickly might startle her as a quick action startles a bird. His irises were a washed out pink. He lowered his hand slowly.

"As you can see," he said, "I am an albino of American Negro heritage and who knows where in Africa." His voice had the clipped, precise notes of the well-educated. "I come," he paused to smile, his entire face crinkly with humor, "bearing a peace offering."

Helen kept her back pressed against the storage room door. She could just make out the hum of continued conversation in there, which she hoped was not just the radio.

"Are you sure you have the right place?" she asked. "We don't have a quarrel with anyone that deserves a peace offering."

"My employer believes he scared you away. No quarrel, just a misunderstanding of what was needed."

If Harry was in trouble with the mob, if some gangster needed more from him than what he was willing to give, was this the time to knock on the door?

"Do you want the owner of the store? I can get him for you."

"No. My message is for Helen. That's you, correct? You match the description." He paused to crinkle up again, the pink eyes almost disappearing into a chuckle. "A fine looking woman, long lustrous hair, great...." He paused. "Excuse me. I'm not trying to be too familiar. I'm just quoting. My employer took quite a fancy to you and was distressed that you did not return."

"Is this the time when I ask who your boss is?" Helen asked. She had eliminated Jessie Murphy the minute the albino said "he," and she did not think that either Joe or Ralph would be anyone's boss. Still, she considered that she did not know how well-placed either of them was with the Nazis.

"No. I apologize, but it is not. Here, however, is the peace offering." He reached slowly into his front right pocket and extracted a small sealed envelope.

Helen stepped toward the counter and took it from his outstretched palm. The stationery was an ivory color, the envelope heavy with linen threads.

"I'll wait while you read it, with your permission. My employer hopes for an answer."

Helen nodded while working the sealed envelope open with her finger. The paper, edges deckled, matched the envelope. The handwritten script in jet black ink was European. Helen recognized the elegance and training that had gone into both the paper and the words on it.

"We had been hoping last night for a chance to talk further," the opening sentence read. No longer heading toward the rocks, Helen wondered what hard place she had to navigate around. She sucked her lower lip into her mouth, bit down on the tender wet interior, and read further.

"I can see that we handled your situation abruptly and without appropriate respect for your concerns. Please accept my apologies on behalf of us all. Would you be so kind as to give us another chance to speak with you? I have arranged for a private dining experience tonight. Also, we can schedule a screen test for you at MGM, since we understand this is something that you might be interested in doing. I have further enclosed twenty dollars to compensate you for your time in this."

The letter was unsigned.

Extracting the twenty from the envelope, Helen sighed, "All right. Tell him I will come to dinner." In her instant assessment, a chance at a screen test was worth another discussion of Nazis in Los Angeles. Maybe whoever this person was could get Errol Flynn and Clark Gable to find out more about the Nazis.

"Most excellent. I will pick you up at seven." He recited Harry and Sarah's address. Helen nodded.

He turned and took two giant steps toward the door. As he did so, Helen had the feeling that she had seen him before. Since she knew she had not ever met an albino Negro who was almost, by her calculation, seven feet tall, the thought was peculiar, as if she'd been dropped in the middle of someone else's dream.

"Wait," Helen said. He turned.

"Now you seem familiar to me, but obviously we've never met."

"Obviously not. Yet and still it is possible that you have seen me."

"A riddle."

"Or a test."

Taking a deep breath, Helen said, "Were you in *The Phantom Empire*, with Gene Autry."

"Also, I've been in the *Flash Gordon* series on occasion." He nodded in approval. "I can see why my employer is so eager to meet with you again. You are not visibly frightened by strange appearances." He pointed his long fingers toward his body. "And, you have a good memory for details. My best to you, Helen, until tonight."

As he left the store, the door banging back against its frame, Harry emerged from the storage room followed by the policeman whose bulk loomed over him. Giving Helen a smile just shy of a leer, the cop exited the shop, banging the door shut behind him.

"Any customers?" Harry asked.

"Just an alien."

"What? One of those Chinamen was in here?"

"No." Helen tried to stop the giggle that was starting, but it was like trying to stop soda bubbles from fizzing. "A *Flash Gordon* alien."

"Are you crazy?"

Helen was still giggling, bracing herself against the counter, tears forming at the side of her closed eyes. Bending over, she wrapped her arms around her stomach and rocked back and forth.

"An actor," she spat out. "He plays aliens."

Harry nodded, walked over to the refrigerator unit and pulled out two Nehis. He popped the caps on both of them, turned and handed one over to Helen.

"Good to see you laughing, Helen," he said. "You're going to need a sense of humor when I tell you this."

Helen waved her hand for him to continue. Swallowing while in a fit of giggles and not having the soda go up her nose required concentration. She squeezed her face muscles tight to force her mood to change. One more deep breath and the fit had passed. She sighed.

"Speak," she said.

"It seems our boy in blue wants a larger cut of my already negligible profit on the ponies."

"Unfortunate for you."

"For you as well."

"How is that?"

"One way I can give him a larger cut is if I don't increase Sarah's home allowance. And if I don't pay you fifteen a week. I could do five, and that is a 'maybe.' Possibly no girl to come in and watch the babies six months from now. And that means no you going anywhere else."

"We agreed to six months and that is when I move on." Helen's tone was defiant but she was no more certain of a way out of this than was Harry.

"I know, Helen, that you don't like me. And that is the way it is. I don't hold it against you, being as how I came and took Sarah away from you. Maybe you don't like me for other reasons, too."

"Like this gambling thing you have going."

Harry nodded in agreement. "Like this and who knows what else. But you don't want Sarah to have a cripple for a husband or worse, to be a widow. That makes it more than a little bit your problem."

Helen looked carefully at Harry to read his expression. He was as serious as if recounting his sins on the Day of Atonement.

"Yes, that makes it a bit my problem," she agreed.

"There are a few other ways to solve this," he continued. "I can shut down the operation, but then I don't have any extra money, I probably lose the liquor store, and you are in the same trap. Or, I can get more business, which is a good way to go."

"What about you just turn this guy in?"

"You are a smart girl. Who would I turn him in to and how would that help me? I'm the one with the illegal bookie operation and he's a dirty cop. Which one of us goes to jail?"

"What if…." She trailed off, out of ideas. "I don't know, Harry."

"Helen?"

"Yes."

"You seem to have a knack for meeting people with money. Could they be a source of more business here? I would just need another hundred a month coming in, all of which I could give to the bozo who just left. Small change, really."

Helen looked down at her shoes and sighed. "Oh, Harry. I don't know. I just don't know."

"Think about it."

"Yeah, I will."

Helen sat on the stool next to the cash register and rocked the Nehi bottle back and forth, watching the sherberty orange liquid slosh up one side and down the other. The rhythm was comforting. She hummed tunelessly. She felt as if she was twelve again, fluent enough in English to understand every threat she encountered at junior high, in the neighborhood, or heard on the radio's news programs, but too young to do anything about most of it except raise her fists on the way to and from school.

> "Fight at school, get expelled, go back to Europe." That was Sarah's dire prediction on the outcome of physical mayhem, and Helen changed direction.
>
> She became an observer of people, whether they were the blonde, blue-eyed bullies in skirts at school or the red-faced, inflated men in the corner pool hall.
>
> Learning to smile like the popular girls in the cafeteria, to say what they said agreeably and in a different enough way that they did not feel mocked but admired, that was a curriculum she studied as earnestly as US History. And by the time she was thirteen she was getting an A in passing as a pretty, normal American teenage girl.

Helen took the Nehi bottle, wiped the wet mark off the counter with a piece of crumpled *Daily Racing Form*, and walked into the storage room. Harry sat by the radio, legs outstretched so that his black socks and an inch of white, freckled flesh showed on each. When he saw her, he drew his legs into a sitting pose. The lower part of his nose was still slightly swollen and his lower left cheek had a green tinge like slime.

"I will try to help with this," she said. "A hundred a month is an awful lot, though. Any chance you could negotiate it down in exchange for...." She waved her hand toward the boxes of liquor. "For cheap booze?"

"This cop doesn't like to work for a living," Harry said. "I don't know if he's going to want to sell scotch or rye. But thanks for the thought." He sounded deflated, as if someone had squeezed him into a much smaller space than he normally inhabited.

"If I'm going to try to help, though, I need some leeway."

"Of what kind?"

"Time off work to meet people and do things."

"What people and what things?"

"I don't know yet." She handed Harry the twenty from the envelope with the mysterious dinner invitation and was repaid with a look of grim puzzlement. "Keep it, Harry. No need to say thanks or anything."

"Right." He folded the twenty into quarters and slipped it into his shirt pocket. "This'll keep the dog at bay for about a week."

"Glad to be so appreciated," she said.

7

WILLIAM PITT, LONG-ARMED AND STOOPED, knocked on the door wearing a charcoal gray uniform with a peaked chauffeur cap. Ben took a single step into the living room at the sound of the knock on the door, waited for the door to open, then, when he saw the man standing there, bolted back into the kitchen, crying for his mom.

"No apologies needed," the chauffeur said to Harry, who did not look as if an apology had been in his thoughts. "Children have that reaction sometimes. It is why I am so good at playing aliens." He chuckled, the laugh smoothly exiting from his mouth. "In my other life, I am as you see me, a chauffeur."

"And you'll take excellent care of my sister-in-law."

"Most assuredly. My employer would not like a hair on her head mussed."

Harry nodded in approval.

Helen walked a step behind William to the cream-colored Cadillac that was not so much parked as dominating the curb outside the house. Across the street, a man walking a bulldog stopped to stare at the car and then gave William and Helen a thorough review as if they were on the sidewalk for his amusement.

Two doors down, a young woman dressed for a secretarial job paused as she was getting her key out of her purse to gaze at Helen and William. Then she dropped her eyes to the lock, put the key in the door and entered the house quickly.

William had the driver's side window rolled down about four inches, enough to let in the cool air tinged with a mix of jasmine, rose, and orange coupled with fumes from the cars on the street.

Helen re-pinned a lock of hair that had slid out of her French twist and rubbed the bridge of her nose. She reached distractedly into her purse and retrieved her compact to powder it. If she was meeting someone who could give her a screen test, she needed to look her best.

She would set aside any plan to return to New York for now until the problem with Harry and the corruption that flowed around his feet like sewage was resolved.

So much for the myth of reinvention by the Pacific. She felt her eyes brim with tears and blinked quickly, biting down on the inside of her cheek, and took three deep, slow breaths.

William pulled into the driveway of the house Sandy had taken Helen to the night before. Four rose bushes bustled with white flowers in varied stages of opening, from tight bud to loose-petaled middle age, flanked the border between the drive and the walkway to the house. A short faded brick path marked a thorn-free zone where motorists exiting their cars could cross to the larger, winding brick path leading up to the door.

Coming around to the passenger side, William opened the door and stood back for Helen to exit. He motioned to the walkway.

"Good luck," he said. Then he returned to the car. As Helen

stepped onto the bricks leading to the door, he slowly backed out the Cadillac, missing a thorny branch by mere inches.

Helen knocked once on the hard oak, rubbed her knuckles, and reached for the brass knocker in the shape of a lion's head. She rapped it once on the brass plate and was preparing to hit hard again when the door opened.

The previous night's host stood there, dressed in a pair of gray slacks, white shirt, and seersucker blue and white striped jacket.

"Hello, Helen. I'm Leon," he said. "Please come in." He stepped aside and motioned toward the living room. She could see that a small round table neatly draped in a pristine white tablecloth, with three bentwood chairs set around it, had been added between the living room and the dining room, which still held the desks, phones, chairs, and filing cabinets.

"At least for now, if you don't mind, we'll dispense with last names," he added.

She stepped into the house. Sitting with his back toward her was the sickly man with the arrogant gaze. He rose and turned toward her. Despite the heat that still lingered in the house from the warm day, he was wearing a cashmere cardigan sweater in an argyle pattern over his shirt. The corduroy pants were wintery as well.

She saw that he was younger than she first had thought, possibly in his mid-thirties. But whatever illness he had aged him.

"I'm Irving," he said. "My wife," he added, "regrets that she has been detained because she would love to meet you. She asked me to assure you that Leon and I are safe to be with." He laughed.

"Your wife is not the woman who was here last night?" Helen asked.

"No, no. Irene and I are longtime associates." His smile was a signal to end that line of inquiry.

"Sandy won't be joining us?" Helen asked. She was surprised at the feeling of sadness she felt, as if she had unwrapped an exquisitely wrapped box and found nothing inside. On the other hand, she felt no sexual threat at all from the two well-dressed Jewish men in front of her. Instead, she was curious, especially about the thin, ailing, supercilious one.

"He is on assignment. And he felt that his history with you might further...shall we say, affect you negatively. And we don't want that," Leon said, motioning her to the table. "Please, sit down and let's have a bite to eat and a chat. Irving insisted that we have the dinner catered, since apparently he doesn't think that I'm able to do more than devilled egg sandwiches."

"Those are the only things you ever put out at our meetings," Irving said with a warmer smile, which lit up his eyes. "What has it been now? Two years of monthly meetings and only devilled eggs?"

"You get plenty of rich food at home. And I wouldn't want any of you to think I'm wasting your money on non-essentials like food," Leon replied, holding Helen's chair out for her.

Helen sat, her knees pressed together, legs slightly tilted away from the table leg. She picked up the heavy damask napkin that matched the tablecloth exactly, and put in on her lap. What she was supposed to say was unclear in the midst of the men chatting to each other in such a seemingly friendly fashion.

"Thank you for the twenty dollars," she said. "I don't think I have anything that I can add to what I said last night that is worth the money, though."

Irving nodded at Leon, a tight little jab of the head, which Leon appeared to take as a signal to sit opposite Helen. Irving then sat to her left, bringing with him a mixed odor of musk and something medicinal that Helen could not place.

"Let's save that part of the conversation for a little later, Helen. First, let's have a little bite to eat," Leon said.

At that moment, the kitchen door opened and a white-haired woman wearing a black housekeeper's uniform with a crisp white collar and white buttons, entered carrying a tray with three oversized soup bowls. The aroma was spicy, slightly tomatoey, and unfamiliar to Helen.

"I hope you enjoy this," Irving said. "It's a specialty of a friend of mine."

Helen looked into her bowl. The rim was an almost translucent pearl color with small, raised turquoise and gold flowers and the initials "I T" and "N T" in ornate cursive ornamenting the large lip. Large kidney-shaped red beans, some type of chopped vegetable she didn't recognize, and what she assumed were chunks of meat floated in a thick sauce.

"What is it?" she asked, dipping a fork in to scoop up the contents. The fork was the heaviest she had ever held, polished to a luminous silver glow, its decoration the same pattern as the china, but engraved into the handle along with a "T."

She blew on the top of the beans and meat, then slid the contents into her mouth. The food had a bite to it and unexpected heat, but Helen found herself pleased. "Hmm," she murmured as she slipped her fork into the bowl for another bite.

"It's called chili," Irving said. "It has garlic, onions, and a spice called cumin."

"That's enough. She doesn't need a lesson in gastronomy." Leon paused with his empty spoon hovering above the bowl.

"No, that's okay," Helen said. She wanted a chance to talk directly to Irving and he'd given her an opening. "Where is it from?"

"You mean originally or just now?"

"Originally."

"San Antonio, Texas."

"It's really good."

"I'll tell David you liked it. It'll have a featured role in his restaurant."

They continued to eat, and Helen wiped the inside of her bowl with bread that had a crisp crust and a soft, white, mildly tangy interior. The two men did likewise.

In the meantime, Helen answered their few questions on when she had arrived in Los Angeles and what she was doing. They avoided any further inquiry into Jessie Murphy or Joe.

"Working in a liquor store can't pay that much," is all that Irving observed.

"No," Helen agreed. "And I'm indebted to my brother-in-law who is also giving me room and board. So, it pays..."

"*Bubkes*," Leon said.

"Nothing," Helen agreed.

"If we are done, let's have some iced tea in the living room and chat a bit more," Leon said.

Irving pushed himself back from the table and got up, briefly resting his hand on the back of his chair. Leon glanced at him and Irving shook his head. Leon helped Helen with her chair. Both men stood until she sat in a tan-colored leather armchair with a crackled seat and arms suggesting years of use. Then they sat opposite her on the matching leather couch, with a cocktail table, ornately carved but oddly out of place with the chair and couch, in between.

The housekeeper entered with three glasses of iced tea, whose color blended with the leather. She placed them on coasters, one in front of each of the people present.

"If that's all, sir," she asked Irving, "I'll leave now."

"That's fine, Bertha. Thank you."

"Do you know much about the Anti-Defamation League, Helen?" Leon asked.

"Not the best place to start, my friend," Irving interrupted. "Start with the threat. We are facing two grave threats to Jewish security in the United States. The first is Communism and its cousin, Socialism. These are not good for Jews or for America. These are systems designed to prevent the individual from reaping the just rewards of his success. Unions..."

He stopped and a slight grimace passed over his face. Whether it was the topic, whatever illness he had, or both, Helen could not determine. "That Sinclair, the one who ran for governor, he would have brought this wonderful state down. And worse, he was an anti-Semite."

Helen nodded and swallowed some iced tea. She had read just the first chapter of the Sinclair book Sandy had given her. How odd, she thought, that Sandy would have given her a book by an anti-Semite. That would not have been like him. And none of her friends in New York had ever said that socialism was a plot against America. But she hadn't listened that hard to their discussions.

"Is that Sinclair Lewis, the author?" she asked.

"No," Leon offered in a mild voice. "He's talking about Upton Sinclair, the politician."

Helen nodded. Now she remembered that Sandy had been very upset about Upton Sinclair's lost election bid. But, she felt she could be excused for not recalling who had run for and not won the governorship of California.

Irving continued. "The other threat to Jews is far more direct. Nazism."

"To be more clear, Nazis and their fellow travelers here," Leon added. "Anti-Semitism is like a deadly bug that lives just under the surface of society. Stir that surface, scratch it in any way, and these fascists will rise up."

"Yes. But we must be careful not to draw attention to ourselves as Jews. We must somehow get America to want to do the right thing," Irving said.

"It is a delicate operation for the Anti-Defamation League. We need non-Jews to be out in front on this," Leon said.

"Hmm," Helen took another sip of the iced tea, now diluted with melting ice cubes, the glass wet with condensation on her hand. She replaced the glass on a coaster on the table. "That's not me." She agreed that non-Jews needed to be in front, as far in front of her as they could be. That could be her exit from this meeting that she now regretted having agreed to.

"Oh, of course. We know you're Jewish, Helen, even though, if you don't mind my saying this, you absolutely don't look it, which is why you could be so very helpful. This was just the broad picture."

"I know the two of you mean well," Helen said, rising from the couch. "But I am just not interested in a lecture on current affairs. Even though," she added, softening her voice, "I know I should be. I'm just a shop girl with a little bookkeeping skill. I'm not whatever you think you need. Really, I'm not. Where can I powder my nose?"

Leon pursed his lips and pointed toward the hall. "Two doors down."

In the small bathroom, whose tub, partly screened with a red shower curtain, was stacked with files, Helen perched on the toilet seat and sighed. She blamed herself for this, the excited amusement she felt after her meeting with William and the feel of the luxe paper of the dinner invitation in her hand. Wanting to peek around the corner to see what was going on. That had always been a problem of hers.

Now she was stuck with two middle-aged Jewish men lecturing her about Nazis and the Anti-Defamation League, neither of which would help her at all with Harry, his corrupt cop, and her desire to return to New York.

She had been mistaken to come to this house. She had been mistaken to tell Harry she would help him. That was Harry and Sarah's problem and they were welcome to it, Glendale, and the whole mess.

"Gentlemen," she said, returning to the room and addressing them as they stood to greet her, "I've had a long work day, and I need to think about getting home."

"We are prepared to offer you a stipend of sorts for further help," Leon said with an affirming nod from Irving, as he slowly sat back down. "And support."

"I don't think…."

Irving cut Helen off. "Twenty-five dollars a week plus expenses, which would include clothing and entertainment, if needed. For part-time work, that is not bad."

"I…"

"A screen test." Irving said this in a flat tone, as if slapping the offer down on the table.

Tilting her head toward him, Helen gave Irving an "oh-sure" look, corners of her lips tilted up slightly, lips pursed.

"That's Irving Thalberg of Metro-Goldwyn-Mayer, Helen," Leon said. At this, Irving nodded.

"You may have seen one of his pictures, possibly *Mutiny on the Bounty*? And I'm Leon Lewis, executive secretary of the ADL. We'd like to welcome you to our little spy ring."

"What exactly do you need me to do?" Helen asked, sitting back down.

8

IN THEORY, HELEN THOUGHT, THE idea was simple. Just accept the next offer from Joe and parlay it into an invitation to Jessie Murphy's house again. From there, ingratiate herself with Jessie and find out who the money was coming from just by observing and being sociable. One or two parties and she would be done. By which time she would also have had a screen test, and maybe a little role in a movie would be in the offing.

Last night, Leon had been adamant that the fascist threat was real. "I was wrong once before," he said, index finger pounding the table. "I thought the Nazi threat was suppressed and scattered after our report to the Special Committee on Un-American Activities and their trip to California to smite these foes down. But no, the threat has reemerged as fresh as the day I thought I had buried it. I will not make that mistake again." He had sat back in his chair abruptly, sending its front legs tipping up then thudding back to the floor.

Stretching her arms overhead, she hummed a little of *You are My Lucky Star* and smiled as she stepped out of the tub and grabbed her robe. As long as she kept her role simple, the Aryan blonde on a man's arm, she would be okay.

Her contact would be Sandy. He'd be a cousin from New York, to minimize any possible concern from Joe. And Thalberg would have an eye on Joe at the MGM studio. She would be done with Ralph, who was just hired help so far as she could tell.

In practice, however, Helen had to wait until Tuesday before Joe called.

"I'm sorry, Helen. I said I'd call last week, but I was so busy the entire weekend."

"That's all right."

"I want to apologize again for my behavior on our last date. I honestly don't know what hit me. It won't happen again."

"Joe, that kind of thing..." Helen hesitated to say he had been drunk since he seemed so very sensitive. "That could happen to anyone."

Helen could hear Joe breathing, a quick intake then a pause. His voice came through the line again."

"So, what have you been up to?"

"You mean besides working ten hours a day and then helping my sister?"

Joe laughed, the sound coming out gravelly from the phone. "Yes."

"My first cousin, Sandy, came into town from New York. He comes here from time to time. You'd probably like him. He's an actor, too. Anyhow, he took me to an Italian restaurant."

There was a bubble of silence. Helen sighed. "Sandy is family, like...a brother to me."

"Sure, Helen. I've got no claim on your time."

"Sandy doesn't either. Like I said, he's family. Like Harry is family." Helen felt goose bumps crawl up her arm as she said that.

"I get it, Helen, really I do. Can I have another chance? Jessie is having another party this Saturday, around one. She told me she'd love to have you come."

Helen wondered whose idea the date had been after all, Joe's or Jessie's.

"Wonderful," she heard herself say in a perfect imitation of the crazy-about-you that she had felt once for Sandy.

When Helen told Harry he'd need to cover all day Saturday at the store, he just nodded.

"What? No comment?"

"Thanks for the twenty. Keep them coming. Enough words for you?"

She consulted the telephone directory under "Apparel-Women's" and looked for the name of the store Irving Thalberg had given her. The ad boasted that the store carried the "finest women's clothing in Los Angeles," and Thalberg had said that he knew the manager quite well.

"How do you suggest I get to Bullock's?" she asked Harry.

"Take the Red Car up on Brand. Ask the conductor about a transfer to the streetcar to LA. Sarah doesn't shop at Bullock's so I don't know."

He eyed her carefully. "It shouldn't take you any time at all to find something that you like there. It's very high end."

"Perfect," she said.

Helen checked her wallet to make sure the five twenties Irving had handed her "for necessary expenses" were still there. How much money could a man who was Louie B. Mayer's second-in-command make, she wondered. He'd just opened up his tan ostrich skin wallet and slid the bills out. Their absence seemed not to flatten the wallet even the slightest.

She'd called a taxi from the liquor store's phone. The taxi driver, a balding, sturdy man whose roughened hands and missing half-a-thumb suggested he'd done heavy labor before retreating into the Yellow Cab system, promised her he'd wait in the Bullock's parking lot. Helen walked through the doors, past the chrome and glass cosmetics counter with a giant floral arrangement of white hydrangeas and equally outsized bottle of Chanel No. 5, and over to a slim woman wearing the classic uniform, white blouse and a calf-length black skirt, impeccably cut. A little pin on her blouse declared her to be "Genevieve."

"I need the right dress for an afternoon soirée," Helen said.

Twenty minutes later, she emerged back through the doors with two Bullock's shopping bags, one for the full-skirted white crepe de chine dress patterned down the bodice and into the hem with scarlet and black parrots, one for the black strappy sandals to go with it.

"You look fabulous, Helen," Joe said. "I know clothes and that is quite a dress."

"I told Harry I just couldn't go to Jessie's party in the same thing I wore last time. And that was one of my best outfits. He advanced me my next week's pay." She smiled and sighed. "I'm just a sucker for nice clothes. This was on sale and I grabbed it."

Joe looked as if he wanted to reach out and finger the fabric to estimate its price. Instead, he said, "Jessie will love it. But isn't borrowing against future earnings a little frivolous? And to spend an entire week's wages on a dress and shoes." His tone was shriveled and paternal.

"Maybe," she said, trying to keep resentment out of her voice. "But I didn't want to look poor, not in that crowd. Isn't Jessie someone you want to impress? And shouldn't I want to impress her, too?"

Joe looked over her shoulder for a few seconds as if scanning the sky for an omen.

"Yes. Maybe I should remember that saying, 'Penny wise, pound foolish.' Let's see if this was money well spent. And I apologize for intruding into your decisions like that. I was just trying to be a friend." His voice was still shriveled and paternal, but he smiled at her.

They did not speak much on the drive to Jessie's home.

Helen started up the stairs to the veranda, which was decorated with a mix of the young and middle-aged, the women shining in the afternoon sun like multicolored crystals, the men dull by comparison. She thought she recognized one young couple, just to the right of the main door to the house. If she could tug Joe in that direction, she would reintroduce herself.

Scanning the crowd, she was relieved to not see Ralph. Maybe today's crowd was safe for Jessie, or maybe she had more than one bodyguard.

"Jessie said to be sure to find her the minute we got here," Joe said in a voice mixing self-importance and puzzlement in equal measure. He had no idea why Helen was such a favorite after a brief meeting and neither did Helen. "It must be you. You're just special," he added, giving her hand a squeeze that pressed her knuckles together painfully.

"I'm sure it's not," Helen said, pulling her hand out of his and then patting his cheek to compensate. "But let's meet some of your friends first."

"Mine?"

"Don't you have friends here today?"

"Not really. I know a few people but... Well, this isn't the crowd I run with usually."

"Aren't there movie people here?"

"They're mostly communists and unionists, Helen," he said firmly.

"But you?"

Joe offered a tailored smile, trim, shaped, and confined to his lips.

"I'm Jessie's eyes and ears at MGM. I know who is pro-American and anti-war-mongering. And she believes in my ability to rise further and further on the production side. Movies," he said, deepening his voice and looking right into her eyes, "are the way to the heart and mind of a nation."

"You are so thoughtful," Helen sighed.

His was a mixture of anger, distress, and craving that Helen understood. The people on the veranda were not workers like he was. Joe was like Ralph or even Harry, a guy trying to get ahead. Maybe having a beautiful woman on his arm was a little like helium in a balloon, floating him higher than he could go just on his own breath.

But it didn't explain Jessie's interest in her.

Helen slipped her hand through the crook of Joe's arm, allowed the breeze to push the silk skirt back against her legs, and paraded Joe along the veranda, nodding and smiling. After five minutes she again spotted the couple Jessie had introduced her to standing in a group of eight. The three couples Helen did not recognize were in their fifties, the men with short-cropped graying hair, in business suits that looked uncomfortable and wrong for the event, the women, also graying, wearing long-sleeved, flower-printed dresses, with buttons up the front and Peter Pan collars, well-suited to their shapeless bodies.

Helen studied the women for a moment, wondering if any of them was even wearing a brassiere. The eight sported matching campaign buttons, all with the picture of a fox-thin, pointy chinned man, with hair parted sharply to the side. Helen had a feeling she had seen him before. But it did not seem to be a good idea to stare openly at the buttons, since it would indicate she did not really belong in this crowd. And belonging was what Helen was recruited to do.

"Didi," Helen said, walking up to the younger woman. "I'm glad to see you here because honestly I don't recognize anyone else and neither does Joe." Didi smiled thinly and the conversation in the group ended.

"Joe, this is Mark," she added at which Joe offered his hand and the two men shook. Then, offering her hand in turn to each of the older women, Helen introduced herself.

She considered the group of three older couples calmly while there was an awkward pause. Then, in turn, the women, followed by the men, gave up their names, the men with the eagerness of well-trained dogs wanting to be petted, the women with the skittish disdain of pedigreed cats.

In order they were Mr. and Mrs. George and Janet Highsmith, Mr. and Mrs. Harold and Henrietta Johns, and Mr. and Mrs. Robert and Matilda Stewart.

Harold owned a fleet of trucks dedicated to moving produce out of the Central Valley and into the grocery stores of the nation. He blinked rapidly and raised a thick left hand, ring finger burdened with a half-inch-wide gold wedding band, to shade his eyes from the sun.

Under his open suit jacket, Robert wore a spotless blue cotton shirt, buttons straining at the holes, through which his white undershirt winked out. He owned land with oil on which grasshopper-like pumps worked tirelessly, while George had an administrative position at a college whose name Helen did not recognize.

"Caltick?" she asked.

"Caltech," George said. "California Institute of Technology."

"That sounds very impressive."

George grinned and turned toward Helen. "A real competitor to MIT, but lately too many Jews."

"One is too many. Like rats," Harold said.

Robert put a hand on George's arm. "Don't monopolize. Let's find out about Helen." The women had slid halfway out of the circle, like moons temporarily behind their planets.

"Helen's brother-in-law owns Forester Liquor," Joe said.

Robert tilted his face toward Helen, raising his mottled, double-chin and gazing down at her as if she had just shrunk a foot.

To Helen's surprise, Matilda said, "A strong middle class is just what the country needs right now, Robert." Robert's face imitated a smile.

"Yes, of course. I just didn't recognize the name of the store, but I'm sure that if he sells German beer, it is one of ours."

"Indeed. The beer of my dear homeland," Helen said.

At that statement, Robert nodded. Then, the men began to talk about politics, especially the unfair attacks launched against the democratically elected Adolph Hitler.

For good measure, Harold threw in comments about market economics and how the flood of good labor from the Plains states was helping to keep costs down for his suppliers. This was altogether a good thing for Americans who needed lower food prices, they all agreed.

Joe began tugging on Helen's arm. Then he whispered in her ear, "We need to find Jessie."

"I have to say hello to our fabulous hostess," Helen said, excusing herself.

She spotted Jessie near the buffet table, pointing out something to a waiter, who leapt to the table, plucked a nearly empty tray from it, balanced the tray high on one hand, and whisked it around the corner of the veranda, toward the rear of the house.

In the sunlight, Helen could see the crow's-feet and lines around Jessie's mouth and the softening skin under her chin that unveiled her in the bright sun as being in her late forties, despite her sleek form and porcelain skin.

Today Jessie was wearing a fuchsia day dress, snug around her hips and flowing to mid-calf. Her height was accentuated by turquoise heels, each shoe with a patent fuchsia bow. Pinned discreetly on her bodice was a "Christian Party" campaign button.

"Hello, Jessie," Helen said, walking up. Joe followed half a step behind. She could feel his fingers tapping on her palm, but she brought her hand forward and up to meet Jessie's, which was being held out.

"Joe, Helen, lovely to have you here. I have a few people I want you both to meet. Where did they go?" She stood on her tiptoes, brought her hand to her brow as if distressed, and scanned the veranda behind Helen and Joe. "I promised Joe that when he stopped being such a lone wolf in the pack, I'd ask him to this campaign party. He's been eager to meet William."

"I apologize, but I don't know more about your guest of honor," Helen said.

Joe leapt into the discussion with the eagerness of a relay swimmer now tapped for his turn in the pool.

"He's amazing. Such a wealth of talent. For example, he won the O' Henry award twice for short stories."

Sandy had coached her, "when in doubt, just look wide-eyed and innocent. This group will jump at the chance to inform you." She thought she'd put his advice to work to see how valid it was. "Oh, my. But I just don't recognize the name."

Joe barked a laugh. "You are such an innocent, my dear. William Pelley. Surely you've heard of him. I mean, he's running for President."

Helen had heard of William Pelley.

On a meat-locker cold Tuesday night, her breath fanning out from behind her scarf-wrapped face, she had walked closely beside Sandy, each of them burying their gloved hands in coat pockets. They'd been heading toward the favored cafeteria of CCNY night students, with its free hot water for tea and large, moist slices of apple pie, crust soggy after a day in the open air.

They reached Convent Avenue and Amsterdam. Sandy commented on the irony that a college that was considered the Jewish Yale would be located on a street named for a convent and within a stone's throw of Saint Nicholas. The sound of traffic was muffled in the cold air.

A man shouted "Get away from here you lousy son-of-a-bitch" about halfway down the block from them. Sandy pushed Helen toward the entrance of a building they were passing.

"Stay in there," he said, whispering in her ear. She took a long step into the meager shelter provided and huddled on the side away from the mailboxes and nearest the door.

Sandy disappeared from her sight, walking in the direction of the shouting.

"Jews get out," she heard a different voice shout. There was the sound of booted feet running toward her and she shrank as far into the corner as she could, her eyes scanning the four-foot-wide opening that separated the sidewalk from her hiding place.

A man about her height, overcoated in black against the cold, dashed by her, his face hidden by the smudgy gray woolen cap pulled down over his ears. A swastika was sewn onto the arm of his coat. As he ran, a campaign button fell off his coat and clattered onto the sidewalk. It rolled on the edge for a brief second, and then fell face up. The fox-faced man who would later adorn Jessie's campaign button looked up at Helen in the glare of the street lamp.

Sandy strolled back, propping up a man with silvering hair who was holding a tan wool Homburg in one hand. With the other hand, gloved in a rust-colored exotic leather, he held onto Sandy's arm as if Sandy were a walking cane.

"Thank you," the man offered with in an English accent. "That man accosted me here on the sidewalk. He wanted to hand me this." He dug out a pamphlet from his coat pocket, letting go of Sandy to do so. It had a photograph of the same man on the front. "When I realized what it was, what he was, I shoved it back at him. Then he started toward me like he was going to hit me. It's when I shouted."

"That was some shout coming from an English professor," Sandy said.

"Chaucer, Shakespeare, they didn't hesitate to use their equivalent of four letter words so why should I?" The man laughed. "But that thing is why I didn't take the visiting professorship in Vienna. And now it's here, this fascist poison." He shook his head.

"Thank you again," he said to Sandy. "I'll let you get on about your night with this enchanting woman." He put his Homburg back on and walked slowly away.

William Pelley, founder of the pro-Nazi Silver Shirts, fascist, anti-Semite, believer in the occult, trying to get on the ballot as a presidential candidate. A dangerous lunatic with a dangerous following. He was the man with the vulpine look.

A young woman Helen gauged as being close to her own age came around the corner from the side of the house. She had the same features as Jessie, but too sharp to be elegant, her nose sitting on her face like a knife with its edge turned out. Everything else about her was understated, as if to compensate. The duckling yellow dress barely touched her body, the linen skirt hanging limply to her mid-calf. Her blue-black hair wilted against her head and neck despite its bob cut. Her lipstick color stained her lips a bubblegum pink.

"Mother," she said, walking up to Jessie and giving her a peck on the cheek, "it's another fine party."

Jessie nodded. "Winona, dear, this is Helen Rice, Joe's friend. Helen, my daughter, Winona Stephens."

Winona offered her hand, which was a bluish-white and clammy to the touch. Helen wondered briefly what illness Winona had that the California sun could not warm her up. She also noticed a large diamond engagement ring on the right ring finger. Glancing down, she saw a thick gold wedding ring on the complementary finger of Winona's left hand.

"Hi, Joe," Winona said. "Norman and I are still hoping you can get over to our place before it's completely done and give us more ideas about stuff for the upstairs. It's just a hodgepodge right now."

Helen turned to Joe and said, "Joe, you have hidden talents?"

"I'm helping Winona and Norman with some furniture ideas, how big, where to place the furniture. That's all."

"Oh, more than that," Winona offered eagerly. "He's helping to narrow down fabric choices and colors. It's so overwhelming to have to furnish a—"

"Very large house that I'm building for them in Rustic Canyon," Jessie said in a tone of voice that shut the door on the line of conversation.

Winona put her hand over her mouth and giggled for a

half-second before taking a deep breath. "It's a lovely area, Helen. Do you know it?"

"No. I'm new to California."

"Helen's father was a hero in the German Army in the Great War," Jessie said.

"And how did you get here?" Winona asked in the tone of a child eager for a bedtime story.

"I was orphaned very young. My older sister and I came to New York. Then, later, she married and moved here with her husband. I have followed."

"But you miss Germany," Jessie added.

"Yes. Although I'm sure I wouldn't recognize anything or even be able to talk much since I was young when I left." This was a semi-true statement and one, Helen hoped, that would discourage Jessie or anyone else from inquiring more closely into her non-existent German past.

"We never forget our native tongue. So you see, dear," Jessie addressed Winona, "many people have it much harder than you ever had."

"Yes, Mother." Helen recognized the tone of voice, since it was the same she had used with Sarah. Give Winona time and she would roll her eyes and stomp off, she thought.

"Helen is exactly the kind of friend you should have. Not the drinking and carousing crowd you and Norman seem to like."

Helen wondered how she and Joe had wandered into this intimate family fight. From Winona's reaction, it was an argument aired many times before.

"Of course, Mother. So, Joe, when you come, do bring Helen." She reached over and patted Helen's shoulder. "I'll be happy to show you around. Maybe you can come to the séance we're having."

"Maybe you'll be able to reach out to your beloved parents," Jessie said in a tone with no trace of humor.

Jessie and Winona shared a passion for the occult sciences, as they referred to séances, astrology, Ouija Boards, and mind reading. They spent the next few minutes discussing mediums who had made appearances at various parties and dinners Jessie had hosted in the past. Winona leaned over and whispered urgently in Jessie's ear. Try as she could, Helen could not hear what she was saying without leaning in closer.

Helen did not believe in the occult. She did not believe in the evil eye, although she thought her mother might have, since her mother wore a *hamsa*, a filigreed hand on a chain, "to ward off evil spirits." Much good it had done her parents.

Helen did not believe that God intervened in lives, either. War, sickness, accident, poverty all intervened, not a beneficent deity. Out-of-body experiences happened when people were starving or inflamed with fevers.

The skilled exercise of cynicism, guarding your expression and your tongue, thwarted anyone who tried to trick you or take advantage of you. And America was the place to be free of all other grandmother's tales. It was the place to be practical and to deal with fear by forging ahead.

"I myself use my intuition at all times. William is so encouraging of my gifts." Helen realized that Jessie was speaking directly to her. "And that is why, Helen, I am so certain of you. My intuition never leads me astray. I am also learning to read people's auras."

"I hope I don't disappoint you."

"Not a chance. I look at you and see myself at your age, as if I am looking into a mirror to the past."

At this, Winona took half a step back from her mother and stared wide-eyed at Helen, as if Helen was an apparition who had sprung out of the tiled patio to haunt her.

"Winona, dear, please see if William is here and has been waylaid by one of his supporters."

Winona stiffened like a puppet pulled sharply up by her strings, said, "Yes, Mother," and walked away, bumping once into the veranda railing and then nearly careening into a servant carrying a tray of empty plates.

Jessie took a deep breath as if she were surfacing from an underwater dive.

"My daughter has habits, indulgences, that I had expected she would give up after she married. But Norman hasn't been quite the stabilizing factor I had hoped for." She took Helen's hand, gripping it like the rung of a ladder, pinching Helen's fingers together. "You have such strength, Helen. I can feel it." She raised Helen's hand, releasing the fingers and resting it, palm down, on her own moist, smooth palm. "Please be a friend to my Winona."

"Of course, Jessie," Helen said.

The look of distress that accompanied the deep breath, deepening the light wrinkles around Jessie's mouth and cratering the skin between her eyes, left, leaving Jessie's face as unmarked as if a light dew had landed and evaporated.

"And Joe," Jessie said in a sharpened tone, "you must not let Winona get near anyone who can be a problem for her."

Helen thought that if Joe could have genuflected, he would have. "No, no," he said.

What people could be a problem for Winona? And, how could that be useful, Helen wondered.

Joe took Helen's elbow and escorted her away from Jessie, who had been greeted by three middle-aged men, each in a suit too dark, business-like, and wintery for the afternoon fête. Jessie gave them a bright smile. "Yes, William Pelley is here," Helen could hear her say.

She seemed to have forgotten her earlier offer of further introductions for Helen and Joe. Helen suspected that Winona was the cause.

Helen and Joe stood on a veranda stair, sipping a non-alcoholic punch. Joe had explained that he wanted to avoid any chance of repeating the mishap of the first party and she agreed. Joe took out a pack of Pall Malls and offered her one. When she declined, he put the pack back in his pocket without taking one himself. She wondered if he had the cigarettes in case someone else wanted one, since she had only seen him smoke once, and then just half of one before he stubbed it out.

Drinking alcohol before sundown was not a bad habit of hers, nor did she smoke. Movies and ads promoted the glamour of smoking, but she didn't have the money and she hated the smell of stale tobacco smoke that haunted most bars she'd been in.

Rose, her radical CCNY friend, told her she was a prude. "No booze, no cigarettes, no sex, no fun," she had said, shaking Helen's arm back and forth in mock frenzy. "What did we have the 1920s for, if not to be free?"

Helen spent the 1920s learning English, going to school, and taking care of herself every afternoon while her sister worked at the garment factory. "Free" was a term she applied to education or, if pressed, to speech and the press, which she had to learn about in Civics and retain for her citizenship exam. "Free" did not apply to behavior that could make you sick, get you drunk, pregnant, or, worse, kicked out of the country.

"How close are you to Winona?" Helen asked.

"Pretty close," Joe said.

"What is her problem?"

Joe leaned in, whispering in Helen's ear even though no one was within five feet of them and couples all around were engaged in their own discussions.

"She smokes a lot of maryjane. That's the crowd she hangs with."

Helen offered Joe a vague, quiet "Oh," the syllable hanging

in the air between them like a round little balloon keeping them apart. He pulled back from her ear, satisfied that she was not going to shout.

Helen knew people who smoked marijuana, mostly hangers-on at jazz clubs in New York or college student friends who took their disaffection with society and turned it into chemical anomie. In her experience, they slowly slid from exerting any consequential effort to languid disinterest, and eventually, to a vanishing act. Whether they ever reemerged on the other side of the curtain of smoke she did not know.

She heard that marijuana wasn't nearly as hard to deal with as cocaine. She heard that snowbirds never came back. And that is what Winona had looked like to her, a little cocaine addict, pale, thin, wired, all mommy's money up her nose.

Helen leaned back toward Joe. "Just marijuana? Are you sure?"

Joe nodded.

"Who does she get it from, Joe?" It was a bold move to ask such a direct question. Helen was counting on her aura to carry the day. Joe had been transfixed by Jessie's insistence that Helen had some metaphysical connection with her.

Joe flushed, pinpoint spots of red firing up his cheeks.

"I don't know."

At this, Helen pursed her lips, gluing them down against the "Yeah, right," that was lurking behind her teeth. Instead, she said, "Let's just go mingle some more."

An hour later, Helen had not seen Winona again. She suspected Jessie's daughter was tucked behind a door in the recesses of the house, avoiding her mother. Or smoking weed.

Helen had only glimpsed William Pelley and Jessie Murphy through an open door. They were standing in the grand foyer and he was whispering in her ear. Three hulking men no older than twenty flanked his rear, each dressed in a silver shirt and dark pants. Helen remembered the large order of shirts that Joe had brought to the cleaners. She was sure these were the same.

The hour had not been without its benefits, however. Helen had flirted her way into four large conversational groups, each dominated by loud-voiced men, who had encouraged their doughy wives to "let the young woman and her beau in." Minimizing her threat to any wife, Helen had glued Joe to her side, using her hand tucked in his elbow, and, when she felt him tugging away in a paroxysm of fear, a firm grip on his wrist, as if he was a toddler about to run into the street.

Social introductions went smoothly. Helen focused on each name, repeated it at least twice in conversation, and then rehearsed the names silently as she and Joe strolled to another group.

Mark Johns entertained his group with tales of the Imperial Japanese Navy's charter ship, *Shoya Maru*, just finishing filling up on the last dregs of California fuel ordered by Japan.

"Three million barrels of the stuff we've sold them. A million for civilian use and two million for military use. What a bonanza! Adolph'll make them honorary Aryans if they get China," he said. Laughter greeted this, and then the men fell silent.

George Highsmith, a wife not in view, strolled up to the group.

"Hey, George, what going on with you? How're you nurturing all those egg-heads?" Mark asked.

"Good."

"How many Jews there, now?"

George glanced at Helen before continuing.

"I think two, but I don't look when they're in the men's room." The men snickered.

"We need to get rid of them."

"That Einstein left for Princeton, but pluck one out and another weed will grow in its place."

"Gentlemen, it was lovely to meet you all," Helen said. Tugging on Joe's arm with enough force to lead him out of the group but not enough to make her seem as if she controlled his actions in any way, she tucked her arm inside his and positioned them against the wall of the house, near enough to hear some of the rest of the discussion.

"He's with that ..." George's voice dropped too low for Helen to hear.

One of the men let out his breath explosively. After that, Helen could just make out something that sounded like "rock." She was directly in George's line of sight when he turned toward Mark to respond to something Mark had said. He stared at her for a fraction of a second too long, his intent unreadable. As if she had felt faint, she put her head on Joe's shoulder.

"I'm getting tired, Joe. Have we done the party enough?" Helen asked.

He looked at her with mild surprise. "I thought you could do this all afternoon. But I'm ready to go."

"Excellent." She smiled. "It's too bad I never got to meet the guest of honor, Pelley, though."

"We had better fix that or Jessie will be upset."

They wove their way back through the seventy or so guests on the veranda. Helen had counted in her head and figured she had met about thirty of them, always targeting the men who dominated their conversation groups. Without exception, they had big, gold watches prominent on their wrists, and wives whose jewelry flamed rainbow colors in the mild sun of an afternoon soirée.

Pelley was tucked in a quarter-circle of admirers clipped off at each end with Silver Shirts. Helen scissored in, Joe in her in wake. Helen felt Joe's hand suddenly snake around her waist as his fingers pulled her back against his side. She was momentarily surprised at the strength concealed behind his shirt sleeves and jacket.

"Joe Miller." Joe offered his hand to Pelley. "I'm responsible here for your uniforms and I'm liaison to some areas of the motion pictures."

"Mr. Miller. Yes, much indebted for all your efforts. As you can see," Pelley nodded toward his men, "we would not be here in such fine feather without your help. And the motion picture industry, well, we will talk about those people another time."

"Mr. Pelley, I'm happy to meet you," she said, her hand drifting up toward her hair to push away a wayward lock. His eyes followed her hand up her body to her face while he smiled vaguely in her direction.

"Helen Rice," she offered. He shot his hand out and she took it.

"Miss Rice, a pleasure, I'm sure."

"Jessie asked me to be sure to find you before I left. She is quite the hostess. And such a capable fundraiser."

"Indeed." Pelley paused, let go of her hand slowly, and looked at her face. His eyes, set deep under the brow bone, were the color of a cloudy morning sky. The black pupils were enlarged, as if straining to bring as much light into their center as possible. His sandy brown hair, generously streaked with gray, was rigidly parted to the side, white scalp demarcating the line as if daring stray hairs to cross to the other side. The voice was low, with the slight vibration of an oboe. His overall impact was simultaneously compelling and off-putting.

"You're running for President."

"Yes. We need to be forces for Light against Darkness."

Helen nodded. "I couldn't agree more."

"God rebuked me," Pelly continued. "I was blaming him for the Great War and the Great Depression which has followed. But I should be attacking the forces in this world that have caused those events."

A thuggish Silver Shirt, triceps bulging under the shirt fabric, said, "Communists."

The Silver Shirt next to him shot his arm out abruptly in a Nazi salute. "And Jews."

The entire phalanx of bleak-eyed men in silver followed suit. Three of the guests, two men and one woman, mimicked them a second later and then, as if on a slow wave, the remainder of the conversation group. A group of four about a yard away, each with a plate of food and a glass of punch, raised their punch-holding hands in imitation. Then, down Helen's line of sight, every guest imitated the salute.

Helen sucked in the tender flesh on the inside of her right cheek and bit down hard. Taking a slow breath, she said, "I look forward to hearing more. And I apologize for interrupting your conversation."

Pelley took her left hand and bowed slightly. Helen heard the faint click of heels coming together. Then he released her hand and Helen backed herself and Joe out of the group.

As Joe was maneuvering his car down the long driveway, Helen looked in the rear view mirror. A man who looked very much like Ralph stepped onto the lawn and stared at Joe's car. Helen's eyes darted away from the mirror as if not staring back meant he could not see her either. She rubbed her hands together.

"Are you all right?" Joe asked, his voice low and oddly tender.

"Sure. Just a little tired."

At the door to Sarah and Harry's, Helen turned her cheek and Joe offered a moist, delicate press of lips.

"If Jessie was serious about you getting to know Winona better, should I call?"

"Of course. Or just call anyhow," Helen said. Her proposed acquaintance with Winona appeared to have nothing to do with Winona's preferences one way or the other. If this was always how it had been, no wonder Winona retreated to a hazy, faded world of drugs.

It was dusk—that time when businesses began to close, shopping ended, children left their balls and sandboxes, and most people retreated from the public to their private lives. People turned on their radios, scanning the dial for the news, and then for broadcasts of *The Lone Ranger* or *The Green Hornet*. In every kitchen, pots and pans clattered, and the aroma of frying onions and peppers floated into the air.

Both children were crying in the kitchen as Helen entered the house. Sarah walked into the hall, a towel tied around her waist as a makeshift apron, her sleeves rolled up above the elbow, wooden spoon in her right hand. She looked at Helen, nodded, and returned to the kitchen, the crying unabated.

"Welcome home," Helen thought.

Sighing, she went to the bedroom, and took off her dress and shoes with the care of a mother removing a bandage from a bloodied knee. She hung the dress in the closet, giving it breathing room on each side. Then, she took out a pencil and a sheet of paper and walked back through the party in her mind, naming everyone she could recall, along with any other information she could think of. That done, she went to help her sister.

9

HELEN DREAMED OF THUGS WEARING silver clothes from head to foot, speaking a language in which German and Polish were muddied together to the point of indecipherability. In the dark room with no hint of sunrise under the shade, she sat on the edge of the bed taking deep breaths and thinking about escape. She had been driven to the end of the continent, with no place to step except into the Pacific Ocean.

After the sun rose, Helen took a shower, not caring if the sound of water in the pipes woke anyone else, and dressed for a Sunday at home. As the coffee percolated reassuringly, she walked outside, picked up the Sunday paper from the lawn, and returned to the kitchen. She enjoyed this small period in the day when no one else was stirring in the shared areas of the house, and therefore, no demands were on her to be, act, or do.

The newspaper reinforced her concerns: anti-Jewish riots continued in Palestine; Greece's liberal government was being threatened by reactionary elements. She turned to the comics, humming *The Good Ship Lollypop*. Shirley Temple was a comfort at least.

Flipping through the sports section, she paused to read a paragraph on the races at Santa Anita, but did not recognize any of the horses' names. Helen folded the paper, putting all the sections back in order, slipped out the front door with her coffee cup, and sat in the thin line of sun that crossed the bricked step to the front door.

Wisps of fog hung in the air, residue of something Harry referred to as "the marine layer." The bricks were chilly and damp, but the temperature was warming.

Helen heard the radio turn on in the living room, announcing that Harry was up. He was the only person allowed to turn it on or off and, when home, the only person allowed to pick a station.

The front door squealed open behind her and Harry said, "Having a picnic?"

"Just enjoying the fresh air."

He stepped out behind her, close enough that his pant leg brushed against her hair. She continued to gaze across the lawn. She felt him step to the side and then saw him sit down.

A day's growth of beard added to his usually gnomish appearance. He had dark circles under his eyes and more gray in both his beard and his hair than she recalled, but then she tried not to look at him hard, so maybe she just hadn't noticed.

"Thanks for the money, Helen."

"You're welcome."

"You're not…uhhh…compromising yourself for it, are you?" he asked in a hoarse whisper.

"Why, Harry, how gallant of you. No, I'm not," she said. "I'm not a lady of the night." It struck her as funny and she started to laugh, the coffee dancing in the bottom half of the cup. "My virtue is quite virtuous."

Harry sighed, his eyes focused on the small chip in the brick between his feet.

"I get that you don't think so, but I am trying to do right here. And to tell you that you are a help."

Helen considered this, her gaze paralleling Harry's on the path. Then she said, "I would like to ask you a question."

His glance flicked toward her and back to the chip.

"Why the hell did you get involved with Dragna?"

Harry nodded and rubbed his chin stubble with a thick hand. "I came out here with good intentions. Run a clean liquor store, raise the kid, try to make your sister happy." He took a gulp of coffee and put the cup down between them. It had a sugar-and-cream aroma.

"But the money it took was money I didn't have. And some of the money was bribery plain and simple. So I looked for a good opportunity, something that was easy, not too dirty. After all, if you can bet at the track, why can't you bet private?"

"Good point," Helen said.

Harry gave her a glance of appreciation. "So I'll make this quick, before Sarah finishes getting the kids ready. That cop? He's a Dragna guy. Like I told you before, Dragna controls all the gambling in LA, and he's got those gambling ships off the coast, too. But the cop's asking me for an unauthorized raise in pay. Something Dragna doesn't know about. Dragna himself doesn't dig into the little guys, like me. There's no payoff for him."

Rachel howled from the depths of the house.

"Thanks for the information, Harry."

Harry stood, picked up his cup of coffee, patted Helen once on the shoulder, and went inside. He left the front door ajar. Helen stretched out her legs and yawned. Then she got up and went inside as well, wondering who had changed more, Harry or herself. Maybe neither.

Sarah busied herself with the laundry and Helen helped her hang pieces on the lines. The actions had a familiar if not comfortable feel: grab two wooden clothespins from the bucket, flick out the damp garment, or grab two ends if it was big, like a bedsheet, drape it over the line, then nail the cloth down with enough pins to counteract the drag of the wet material toward the earth. It was a tedious job that she, Sarah, and their mother had done together from the time Helen was three and able to grab two, and just two, clothespins.

"How was your party?"

"Good. Joe is okay, not a pushy kind of guy, you know." Helen offered that as reassurance.

"That was some dress you had on."

This was in a neutral tone but Helen knew what was behind it. She squinted as she turned toward her sister, who had her back to the high, late-morning sun.

"Sandy knows a guy who knows the manager of the dress salon at Bullock's."

Sarah pursed her lips, cocked her head slightly, and gave her "let's see where this is going before I decide to yell" look.

"So the guy told Sandy that he would introduce me to the manager, who is looking for someone to model the clothes. I went there and I told him I had this invitation to this big party. He said I could borrow the dress and I needed to tell anyone who asked it came from Bullock's and who the designer was."

"So did anyone ask?" This was spoken in a tone as dry as the air around them.

"Yes, two women. But the dress wouldn't have looked good on them at all. Anyhow I told them where it came from. Then, I couldn't remember the designer's name, so we all had to go into the bathroom at the house, and they unzipped the back and looked in." Helen hoped that this last little detail was enough to convince her sister.

"And the sales tags are still in the dress?"

"No. The manager took them off but he said it was no problem to put them back on."

"I've never been to Bullock's."

"Maybe I can take you when I return the dress."

Sarah turned away from Helen to pluck another wrung-out blouse from her pile and put it over the line. "Sure, Helen. Maybe you can."

At four, the phone rang. Harry answered it. They had all been sitting in the living room, the music playing quietly on the radio so as not to wake the napping children. Bing Crosby had just finished singing *You're Getting to Be a Habit*. Helen had read every section of the newspaper, including sports. Sarah had dozed off, startling like a napping child at the sound of the phone.

"For you, Helen. Sandy," Harry said.

"We need a report," he said without preliminaries. "So I'll pick you up at six tonight unless you have other plans."

"Sandy, how nice of you to call again," she said, smiling down the hall at Sarah, who was staring at her.

"What?" She paused. "Dinner tonight? Oh, I need to ask Sarah if that's okay. You know it's the only real family time we all have together."

The corners of Sarah's mouth twitched up toward a smile. Sarah had once played guys along, never saying "Yes" until asked at they asked least twice for a date, but never saying bluntly "No" either if she had liked the guy.

Helen put her hand over the mouthpiece and said to her sister in a stage whisper, "You okay with this? He's going to leave LA and go back to New York."

Sarah nodded.

"Yes, I told her you were leaving soon and that this was important to you. So, I'll see you at six. And I also told her that your friend had sent me over to Bullock's so I could see about modeling there. Guess what?" She paused. Sandy said nothing.

"He lent me a dress to wear. Now, Sarah wants to go to Bullock's with me to return it." She paused again. Sandy said nothing.

"I knew that would be okay with you. See you at six."

Sarah's eyebrows tugged upwards in a comic expression of surprise. Helen knew Sarah was exaggerating for effect, but maybe the monologue would satisfy her doubt over the source of the dress for now.

Helen did not want her sister probing and prying into her business. Sarah had done that so effectively in the past that Helen could still feel her earlobe throbbing as Sarah tweaked it after catching her in a lie. Now Helen had two stories to balance about the dress, one to Joe and one to Helen. The quicker she got rid of the dress the better. But it was so lovely.

Sandy declined a cup of Folger's and a home-baked cookie. Smiling at Sarah, he promised to have her accompany Helen to Bullock's "whenever Helen is ready to return that dress." He then gripped Helen's hand with a little more force than Helen thought necessary and moved her toward the door.

"What was that all about?" she asked when she was seated in the car. She rubbed her fingers together, watching the pressure marks fade on the top of her left hand.

"You can't call the plays in this."

"What?"

He spoke slowly, each word coming out flat and stern, as if pounded by his vocal cords.

"You cannot bring someone else into this, even if it seems harmless. Or clever."

"I can't take my sister to Bullock's to return a dress?"

"Who calls the manager at Bullock's to arrange for the return of a dress that was actually paid for? Who convinces the manager to say that you are now modeling clothes at different events? And what if Sarah decides she now wants to go with you to see you model? You see now that this involves more than just me agreeing with your story."

Helen stared out the passenger window, cheeks flushed. "I haven't gone to spy school."

"No, you haven't."

"Sarah and Harry both think I've become a prostitute. They can't imagine how else I got the money for that dress."

"I admit we need to get you a good reason for that."

"So, what is the matter with the one I offered?"

He reached over and patted her thigh. "As a story it's okay. We need to give you the background, find the person at Bullock's who can help with this. And we want people there who help not just for money but for the right reasons. They need to be motivated."

Helen continued to stare out the window, her eyes barely registering the smooth taupe-colored trunks of the palm trees lining the street and the occasional lone pedestrian.

"You're a great liar on the spot," he said. "It'll help you."

"Thanks." The view blurred and she blinked her eyes, surprised to feel a tear trickle down her right cheek. Swiftly she wiped it away.

"Those Silver Shirts are a creepy bunch," she said.

"Let's save it for the briefing."

They walked up the steps of Leon Lewis' home and Sandy knocked at the door. A small woman in her early thirties, luminous brown eyes framed by wavy russet hair in a fashionable bob parted smartly on the left, opened the door. She wore light grey linen slacks and a grass-green short-sleeved silk shirt that set off her eyes and creamy skin.

Holding out her hand to Helen, she said, "Hi. Irving insisted

I come today to meet you and to protect you from all these guys. I'm Norma."

She stepped aside for Helen to enter.

As Helen stepped into the living room, she said, "Are you Norma Shearer?" Helen recognized her from the film, *A Free Soul*.

"Afraid so. Just call me Norma. And are you Helen Rice, ace spy?" Norma's smile was quiet, as if it was a whisper directed only to Helen.

"Indeed she is," a voice from the living room said. Irving stood up. Even in the transition between the bright outdoor light and the dim living room, Helen could see that he stood straighter and was dressed for the warm day. As her eyes adjusted, Helen also saw Leon walking into the living room from the kitchen, carrying a tray with a pitcher and five glasses.

Helen and Sandy sat on the couch drinking tepid tap water. Helen's right thigh pressed up against Norma's linen clad leg and Helen scooted toward Sandy, only to have her left thigh steam against his.

"You're always right, Irving dear," Norma said. "But, Helen is much taller than I am. She's Kate Hepburn's size." She reached down, lifted Helen's arm, and then held hers out. Helen's knuckle bone hung at least four inches past Norma's.

"We can't use her as a double for me, but I know we can find something for her when my film after *Romeo and Juliet* comes up. That is, of course, if you don't mind, Helen."

Helen was in the process of shaking her head to show she did not mind at all, when Leon said, "Can you find her some clothes that will fit? That'll save us money on wardrobe for infiltrating this Nazi group at the top level."

Norma nodded. "Good idea. When is her next performance?"

Before Helen could answer, Irving said, "We need to have her focus on getting specific kinds of information. For example, I need to know how compromised the studio employees are by the actions of this weasel, Joe Miller. That's his name, right?"

Helen nodded.

Leon said, "The studio employees are not our biggest priority, Irving."

"Hollywood gets a strong message out, Leon. We can't afford to have it compromised by fascists."

"Let me find someone to keep an eye on him at the studio, then. There's no shortage of concerned Jews there. You and Louis B will be in the loop, I promise."

At that, Thalberg nodded.

"What we really want is to track the money, because money is the message. And if Pelley makes a good showing in the election or, worse, if Lindberg, who actually has a chance of winning, decides to run, money is key," Norma said.

"Yes, that is important, but we need to be on top of any groundswell of support from ordinary Americans for Lindberg or his ideas," Leon said.

"Excuse me," Sandy said in what Helen recognized as his stage voice, designed to carry into the balcony seats. Leon, Irving, and Norma looked at him in surprise.

"I actually am a spy. This is my area, and if anyone needs to assist Helen in finding her way into this group, it is me. Always with thanks, of course, for wardrobe help and for money. We need to hear from Helen what she found out, what she saw, who she met. That will let us figure out what possible new avenues she should explore."

After his outburst, Sandy stayed quiet, once excusing himself to go to the bathroom, then returning and taking up the same position, thigh to thigh, next to Helen.

Over the next hour, Helen went through the details of the party, focusing on who was there and what was said. George's position at Caltech was worthy of note, especially when Helen told them about his sotto-voce conversation, during which only the word "rocks" was clear.

As she responded to each question with detail, she began to realize just how much information she had absorbed during the party. When she finally finished answering Leon's last question, she took a deep breath.

"Here are my thoughts," she said. "Jessie wants me to get close to her daughter. If I do that, it will help me stay in Jessie's good graces. My 'aura' will remain golden or whatever color Jessie thinks it is. I'll get asked to more gatherings by more people."

"Jessie is a key figure in Los Angeles. Kuhn is in contact with her, too," Leon said.

"Who's Kuhn?" asked Helen.

She took another sip of water after shakily pouring it into her glass from the ever-warmer pitcher. The liquid was hard to swallow even though her mouth was dry. It was as if she had to tell her muscles what to do.

If Flash Gordon had landed his spaceship in the narrow expanse of front lawn that Helen could see through the windows, she would not have been surprised. The whole experience of being a spy seemed like something out of a movie, helped by the knowledge that she was sitting with an actual studio head and his movie star wife.

"Kuhn is a naturalized citizen from Germany who now fancies himself Hitler's aide-de-camp in America. He's starting groups he calls 'Bunds,' and I quote, 'sympathetic to the Hitler government,'" Leon said.

Norma, who had poured herself more water as well but with a firmer grip than Helen's, nodded. "I heard him in New York. Claims he has hundreds of thousands of followers."

"And Schwinn. Let's not forget him."

"Schwinn?" Helen asked. She could feel the corners of her mouth tipping downward as she heard another name to keep straight.

"Another German import, naturalized, and in charge of the Bund's 'Western Division.'" Leon said. "Thinks he is charismatic. Likes to play ladies' man."

"It's getting late. Let's try to focus. It's not an NYCC debate; it's a spy operation," Sandy said.

Leon nodded and Irving and Norma sighed.

"Go for the daughter, Helen. And good work on this other stuff," Sandy said.

They agreed that Sandy would check in with Helen daily by phone. Norma went into the dining room and Sandy followed, leaning over the desks still piled high with notebooks and type-writers to talk to her.

When Norma returned to the living room, she said, "I'll see what I might have for you among my taller friends. I'll reach out to Kate. And I'll tell the manager at Bullock's that it's no problem if you return the dress. And he'll keep the story straight for your sister, who, Sandy tells me, is quite eagle-eyed."

Helen smiled, feeling it grow on her face from polite to genuine as she looked at Norma.

"Thanks."

For three days Helen had nothing to report, but she kept Sandy on the phone each time she called while she aimlessly chatted about her niece, her nephew, and her day at the liquor store.

"Is this some kind of code, Helen?" he asked, his exasperation skittering through the line in his tone of voice.

"No."

"Afraid?"

"Maybe." She whispered into the receiver looking down the hall to see if Sarah or Harry were nearby. The noise of a marching band played loudly in the living room. Then there was static until Harry settled on another station.

"It'll be okay. And, Helen, I'm sorry you got dragged into this." Sandy's voice was low, too, with a tinge of the intimate warmth it had when they were dating. "Remember, I asked you to stay in New York."

There was no sense in going down that path. "Sandy, you told me not to go to Los Angeles. That's different. Don't worry about me. I'll get something out of this."

"Besides knowing that you are doing the right thing?"

"Yes. Besides that."

"Pleasant dreams, Helen." With that he hung up.

By Thursday, Helen felt the strain of waiting for something to happen tearing at her neck muscles and creeping down each of her legs. When her lunch break came at the liquor store, she told Harry she was going for a walk. She strode down the sidewalk toward the dry cleaning store where she'd first met Joe, dodging the only other pedestrian for two blocks as he exited from a shoe repair store.

The dry cleaning store was also empty of customers. Glendale seemed to Helen to be the most unpopulated big-little city in the world.

In New York people were everywhere all the time, bumping into each other like billiard balls on the street, on buses, and the subway. Here, it was as though the game was over and everyone had gone home.

The bell tinkled as Helen opened the door and Elsa emerged from the rear. The air in the store had the warm, steamy scent of clothes being pressed with an iron somewhere behind the curtain.

Elsa's face was damp, and she wiped her hands on a towel with a faded flower pattern that hung from a hook next to the cash register.

"May I help you?"

Helen had walked in with a vaguely formulated plan. As a result, she stammered her way through a request to know if Joe had been in recently, because she had accidentally left her sweater in his car and had no way of getting in touch with him.

"And when he has found the sweater in his car, why would he not call you?" Elsa asked.

Helen flushed. "Ummm. You're right. So sorry to have bothered you." She turned to leave. If she couldn't get information from the owner of a dry cleaners, how could she get information from Jessie Murphy or even her drug-addled daughter?

"Wait, Miss."

Elsa's face bore an expression between smile and smirk. "I think that Joe would like to hear from you. He is not bold with women."

"Do you know him well?"

"Oh, yes. He is my nephew. My littlest brother and his wife. That part of the family."

"I didn't realize you were family. And Joe's parents. Are they here in America, too?"

"Dead in the war. His father in the trenches and his mother of the fever."

"I didn't realize Joe was an immigrant."

"He is not. His father died in the American Army. He was the immigrant. To join the army and fight against his Fatherland was the way to get papers."

"Citizenship papers?"

"Yes."

Helen left with Joe's phone number written on a torn corner of an old newspaper crumpled in her fist. She thought it was nail-bitingly strange that she and Joe were both orphans because of the same horrid war and influenza epidemic.

It was almost one in the afternoon and she ran the last few steps to the liquor store. As she pushed open the door, she saw a thickly muscled figure standing by the counter. Harry was leaning toward him and they fell silent as soon as she entered.

"Hi, Helen," Ralph said as he turned toward her.

"Ralph was just saying that he thought he caught a glimpse of you at a party last weekend."

Ralph hung his head and offered the movie version of a sheepish smile. "Guilty. I'd just come in to do my security work, like I was telling Harry, and this knockout is getting into a car and leaving. Some kind of bird on the dress that looked like…"

"A parrot. Yes, it was me."

"I got to tell you, no other woman there could touch your sister-in-law in the looks department," Ralph said to Harry in a loud whisper.

The stagey act worked on the muscles in Helen's neck like a screwdriver on a loose screw. It was all she could do not to reach up and begin to rub but she did not want either of the men to sense that she was distressed.

"If I had known you were there, Ralph, I would have come and said 'hi' before I left."

"I'm sure you would have. In fact, I'm so sure that I have come to ask you if you'd like to go out with me tonight." His smile touched the surface of his lips but not his eyes.

Helen was aware of her shoulders creeping toward her ears, the muscles continuing to tighten in her neck, and the slight backward tilt of her torso, as if her body wanted to take flight back out the door. In the hand that held Joe's telephone number, her nails bit into her palm.

She drew her open hand up to her forehead, smoothing back a stray lock, and sighed.

"Tomorrow is a work day."

"This is possibly a once in blue moon chance. I've got a job out on a gambling ship. I thought it would be interesting to you. You could see what that's all about."

"I don't think I can."

"Let me be straight with you."

"Please do."

"I need a pretty girl to escort onto the ship so I don't look so out of place and I can nose around without getting stares. It's not that I couldn't ask another girl, but you are the prettiest one I know."

"I've heard of the guy who owns this ship, Helen. You should go," Harry said. He was standing behind Ralph so Ralph did not see him mouth "Dragna."

"Well, if it's okay with Harry how can it not be okay with me?"

"That's what I told Harry when we were talking about what a small world it is. How you know a guy who knows a guy who knows a guy and boom."

Ralph turned toward Harry and said, "Great chatting with you." Turning to Helen, he added, "I'll pick you up at ten tonight. The fun doesn't really start until then. The women there specialize in looking good, so that dress with the bird…"

"A parrot."

"That's the one. You could wear that."

Ralph walked over, kidnapped a Nehi from its cold resting spot, swung the door open, shivering the glass, and left.

Helen sat on the stool behind the counter, rolling an icy bottle of Schlitz up and down her neck and across her shoulders, stopping only when she got to her bra strap. She did not care that her blouse had damp spots.

"Really, Harry. Now I've got to go out with Ralph again because he works for Dragna? I was going to never see him again. This guy specializes in working for the worst kind of people."

Harry stood with his hands folded on top of the counter across from her. Helen could see that he was gripping his fingers as if they would disappear if he let them go. He'd been absolutely silent since Ralph had left. The silence had a life of its own by this time. Helen wondered if he would ever speak.

Considering the few options Harry seemed to have, Helen almost felt bad for him. It was as if he, Sarah, and the babies were tottering at the top of a high mountain, with Jack Dragna's rogue cop about to shove them over the edge, sending them all sliding down to oblivion, like rubble.

"Just go with him. It's not Dragna he's working for, and the guy he is doing this job for doesn't give a damn whether it's you or some other girl, just so long as Ralph can mingle okay."

"He tell you that?"

"Pretty much. The guy doesn't even know you're my sister-in-law. Doesn't care. Ralph just talked you up to him."

"According to him."

"It's what he said."

Helen returned the Schlitz to the cooler without opening it and grabbed a Coca-Cola. Opening it, she took a long drag, swallowed, and took another.

"It's too hot for a spring day, Harry." She grabbed her purse from the shelf near the register. "I'm leaving now. Got to see a man about a dog."

He looked at her and nodded.

Helen considered going back to the house but there was no way to use the telephone without Sarah either overhearing or asking questions. She didn't think she could keep her composure if Sarah started in on her.

And Sarah would want to know why she was wearing the dress again if she was supposed to return it to Bullock's. Before she went to the house, she needed an answer for that and a plan.

Helen walked along the boulevard humming *Did You Ever See a Dream Walking?* to keep her pace even. It was a better choice to keep her mood up than *Stormy Weather,* which was the first song that had come to mind. Those lyrics evoked the pressure of Sandy's thigh against hers. Since she needed to call him about the latest developments, a clear head and a calm body were in order.

She found a pay phone booth at a Rexall Drug Store four blocks away from the liquor store. The booth was tucked at the rear of the store, so Helen passed the inspection of the middle-aged man at the register, walked past shelves stocked with Band-Aids, Mercurochrome, and hot water bottles, turned right when she was almost at the fountain counter, with its stools and fading aroma of hotdogs and burgers on the grill, and entered the booth.

The booth smelled like dirty socks. She shut the door firmly behind her, hoping for as much sound proofing and as little foot traffic as possible.

Extracting the folded, slightly damp paper with Joe's phone number on it, she dialed, thinking it would ring and ring in an empty apartment, but willing to spend the money just to be able to tell Sandy she had tried.

"Hello?"

"Joe?"

"Yes. Who is this?"

"Helen." She heard the receiver being muffled by a hand, murky vowels floated into her ear, and then he came back on the line.

"Helen. Wow." His tone had the intonation of a ten-year-old just given a new comic book. But underneath, Helen detected worry.

"Is this a bad time to call? Actually, I'm a little surprised to even get you now."

"No, not a bad time. I'm home because…" The phone was suffocated again, giving over to more high pitched vowels. "Because we're in between films so everyone got a few extra days off. Winona dropped by."

"Really!" Helen infused the word with warm and giddy delight. "I'd love to see her again."

"Yeah, sure. That's kind of what she and I were saying when I told her it was you. Is that why you called?" Joe sounded puzzled. "And how did you get my phone number?"

Helen did not want to give Joe the particulars of her conversation with his aunt. What she wanted was his address so she could call a cab if necessary and get there before Winona left.

"Oh, golly. It's a bit of a story. Let me tell you when I get there. Where are you?"

Joe lived six blocks from the drug store, an easy walk. She told him she would be there in about fifteen minutes. Then she got change from the middle-aged man at the register, buying a pack of Wrigley chewing gum to force the issue of dimes.

Sandy had told her that if he did not answer the phone, an answering service would. When she expressed surprise, he said they were specially trained and trustworthy. "Feel free to tell them anything," he said.

Helen considered telling the woman who answered the line exactly how she felt about getting dragged into spying on Nazi sympathizers and being dragooned into a game of peek-a-boo with gangsters. But the woman sounded grandmotherly.

"You're one of Sandy's people?"

"I am."

"What can I tell him for you? I have my pencil ready."

"Tell him I'm on my way to meet Joe and Winona. He'll know who they are. Tell him that I have gotten trapped into going to a gambling ship tonight owned by Dragna with that creepy bodyguard guy, Ralph. If he doesn't know who Dragna is, tell him to ask one of his local buddies. Tell him...." Helen paused to consider whether she wanted to say she was angry or afraid. "Tell him that's what I have to report."

"Okay, dear. And be careful." The line went dead. Helen hung up the receiver.

Helen walked to Joe's apartment at the pace of a New Yorker about to miss the last train uptown. She looked around for a building more than one story high, something massive against the sky, and was disappointed and worried. She double checked the address she had written down in the phone booth and then proceeded down the indicated block.

At the address that Joe gave, a set of three single-story units sat in the middle of a grassy area patched with brown dirt. A garden hose snaked out from behind the first building, a small muddy puddle beneath it.

Each building had rounded corners, into which frosted glass brick windows were inserted. The windows began at Helen's eye level. Identical twin doors, painted mahogany red, with small brass numbers, were set midway into the first building's front. Helen assumed the same was true of the two other buildings. Next to each door was a clear glass window, draped on the inside to prevent anyone from looking in.

Helen walked up the concrete path that led to the last building and knocked on number six.

"Helen," Winona said, opening the door wide. An acrid odor, something like Marlboro cigarettes but more vegetal, that Helen recognized as marijuana, hovered around her.

Winona's hair was tousled and snarled. She was wearing an orchid-purple blouse with an over-sized Peter Pan collar and high-waisted linen pants. The clothes, well-made and expensive, looked as if she had grabbed them off the bedroom floor or possibly even slept in them.

Her eyes were red-rimmed. A large bruise that was just beginning to turn purple adorned her left cheek bone, and a cut whose redness indicated the blood had just begun to dry puffed at the side of her mouth.

As Helen stepped into the living room, however, she realized that no one had been smoking reefer in the immaculate living room. And no one had been beating on Winona there either.

The simple room, painted a stark white, contained an area rug patterned in faded hues of gold on a white ash floor the color of morning sunshine. The mantle over a brick fireplace, painted white, held a single large silver bowl on one side and a tall, ornate silver candle-stick on the other.

Two thickly padded leather chairs with geometrically squared off arms and heavy braiding on the sides faced a low, round table with an oval glass top. A third leather and metal chair with open arms completed the arrangement.

Against the wall a triangularly shaped table with a square, highly polished wooden top held four books, laid flat. The top book read *Le Corbusier* and featured a photograph of a sleek leather sofa on the cover.

As Helen stepped away from Winona, she felt a light breeze blowing in from the rear of the apartment where she could just glimpse a refrigerator.

"Joe just went outside for a minute. He said he needed fresh air." Winona giggled. "I think he just feels that I stink."

At that she sank into one of the chairs and put her head between her hands.

"I told Joe it was okay for you to come over. The Mother Figure thinks you would be good for me. I need a friend. I've worn Joe out."

Helen sat down in the matching chair. The leather was supple and the back of the chair cushioned her in comfort.

"Tell me what's going on, Winona."

"I rattle around in that infernal ranch house that Mother had built for us there in Rustic Canyon. It's so isolated."

Winona lifted her head out of her hands for a second, then dropped it again, nestling her cheek bones into her palms. Helen had to lean forward to hear her.

Helen wondered how much of this confessional talk could be chalked up to the pot and the lack of sleep and how much was caused by the beating she had taken.

"The house is weird, Helen. Mother's architect put in all these buildings that seem just useless. And it needs a fucking army to take care of it."

"That cut on your lip could use some ice," Helen said. "It's going to start to bleed again." She got up and walked into the kitchen.

As she expected, the refrigerator was in pristine condition, ice cubes smartly tucked into trays in the freezer. She plucked a tray out, walked to the sink, pressed the ice cube release bar and it worked like a champ. Cubes spilled into the sink.

She grabbed four, tucked them into the clean tea towel that hung near the sink, and went back into the living room. Given Joe's standards of hygiene, she suspected he knew how to get blood stains out of a towel.

"Here," she said. Winona lifted her head, took the towel, and pressed it against the side of her mouth. Something about that act braced her, and she sat up.

"I need you to take a look at my rear, too." Winona stood, turned her back to Helen, and dropped her pants and panties to the ground in three quick movements. Her right buttocks had a large hand imprint, red now but threatening purple and green in the next twelve hours.

"You'll have a bruise there for sure," Helen said. She went back to the kitchen, grabbed a handful of just-melting ice cubes from the sink, found another towel and returned.

"You can sit on this," she said, waving Winona back to the chair.

"Do you want to tell me who hit you? I'm guessing it wasn't Joe."

"No. It wasn't Joe. I don't want to tell you."

"Joe knows and he's tired of it, is what you said. So, it's your husband or it's your lover." Helen was not sure she wanted to know except that knowledge was always useful, if not to her then maybe to Sandy.

Winona smiled, winced, pressed the pack more firmly to her lip, and shook her head.

"Nope."

Winona was playing games with her. Helen didn't know if it was just her nature or if the marijuana or the stress brought it out. Whichever, it was annoying, and Helen had no time for it.

"Wait here," she said to Winona.

She got up, walked into the kitchen and then into the bedroom in search of a clock. A hexagonal one, edges decorated in emerald green and black alternating triangles, sat on the top of a dust-free bedside table. Helen picked it up and carried it back to the living room, its steady ticking a comfort to her ears.

"The time is now 2:55, assuming Joe's clock is accurate. I have to go out tonight to help a friend. So, Winona, as much as I would like to listen to you, I have to leave in about thirty minutes. And, I really came to see Joe anyhow."

The last statement was true, although Winona was a more promising entry into the world of Nazi-sympathizers in Los Angeles than Joe was, at least at the level of money and power. Irving Thalberg could monitor Joe as closely as he wanted without Helen.

Winona looked at her and then at the clock. She took a deep breath, then another.

"Norm has many problems, but smacking me around is not among them. Our sex life is sort of blah, but that's probably me, not him."

"So how can I help?" Helen knew there was more to the story, but it would have to wait for Winona to be willing to tell her. That was how friendship usually worked.

Winona lifted the ice pack off her lip and waved it at Helen. "You have."

"More than that?" Helen tried to insert more warmth into her voice. That brought another smile to Winona's lips.

"Come up with Joe to the house this Saturday. You can be an approved guest. You'll rescue me from death. Or boredom, its kissing cousin."

Helen agreed with Winona on the boredom issue. The years she'd spent as an office girl in New York were a dense, white emotional fog. But spending the day at a strange house with fascists felt like diving into a lake knowing rocks were submerged there but not knowing where.

Winona lifted her hand and grabbed Helen's. The hand was cold as a ghost's.

"All right," Helen said.

"Good. Joe is next door with his friend. Just go knock. I'm leaving and you have ten minutes left before you need to go." Winona picked up the clock and handed it to Helen.

A tubby man in his early thirties answered the door at number four when Helen knocked. He was as tall as Helen, five feet nine inches, with a full growth of red beard and a mustache. When he spoke, he had a Southern drawl.

"Yes?"

"Is Joe here? I'm Helen, and I was told I could find him at this number."

"Helen, come on in."

She heard Joe's voice call out to her. The man opened the door wide for her to enter.

It was hard to believe the two apartments were identical in size. This one held a large, overstuffed plaid sofa, facing a heavily carved dark wood coffee table. Two rifles leaned against the corner of the fireplace and six boxes were stacked one on top of the other beside them. She could see labels with pictures of bullets. Above the mantel hung a Confederate flag.

Joe stood when she entered. "Winona?"

"I helped with the ummm." Helen patted her lip. Joe nodded.

"And she's gone home," Helen said.

"So, Ted, thanks for the break and the coffee. We'll get together soon," Joe said.

Helen walked with Joe back to his front door.

"I gather Winona has come here before with the same problem," she said.

"Ongoing. I don't want to talk about it."

"Sure. It's Winona's life."

"You could say that. How did you get my phone number, Helen? You never did say."

"Your aunt, Elsa."

"Elsa, of course." Joe's voice was flat.

Helen could detect no emotion that would give her a clue as to what to say next. She remained silent.

"How did you leave it with Winona?" he asked.

"She invited us to her house for the day."

He looked at her, a flush starting from his neck and creeping to his cheeks.

"Sure, that should be fine. Are you available? It's best to grab this opportunity. It'll be good for Winona."

"Joe, Winona said I would be an approved guest. What does that mean? Who does the approving?"

"Jessie."

Helen wondered about a relationship between a grown married daughter and a mother who approve the daughter's guests.

"So Jessie would be happy if I went?"

He nodded, once down then up, as if offering half a "yes."

"The house is rustic, like the name. It's not grand. At least not yet. It's casual. Near the beach."

"I've never seen the Pacific."

Helen decided not to tell him that on those rare occasions when the New York sun coincided with a weekend day and all her friends went to the beach, she put on her suit and sat on the towel with her back to the water and her gaze on the land.

"You'll see it soon. I'll pick you up Sunday morning about 10."

On her walk back to Sarah and Harry's, Helen thought about Joe's relationship with his aunt, Elsa, and Winona's convoluted dealings with her mother. She did not understand how Norman fit into all of this. And it remained unclear how, if at all, working her way into the inner circle of the Murphy household would enlighten anyone on the Nazi threat to the United States.

10

RALPH CALLED TO SAY HE would pick her up at eight thirty instead of ten, since they had to make their way through Los Angeles down to the harbor and from there onto the ship, which was three miles and one yard off the coast. This allowed the gambling to go on unimpeded by the LA cops or federal agents, but it made for a longer trip out, he explained.

Helen had weakly offered that Bullock's was willing to sell her the dress at wholesale, so she decided to keep it. Sarah rolled her eyes.

Now, wearing the parrot dress with its tropical colors, such an affront to the middle-class safety of the living room, Helen endured Sarah's cold stare for as long as she could.

"Out with it, Sarah." At the sharp tone of her voice, Harry looked up from the sports section of the *Herald Express*, folded the paper, got up from his seat and walked into his bedroom. During this entire process, Helen and Sarah sat in their chairs, knees pressed together, staring straight ahead.

"What did I bring us to this country for, Helen?" Sarah said, her voice raspy with anger. "Not for you to hang out with hoodlums or to be whatever it is you are now."

At the word "hoodlums," Helen laughed once, the sound slicing through Sarah's remaining words.

"I am not the one here married to a bookie." When Helen said that, Sarah's mouth twisted and she clamped her hand over it as if to stop a demon from flying out.

"Sarah, forget that I ever said that." Helen rose and went to her sister, putting one hand on Sarah's shoulder, lightly at first, worried Sarah would just push it off. Sarah was shaking, but she put a hand on Helen's and they stayed that way for a few more seconds.

"Listen to me. Believe me when I say I am not a prostitute. Joe and Ralph are not hoodlums. It's really too bad that Harry is in trouble over the horses. But I don't hold that against him or you."

Sarah patted Helen's hand softly and took a breath so deep Helen saw her stomach rise and then fall again as the air released through her mouth. Then she got up and walked into the kitchen.

> Steerage was all Sarah could afford for herself and Helen. When the agent handed her the two tickets, Helen watched her slide them into the safest place she had, the bodice of her dress. There was no one to ask what to expect.
>
> Sarah took the lower bunk and Helen, the upper. For safe keeping, she put the little money they had left under Helen's mattress. In the bunks next to them, a Polish farmer with broad, raw hands, and his wife with a sunburned face and chewed nails, tucked in with three children. The oldest shared a bunk with the father, the two youngest slept head to toe with their mother. Before the ship left the harbor, the middle child began to throw up.
>
> Helen could not stop shaking. "There isn't a window."

Helen's body trembled in the bunk so violently that Sarah asked, "Are you having a fit?"

When Helen shook her head "no', Sarah pulled her onto her feet and took her up the steps. On deck, passengers hung onto the rails, looking down at the waves or forward toward America, as if they could see the Statue of Liberty through the mist.

Sarah found a ship's mate. He was a pimply faced young man, just out of adolescence.

"How much for a second-class cabin," she asked in a choked voice.

He motioned toward the door leading into the second class deck's cabins. "Come with me," he said. His voice had a thick Dutch overlay, phlegmy and coarse.

Sarah pointed Helen towards the deck. "Sit. Don't move. Wait for me."

Sarah waited until Helen was sixteen before she told her the rest of "my immigrant story," in a tone like bitter lemon.

There was a narrow cabin with bunk beds and a high porthole, its window clamped shut. A wash basin sat on a narrow stool. Each bunk had a single sheet and a thin wool blanket.

"How much?" Sarah had asked.

"Too much for you," he said. "But you give me sex, I make sure no one bothers you here."

Sarah met him every night of the journey behind the second class dining room, where barrels of flour and apples were kept. Young girls had endured worse. At least this dry and painful debacle was her choice.

When they left the ship at Ellis Island, he found her.

"Here," he said, putting a wad of Dutch guilders in her hand. "You are nice girl. I feel bad now. What I make you do."

He turned and walked away. She never asked what his name was.

Sarah returned to the living room, holding a half-full glass of water, from which she took a sip.

"I never should have asked you to come. That cop who comes to the store is a *momzer*," Sarah said.

"Yeah, he's a creep all right." Helen was surprised at the Yiddish. The guy *was* a bastard, but for Sarah to revert to Yiddish she had to be more upset than Helen knew.

"And too big to fight."

"Sarah, did he try to force himself on you?"

Sarah turned her head away. "I should never have asked you to come," she repeated, her cheeks flushed. But she could not be persuaded to talk about anything she did not want to talk about. Helen knew that very well.

"The dress, the dates with Joe and Ralph, even having Sandy around, those are chances for me, Sarah. Joe, Sandy, even Ralph have connections to the movies. Maybe that will work out for me. Or this modeling job for Bullock's will turn into something bigger.

"The cop looks at me, that's all he does. I managed all this time in New York, which has just as many *momzers* as here, maybe more." Helen paused.

Sarah sighed again. "Okay. I get excited. I worry it is not good for you. And it is my fault to bring you here."

Helen leaned down and kissed Sarah on the cheek. They had not kissed each other since Helen was a young adolescent and the imitation of mother-daughter affection felt forced to her. But Sarah smiled.

Helen composed herself as the doorbell rang. Ralph was wearing a three-piece taupe suit in a lightweight fabric cut for his boxer's torso. A trifold honey orange handkerchief was tucked in the breast pocket, and the tie's polka dots on a peach background blended with the pale blue color of his shirt. He wore a white fedora.

"You look beautiful, Helen," he said.

"And you look quite good yourself."

At that he smiled and offered his arm. They walked out to his car, and she settled into the passenger side while he quietly closed the door.

For several minutes they drove in silence. The streets were quiet. Yellow-hued splashes of light from the street lamps relieved the darkness.

At a long red light, Ralph said, "I thought it might get chilly on the boat going out. I didn't know if you'd brought a wrap, so I threw something I had in the back seat just in case."

Helen had not brought anything, preferring to freeze rather than wear her frayed New York coat. She turned and saw a dark mass on the seat, which, at her touch, turned silky and warm. Grabbing a fist full, she pulled it onto the front seat. The hue was a mysterious inky blue in the limited light but the material was cashmere and Helen stroked it languorously while it sat in her lap.

"I think the color will go with the bird," he said.

"How did you come by a cashmere wrap?" Helen's voice was teasing. She wondered, though, if a girlfriend of his had fled the house, leaving her prized possession behind.

"The same way I came by this car. Bought it off a guy who was down on his luck."

"His wife must not have been happy."

"I suspect that the cashmere was the least of it. I picked up a pair of sapphire earrings, a gold and topaz broach, and this long black enameled cigarette holder with little gold filigree around it."

"Did he sell you any of *his* stuff?"

"Nope."

A flicker of dismay, as brief as the spark on a lighter, passed over Helen's features. Had they talked about the sale of her jewelry, this unknown woman and her down-on-his-previously-great-luck husband? Did she come in one night to put them on for a party and discover they were gone? Or was partying with jewelry on already a thing of the past? She patted the cashmere again.

"What will you do with all of it?"

"I'll hold onto it a little longer to see if he wants it back."

"And?"

"If he does, great. He'll give me a little extra for storing it for him."

"Ahh. And if not?"

"I'll pass it on at a profit to those who can still afford it. Unless I like it myself. It's how I got the car."

"I remember."

So Ralph had an extralegal pawn operation going. People came to him who didn't want to go to a place where everyone else's tragedies were lined up in a glass display case, and three balls hung over the door.

Helen wondered how he had gotten his clientele. She could think of three ways: through his boxing, through his work on the movie sets, and through his security work. All of those would put him in the path of men on the way up, on the way down, and clawing to stay where they were. Her fingers continued to absently stroke the cashmere.

"It's a long drive to the dock," Ralph said after a few minutes of silence during which Helen heard the motor in the car hum and felt the wheels moving with an occasional bob up and down on the pavement.

"Maybe we should make polite conversation," he added.

Helen turned to him. "Let's talk about when you took me to your house," she said.

He shot a glance at her; then his eyes returned to the road, tracking the headlight beams of the car. They had passed a very few cars on the boulevard, and no one seemed to be in their lane. In this section of Los Angeles, everyone was decorously indoors.

"It is true that I saw the gun, and it upset me. But now I understand it's your job."

He nodded. Helen watched his hands moving the steering wheel patiently around the curve on the street.

"How do people hire you for these sorts of things?"

Maybe in Ralph's answer Helen could find out if his sympathy was with Jessie and her fascist friends and why the brochure from the Nazi-oriented bookstore was on his table. If he was just hustling for a few sawbucks like everyone else, she could relax a little.

"I applied to be a house dick when I had to get out of the ring."

"A what?"

"A hotel detective. Too many hysterical dolls, cheating husbands, heart attacks at two a.m., and drunken s.o.b.s at all hours. So then I went the cinder route."

"Which is?"

"Being a railroad detective. Private security work is more manageable."

"But maybe more dangerous?"

"Running after a guy in a freight yard at midnight is dangerous. Carrying around a gun and watching for mostly non-existent boogie men, not so dangerous."

"The pamphlet in your room. What was that about?" She kept her voice calm and disinterested as if asking about Nazi pamphlets was the natural segue from asking about guns.

"Yeah. I picked that up at one of Jessie's parties, if you could call it that. Bunch of stiffs, collars up to here," he paused and slapped his hand under his chin to illustrate. "I took it home. It's just the same stuff I overhear at all those shindigs. Crap. I just forgot to throw it out."

Helen shifted in her seat, crossing her legs. Ralph took his eyes off the road to watch, then refocused.

"You don't wear perfume," he said.

"That's a change of subject."

He raised a finger in a silencing gesture.

"Your hair isn't bobbed, you don't wear perfume, you are smooth but you are not a broad, if you know what I mean."

"I come across as a slightly old-fashioned girl who dresses nicely."

He smiled. "Exactly. For the job tonight, it's what I need. The guy I am keeping an eye on for another guy…"

He paused, Helen nodded that she understood, and he continued. "The first guy is always worried about being chiseled or worse, so I can't go alone because he will for sure have his boys on me the minute I come aboard. And if I arrive with a low-class twist on my arm, it will attract bad attention because this is a high-class operation."

"And if you go on the ship with me?" Helen was not sure that being excluded from the category of dolls and kittens was what she wanted, especially if that meant she was instead in the category of good old-fashioned girls.

"He may not notice me. Even if he does, he won't necessarily think I'm there working. He'll see you're a looker, which he would expect, but not the kind of looker he expects." At that, Ralph grinned.

"He who?"

"Jack Dragna." Ralph said the name in a tone as flat and hard as an anvil. His eyes stayed on the road, tracking the headlights weaving their yellowish way through the fog.

Helen found that tender spot on the inside of her lower lip and bit down, sucking the flesh. She was not sure if she completely believed his statement about the pamphlet but the tone of his voice gave no doubt about his feelings toward Dragna.

"But what is it you are supposed to do? I don't want to get in your way. Wouldn't it help if I knew?"

"I'm just a little extra protection for Bugsy Siegel. They are having a meeting, Bugsy and Jack, over their mutual futures. I am just there with other guys to keep the place calm. It'll be an ordinary night. Just relax."

"I heard you tell Harry you didn't associate with gangsters."

Ralph shrugged. "I don't associate with them, Helen. I am an independent contractor who does very specified and limited work for them as a bodyguard. That's it. No thuggery involved."

Helen twisted her hands together in her lap. "I can't do this, Ralph. I don't know what gave you the idea that I could or would. Please, you can just drop me off at a hotel or someplace where I can get a cab home." When she raised her hand to rub her cheek, it trembled.

They were driving into a low hanging mist that thickened as the car pillowed into it. Ralph rolled down the driver's side window and ducked his head out.

"I'm just trying to keep that center line in view. We're about at the pier."

"Ralph, I just want to go home."

"Listen, kid, your brother-in-law and I had a good talk. First about people we knew in common, then my boxing career. Finally, we got onto gambling and protection. So I know he has problems with that cop."

Helen grabbed her left trembling hand with her right. Icy shakes were now sliding up her arms and her teeth began to chatter. She wrapped herself in the cashmere stole, cocooning herself to her chin. Then she slumped against the passenger door, half hoping it would open and she would just fall out.

"Yes. He has problems with that cop," she said.

"I'll help him with those problems."

"You and Bugsy Siegel?"

"Bugsy's got no control over stuff like that out here."

"Yet."

He nodded at this. "You are also quicker than the average twist. Anyhow, the point is that I can help Harry due to my connections."

"And I'm your payment for helping?"

He paused, gripped the wheel a little tighter, and sighed. "You are here to accompany me to an evening on one of LA's finest gambling ships. You can hoity with the toity. Don't worry. I'll give you twenty and you can blow it on one spin of the wheel. Or you can slip into the Ladies' Room and just sit there until I'm done in about two hours. I just need you to be with me on the boat going out, so the cops that patrol and keep notes on who goes out to those ships don't notice me too much, and let Jack see you with me."

"That's all you need."

"Yes. The other thing I'll do as a favor to Harry."

"Why?"

Ralph shrugged, shoulders creeping up his mountainous neck, then down.

"Why not."

Ralph opened the car door for her and gave her his hand. The air was salty, moist and translucent with fog. Her high heels sounded like the dull thuds of a mallet on the wood pier planks. Helen looked down to avoid wedging a heel into the spaces between the boards, and because the first glimpse of ocean always evoked quick, nauseous swallows for a few seconds even in a wave-free harbor.

He walked her to a small canopied boat. "We get in this."

The tender, with its blue canvas roof, was held against the pier with thick ropes. Ralph handed Helen off to a ship's hand, who grasped her firmly around the arm, almost lifting her into the cabin. She took a seat on a dry, cushioned bench, where Ralph joined her.

As the tender bumped against rubber tires that decorated the side of the pier, she forced her hands into her lap, and focused her attention on the other passengers.

Two other man-woman pairs were also in the boat. Helen did not know if they were couples, as such. One balding man in a tuxedo had his arm draped over a blonde, blue-eyed woman with a plunging neckline. His eyes were fixed on something only he could see in the vicinity of the woman's left breast. She looked young enough to be his daughter. The woman in the other couple stared toward the bow of the boat, while the man gazed down, twisting his wedding ring back and forth.

Just as she was going to turn to Ralph to ask a question, a voice boomed in from the open gangway.

"Good evening, ladies and gentlemen."

A firm step on the gangway caused the boat to dip slightly in the direction of the dock.

"I don't mean to disturb you."

A uniform came into sight, then a head topped with red hair and sporting an LAPD cap. The policeman was smiling and looking carefully at each passenger.

"I'm your local police. I just want to be sure you have a safe, legal journey out and back. Don't fall overboard. Thanks for your cooperation." He moved back onto the dock.

Small lights lit up the gambling ship in the multi-colors of a Christmas tree. In the fog, the ruby, sapphire, and emerald tones shimmered.

A gangplank stretched up two stories to the top deck. A door swung open, releasing the sound of laughter before it shut again.

Helen climbed up the ramp and was handed off to the deck by a clean-shaven young man in a white uniform. Ralph followed. He took her arm and they walked to the double doors. After the small boat, the ship felt like an island, calm and steady. Helen's legs shook nonetheless.

When they entered the room, Helen coughed because cigar and cigarette smoke hovered in the air, duplicating the fog outside. But while the fog had seemed to muffle the ocean and the noise the insignificant tender made on it, inside there was a symphony of sound, high-pitched laughing and talking, the click-click of a ball skipping on the roulette table for percussion, baritone shouts at the craps table.

In the center, a group of silent gamblers sat around a table.

Abruptly, one the men at the table threw back his stool, said, "Fuck this," and walked away.

As he shoved by Helen and Ralph to get to the door, he muttered, "Watch it, sister. The game is rigged."

Ralph smiled amiably and glanced around the room. "Let's just walk a little, shall we?"

As they walked around the large room that appeared to occupy the entire top deck of the ship, Helen focused on the women more than the men. Except for a handful of older women, every one had bobbed hair in tight waves. Helen had seen her few women friends wrapping their hair onto curlers every night, then tossing in their sleep until morning to achieve just that effect.

Those in dresses wore frocks with wide shoulders, deep decollates, and sharply nipped waists, while the men hovered around them like decorations attached by invisible threads. Other women had on short bolero jackets or cropped capes over geometrically patterned blouses tucked into long skirts or pants made of satiny material.

One woman about Helen's age, hand up to her mouth, tottered past her on high heels in an ocean blue chiffon evening dress cut daringly low in the back, her escort wobbling next to her, a martini glass in his hand.

"I'm done with the fashion show," Helen said.

"Let's go over to the bar, then."

They walked toward the rear of the room, where Helen could

see a long mirror and an oak counter. As they got nearer, she saw that high-end alcohol was being served. Seagram's Crown Whiskey, Martini and Rossi, even Cinzano could be had.

"They water it down, but booze makes those wallets slide out of the pockets much easier," Ralph said.

A table for two was empty and Helen slid into one side of the banquette, happy to get off her feet. Ralph sat down next to her.

"Have you seen who you want to see, Ralph?" She leaned over toward his ear to ask the question.

"At your two o'clock, Helen, but don't stare."

She smiled and glanced casually toward her right as if thinking sweetly about a compliment he had just given her. A man who looked like the Italian grocer she had bought her rare orange or tomato from in New York sat there. She had enough time to take in his black and silvery hair, brushed back from his forehead, and the deep creases around his mouth before she turned back to Ralph.

She looked down at Ralph's right hand resting on the table, placed her left over it, intensified her smile, and leaned in almost grazing his ear with her lips. "I gather that's Jack Dragna."

Ralph tipped his head up, so his mouth was next to hers. "Uh huh." Then he kissed the corner of her mouth quickly, and moved his mouth closer to her ear.

"Now, where's Bugsy?" he asked.

Helen withdrew her head, patted his cheek with her right hand, and sat back in her chair. His kiss had been a surprise, although lacking any demand, and his cheek was smooth.

That close to Ralph she could detect ridges in his nose, as if the bone beneath had been broken and re-broken and the pieces never lined up again. It reminded her of poorly mended china. He had put on aftershave which had a lemon and lavender scent, refreshing after all the smoke in the room. She had not noticed it in the car.

No man in the vicinity of Dragna looked young enough to be Benjamin "Bugsy" Siegel, she thought. As a thickset man in a suit plastered on him twenty pounds ago trudged toward Jack Dragna, she said, "I need to go powder my nose."

The action of unfolding herself from the bench, smoothing the dress down over her hips, and sidestepping onto the floor caused Dragna and the man, now done with trudging and stationed by Dragna's right shoulder, to focus on her like sailors with a telescope.

Ralph gave her a bland smile, patted her hip, and said, "Hurry back, dear," in the slightly-too-loud voice of a man at the outer edge of drunk. Ralph, she knew, had had nothing to drink since he'd picked her up two hours before.

As she moved away from the table, Dragna nodded to Ralph and the man at his right shoulder started to advance toward their table.

"It's that way, sweetie," Ralph called, waving his hand toward the bow of the boat.

At that she turned her back to the table and walked away.

Helen slid around a coven of well-dressed women cluttered at the door to the Ladies' Room and into the two stall space, which smelled of cigarette smoke, sea water, and something chemical that she couldn't place. She decided she'd be better off taking a deep breath on the deck, so she turned, pushed the door open, and banged it into a porcelain blonde, seashell white skin, silver silk cut on the bias, and arctic fox fur.

"I'm so sorry," Helen said.

"S'okay," the blonde replied out of a scarlet-lipped mouth in a Bronx accent.

"You're from New York."

"Got me. You?"

"Yeah. Just got here in the last few weeks."

"Wow. You don't sound New Yorky at all."

"I'm working on the accent. To fit in," Helen said.

The woman nodded. "I'm Vivian." She held out her hand and Helen shook it. Vivian's grip was firm.

"There you are." A man with thick black hair and eyes the color of blue agate stood just behind Vivian. He was about six feet tall, dressed in a navy cashmere jacket, with gold buttons, and grey slacks, both impeccably tailored. Taking Vivian's arm, he drew her toward him while smiling at Helen as if he wished it was she he had by the hand.

"Who's your friend, dear?" he asked.

"We just met."

"Well, then, it's introductions all around. I'm Benjamin Siegel. This is my friend, Vivian Halls." Bugsy Siegel held out his hand to Helen.

"Helen Rice," she said.

His grip was tender, as if he was holding a small bird. He held her hand then let it slip carefully out of his.

"Miss Rice, a pleasure," he said.

"Mr. Siegel, Miss Halls, I need to rejoin my date for the night before he calls out the Coast Guard." She'd seen Bugsy and now all she wanted was to sink back into the crowd and become invisible.

"Let us walk you over. I'd like to meet the man lucky enough to have you to himself tonight."

"Hardly to himself with this crowd."

"Indeed." Bugsy offered one arm to Vivian and the other to Helen. As he walked them through the gambling salon and toward the bar, people stopped talking and slid out of their way, regrouping behind them and whispering.

"There he is," Helen said. Ralph was sitting at the table appearing to nurse liquid in a Scotch glass.

"I'll let you go then, having delivered you safe and sound."

Bugsy slid his arm away from her. Ralph looked at him, then got up.

"Baby," he said loudly, "where did you go?"

"Powdered my nose."

"Oh, yeah." He shook his head. "Forgot." He picked up the glass. "Who's that with you?"

"Benjamin Siegel and Vivian Halls."

"Okay, fine. Come here and sit down." Ralph patted the seat next to him.

Helen looked quickly at Jack Dragna. He was looking at Bugsy Siegel and Vivian. Ralph was a forgotten side-show, which Helen assumed was what Ralph wanted.

As she slid in next to Ralph, he leaned over, the liquor in the glass rocking like its own stormy sea, and whispered in her ear, "I see you found Bugsy." Then he planted a wet kiss on her neck.

"Eeew. I think you've had enough," she said, wiping the spot with a napkin. Her voice was just loud enough that Dragna looked over, shook his head, and went back to watching Bugsy saunter across the room toward him.

She felt a second glass between them into which Ralph poured liquor from the glass in his hand before returning it with a thunk to the table.

Dragna's bodyguard flicked a glance toward Ralph then returned to watching Dragna and Siegel as Siegel took out his wallet, handed Vivian some bills, waved her toward the roulette table and then sat in a chair next to Dragna.

Ralph stood up and Helen followed. He walked her back toward a blackjack table, sat her at a chair, put down a twenty, and motioned to the dealer to give her cards. He stood in back of her, with a clear view of the Siegel and Dragna discussion and the position of Dragna's bodyguard.

"Ask for a card," he said to Helen, glancing quickly at the cards at her spot where the four of diamonds and six of spades lay exposed.

Helen had never gambled for money but she had seen it done in movies. "Hit me," she said.

The dealer took a card off the top of the deck and turned it over as if unveiling a work of art. The queen of hearts dropped on the others.

The player to Helen's left took a card, then the dealer, whose cards now totaled nineteen. The dealer plucked the twenty off the table and put two black chips in front of Helen.

"Leave it there," Ralph said without taking his eyes off the gangsters, who were still deep in conversation. Helen looked over. Dragna's bodyguard had his back turned to the blackjack table, one hand visible and one hidden by his torso.

"I'll be back. Just play."

Ralph walked quickly toward the bar area, abruptly changing his pace to a stagger as the bodyguard turned to look around. One hand slapped at his jacket pocket. He staggered again, reaching the booth where he and Helen had sat, and went down to his hands and knees.

"Miss, do you want another card?" Helen looked at the dealer and then down at her hand. She had a nine of diamonds and a seven of hearts. The forty dollars in chips sat in front of them. What she wanted was to take the money and go home.

"Okay."

The dealer stood there, cards in his left hand, waiting.

"Oh, hit me."

The dealer shook his head, pealed a card off the deck, and put down a five of hearts.

"You have twenty-one, Miss," he said. "You don't want to do anything else for now."

After he finished with the other players, he swept the cards off the table and put three black chips next to Helen's two. "That's one hundred dollars in chips. Twenty dollars each chip." His voice was patient.

"Why don't I change two of those for ten dollar chips? That way, if you want to put down less or if you want to tip those who brought you luck, you'll have something to do it with."

He smiled as if expecting or not expecting a tip was just a thought that floated through to which he had no attachment.

"Thank you." Helen was leaning to the right to catch a glimpse of Ralph who had disappeared from sight.

Dragna's man moved toward the last spot where Helen had seen Ralph on his hands and knees.

Ralph stood up, and Helen was surprised at how relieved she felt. He held something up in his left hand for the gangster to see. Helen saw a tiny flame flicker on and off.

The bodyguard held out his hand, and Ralph dropped something gold into it. Ralph pointed out something on the object, while the bodyguard peered down. Then the bodyguard shrugged and dropped it back into Ralph's outstretched palm.

Dragna looked over and his bodyguard raised a hand and waved as if signaling "all clear." Suddenly Ralph stumbled into the guard, pushing him off balance. They grabbed at each other in a two-step, then regained their composure. Ralph smiled, patted the man on the shoulder, and wobbled off in Helen's general direction.

She looked down at her chips, pulled seventy dollars in chips off the table, stuck them in her purse, and focused her attention on the next hand. She had eighteen, the dealer had twenty, and next thing she knew, thirty dollars in chips had slipped away from her in thirty seconds. More than two weeks' wages on a flip of a piece of cardboard.

Helen dropped off her stool and began to walk toward the exit doors at the stern.

"The cashier is mid-deck," Ralph said as he caught up to her. "Makes it more tempting to stop and play more before you leave."

"Are we done?"

"Not quite. Just give it ten more minutes. I can't stand here and chit-chat. Must keep my eyes on…"

"Yes. I'll just go to the ladies' room again, then and sulk for a while."

"Good plan." Ralph raised his voice and said, "I brought you here, and you're not leaving without me."

He grabbed her upper arm, face contorted with force, but his fingers locked a hair above her skin. She winced as required, and stomped her foot on his toe. He let go and she did her best to flounce off toward the bathroom.

Helen spent the short trip back to shore buried in her wrap, face turned away from Ralph, fingering the cash she'd exchanged for the chips, and avoiding thoughts of the ocean beneath her feet. They kept the pose of quarreling lovers until his car was clear of the parking lot.

"Was that supposed to be fun?"

"Well, you did get to meet Bugsy Siegel and you're seventy bucks ahead of where you were when I picked you up."

"True." Helen relaxed into the seat. "What kind of bodyguarding was that? You weren't ever within five feet of Bugsy."

"Do all of Roosevelt's secret service men hover around him like a swarm of bees?"

"Do I know? I suppose not."

"You suppose correctly. And part of my job is to create distraction at certain moments."

"The lighter trick?"

"Yep. And the little fight with you."

Helen shivered and wrapped the creamy texture of the cashmere closer around her shoulders. The car's heater was on, blowing too-dry air against her legs, but it failed to warm her enough.

One glimpse of Dragna and Bugsy Siegel was enough for her. "One can smile and smile and be a villain" floated into her thoughts. Some Shakespeare play, *Macbeth* or *Othello*, that she'd read in high school. All she could recall was that in both plays the women ended up dead.

"How do you plan to help Harry?"

"I did a little horse trading."

He stared out the window into the light fog. The car's head-lights beamed soft white into the ghostly vapor. The car motor hummed.

Helen considered that for a moment as she slipped off her shoes, arching her feet. "You traded tonight for Bugsy telling Dragna what?"

He grinned. "You are one sharp gal. One night of my life that I got to spend with you in exchange for Bugsy telling Dragna that, among other issues that Dragna has and will have with his opera-tions in LA, he has a rogue cop asking for more than what Dragna considers a fair cut."

"And holding out on Dragna."

"That too."

"What's to keep Dragna from just taking the extra money?"

Ralph shook his head, rolled down his window to signal left, and a wisp of fog slid into the car, moistening the window and dampening Helen's cheek. The car turned onto a wide avenue. The fog vanished.

"He won't want that cop to think he can set policy. And there's a certain code…"

"The criminal code of ethics?" Helen laughed.

"Yeah, well, he was fair to me when I was in the ring. Left me alone to win or lose. Sent his guys around for a ten percent cut of the fight money. Still, he's a real son of a bitch."

"Dragna took a cut?"

"You sound shocked, Helen. Did you think boxing was a clean sport?"

"No. I actually did not think about boxing at all."

He looked over at her. She stared straight ahead. The sharp-ness in her voice had surprised her as well.

They continued in silence for a while. Helen wiggled her toes while staring out the passenger side window at passing buildings and empty lots.

"He didn't say 'hello' to you." Helen's voice was almost a whisper.

"No. But Marty did. Said that 'the Boss' sent his greetings. Complimented you and so on and so on. Said he hoped I was having a nice night off. Maybe he was being ironic."

Helen figured that Marty was Dragna's visible bodyguard. Who knew how many others there were floating around that night.

"Why didn't you tell Dragna about Harry yourself?"

"First, not my place. Second, heard better from higher up. Third, don't want him to know more about my business than is absolutely necessary. Like I told you before, I am not a gangster."

"This is the part where I say thank you and what else can I possibly do to show my gratitude and that of my family?"

"I did it to help Harry for my own reasons. So, thanks accepted. No other offers of gratitude are expected."

"For a boxer, you have quite a chivalric sense."

"For a former boxer, who makes his living as best he can, I try to."

At the house entrance, Ralph paused. Helen stood with her back to the door unsure whether she would accept a kiss or turn her cheek. To her surprise, Ralph took her right hand with his left, reached into his pocket with his right, and pulled out a card.

"My business card," he said. "If you need me, just call and the answering service will let me know."

"And I would need you for?"

"Escort, protection." He shrugged. "You be careful." He smiled. She found she was beginning to like the lopsidedness of that smile, with its slightly swollen lower left lip and a glint of teeth. "Or, you could want to see me."

Helen held the card between her thumb and index finger and

stared at it as if studying it for clues. It was just a simple, white card with black print giving Ralph's full name, a telephone number, and, in the lower right corner, the words "Private Detection and Personal Safety Services."

"Thanks," she said and slipped into the house.

In bed, she churned over the night's events, the top sheet twisting around her as she hunted for a comfortable position. The more she thought, the less likely it was that Ralph had told Bugsy Siegel about the cop's rogue demand just to do Harry a favor. By 3:00 a.m. she had decided that Ralph gained points with Siegel by giving him a tidbit about Dragna's owned man going astray.

That way, Siegel looked like he had a finger already in Dragna's operation and Dragna looked weak. She could not figure out Ralph's relationship to Dragna and Siegel exactly. Maybe Ralph traded information like he traded other baubles, cars, and cashmere wraps. And maybe, as he told her, he just provided security. With that, she sighed, plumped up the pillow, and slept.

11

CLOUDS WITH THICK, SHADOWED CENTERS hung in
the sky, barring the sun's early-morning rays. The flowers did
not open, as if protecting their tender spring color. The air tasted
wet.

Helen pulled her sweater tight across her breasts and kept up
her pace with Harry on the morning walk to Forester Liquor. She
had slept all of four hours. Her hair felt too heavy for the French
twist that she had rolled it into just minutes before. As if to prove
it, a hank fell morosely out of its pin and onto the back of her neck.
She tucked it quickly and fiercely back, scratching her scalp with
the tip of the bobby pin.

Harry was silent as usual, trudging like a bulldog. When they
arrived at the store, he slid the key into the door lock and the second
key into the bolt lock, turning them simultaneously and pushing
with a slight grunt on the door. A small box wrapped in butcher
paper lay askew on the floor.

The box's position suggested that it had been dropped through
the mail slot, which was almost never used since the mailman preferred to hand Helen the magazines and bills and smile at her.
Helen picked it up and gave it to Harry. Something rattled in it.

"Too small to be money," Harry said.

"Were you expecting something?"

"Nope."

Last week's accounts hadn't been fully entered, so Helen took the ledger book, sat on the stool near the register, and began to sort through the daily cash totals, which she slid under the changer tray each night. She had just finished Thursday when she heard Harry mutter "fuck, fuck, fuck" in a low, urgent voice.

"What's the matter?"

"Just come here."

The box was open, sitting on the counter near the vodkas. Harry was leaning over it, shaking his head slowly back and forth.

"Before I show it to you, you have a steady stomach, yeah? Don't faint easily or anything? You don't seem like that type, but I should ask."

Helen drew the tender inner side of her mouth between her back right teeth and swallowed. She ran her tongue against the smooth flesh her teeth held before answering.

"Yes. I'm not that type."

He slid the cardboard container, with its butcher paper flapping open, toward her. Helen looked in and saw a man's thumb, severed at the knuckle, nail intact.

"It's real?" she asked.

"For sure."

"And so we think it belongs to the cop?"

"Shh. Jeez, Helen, yes, we think it belongs to the cop."

"So he won't be bothering you any more about that extra money." Helen sighed. "I think I need a drink."

She walked over to the cooler and pulled out a ginger ale. That would be the thing to settle her stomach, which was acting rough between the late night and the early morning surprise. She popped off the cap with the bottle opener and took several long gulps.

"Do you want one, Harry?"

"No. I need something stronger." He picked up the little box, opened up the door to the back storage area, flipped on the light, and went in. Helen waited.

"Any dead bodies in there?"

"No. And I'm taking this out to the dumpster in back and shoving it way down."

"Good plan," she said. Her hand on the counter was flattened and white with the pressure of her body leaning against it because her legs were too wobbly to help her stand on their own. All her strength was in her voice, but there was no need for Harry to know that.

When Helen was six, men re-appeared in her village. She would have said one-by-one, but it was more like nine-tenths by eight-tenths. Where legs had been, there were stumps, pant legs folded and pinned up to reveal air where flesh, blood, and bone had once been. Patches stood in for eyes, empty sleeves for arms. One of the older children told a ghost story about all the amputated body parts walking in the darkest night through the woods to the village to find their owners. At the time, Helen slept with Sarah, and awoke screaming and pointing toward the foot of the bed. "Poppi's leg. Poppi's leg."

She remembered the vision even now, and despite knowing it was the nightmare of the six-year-old she had once been and would never be again, it had the power to make her shiver. And now there was a body piece taken from a still-live man tossed into the garbage in the alley behind Forester Liquor in Glendale, California.

Helen and Harry slid carefully around each other in silence

all morning. The two customers who came in, one for the morning paper and a bottle of gin, one to place a small bet, were welcome distractions. Helen could almost smell the normalcy on them like perfume. She finished the ledger entries, then read the morning paper, starting with each story on the front page.

Just before noon, the door opened again and a man in a pressed and almost new police uniform entered. He was slim, with chocolatey brown eyes that were level with Helen's own, black hair, tanned skin, and a light step.

"Hi," he said.

"Hello," Helen said.

"I'd like to introduce myself to the owner. I'm Officer Roger Tamp and I'll be on this patrol for awhile."

"Let me get Harry."

Harry was sitting at the table in the storage room with an open half-pint of Scotch in front of him. He seemed more interested in swirling the bottle from side to side than drinking it, but Helen had not been in to see what had occurred before.

"New cop in front. His name is Roger Tamp."

"Okay." Harry stood, brushed his hand quickly through his hair, then retucked his shirt into his pants. "Presentable?"

Helen nodded.

"Glad to meet you, Officer Tamp. We're always happy to have our men in blue stop by."

Roger nodded, then turned slowly to survey the panorama of liquor in the store. "Seems like a fine, upscale place to me, Mr. Forester. We don't want the kind of establishment that attracts the wrong element."

"Of course not."

"I'm not sure if Officer Bladgett will be returning."

"Really? Why not?" Harry's voice was low and incurious. He sounded as if someone had just told him that he needed to switch one light bulb for another.

"He's recovering from an injury sustained off-hours."

"What a shame. Will he be all right?"

"Yes. I don't suppose he ever spoke to you about anyone who might want to harm him?"

"No. He'd come in, of course. We'd offer him a Coca-Cola on the house. He'd chat for a bit but never about enemies. Just the usual, like 'be sure you lock up good and tight.' Or he'd let us know if there had been a burglary nearby. A good beat cop, if you know what I mean."

Tamp nodded. Then he looked at Helen, who lifted the corners of her mouth in a sad smile.

"That is too bad about him," she said. "Would you like a soda?"

Tamp shook his head. "No. I'll just be on my way."

Sandy called just after Helen, Sarah, and Harry had finished dinner. Sarah was bathing the kids and Harry was in the living room, the radio volume low, and a whiskey shot in his hand.

"What's new?"

"I have an invitation to the Rustic Canyon place."

"Good."

"I'll need the right clothes. New slacks, a bathing suit, maybe…"

"Okay. Go to Bullock's and see the assistant manager. He'll fix you up." Sandy's voice was flat, like he was running through lines in a play just to get them over with.

Helen controlled the urge to sigh. If Sandy was disinterested, she would be too.

"Keep your eyes open for new people," he said.

"Like who?"

"We want to find out more about some Nazi named Schmidt."

"Schmidt? There's a whole country full of Nazis named Schmidt. It's called Germany."

"Obviously, Helen, this is a special Schmidt out here in LA."

She snorted. If Sandy knew what she'd already weathered on only four hours sleep, he might not be so condescending.

"We think he is a full-fledged Nazi spy, with links to the Silver Shirts, your friend, Jessie Murphy, and, of course, to the German American Bund. Fritz Kuhn's thing, that Bund, has grown since we thought we put a stake in the heart of the Friends of New Germany."

"Watch for Schmidt. Is that all? What is he going to spy on, Sandy? The movie industry?"

"No, Helen. We have the movie industry pretty much locked down." Sandy's voice rose from tepid to simmer. "There's still the entire west coast, a Naval base…" His voice cooled. "I need to brief you. The phone is not the best way. I'll be there in twenty minutes."

"No, I'm…" The dial tone buzzed in her ear.

Sarah glared at Helen when the doorbell rang. The children were sleeping, a sacred time in which adult actions were hushed, the radio was low, and the house drifted into a drowsy lull.

"Sorry! It's just Sandy."

He entered with a bear hug for Sarah, as he slipped something into Harry's open palm that was dark brown, cylindrical, and pungent. "Cigar from Cuba, Harry. Friend of mine brought a box over. It's hand rolled by pretty señoritas. Enjoy."

"Sarah, did Helen tell you she has a callback to Bullock's for modeling? They want her to do resort wear. Do you want to go with her this Saturday morning?"

"The children. No one to watch them." Sarah shook her head.

"Of course. Anyhow, I wanted both of you to know she has to go in for this. You okay with that, Harry?"

"Sure, sure." Harry was sniffing the cigar. Whatever he thought of two unexpected presents in one day, Helen's role was clear and her ability, now, to take whatever time she needed was almost absolute.

Only Helen noticed that Sandy made no eye contact with her as he held the door open for her to go out to the car.

The day's damp had become a light drizzle, like a spider's web of rain that Helen swept away with her hand as she walked down the sidewalk to Sandy's car. Her wet calves were goose-bumped and she leaned down to rub them, as she slid into the car.

She sniffed at a grassy aroma with a sweet underpinning and looked over her shoulder. A small wooden box with a sliding lid sat on the back seat. Even in the dim light of the street lamp she could make out a large decal of a smiling Spanish woman, with crimson lips and a large white flower in her hair, decorating the top of the box.

"Those are really high-end cigars," Sandy said as he sat down in the driver's seat. "Thalberg brings them in."

"About this spy business," she said.

"Thalberg and his group have a good handle on Joe's 'interests' shall we say. You identifying him as a pro-Nazi infiltrator is proving very helpful." Sandy cut her off while the car accelerated. "Now Mayer and Thalberg can simultaneously fend off unionists and Nazis. It'll keep them busy and out of my hair."

"Your list of people at Murphy's shindig for Pelley was also helpful. I've got people working on them and whatever other connections they might have in Southern California. There's a lot of money here. We need to follow it and shut it off."

"Hooray," Helen said. "Can I call it quits, please? I don't like the ocean or ranches, Winona is a crazy girl, and Joe gives me the creeps."

"We don't think Joe is a direct threat to you."

"We don't?" Helen wanted to kick Sandy for the imperious tone and the insufferable emotional distance.

"No. Joe's interests lie elsewhere, as they say. And, in so far as we can find out, he's always had a friendly, even protective, interest in women that doesn't involve…"

"Sex?"

Sandy paused. "That's right. Ralph, on the other hand, seems quite attracted to women." His tone seemed mildly curious, but Helen chose to ignore the implied question.

"Ralph has ties to Dragna and Bugsy Siegel," she said.

"Yes, he does." The information was obviously not news to Sandy. "Siegel, in particular, wants very much to be a player in LA's glamorous side."

"The movies?"

"The movies, two big race tracks, that kind of thing."

"I don't want to find out any more about any of these people."

"You want to go home?"

She blurted out "Yes" before she could think.

"And where might that be, darling Helen?"

Home was a fluid concept for the first three years that Sarah and Helen were in New York. Referred by the Hebrew Immigrant Aid Society to a factory that was hiring and that had a good contract with the Amalgamated Clothing Workers of America, Sarah worked forty-four hours a week and got decent wages. The ACWA had low-cost cooperative housing but an enormous waiting list.

So Sarah rented a room for them in the Seigelmans' apartment on Orchard. It had a double bed, an armchair, and a serviceable chest of drawers. The Seigelmans gave Sarah a shelf on which to put two plates, two bowls and some flatware, and specific kitchen privileges.

The matriarch, Ruth, presided over her husband, two young adult daughters, both of whom worked in the garment industry, and her shy adolescent son. Her talk was peppered with Yiddish swearwords and complaints offered with a moan. She told Sarah she'd keep an eye on Helen after school.

Helen's response was to enter the apartment daily with her key, walk quickly to the bedroom, open the door, and then lock it from the inside.

By the time the cooperative housing came available, Helen no longer needed any looking after. The small apartment had a bedroom, into which they crammed two single beds, and a parlor space open to the kitchen.

The fact that they shared the bathroom with four other families did not bother Helen at all. She developed a special way of locking the bathroom door, by using her bobby pin strategically, and she threw her towel over the door knob to stop any unwanted efforts to spy on her.

She blamed the ACWA for introducing Harry into their lives. The union hired a bunch of Long Island thugs to intimidate strikebreakers. The next thing Helen knew, Sarah brought Harry home from a union meeting and said she was going out dancing with him.

Sandy parked the car on a dirt turnout on one of the hills above Glendale. The street going up was paved to a silky smoothness with a bright white line separating the traffic moving up and down.

In the headlight's beam, Helen saw bulldozed piles of earth and a football-sized empty lot about twenty feet beyond the car. A chained gate had a sign reading "No Trespassing," and a small billboard stationed at the beginning of the lot said "Residential Lots For Sale," with a number to call.

Sandy turned off the motor and the windshield wipers. They came to attention pointing straight up, curved streaks of wet and dry glass on either side. Helen watched the raindrops erasing the streaks. Except for one car passing by to their rear, the area was deserted.

"We're not prepared for war," Sandy said. "There are lots of people who don't want us to even think about another war. Lindbergh is one, but the government is chock full of them. War is coming though. First in Europe and then here."

"You're sure about this?"

He nodded, his gaze fixed someplace past the windshield. "I'm sure because so many people whose opinions I respect are sure. And things are getting worse and worse for us in Germany, as you know.

"Southern California has a growing airplane manufacturing industry, a large and underutilized naval base in San Diego, and research facilities, notably the California Institute of Technology over there in Pasadena." He pointed vaguely toward the east.

"These are three areas where active spying could gather crucial information to help Nazis before the United States enters the war to come. Before we have a chance to gear up, all our secrets could be gone."

Helen shifted in her seat. Now that the car had stopped, the heater was off and she was chilled again. She shivered slightly.

Without comment, Sandy slid next to her and put his arm around her, bringing with him the smell of a starched, ironed shirt and the light orange and lavender fragrance of Lentheric aftershave.

She tried to keep a space between her body and his, wrapping both her arms around her torso just as she had earlier in the day on her walk to work. Digging her fingernails into her upper arms for composure, Helen sat upright, staring into the window, which, in the nighttime gloom, reflected back her face and Sandy's as if in a distorted mirror.

"You're shivering," he said. His right hand began to gently rub her shoulder.

"For crying out loud," she said. "Do you want to tell me the world is coming to an end or do you want to neck with me?"

Sandy laughed and removed his hand. Helen wasn't sure that was the outcome she had wanted.

"If we were to kiss, maybe I wouldn't care so much if the world was coming to an end," he said.

As tempting as it was to turn her face toward his, Helen continued to resist.

"I don't think this is helping," she said.

"Right." His hands were now clasped in his lap and he edged back toward the driver's side, leaving a warm, sad space between them.

"The man you wanted me to find out more about, do you know if Schmidt is really his last name? It sounds too easy, like Smith would be."

"Good point. No, we're not sure. But we are reasonably sure the person is a male, who legally emigrated from Germany at some point, and is now in Southern California and in contact with Jessie Murphy and her bunch."

"Age?"

"Probably between thirty-five and fifty."

Helen thought about the men she had met at the two parties. Many were in that age range, but none of them seemed to be German immigrants based on their accents and all-American presentations.

"We think he wouldn't want to be visible to many people. And he may be looking for an entrance into military or research areas. Or, he might have a way in already. Were any of the people at the party associated with military or research?"

Helen mentally reviewed the people at the second party. "George Highsmith works at Caltech in administration. He's not a scientist, for sure. He was talking and the only word I could make out was 'rocks.' And, Winona's husband, Norman Stephens, is a mining engineer. I didn't meet him. He doesn't seem to be around much."

"Well, start with Winona, then. George, if you see him again. Also, since he's attached to the Silver Shirts or the American Bund or the old Friends of New Germany---I wish they'd stick to one name-- try getting some information out of what's-his-name."

"Joe?"

"Yes."

"I thought you were already keeping an eye on him."

"We are, but that's for his studio agitation. And 'keeping an eye on him' is all we can do. We're not in any place to ask him for information. You are. So see if he knows anything about this Schmidt."

Helen tucked a thigh-skimming romper in an orange hibuscus print along with an extra-large towel, both "the height of resort wear" according to the Bullock's sales woman, into a straw bag. She smoothed down the pant legs of the sage linen high-waisted trousers, tucked in the coordinated blouse more firmly, and slid her arms into the peach cashmere sweater.

She had adamantly refused to even consider a bathing suit. If she did not have one, she had a valid excuse for not going near the waves.

An afternoon dress, with the option of going "cocktail," according to the sales woman, hung in her closet now. The calf-length skirt was black, with a white ink-spot pattern, and the attached top pleated white organza, with a bolero jacket in the same print as the skirt. The outfit was belted tightly with a green crepe cummerbund.

"You look better in it than the model we had for the *LA Times*," the woman said to Helen as Helen swirled the skirt in front of the dressing mirror.

Helen replied by telling her to put it on the tab. The seventy dollars she had won on the gambling ship, and did not now have to hand off to Harry, and the open account at Bullock's made her almost giddy. But if she had once thought money would make her feel safe, her current situation put the lie to that. Maybe they'd put the new dress on her corpse.

Joe escorted her to his car, one hand flickering at her waist like a moth above a flame. His fingers landed for an instant at the small of her back, then pulled away, leaving a filmy impression on her skin under the pant waist. Popping open the trunk, he placed her straw bag in, and then banged the trunk lid closed. The noise made Helen startle even though she was expecting it.

"The place where Winona and Norman live is unique," Joe said as he pulled out of the parking spot. "Not just because it's in a canyon with fifty-five acres of land, but because it is such a work in progress."

"I thought it was a ranch house."

"It will be so much more than that. The plans that Jessie talks about are phenomenal. Four stories, twenty-two bedrooms, an indoor pool, and even a movie theater."

That sounded like far more than a ranch to Helen. She had never heard of a house, a mansion, or a castle with twenty-two bedrooms. Who in the world was Jessie planning to entertain there? It had to be Jessie because Winona did not act like she knew four people outside of her mother, Joe, her husband, and the mystery abuser, if he wasn't one of them.

"So what is it now, Joe? I don't want to be surprised in front of Winona and Norman."

"Ahh, Norman won't be there. Out of town."

Helen nodded. Norman was more about what he was not than what he was. Not at the party, not the person who hit Winona, and not there today. Possibly he was with the elusive Herr Schmidt, if Schmidt was a real person.

"And the house?"

"You should know they started with raw land and now they have terraced gardens to grow food, their own power station, and water tanks," Joe said.

"Admirable."

Helen took a deep breath. That was possibly too high hat. A quick glance at Joe suggested as much. His lips were clenched together and his eyes were rigidly looking ahead.

"Joe, that was unkind of me." She sighed, raised her hand and brushed strands of hair away from her forehead. "I'm nervous about this whole thing, you know. This class of people, the money. It's beyond me." She put both hands to her mouth.

"I get a little mouthy when I'm…" she said.

"Worried?"

"Yes. Or out of my element."

"You'll do just fine." Joe reached over and took her left hand as she lowered it from her face. He stroked her palm as if it were a small kitten.

Helen recognized that this was a role Joe knew well, comforter of women in distress.

"Thanks," she said. Her lower lip trembled. In fact, she really was afraid and feeling out of her element.

Joe pulled off a winding two lane street. A seven-foot-high iron filigree gate covered on both sides with chicken wire blocked entrance to a dirt road that looked as wide as a New York sidewalk. The gate was padlocked shut.

"Welcome to Rustic Canyon," he said as he got out of the car. He took his keychain from his pocket, flicked through six until he came to the one he wanted, walked over and inserted it into the bottom of the padlock. It fell open.

As he tugged the gate open to let the width of the Ford through, the gate dragged in the dirt, kicking up red dust that settled on his shoes and drifted up to smear his cheek a light pink. The smell of sage and eucalyptus filled the car from the open driver's door.

Helen recognized oak trees, a bit like those she had become familiar with in New York, staggered along the narrow dirt drive. The deep green leaves had a spoon shape. When they swayed, a light gray underside flipped in and out of sight.

There was a saltiness to the breeze because the canyon was less than a mile from the ocean. To emphasize its closeness, seagulls flew overhead. A bird, whose call was unrecognizable to Helen, sang "chit-chit-chit" from its perch in a tree.

A slurry of dust followed the car up the track. One sharp turn, then the Ford climbed up a steep grade, groaning until Joe slid into second gear.

Then they arrived on a concrete driveway. Facing them was a two-story house, painted the color of fresh snow, with eight tall rectangular windows on the second story, a matching set of six on the first floor, and entry doors, transparent glass covered by black filigreed wrought iron, tucked into a deep porch that angled out. To one side, there was a two-car garage. To the house's right and left, Helen saw grayish green hills whose slopes dropped sharply down as a continuation of the canyon she and Joe had just maneuvered.

Joe parked on the side of the concrete to the left of the main doors. He opened the door for Helen. As she stepped out, he returned to the rear of the car, pulled her straw bag out of the trunk and tucked a manila folder under his arm.

"What's in the folder, Joe?"

"Just something I worked on with some of my fellow employees at MGM."

"Movie stuff?"

"Sort of. More political. You know, concerns about unemployment…" His voice trailed off and he transferred the folder to one hand. "I'll let you read it in the house, if you want." He sounded unsure, as if he had written a poem and now had been asked to read it aloud.

"Great." Helen smiled at him.

Winona was standing at the open door when they approached. Helen had the sense that Winona had been standing there for several minutes, checking her watch, gazing at the narrow dirt path, willing them to arrive on time.

"Oh goody," she said, sounding like a child whose best friends had just come to play, relieving her from a long day of boredom.

"Helen, come in. Just turn right, there's a dear. It's the living room."

The porch held twelve white Adirondack chairs, three white wicker side tables, a hammock at the far corner, and assorted foot stools in bright primary colors. After the front door closed, she saw there was no grand foyer, just a stubby hall and narrow staircase to the second floor. French doors closed off whatever rooms lay to her left. Helen obediently turned right. Joe put her straw bag down just inside the front door and followed her.

"Oh, Joe," Helen said, turning to speak to him, "I can see your hand in this all right."

The room was not quite square, at least thirty by forty feet. The walls and ceiling were a uniform vanilla color, which seemed to pick up the light coming in from the windows and reflect it all over.

At the far end, a set of three alcoves nestled into the wall, each filled with books. There was a large fireplace, flanked with gray stonework and taking up at least a third of the wall opposite the windows. The mantle was of matching stone and each corner held a tall Art Deco bronze sculpture, one of a dancing woman, the other of a bullfighter. Helen walked over to look at them more closely.

Above the mantle hung an oil painting of Jessie and Winona, done, Helen thought, when Winona was in her coltish mid-teens. Jessie's hand was firmly on Winona's shoulder as if to keep her from leaping out of the frame.

The floors were a dark wood and the furniture had a strikingly square, simple appearance, enhanced by a dark gray tweedy fabric on the sofa and chaise lounge and a deep gold corduroy fabric on the two chairs.

A low, outsized, rectangular table of ash-toned wood sat in front of the sofa. On it, a tray held a pile of grapes, cheese, and an array of crackers. A carafe of coffee sent its acidic aroma into the air. Three large mugs sat near it.

"Sit down," Winona said, waving in the direction of the couch. "I don't want the coffee to get cold."

After Helen had paid her compliments to Winona on the house and Winona had said that the building would eventually be guest or servant quarters, Joe reached for the folder which he had put on the table.

"Would you take a look at this, Win, before I show it to Jessie? She was going to run it by Kuhn and then let me know if it is a go or not to distribute."

"Not Schwinn? After all, he's more local."

"Maybe him, too."

Helen sipped her coffee and reached for a grape. Winona sat to her left and Joe just to her right, on the chaise section of the couch. Anything that Joe handed Winona would pass right over her. If it was important, she'd never know.

"I've found that sometimes if I read something aloud to people it's easier to catch the mistakes than if I just read it to myself," Helen said.

This was a statement that Anna Sessler had made when talking one night in the deli in New York about her doctoral dissertation.

She'd then proceeded to read an endless passage about Kafka and Kabbalah to the gathered dozen or so students and Helen, the hanger-on.

"Good idea," Winona said. "Read it to us, Joe. And it'll help you get over this shyness thing you have."

Helen considered that Winona might consider taking her own advice, since she'd never seen Winona speak firmly to anyone except Joe.

Joe picked up the paper, cleared his throat, and began.

"Unemployment in the Motion Picture Industry is reaching tremendous proportions. Not more than fifty percent of the capacity is working today. These American workers are demanding to know the true reasons for this alarming condition whereby their families are kept on the verge of starvation, while the Jewish monopoly of the Motion Picture Industry brazenly discharges non-Jewish men and women and replaces them with refugee Jews from Europe." He paused.

Feeling color rising in her face, Helen said, "You are so articulate, Joe. It does make one angry just thinking of it." She could hear her voice tremble.

"Dear, you are so right to be upset over all of this with the Jews." With that Winona patted Helen's hand. "Do have a little piece of cheese."

"I'm not done," Joe said.

Helen cut herself a sliver of cheese, put it on a cracker, and sat back.

"This is done to antagonize friendly, anti-Jewish governments in stirring up international war for Jewish vengeance and profit."

"I'd say that last little bit needs some work." Winona picked up a handful of grapes and began popping them into her mouth.

Helen wondered how she had a chance to chew them before swallowing.

"Have Mother or Schwinn take a look at it. But if you tell them you know it needs polish, they'll be more receptive."

"And less likely to think I'm just a footstool," Joe said.

"Joe, they know how much you care about the cause and, really, you are invaluable to them in your placement in the 'motion picture industry,'" Winona said this with little quotes in her voice. "And now, with Helen, Mother won't be on you about bringing a woman around. Really, I don't know why she bothers you about that. You just needed to find the right one. I mean, that's what she told me about Norman." The edge in her voice sliced at her husband's name.

Helen, who had sat with her back pressed against the couch, leaned forward, smiled at Joe and then at Winona and said, "I thought it was very well done, Joe. I don't know Mr. Schwinn, but I am sure that Jessie will help. I think she likes to be in that role. Am I right, Winona?"

"If by 'helpful,' you mean 'in charge,' absolutely." Winona pushed the tray of food a few inches back on the table. "Let's do something else, now. Did you bring play clothes?"

"Yes."

"Swimsuit?"

"No."

"You can borrow one of mine."

Helen doubted that, since Winona had the build of an elongated eleven-year-old, but she nodded in agreement.

"We'll change upstairs."

Helen climbed the steep stairs behind Winona, using the exercise to breathe in and out in short puffs, as if that would rid her of the dread she felt inside. The German-American Bund did have ties to anti-Semitic behind-the-scenes Hollywood. No matter how important Jews were, they were vulnerable to attack. Maybe she should finish reading *It Can't Happen Here*, because maybe it could.

Entering Winona's bedroom, she sank into a fussy pink satin boudoir chair and tried to think of something to say.

"I understand there are great plans for this property,"

Winona tossed first one, then two, and finally a grand total of six bathing suits onto the bed for Helen to look at. The double bed was unmade, but the left side of the shiny pure white sheets was still tucked in, suggesting that only one person was responsible for the scramble of white quilted blanket, sheet, and pillow.

The undraped windows framed a view of sage green and gray hills, oak trees with fluttering leaves, and a brilliantly copper-backed hummingbird sipping from a bird feeder. A diaphanous mist blanketed the tops of the trees.

"Mother spends a lot of time sketching out her ideas. Grand entrance with a horoscope design in mosaic tile, that sort of thing. Now she needs a master architect."

"When will that happen?"

Winona shrugged. She was rummaging through the top drawer of the twelve drawer mahogany chest, whose ornate carving was out of a Grimm fairy tale, so discordant with the living room below.

"Nice chest."

"Mother bought it. She said it's more what he'll like when he comes."

"He?"

Winona turned. Her face had the look of awe coupled with fear that Helen associated with seeing five Polish Calvary officers gallop their horses down the paved street just when the Great War ended.

"The Führer."

"Hitler is coming *here* for a visit?" Helen was glad Winona's state of mind gave her cover for her shock.

"You should talk to Mother about that. But I'd say the odds are he'll come for more than a visit. Schwinn, he's the one who got Mother to buy this place and invest most of her money in it, says Hitler will win the war."

"Most of your mother's money is in this?"

"Yes, my inheritance, if you want to look at it that way."
Winona patted the top of the bureau with three firm thunks.

"How does Norman feel about that?"

Winona's hand was inside the drawer of her bed table. An
abrupt tug and the drawer slid out. Untaping what looked like a
small sachet, Chinese red and embroidered with a garish dragon's
head in gold, from the underside of the drawer, Winona turned
toward Helen. She opened the packet, took out a stubby pre-rolled
reefer, and said, "Care to join me?"

"No, but thanks."

Winona shrugged to indicate it was Helen's loss.

"Norman says that Hitler will win the war and we will be
so very well-placed in his American regime that who cares if the
money is in the property now."

"So Norman thinks that Hitler will bring the war to America?"

Until now, Helen had thought a war would stay in Europe. A
Europe that did not care what happened to Jews, that wanted the
Olympics in Germany, but a Europe that was far away. Her shudder
did not escape Winona's gaze.

"Oh, there won't be a war here," Winona said in a tone better
suited for placating a five-year-old who had just been told she'd
have to wait until after dinner for dessert. "Everyone will just see
how good Hitler is at calming a country, putting its finances back
in order, and cleansing it. They'll vote Pelley's Christian Party into
office. It's simple, really."

"And that handbill that Joe is writing?"

"All part of getting the working man to realize what is really
needed here. They saw it clearly in Germany."

Helen inserted a smile over her lips. Right around now Sarah
would be taking Rachel and Ben for a walk over to the nearby park.
Sarah would take the comics section of the Sunday paper with her,
folded-up in Rachel's baby stroller, so she could practice reading
English while showing Ben the pictures.

She would put Ben in the baby swing, with his legs dangling out of the opening, his plump bottom firmly hugged by the bucket seat, and push him until he giggled. Then he would run over to the short slide, clamber up with his stubby, but determined legs, and catapult himself down, willing his mother to catch him before he hit the sand at the end. The three of them would spend an unmolested hour there, breathing, playing, reading the funny papers.

"And if they don't vote the Christian Party in?"

Winona struck a match and sucked in on the joint. The smoke was more pungent than a Lucky Strike, with a burnt overtone that made Helen cough.

"Isn't that a bit harsh on your throat, Winona?"

"Yes, it's a little harsh. Maybe Lindberg will run. I don't know, Helen. Now, let's get dressed."

Helen convinced Winona that it would be immodest for her to try to fit her upper body into Winona's swimwear, none of which had space for breasts bigger than apricots. Helen walked downstairs in her romper, followed by Winona, in a bathing suit that would have been daring if Winona were built differently.

The suit barely covered the bruises on Winona's hip. A thin bluish-black line winked out on her left side when she walked.

Joe had changed into Bermuda shorts; He did not like to swim either, Helen concluded.

"Oh, Joe, don't be such a noodle about this. Go put on your swim trunks."

"OK, Winona." He walked away from the living room toward the other wing of the house. "It'll be just a minute."

With the sound of a car screeching up to the house in the wrong gear, Winona strode over to the front door and looked out between the iron fluting.

"I can't get a moment to myself," she said, turning to Helen with the adolescent flounce Helen now associated with her.

"Your mother?"

"Oh, yes. She's getting out of the car now with a roll of paper under her arm for another round of house plans."

Helen considered whether Jessie was there to be sure Winona was doing what she was supposed to do, which seemed to be to occupy the house and not be trouble.

Winona had turned to survey Jessie's progress toward the door. "Hermann is with her. Thank God he didn't bring his dog with him."

She swallowed twice as if her throat had suddenly dried, then licked her thin lips, the tip of a carnelian tongue flitting back and forth.

"Isn't the dog housebroken?"

"It's a vicious German Shepherd named Lump. Why would anyone name a dog that?"

"It's German for 'rogue,'" Helen said.

"Ahh," Winona said, as her hand drifted down toward the bottom of her swimsuit, which she tugged at. Helen saw her wince.

"I'm going back up to change. You're fine." Winona took the stairs two at a time, reaching the upstairs landing just as Helen heard a knock at the door.

"She's got her own key. That's just to be sure I'm not lying in the living room, naked, with a bottle of Scotch and a reefer."

"How very nice to see you again, Helen. I'm glad that Winona asked you over and we didn't realize we'd intrude on your plans. I'd like to introduce you to Hermann Schwinn. Hermann, darling, this is Helen Rice, Joe's girlfriend."

The man standing just inside the small foyer had eyes the color of black walnut, almost indistinguishable from his pupils.

Helen had the eerie feeling that he was not so much looking at as consuming her.

Slim, taller than Jessie by a few inches, Hermann had a narrow face, interrupted by a black pencil mustache above reddish lips, and ending in a sharp chin with a tiny cleft. He wore a brick red colored polo shirt banded with cloudy blue and tucked into stylish, loose fitting trousers in a color reminiscent of cement. Helen judged him to be around thirty, his smooth, lightly tanned skin unmarred by wrinkles or crow's feet.

"Delighted," he said in a light German accent. He took her right hand, bent over it, and then stood erect. The gesture was all theater, the confidence of a man who charmed women, the playing out of a European charade.

Surprisingly muscled in his arms and legs, as if he worked out routinely with weights, Joe had made a momentary appearance in orange plaid swim trunks and retreated down the mysterious hall to change again. Winona remained buried in her bedroom wardrobe, apparently excavating for Mother- and Schwinn-suitable sports attire.

Jessie led them into the living room, where Helen sat at the edge of the end of the chaise with her legs scissored together and angled toward the remainder of the sofa to create a border. When Jessie took the far end of the couch, Schwinn slid into the middle, his back board-straight, feet parallel and directly under his knees, as if he were imagining a military review.

"I am told you are also from Germany," he said. "I immigrated in 1924, at age nineteen. My luck was I had studied English in school, but here you see I still have my little German touch. You have none."

Accents were tricky. To Joe, with his naïve all-American ear, Sarah's was as good as German, but to someone like Hermann Schwinn, it would be a problem. The Yiddish inflection would grate, even though neither Schwinn nor Sarah could roll their "r's."

Helen smiled a brilliant Pepsodent smile.

"Mr. Schwinn…"

"Please call me Hermann."

She nodded. "Hermann, then, I was eight when I arrived. The American public school system knocked any accent out of me. I've worked hard to be an American."

"I, too, have my citizenship papers. This is a true land of opportunity, if only we can turn it to the good. I only meant to say that America can take the accent away from us but it cannot disrupt our love of the Fatherland."

"Of course not." Helen felt light-headed, as if Hermann's steady black gaze was sucking air from her.

"You should come to the Deutsches Haus. There's a wonderful restaurant serving good, home-style German food. It will remind you of home."

"When my sister and I left, after my mother died and my father, sadly, had already perished in the Great War, we were down to a potato and a turnip for soup each day but Sunday. I don't want to be reminded of home."

Helen stared directly into his eyes, willing herself into a slow, even breath, staving off the nervous biting of her inner lip.

He nodded and smiled, teeth hidden behind his lips. "If you returned today you would see such a vast improvement in Germany's situation."

"So I've been told."

"Do you like beer? We also have a beer pub."

"I find beer not to my taste. Too heavy."

Helen could detect a slight flicker around Hermann's mouth, whether amusement or anger propelled it was unclear. But it was her sense that men who viewed themselves as powerful, even charismatic, were excited by the chase and preferred prey who were not easy.

"Do you like movies, perhaps?"

"Doesn't every American like a good movie? And, we are right next to Hollywood."

"We show movies every week or so. They are free and quite informative, also."

"Travelogues?"

"More informational. Topics that the American voter needs to be aware of."

"Possibly, then," she said. "If the movie is not too long and boring."

He smiled.

Winona entered the room. Her attire had taken a turn to the demure, with a calf-length sleeveless dress that failed to cling to any part of her, as if challenged to find flesh under its cloth. It was a sodden grey color, with flecks of white like dust bunnies in the pattern.

Hermann stood. "How lovely you look in that, my dear," he said.

As Winona raised her hand for him to take, it trembled in imitation of the leaves on the oak trees. He began to rub it between his two palms, while Winona stood, lips parted, her shallow breath audible.

"Is your asthma acting up?" Jessie asked.

"No."

"You're pale and those bruises on your face..." Jessie sighed.

"Winona and Joe and I were just going to sit out in the sun when you arrived. This seems to be the country that winter forgot," Helen said.

"If you like this weather, you would love Palm Springs. Now that is a town that winter never visits," Hermann said.

Unleashed from his, Winona's hand returned to her side. She slid onto the couch as if she were boneless.

"I find the idea of a complete absence of winter troublesome. More suitable for cactus, if that's the name of the plant with needles all over, than for humans. We need a rest from the sun's perpetual rays, don't you think?" Helen said. She sat back, waiting to see what this small verbal challenge evoked in him.

"That is what night is for."

As if she were lost in contemplating his *bon mot*, Helen pursed her lips and looked into Hermann's eyes. They were just eyes, she told herself.

"Hermann," Winona said.

Helen looked over. Winona's face was pale, her lips puffed out and pouty. Her shallow breath and shivery body were driven by sexual longing that even a shapeless dress couldn't camouflage. If Jessie didn't see it, she was certainly blind to the color of her daughter's true aura.

"Yes," he replied, voice as calm as bathwater.

"Shall we go outside and sit by the pool?" Winona swallowed and ran her tongue quickly across her lips.

"Excellent idea," Jessie said. "Joe, I want you to go over these plans with me."

Tucked under a large straw hat provided by Winona, Helen put her head back on the cushioned chaise, closed her eyes, and listened. Joe's voice adopted the pleading and placating tone she had heard him use with Jessie before. They were discussing Zodiac signs.

Winona, who had settled into the chaise next to Helen like a child taking a reluctant nap, turned on her side and whispered to Helen, "What do you think of him?"

Without opening her eyes, Helen whispered back, "Of Joe or Hermann?"

"Hermann." The tone of her voice reminded Helen of high school.

High-pitched whispers in the hall, a giggle here and there, triumphant engagement announcements and ill-timed pregnancies.

On the latter, Sarah had been absolute. There was to be no hanky-panky, no "giving the cow away for free," a saying she had managed to pick up in her job at the factory. It was an Americanism she grabbed onto and repeated weekly.

When Helen saw two of her good friends' futures felled by pregnancy and quick marriages to men with doubtful futures but potent sperm, she adopted it as her own. No intercourse before marriage.

"He's interesting," Helen said. She turned her face toward the sound of Winona's voice and fluttered her eyes open, trying to convey empathic disinterest and an absolute lack of threat to whatever Winona believed her relationship with Schwinn was. To accomplish this, she had to battle a feeling akin to opening up a packet of rotting meat.

"Isn't he, though? Very powerful, too." Winona rubbed a spot on her upper thigh through her dress, the fabric moving up and down like a wrinkled dishrag.

"Are you and he…." Helen let her voice drop off the edge of the inquiry into silence.

"Shhh." Winona gestured with her pinkie finger toward her mother, Joe, and Schwinn, engrossed in plans for Hitler's California post-war summer castle.

"Take a little walk with me." Helen sat up and rose from the lounge, causing Schwinn to momentarily glance up from the plans with a startled, appreciative look.

Winona managed to stand with the fluidity of a rag doll. Helen grasped her under the elbow. "I'm getting a little tour of the outside."

"Watch out for rattlesnakes," Joe said, looking up from the blueprints, Schwinn's hand directly above his on the stiff paper, holding it taut in the light breeze.

"Seriously?" Helen said.

"Most certainly. Take a switch." He pointed to an umbrella stand stuffed with dead branches, which Helen had taken for a decorative statement.

"It's clear that Hermann only has eyes for you," Helen said as she and Winona walked up a narrow, dirt trail heading away from the pool area and toward a half-finished structure, all metal beams and concrete against the canyon wall.

"Do you think so?"

"Yes. How long have you and he been..." Her brain tried to find the blandest term for lovers that it could. "Such good friends, if I can ask?"

"Since shortly after Mother and I met him. Norman is out of town so much for business..."

"I'm sure it is lonely out here. And, I must say, it's a little dangerous for a woman all by herself." Helen moved her switch back and forth, concerned about a snake lurking in the underbrush. None appeared.

"Very. And Hermann needs a secluded place." Winona seldom seemed to answer a direct question with a direct answer.

"For?"

"I really like your company. Call me and come over again. Take my number when we're back at the house." Winona reached over and took Helen's hand, wrapping her damp fingers around the palm. Helen squeezed in what she hoped passed for a friendly manner.

"Does he come to get away from things?" Helen tried again.

"He comes mostly to see me." Winona's voice had a little "huff," whether of wounded pride or exertion it was hard to tell.

"That must be great."

"Well, he has these meetings, too."

Helen decided to wait Winona out. A long thirty seconds or so of silence, interrupted by Winona's little puffs of air and the whiskering of the switch back and forth, passed.

"Sometimes it's people I sort of know, like George Highsmith. But George never comes with his wife and he and Hermann just hide out with a bottle of scotch in the living room."

George from Caltech was coming for a secluded rendezvous with the leader of the Bund movement in California. What did rocks or Jewish scientists have to do with it? Helen made a mental note to ask Sandy if Leon had made any progress on the Caltech issue.

"Scotch and not good German beer?" Helen said.

Winona giggled. "Neither one of them really likes beer. But it's okay because soon the whole world will be Hitler's and all the liquor will be good German stuff."

"I'll be sure to tell my brother-in-law. It'll save a lot of effort in displaying merchandise."

There was another minute of silence.

"Once in a while ship captains come up. They mostly only speak German and it's hard for me to understand them. Hermann comes to chat with them. And sometimes their crew brings in supplies, boxes of stuff. Mother says it's all books and pamphlets."

Helen considered changing the subject so that Winona didn't think she was too interested. But it was clear that Winona had a limited sense of her audience of one, just a doped-up sense that someone was thankfully listening.

"That's a lot of company."

"Yeah." Winona stopped trudging up the sloping trail and wiped a trickle of sweat from her left cheek.

"A friend of mine wondered if John Schmidt ever came here. I told him there were so many John…"

"John? Sure. He always tries to corner me and talk about how much he misses Germany."

"Well, isn't it just a small world. He comes here? And, you are so sensitive to people, Winona. I bet he really enjoys the time with you." Helen held her breath, hoping the praise would tug out more on Schmidt from Winona and keep her from asking who knew Schmidt and from where.

Winona turned her head with the thankful look of an inept ten-year-old whose manners have just been praised. "He was in the German Army, you know."

Helen shook her head and widened her eyes. "I've never met him. He's just someone that someone I know knows." She hoped she'd spun the invented web of relationship between her and Schmidt so thin that it disappeared in Winona's mind.

"Well, John came here and enlisted in the United States Army and became a captain. He fought on the US side in the Great War. Hermann thinks the world of him, even though, you know, he wasn't on the right side last time. But he's making up for it."

"I'm sure he thinks the world of Hermann, too."

"I'm tired of this. Let's talk about something else." Winona's mood shifted toward dark.

Helen obliged. She was worried that any more questions about now-retired Captain John Schmidt might trigger Winona's suspicions even though it appeared that Winona, rather than having a sixth sense, had almost no sense. No wonder Schwinn sequestered her when he had important people to meet. Winona was like a leaky sieve.

"Tell me about this building. What's it going to be used for?" Helen pointed to a one-story cabin, with a padlocked door and two barred windows, set several yards away from the path they were on.

Winona shrugged and circled again to personal matters.

"You know almost all my dirty little secrets now. Now tell me something about you." Winona had dropped her voice to a whisper and pulled Helen's arm close into hers.

Helen squeezed back, clenched her teeth and smiled in an imitation of friendship.

"I'm not married, you know. And I've never …." Her voice dropped off and she allowed herself a deep sigh, trying not to cough in the dust being kicked up by their trek up the path.

"Really?" Winona's voice pitched high and thin.

Helen wanted to clamp her hand over Winona's mouth. Instead she said, "I'd only ever tell you the truth. What is it like?"

Winona stopped on the path, resisting Helen's slight tug as if she were a recalcitrant puppy on a leash.

"Joe won't be at all like Hermann. Men are different. Hermann is soldierly and stern. He wants me to behave like a good German woman."

Apparently the fact that Winona was married and the daughter of a wealthy woman who was funding his delusional vision of a summer palace for the Führer didn't stop Schwinn from having sex with her. But maybe that was what good German women did. Winona rubbed her right buttocks, very near the bruise.

"He's the one who hits you?"

Winona dropped Helen's arm. "I am a bad girl. Mother says that, too. If it will help me be the right kind of woman, I am okay with it. And afterwards he takes me in his arms, holds me on his lap, kisses me so kindly, and asks me to promise him and the Führer that I will be good."

"I see. What about Norman?" Helen felt a twinge of an emotion close to sympathy for Winona. She could sense it in the same way she could sense a sneeze that almost came but didn't.

"He wants me to be good, too."

"I don't think you are bad."

"You don't know me that well and you are my friend."

"I meant what about Norman, because you are married after all."

"Oh, that. Norman doesn't care. I see your eyebrow went up at that. Norman is just not into sex with me. I think he has a mistress." She shrugged. "And, I'm not into sex with him or even, really, with Hermann. Norman cares about engineering and he cares about the fate of America, and he cares about overseeing his projects."

Helen stepped closer to Winona and gave her a soft, enveloping hug. At her touch, Winona slumped against her and Helen had to lock her knees while Winona hung, heavy and limp as wet sheets, on her arms, her chest heaving with a locked-in sob.

In discomfort, this ran a close second to the image of Winona and Schwinn naked on a bed, Schwinn raising a flat, Heil-Hitler palm above Winona's reddened and bruised rump.

Abruptly Winona straightened and stepped away.

"We should get back. They'll wonder where we've gone."

"Where could we go?" Helen looked around, seeing only an incomplete building, half-framed against the blue-gray sky.

"Nowhere, I guess." Winona took her hand and turned back down the path.

12

"LEON HASN'T HAD MUCH LUCK yet finding out who at Caltech is working on mining, drilling for oil, or metallurgy, or other issues related to rocks, and what that might mean."

Sandy looked at Helen for the briefest of moments before turning his focus back to the three pedestrians crossing the street, his hands gripping the steering wheel. She wanted to tug his right hand off and hold it, but she fended off the impulse.

They were driving in a long-looped pattern around Glendale in and out of shadows and late afternoon sun, which glared into Sandy's eyes whenever the car turned into a west-facing lane.

"So our elusive Schmidt is this immigrant who is now retired U.S. Army Captain John Schmidt, which gives him access to our bases and our guys. Great." His hand floated off the wheel and then returned to the three o'clock position with a slap.

She could not tell whether *great* was praise or frustration.

"Leon is sending Captain John Schmidt's name over to our friends in the F.B.I.," he said. "And, someone will need to work on monitoring George more closely. See what departments he is responsible for or takes an interest in."

"I'm glad." Helen wondered who would get the tedious task of watching a bureaucrat push paper.

"Caltech research and talent is vital in gearing up for the coming war."

"The war America doesn't want."

"The war America will have to fight."

"I could have misheard the word," Helen said.

"Have to fight?"

"No, I meant maybe it wasn't 'rocks.'"

"Hmmm."

Sandy shoved his arm out the window in the "L-shape" for a right turn and swung the steering wheel over. The car lurched around the corner onto another residential side street, verdantly green lawns carpeting the space between the sidewalk and neat front doors. Helen rolled down the passenger side window with three full turns of the handle, and the scent of fresh cut grass entered on a cool breeze.

"That would widen the search to all the departments, then," he said. "Try to narrow that down for us."

Helen looked at the passing panorama of houses tucked into lots bordered by driveways leading from the street to garages with doors painted a brisk white.

Sticking her hand out the window, she spread her fingers so the air whipped between them. Those houses, so safe looking, were as out of reach to her as they had been when she looked at them on the postcards Helen sent. She brought her hand in and rolled up the window.

"I have some things for you from Norma in the trunk. Maybe they'll cheer you up," Sandy said.

"Maybe." Helen rested her head against the seat back and closed her eyes.

"Try getting in touch with Winona without Joe's help. Reinforce her feeling that you are her friend. Get more information."

"It was too easy to get this information. I think it may be all that Winona has to offer, anyhow. She was clear that Schwinn's meetings with George were in a huddle away from her. It made her fretful, to say the least."

"All the better. Tell her that the next time Schwinn is over and he says he's got George coming up, you'll come over and keep her company so she won't be so sad and lonely. Maybe add that you'll help her stay sober that night."

Helen opened her eyes as he gave her his marching orders.

"That's the plan," he said.

"And I will get the information about Caltech how?"

"You'll figure it out. Something will hit you and you'll know."

"If I'm caught?"

"Give them that look of yours and make something up. Get flirty."

"I'm not impressed with my skills in that area."

"I am."

Sandy helped Helen carry two tight-woven wicker laundry baskets, each piled to the rim with folded up clothing, into the living room. Sarah, a red gingham apron around her waist, stood at the door between the kitchen and the living room, one hand on her hip, the other holding a wooden spoon, bowl tipped up and pointing toward them like an extension of her finger.

"What is that for?"

"Hi, Sarah," Sandy said. "These are from the woman I told you about. The one with connections in the motion picture business. She's getting rid of them and wanted Helen to have any she wanted. Or you."

"Okay. I thought you were going back to New York, Sandy." Sarah continued to hold the spoon, pointed toward his chest.

"Yeah. Well, more auditions." Sandy shrugged. "It's the business."

Sarah nodded, put the spoon on the counter next to her, untied the apron, and hooked it over the nearby kitchen cabinet door handle. In three steps she was kneeling next to Helen, the corners of her mouth beginning a slow upward course, her hands moving over the peach-colored raw silk of the blouse on the top of the pile, with its eighth-inch round buttons in mother-of-pearl.

"Look at this skirt! It would go perfect with that." Helen held up a mid-calf-length skirt in cream with half-finished tiny cubes in shades of orange and pink distributed in a seemingly random pattern across the fabric. "You have to try this on."

"I have no place to wear anything like this." Sitting back on her haunches, Sarah put her hands, knuckles down, on the floor next to her, as if she were too weary to rise up.

Helen walked over, picked up the blouse, threw it over her arm on top of the skirt, and said, "Get up. We'll find you clothes and then Harry will take you out to a restaurant and a movie or even dancing. I promise you, Sarah."

Shaking her head in disbelief, Sarah stood. Helen picked up one basket and said, "Sandy, thanks for the ride and the little talk. And for bringing these. I'll see you later."

"You won't forget to do what we talked about?"

"How can I?"

After dinner, Helen pulled Sarah into the bedroom, where the clothes were now heaped on Helen's bed. She unbuttoned Sarah's housedress, slid the shoes off her feet, and re-pinned her hair in a chignon with a deep bang that flowed across her forehead.

After ten minutes of trying on clothes, staring first at the top in the bureau mirror and then standing on the bed to see the waist down, Sarah relaxed. Fifteen minutes into the exercise, she shouldered Helen aside and sorted the clothes into potential outfits, pushing aside the long, sequined, black evening dress, with a décolleté that hovered four inches above her navel, two cotton rompers, one in red gingham and one a sunlit yellow, one orange swimsuit, and a low cut satin blouse with a matching high slit skirt.

Shyly at first, she tried on three of the nine remaining sets. By the fourth, Sarah was smiling, pushing her bangs out of her face, and striking poses as she stood for Helen's approval. They began to giggle like school girls, stroking the two cashmere sweater sets, then twirling each other about the room.

This was the America they had come for. Good clothes, an O'Keefe and Merritt stove, a backyard with green grass and enough space for children to run around in.

"I need to get my hair cut," Sarah said, pushing the grey strands under the darker red strands along the side of her head. "A little trim."

"Okay."

"I want to show Harry this."

Sarah left the bedroom wearing a sleeveless summer dress, the shade of begonia leaves in the rain, full-skirted, fitted across the bodice, with a v-neck, and cinched at the waist with a matching belt. Helen waited, then walked quietly toward the living room. In the lamp's glow she could see Sarah and Harry dancing while Bing Crosby crooned on the Philco.

Retrieving the phone number that Winona had given her from her nightstand drawer, Helen dialed. When Winona said "Hello," Helen cupped her hand around the receiver and threaded her way through Winona's non sequiturs until she had a promise that Winona would invite her and Joe over for dinner the next time Hermann came.

Helen thought the chances were good that George would come for a *tête-à-tête* or a German ship's captain would turn up. She doubted that Hermann's interest in Winona extended beyond the use of her house for very private meetings and the use of her body.

"That way, if Hermann has, ummm, other guests, we can sit and chat with you until they are gone. I could see how sad that made you." Helen whispered into the phone.

"You are just too kind. Mother was right about you."

Haunted by the ghost of the finger in the box, Helen pushed the Forester Liquor front door open in a slow sweep. The door hit nothing and, relieved, she stepped inside.

She had agreed to staff the store alone for an hour that morning. Harry needed to "see a dentist about my back tooth, here, which is killing me," as he had muttered while holding an ice cube wrapped in a kitchen towel against his jaw. Sarah had put her lips against his forehead to check for fever. Ben banged his cup against the kitchen table rhythmically as Helen left.

The first half-hour she entered numbers into the account ledger and opened up a short stack of bills. Based on what she could see, Harry's legal business was turning around, profit inching up. That was good because it was between racing seasons, ponies resting in stables nestled against the San Gabriels or down where the surf met the turf and a new race track was being built.

The new cop hadn't been around since his one and only appearance. It was unclear to her what Harry's position was with Dragna now.

If she just sat on the stool, the fan moving the air so it flowed across her cheeks without ruffling her hair, and looked out the window, she could pretend that the California sun created no dark shadows for Nazis to hide in or alleys where gangsters could lurk.

A thick figure passed by the window, the door opened, and Ralph entered.

"Is Harry here?" Ralph asked, as if he and Harry were the kinds of pals that saw each other daily, neighborhood guys who hung out on the corner together or went to the bar to grab a drink after work.

"At the dentist."

Ralph nodded, walked over to the case where the cold drinks were kept, reached far in and brought out a Pabst. Sticking his nubby thumb against the cap, he pushed, pushed a little harder, and the cap popped off. He tipped the bottle into his mouth and took three long swallows.

"You must be thirsty," she said.

"Let me check the time." He made a show of looking at his wristwatch, held on his wrist by a thick gold band. "I've been up all night on a job, so let's just call this my after midnight drink, shall we. Yes, I'm thirsty and hungry, too. I thought maybe Harry would like to join me for a huge breakfast, but that's not to be. And I suppose you are stuck here?"

"I am."

"I guess if the mountain won't come to Mohammad, I will have to get take-out and eat here."

"Is my ongoing company part of some deal you and Harry came to?"

"Your company…." The edge to his voice made her draw back as if he had clenched his hand into a massive fist. When he saw her shift on the stool, he shook his head. "You need to know that Jessie asked me to look into you and your family to be sure you are the 'right type of person' as she so delicately put it."

"So she doesn't just trust her paranormal abilities?" Helen tipped her head and rubbed the bridge of her nose. The news upset her, more because Harry didn't want anyone to know they were Jewish than because it would sucker-punch her spy career.

"No."

"And what did you find?"

"That you and Harry are what you say you are. As am I. It's America and that's what we're entitled to." Ralph took three steps back toward the door, then turned around and said, "I'll leave, Helen. Just tell Harry I said 'hello.' See you around."

One customer came in, grabbed a cold bottle of soda and the newspaper and left. Dust motes bobbed in the breeze from the overhead fan. Helen went into the storeroom to get a dust rag. She heard the front door open, and Harry called out, "Helen" in the muffled tone of someone with cotton batten in his mouth.

She peeked out the door. He was alone, his elbows propped on the counter facing toward the storeroom door, his jaw visibly swollen.

"Hey," she said as she stepped out with the rag in her hand. "What did the dentist do to you?"

"Pulled the tooth. Novocain hasn't worn off."

"It's been quiet here, Harry. You can go home if you want."

He shook his head and pointed to the storeroom. "I'll sit in there."

"Ralph was here."

Harry's eyebrows raised a fraction of an inch and he tilted his head.

"What for?"

"He said he wanted to have breakfast with you. I told him you were at the dentist. He went away."

"Mad?"

"Miffed because I didn't want him to hang around me. Was I part of the bargain, Harry? He gets Dragna to pull that cop away from you and Ralph gets to hover around here, ask me out?"

"Nah." Harry's voice grunted hoarsely.

"Okay. Let's say I believe you and leave that alone for now. What is the deal between you and Ralph, then? Why the favors?" She considered telling Harry about Ralph's guard service for

Nazi-lovers and decided it would be useless. "It can't be just that you recognized him as a former fighter or his attraction to your good looks."

A little barking laugh slid from Harry's mouth. "Hurts, Helen. Don't make me laugh."

"You've got Novocain. You can't be hurting. Try another line out."

"He's a Long Island boy. Grew up just a few blocks away from me. His older brother was a classmate."

"That doesn't make for such a strong tie."

"We know the same people."

"Still..."

"We keep the same secrets, Helen. That's all. No more." He slid around the counter, opened the storeroom door, entered, closed it behind him, and Helen heard the click of the lock being thrown.

Three days passed during which Helen did not hear from Joe, Winona, Jessie, or Ralph. Sandy checked in by phone, ending the discussion when she said there was nothing to report. She and Sarah continued to play dress-up in the clothes Norma Shearer had sent, and Helen wore two of the less dramatic outfits to work. The woman with the big diamond ring and heavy betting habits was impressed.

"Phone for you, Helen."

She put the bottle of Johnny Walker on the shelf above her head, plugging the hole in the lineup of Scotch that had been made when a scraggly, ill-shaven regular had purchased two bottles just after ten that morning. Walking behind the counter, she picked up the receiver.

"Hello?"

"Helen, I hope I am not bothering you." The formality of the grammar gave Schwinn away as much as the German accent.

"Hermann?"

"Yes, yes. It is I. I want to know if you can come this Friday night to a dinner at the Deutsches Haus at eight. A program follows at nine-thirty by my good friend, Paul Themlitz, who owns the Aryan Bookstore. You will be interested."

This was stated with the firmness and authority Helen had last associated with her sixth grade teacher, a martinet of a woman, thickly built with a ruddy complexion that bloomed into scarlet when she was upset with a student's behavior. Fighting the impulse to scream "No" and slam the receiver down, Helen asked if her very dear friend Winona would also be there.

The question created a little eddy of silence on the other end. "Would you like her to come?" finally crackled across the phone line.

"Yes, indeed."

"Then of course I will be sure she is there."

"Then I will come. Winona can pick me up."

"*Sehr gutt. Auf wiedersehen.*"

"*Auf wiedersehen,*" she said to a dead line.

"He told me, Winona, that he wanted you to have a little company at this talk because he would have to introduce the program and everything. Really, he sounded so concerned about you that I couldn't say no."

Helen's voice had the high pitch and breathiness she associated with exchanges she'd overheard in the girls' bathroom at high school between cheerleaders before the homecoming dance.

She had avoided all entanglements back then, finding the boys to be boys, and only that. The ones with prospects were already focused on college and the ones without were not the ones she would date. This gave her the reputation of being peculiar and stuck-up, but it relieved her of any issues with other girls over boys. The last idea she wanted in Winona's addled brain was that Hermann was now interested in Helen.

"Oh, Helen." Winona's voice sounded like a dam with a crack through which tears leaked. "I'd divorce Norman in a minute if Hermann only would act like he was committed to me."

"It's so hard on you! Has he called to say he's coming over?"

"I forgot to tell you. Dinner this Sunday at six. Can you ask Joe?"

"I'll call him right now."

Behind Joe's voice a phonograph record needle hit the end of the song to produce a cat's claw scratch as it slid over the paper label.

"Get that, will you?" Joe said to an unnamed guest. There had been a sliver of silence when she asked him to go to Winona's for dinner on Sunday night. Possibly the guest was the reason since Helen had heard a "damn" in a low register just after Joe had said Sunday night at six was fine for dinner and he would pick her up at five-fifteen. She assumed Joe and the "damn" person would work it out.

The abrupt uptick in scheduled contacts between Helen and Schwinn were duly reported to Sandy, leading to an immediate invitation for dinner "with someone you already know" that night.

When he picked her up at the store, Helen sensed a little whirligig of tension behind his immaculate greeting to Harry, as if he were afraid he would blow his lines before the act was over.

As they walked down the block toward his car, Sandy whistled tunelessly, his stride outpacing Helen's.

Trying to keep up, she grabbed his arm. "Hey, slow down," she said.

"Sorry. You need briefings on Themlitz and Schwinn with more detail than you've had. I'm trying to sort what's helpful from what's not."

"Why don't you let me figure that out?"

He opened the passenger side door for her and helped her in as though she had twisted her ankle, followed by a sad pat on her hand.

"What's really the matter, Sandy?" she asked once he was settled into the driver's seat and they were moving along the street at a comfortable speed.

"These are dangerous men plotting to get weapons, to turn the National Guard into their private army, to…" He paused.

"To take over the world. I understand that."

"Two years ago, Schwinn got orders from his higher-ups to negotiate with the Nazis to ship German arms here for the Silver Shirts. We're sure he got them and stored them somewhere. But we don't know what kind or where."

He stared out the window, fingers tapping on the stick shift as if typing out code.

"I'll see what I can find out."

The car crawled in the traffic, threatening to stall out in second gear. Sandy squinted in the glare of the sun through the windshield. His fingers continued their desperate coding.

"Okay," he said. "Schwinn and Themlitz. There were threats to have fifty storm troopers come into Los Angeles from the ship, *Schwaben*, to 'protect' the local German Day parade from possible 'anti-Hitler' demonstrators. They were active players in that.

"These ersatz storm troopers meet and drill at the Aryan Bookstore. Uniformed SS troopers, who are passengers from

German ships which freely come and go to the United States, show up and train them. And they bring money and Nazi propaganda. But where do they practice firing?"

"The ranch?" Helen said.

He shrugged. "Probably."

The car eased to a stop in back of a delivery van belonging to a furniture store. The van driver stuck out his hand and waved at them to pass so he could wiggle his way back into the parking space Sandy's auto was now blocking. Helen looked at her wristwatch. At just past five p.m., it must have been his last delivery of the day.

Sandy checked the driver's side mirror, leaned his head out the window to double check, stuck his hand out in a left-turn posture for extra magic and moved into the opposite traffic lane and around the truck.

When the car was safely deposited in the correct lane, he sighed and reached over to squeeze Helen's shoulder.

"We have people, a few people, who are there at those meetings. They aren't close enough for big secrets yet, just piddly stuff like whether a new batch of Nazi bullshit has been delivered for distribution. As if the Silver Shirts couldn't manufacture that here all on their own. But we haven't got anyone like the shooting star you are."

"And your message to me is what, then?"

"Be smart, Helen, and be careful. We'll try to keep an eye on you. And here's our dinner spot."

Her whole life had been lived as dark waters stormed around her. California was a chimera. Despite the bright sunshine and flowers in every hue, its true nature was as seaweed- strewn, dank, and stinging with salt as anywhere else. She sighed.

They parked in the rear of the restaurant and entered through the back door into the kitchen, which boasted a large grill on which steaks sizzled, tended by a man with a Navy anchor tattoo on his right bicep and a white chef's hat on his head, and a cooktop where large enameled pans full of bubbling sauces released the savory odors of tomato and garlic.

They entered a room marked "Private." A round table was overlaid with a smoke-colored tablecloth on which sat place settings for three.

Leon Lewis was in one chair. He stood up when Helen stepped in and pulled out the chair next to him for her.

"I ordered three rib eyes. I hope that's all right. You don't keep kosher do you, Helen?"

She shook her head. Dietary laws were left in Europe, on the empty plate with hunger.

"Good. I mean because if Schwinn and that bunch want you to eat with them at the Deutches Haus, it won't be kosher chicken." He laughed dryly.

"I could always say I was one of those vegetarians."

"We hear Hitler is one. But I don't think the Deutsches Haus menu has that option." He smiled at her as if she were a well-loved niece who needed career guidance.

The door opened and the cook entered balancing three plates on his arm. Each had a steak at least two inches thick and a large baked potato. When the plate was in front of her on the table, Helen saw that her potato was already split, a pat of yellow butter melting into the white interior, a tablespoon of sour cream sitting shyly on the lip of the plate in case it was also wanted. The conversation stopped while they cut into their medium rare steaks, releasing pink juices onto the plates.

"Best steak in town," Leon said, after they'd each had a chance to swallow their first bite. "But, we need to brief you for your adventures to come, Helen." He laid the knife across the lip of the plate farthest away from him, its sharp edge facing out, and leaned down to pick up a briefcase that had been hidden under his chair.

"These are court documents from an LA Superior Court case in 1934." He placed a ream of single-spaced typed paper on the table.

"They document testimony by members of the German-American Alliance against Bund and Silver Shirts like Themlitz and Schwinn. Alliance members were suing because their group had been 'illegally' usurped by the Nazis. It got thrown out of court but not before we could get a good glimpse into their inner workings. And the Bund balance sheet, which was at least $30,000 at the time."

Sandy put a hand on Leon's. "Respectfully, Leon, let's just tell her a little about the list of authors that Themlitz wanted expurgated from the LA libraries. That will be something she can talk to him about."

Leon narrowed his eyes then gave an exaggerated shrug. "Okay. He and his cronies petitioned the library to eliminate about a thousand authors. From Adler to Zweig, the finest minds in the world were on the list."

Helen picked up the nineteen pages he handed her. Column after column of names, and she recognized a handful at best. Sandy plucked it from her.

"Adler and Freud, do you know them?"

"Freud," she said.

"Okay. Did you read the book I gave you by Sinclair Lewis?"

A slight flush slipped up Helen's neck as if her body secretly conspired to embarrass her.

"A few pages. The first chapter."

Sandy pressed a finger against his nose like the air had just developed a slight odor.

"May I ask why?"

The long train ride, the windows framing one scene of America after another, from cabbage fields to garbage dumps, from sere prairie land to mountain peaks, had provided its own entertainment.

People had wandered up and down the train aisles, and a few had paused to chat with her. One thin, beardless middle aged man in a wrinkled white shirt, a wedding ring prominent on his left hand, stood, his hand clutching the seat in front of her for balance, and chatted with her about California.

Looking down, he saw the spine of the book, *It Can't Happen Here* in large graphic type.

"That's kind of a Commie book, isn't it?" His voice was casual and curious. Helen could detect no sharp edge, but the question itself alarmed her.

"Is it? Someone gave it to me to read on the train."

"Ahhh. Good friend?"

"No. A girl who lived down the hall from me. She was just passing it on, she said. I asked her what it was about but she hadn't read the whole thing. So I just shoved it in my bag in case."

"In case of what? You needed a door stop?" He laughed and she forced a short "ha" out of her dry throat.

"In case I got bored or something."

"No chance of that for someone who looks like you. But I gotta go and see if the missus has woken from her nap. Bye now."

Helen shoved the book further down in the bag and tucked her sweater over it. She stayed with her movie magazines for the rest of the trip.

"I was concerned that if I read it on the train, people would think I had Communist leanings." She looked into Sandy's eyes, only inches from her own and tried not to think about his mouth, also only inches from her own.

He nodded and pulled back, leaving a ghostly sense of his former closeness. Helen looked over at Leon, who was chewing on another bite of steak. She rapidly cut another bite for herself and began to chew also.

"That's good," Sandy said. "Tell me more."

"This man saw it and said he'd heard it was a 'Commie' book."

"And you said?"

"I said I didn't know anything about the book. A friend had given it to me."

"Perfect. That's what you say to Themlitz. Someone gave you the book to read but it scared you because you heard it was a Red book. And ask him if Lewis was on his list of authors to be expunged from the library. He'll say 'yes.' Then you bat those eyelashes of yours and ask him to tell you more."

"That'll work?"

"He's a man. It'll work. And, since Schwinn is also interested in you, it'll increase his desire to have you around him, not Themlitz. So there'll be an even better cover for you when you and whosis—"

"Joe?"

"Yes, him. When you and Joe go back out to the ranch for dinner on Sunday, you can play this out."

Sandy leaned back in his chair, put a piece of meat in his mouth, his eyes on his plate as if looking for Delphic omens of the future in the swirls of meat juices.

"The Caltech issue is very important. Find out why Schwinn meets with George," Leon said.

"It's possible some other Nazi creeps will be there," Sandy said.

"Who?" Helen put down her fork, which felt too heavy to lift to her mouth.

Sandy shook his head and stared at the swirled pattern on his plate. "We don't know yet."

There was a knock at the door. Leon looked at his watch, nodded, and got up. "I have another meeting. That's my ride. Sit and finish eating, my dear. As I said, the steak here is out of the ordinary."

Helen called Winona at nine in the morning to talk about ar-rangements to pick her up at the store for the Deutsches Haus meet-ing. Winona's voice was blurry with sleep and Helen worried until five o'clock that she hadn't registered what she was being asked.

But, at five sharp, Winona opened the Forester Liquor door and walked in wearing a bubble-gum-pink cotton dress whose skirt fell loosely to mid-calf and whose bodice, designed like a sep-arate blouse, featured elbow length sleeves and an austerely white Peter Pan collar that outdid her skin color for pastiness. She looked like a sick school girl who should be taken home and put to bed.

"You look great," Helen said.

Winona twirled around, the skirt flapping against the stacked bottles of Scotch on display.

"It's new."

"I hope I'm dressed all right." Helen had chosen her most con-servative spring outfit from New York, a calf-length periwinkle blue dress, whose sleeves billowed slightly before being pulled in tightly around her wrists.

Winona wrinkled her nose, scrutinized Helen as if she were a store mannequin, and said, "It's a little dated, but I think it is per-fect for tonight. And anyhow, dear Helen, you can wear anything and make it look good."

Helen went to the storage room door and knocked. "I'm leav-ing now, Harry."

"Okay. Have a good time," he said, his voice muffled through the door. Since Ralph had taken care of his Dragna problem, Harry was markedly more mellow and disinterested in Helen's comings and goings as long as she put in time at the store and kept the books.

Helen wished she could say the same about Sarah, who, full of concern, hovered around her like a clammy fog.

A shiny, grass-green Ford sedan was parked down the street. Its outward appearance was marred only by a prominent dent in the fender, giving it the look of a lovely creature with a bandage on its jaw.

Winona and Helen walked toward it, their images mirrored in the storefront windows as they passed by. The air stank of exhaust fumes from three cars idling as the light turned slowly from red to green.

Winona coughed twice as each car accelerated, leaving more traces of their machine presence to smell.

"I'm a little asthmatic," she said as she unlocked the car door and opened it for Helen.

The interior of the car looked like the playpen of a slightly demented two-year-old. Three stuffed Teddy bears and a Raggedy Ann doll sat propped up in the back seat. The floor of the car was littered with candy bar wrappers. A Tootsie Pop wrapper stuck to the bottom of Helen's shoe, and she tugged it off. Necco wafers lay crushed to pastel powder on the floor. Before she sat down, Helen brushed her hand over the seat to dislodge a dried up bite size piece of an old-fashioned donut.

"I've got no time to clean the inside. And I don't have many passengers," Winona said.

"It's very nice."

As they headed toward downtown Los Angeles, Helen wondered if Winona had few passengers because no one who knew her was foolish enough to ride with her. She braked sharply at lights, stalling the car out on five separate occasions, once flooding the engine so that they had to sit for five minutes while "things settle down," as Winona put it.

Other cars moved angrily around them. When the car started

up again, Winona gripped the steering wheel with white fingers and red knuckles, her breath so raspy Helen could hear it.

"I just love to drive," Winona said.

"What a wonderful skill to have. I'm jealous."

"If you want, I can teach you."

"How kind of you." Helen hoped Winona would forget she offered.

They were now entering an area with densely packed buildings several stories high. They had the gray stone façades and chiseled features Helen recognized as a downtown. She sat back, satisfied that she was now in the real Los Angeles, and looked around for people going about their business. There were none.

Winona maneuvered the car on a four-lane avenue up a low hill and then down again. For six thirty at night, the sidewalks remained stubbornly empty of pedestrians. They bumped across trolley tracks at an intersection.

"Help me find 634 West Fifth Street," Winona said. "It should be around here someplace."

"Do you have a map?"

Taking her right hand off the steering wheel, Winona leaned over so far toward Helen that she could see the road only with a sideways glance of her left eye. She patted the glove compartment.

Helen wondered if anyone had ever told Winona to use her words. Grabbing a map of Los Angeles out of the pile of debris in the compartment, Helen opened it onto her lap. She traced their path with one finger: they were driving down Grand Avenue and had just jerkily moved through the intersection at Third Avenue.

"So, Fifth is coming up. Try a right."

Winona nodded, breathed so deeply Helen feared for the buttons on her bodice, increased her grip on the wheel, and made the turn.

"There it is," she said. A triumphant grin lit up her face.

"You know I once hit a little pickaninny driving. Mother was so upset that she had to pay for the cast and the crutches for the broken leg."

"Pick...?"

"You know, a Negro child." Winona emphasized the words "Negro" and "child" then giggled, the laugh sucking all the dignity out of the terms. "Good thing I didn't kill it. Mother would have had to pay even more money and boy would she have been mad."

Winona's efforts to parallel park relieved Helen of the need to respond.

Helen took three deep breaths to calm her stomach. It was useless to worry about what might happen in an hour, when Winona drove her back. She could only focus on how to respond to the now and plan for the moment just after.

The Deutsches Haus Tavern was unprepossessing on the inside. Eighteen tables, most set for parties of four, were covered with red and white checked oilcloths. They held two or three people, at most. The majority of the diners were men with beer steins in front of them. Several looked up when Winona and Helen entered then returned their gazes to companions at the table. There was a bass murmur of male conversation.

To the rear, a dark wooden bar stretched the length of the room. Badly lit landscape paintings hung on three of the four walls.

A white-shirted bartender wiped off the counter then put a mug of beer down with an audible thunk in front of a man who looked familiar to Helen.

"There's Mark," Winona said. "I'll go say 'hello' and see if he wants to sit with us. You grab a table." She pointed toward an empty table that would seat four.

Mark and Dodi had been at the first and second parties at Jessie's. What did she remember about them other than that they both liked the last Astaire-Rogers movie? Did Mark's father own an oil field?

As Winona approached Mark, he looked up and then smiled at her, nodding as she leaned in to say something in his ear. He grabbed the mug by its handle, slid off the bar stool, and walked with Winona over to the table.

"I think the three of us have dropped the average age in the room by half," he said as he sat down next to Helen. His chair scraped against the floor as he pulled it in.

"It is an older, more settled-looking group," Helen said.

Mark laughed. "Tactful."

"Dodi isn't here?" Winona looked around.

"She's not the meeting type. At least not these kinds. Garden club, bridge club, more to her liking. So, are you interested in politics, Helen?"

"I'm here because Winona wanted to come. I think when I met you, you said your father and you were in the oil business, but we never had a chance to talk more about that."

Helen counted on her maxim that the second a man was asked about himself he lost interest in her, except for what she looked like.

For the next several minutes Mark described Dominguez, populated by oil derricks and oil pumps, Mexican laborers battling it out with dust-bowl refugees, and slippery men, greasing their way into the California legislature to deprive his family of their claim to thirty acres of prime liquid fossils.

His beery breath was a warm, yeasty breeze on her neck. Helen nodded like a metronome.

As Mark held forth, Winona swiveled her head from right to left every half-minute or so. "At last," she said.

A smiling Schwinn, decked out in mock military garb, so starched that even his hair follicles seemed stiff, walked toward them. With him was an overweight man in his early fifties, Helen guessed.

The man had sandy gray hair combed over a bald spot, and eyes whose color was fogged behind thick glasses. He wore an ill-fitting black suit, the jacket straining at its buttons, a white shirt, and a thin black tie. A silver swastika pin decorated the jacket lapel.

The man offered a plump hand to Helen and she shook it. The skin had the texture and temperature of a raw plucked chicken leg just out of the refrigerator.

"Paul Themlitz at your service," he said.

"Mr. Themlitz, I have been looking forward to meeting you."

"Paul, please."

Helen nodded. Themlitz shook hands with Mark, who speedily vacated his chair for the stars of the local American Bund.

Picking up the chair and placing it so it faced squarely toward Helen, Themlitz said, "Hermann was right about you." He tilted his head up and stared at her through the bottom of his spectacles.

"In a good way, I hope," Helen said.

Themlitz moved his head back and forth as if Helen's face was an old manuscript he was scanning with his near-sighted vision. His hand floated up wraith-like toward her cheek, then dropped down. "Beautiful Aryan features," he said.

Helen spoke quickly, hearing the tension in her voice. "I don't mean to take advantage of your expertise, Paul, because we've just met after all..."

He waved his hand to indicate that was of no importance.

"But have you heard of this Communist book, *It Can't Happen Here*? Someone I barely knew in New York, a neighbor, handed it to me to read on my trip out here and I found it to be dreadful."

"Exactly so. One of the books that should never have been published let alone freely circulated in our public libraries."

"Dangerous ideas," Helen said. "I hope to be able to visit your bookstore for some good reading material."

Themlitz covered her hand with his cool, scratchy palm. His nails were manicured and shiny even in the dim light, like deep-water fish at the New York Aquarium. "I look forward to that. Let's make a date for tea, in fact."

Schwinn had taken the fourth chair. "Beauty and brains, just as I said."

Themlitz's murky vision swung to Schwinn, leaving his invitation to the bookstore unanswered.

Helen felt a light thud as Winona kicked the table leg. Then she grabbed Helen's thigh under the table and squeezed and twisted with surprising force. When Helen turned, Winona had a kewpie-doll smile on her face. She let go of Helen's thigh and gave a brief nod.

"Winona is such a mentor to me. She is so knowledgeable about the cause. And devoted," Helen said.

She was certain Winona had left the red marks of a grade school bully under Helen's clothes. For all her drug-addledness, Winona was a force that would call Helen to account for any deviation from the course Winona had sighted out for her.

Winona smiled and replaced her hand on the table. "Helen's boyfriend, Joe, is one of our people in the movie business," she said. "Helen and Joe will be joining me for dinner this Sunday night."

Helen tried to relax into a smile as she rubbed her thigh. "Such a gracious hostess."

"Well, I might just see you all there if Winona wants to add a fourth," Schwinn said.

Winona looked as if she had been given a surprise birthday party. "You know Norman is always gone for business. It is lonely and I welcome the company."

Winona also had a gift for acting or lying or both, Helen observed.

Schwinn apparently did not want Helen to know he was already going to Winona's. That would be consistent with flirting with Helen, or it might be because he did not want Paul to know that he already had plans to see Winona at the Murphy Ranch that particular night.

Schwinn, she considered, loved drama, dress up, and secrets. How appropriate he lived so close to Hollywood. It was as if he could be the lead in his own movie about the end of democracy and the downfall of the Jews.

"So it's set," Helen said.

"Will there be other guests?" Themlitz asked.

Schwinn gave him an uncomfortably long look.

"No," said Winona.

"Well, then," Themlitz said as he turned his torso to look out over the room, "just an intimate dinner for four. I see our crowd has grown. Must be time for the talk now." He rose and made his way toward the bar.

Themlitz had a voice that scratched and wheezed as he tried to project it into the restaurant. Nonetheless, the fifty or so patrons quieted and turned their chairs to face him, the men sitting with legs planted in front of them and arms crossed over their bellies, the women sitting with crossed legs, hands on top of purses in their laps.

The night's topic was the growing nationwide appeal by Jewish leaders to have German goods boycotted.

"These Shylocks want to strangle the good German manufacturers, already devastated by the impact of the Great War. Their efforts to control the world's economy must be stopped. Write your congressman and the newspaper," Schwinn said in summary at the end of twenty minutes of reciting what seemed to Helen to be a city-by-city store-by-store account of the effort.

The end of his talk was punctuated with a last wheeze that sounded like air sizzling out of a bicycle tire. Then he wiped at his face with a large, white handkerchief, smiling at the applause.

Helen thudded her hands together in imitation of applause, her lips pursed.

"Wasn't that a marvelous talk?" Schwinn leaned across the table to capture Helen's attention. He began to scoot his chair around toward her, the sound of the wood scraping on the tile floor adding to the din.

"Yes," Helen said. She hoped the flatness of her reply would be lost in the overall noise.

"Dear, you don't look well at all. You should make your apologies and we should leave." Winona said. She had leaned in toward Helen, with her mouth at Helen's ear. Her stale beer breath added to the stink of the cigar smoke that smudged the air.

"Helen needs to leave now," Winona said. She stood, pulling at Helen's arm.

Schwinn stood. "Just let Paul say *auf wiedersehen* to our guest."

Winona dropped Helen's arm abruptly. "Of course. I was just being..."

"Solicitous. It's been a long day for me, with work and all." Helen forced a smile onto her lips, turning it first to Winona, who nodded, and then to Schwinn, who shrugged and smiled in return.

She would need to be more careful of Winona, whose noxious jealousy was like her horrific driving. Helen could end up with a broken leg or her head through the windshield.

Themlitz was making his way back to the table, stopping to shake hands with a few of the men, patting some of them on the back. Helen noticed that none of the women offered their hand. Did his cool, prickled skin distress them, too?

"Our beautiful women are leaving us, Paul," Schwinn said. "Helen worked all day and has another work day tomorrow. And Winona has graciously agreed to drive her here and home again." He leaned over and whispered something in Winona's ear at which she sighed.

"Work?"

"Her brother-in-law's liquor store."

"Be sure to give him this, then." Themlitz reached into the

pocket of his jacket and pulled out a tri-fold mimeographed flyer. "It's the information my talk was based on."

Helen took it, folded it in two, and stuffed it into her purse. "Thank you so much for an enlightening evening. And I look forward to coming to your bookstore another time, if my work schedule permits it."

Helen walked silently next to Winona until they reached the car. When they were in the car and Winona had negotiated her way onto Grand Avenue, Helen said, "Thank you for bringing me."

"Hermann is chivalrous with all women," Winona said. Her voice was nasal and clipped.

"I can see that."

"Don't take his kind words and smiles for anything more than that."

"Of course not."

"Are you really still a virgin? In this day and age?"

"Yes."

"Waiting for what?"

Helen thought about dates, corned beef sandwiches, and pickles, dances in large, steaming halls, and groping, teeth-clashing kisses with a dozen young men. Only Sandy had made her not want to pull his fingers away from her breasts, surprising her with a moan she realized came from her own throat. It was only when his hand crept onto her inner thigh and began to stroke her that she gripped it and pushed it away.

"The right guy." Helen was thankful Winona had only had a half a mug of beer and that the streets were vacant.

"Is Joe the right guy?"

"I don't know."

"Hermann isn't." Winona pulled to a stop at a light and stared at Helen, the red of the light suffusing her face with a devilish glow. "Don't mess around with him. And don't tell him you're a virgin."

"I never even thought—"

Winona slammed the car into first gear as the light turned green.

Helen decided not to finish her sentence. The car straddled the mid-line of the street until Winona yanked the wheel to the right. A lone car trailed behind them at a half-block remove, as if afraid to come closer.

A few blocks later, at another stop, Winona sighed. "George will be coming over, too. But Hermann promised me it would just be for dessert and a brief one of his private talks. Then he'll go and the four of us can sit and chat."

Helen turned the topic to clothes, and Winona talked, shifted gears, stalled the car out three times, and finally deposited Helen in front of the liquor store.

The windows reflected Helen's image as she slid out of the seat and stood on the sidewalk, wrapping her coat around her in the late night breeze. The street was deserted except for them and two other cars waiting out an unnecessary red light.

"You're sure you want to be left here?"

"Yes. Quite sure." Helen did not want Winona anywhere near Sarah and the children. It was regrettable that Joe knew where Helen lived and that any of them knew where Forester Liquor was.

Helen took the store key, opened the door, waved goodbye to Winona, and shut and locked it behind her. She walked to the store phone and dialed Sandy's number.

When he answered with an abrupt, "Yes," she said, "Come and get me at the store."

Sandy knocked at the door in the tat-tat-tat pattern he had told her to listen for. She tipped the yellowing store blind back to peer out, then unlocked the door.

They moved over to stand by the counter. Helen opened the storage room door, turned on the light there, and then shut the door to a small crack, allowing enough light to just make out San-dy's features.

"You got back safe and sound," he said. His hands were resting on the counter, his body posed as if he were just going to order a beer.

"These are terrible people."

"They are Nazis, so it goes without saying. What did you find out?"

"Here's a pamphlet on the talk." She took the trifold out, but he waved it away.

"Just dump it someplace. We've got plenty of those. That part of what Themlitz and his group do is 'an open book,'" he said.

"Clever," she said, acknowledging the wisecrack. "Winona is a crazy, jealous, violent girl." She slipped the paper back in her purse. Dropping it the wastepaper basket in the store was not an option.

"Surely you've met her type before."

"Not ones who grind at my leg with their fingers and who have access to guns, no."

"Do you need a bodyguard?"

"Are you volunteering?"

"Me? No."

There was a pause. When Helen realized Sandy wasn't saying anything else, she added, "George will definitely be there Sunday night."

"Good. And you will find out what is going on at Caltech that is a subject of such interest."

"That will end my part in this?"

"It will."

"And I can count on —" She was going to say something about his good will, but he cut her off.

"A screen test and everything else we promised. Thalberg's a man of his word." Sandy touched her arm. "It's important. We have to stay ahead of them. We have to use our resources well."

The place where his fingers touched her sleeve felt warm. She reached up and briefly pressed his hand. "I know."

He brought his other hand up to meet hers, brought her fingers to his lips, and said, "Ah, Helen."

They stood as if his light kiss had frozen them in time. Then he dropped her hand and said, "I should get you home."

13

S ARAH WAS FEEDING THE CHILDREN breakfast when
Helen walked into the kitchen the next morning. The aroma
of the coffee mixed with the bland, heavy smell of the Cream of
Wheat. Rachel was splayed out on the floor, a half-empty bottle
propped up by a twisted kitchen towel next to her as she contentedly sucked on the nipple. Only Sarah would have kitchen floors so
clean that she did not hesitate to put her baby down on them, Helen
thought.

"Harry is already to the store," Sarah said. "The beer truck
comes early." Her back was turned to Helen, her arm moving in
small deliberate circles as she stirred the cereal she was feeding Ben
with a small baby's spoon.

Ben was enthroned in his circus high chair, Cream of Wheat
spread over his face like clown make-up. His mug was on the floor
and Helen grabbed it and placed it on the kitchen table.

"Did you have a good time last night?" Sarah asked. Her eyes
were focused on her son as she tried to get a spoonful of cereal
into his mouth while he swiveled his head back and forth. Helen
had noticed that in this family the babies ate all the food Sarah

provided to them, willingly or not, because their mother acted as the 'clean plate' enforcer.

"Not really. Winona drives like a maniac."

Sarah nodded. "These are not so good people. You should not be with them anymore."

"Because Winona is a bad driver?" Helen felt her stomach twisting into a familiar little knot. She went to the stove and poured a half cup of coffee from the percolator.

"Because, my sister, Benjamin found your purse this morning."

"And?" Helen waited.

"He is pulling out things and I stop him. So here is this thing." Sarah's mouth wrinkled up between a sob and distain. She pointed to the sink.

Before Helen stood up, she knew she would find the trifold from the Themlitz speech lying soddenly in the sink, as if Sarah had tried to wash the words off the paper before she confronted her sister.

"You are right," Helen said. "These are horrible people."

She walked over to Sarah and laid her hand on her sister's shoulder. Sarah placed her free hand on top of Helen's. Her fingers were ice cold even though the kitchen was warm.

A sob exited from Sarah's mouth, low and indistinct, but enough to make Ben startle and blow the cereal in his mouth out onto the tray and Sarah's arm.

"What are you doing with them?" she asked.

"I just need to…"

Sarah gripped her fingers tightly.

"You need to not do this whatever. And for who do you do this?"

Benjamin's eyes were intent on his mother's face. Then his gaze bobbled down to the bowl of cereal and the spoon gripped in Sarah's hand.

"Mo ceelel," he said.

In response, Sarah dropped the spoon handle and shoved herself away from the highchair. Left alone, Benjamin slid a hand into the cooling porridge and brought a full palm up to his mouth.

Sarah pulled the bottle nipple from Rachel's mouth, eliciting a cry of protest to which she did not respond except to pick Rachel up and place her in burp-position on her shoulder. Patting her back rhythmically, Sarah paced the small kitchen.

"Come, sister," she said. She stepped into the hallway as if to protect Ben against a further outburst. Helen walked with her and stood a foot away, her back to the living room.

"What is it you do?" Sarah said. Her voice hissed out like an angry snake.

Helen waited until Sarah took a breath, then offered in a low voice, "I told some people in the Anti-Defamation League that I thought Joe knew some Nazi sympathizers here. They asked me to just go to the restaurant and hear the speaker. Nothing that would get me in trouble."

"I bring you to California to be safe, for a job and a start away from that cold city. You do this?"

When Sarah was in her full protective sister mode she could take on the Indian goddess Durga, with her many arms, she could beat back a thousand frightful clowns, she could take Helen to safety from the devastated post-war continent. Helen wanted nothing more than to agree with Sarah that she should stop.

"Not on purpose."

Sarah rolled her eyes. "You are a spy by accident?" She banged harder on Rachel's back, finally eliciting a soft, gurgled burp and a dribble of milk from the baby's mouth.

A spy by accident seemed to describe exactly what had happened. But she could have exited at any time, could have told them no instead of being lured by a screen test that she certainly would not pass and money that Harry no longer needed. She could have stopped after the first party or the second, or told them to find some radical Jewish college students to run around. They could probably use the excitement. She could not.

These Nazi sympathizers were bumbling, pompous, crazy, bad people who, in their farcical way, in their imitation of real evil, were evil enough. People had thought Hitler was a clown, or so the newspapers and the radio said, and yet there he was, still Chancellor of Germany.

"Yes, but you and I have moved as far away from the slime of Europe as we could and it is still following us. So, here at the Pacific Ocean..." Helen said.

Sarah stepped around Helen without saying a word. She entered the kitchen, put Rachel back on the floor, and wet a tea towel so she could begin to clean Benjamin up.

"My babies need to be safe," she said. "No Nazis here at my house or at the store. You tell the ADL that."

"Sarah," Helen said.

Her sister did not turn around.

"Will she tell Harry?" This was Sandy's first question after Helen finished her thirty-second summary in a whispered voice. Her eyes were fixed on the storage room door, slightly ajar, and where she could see Harry in slivers as he moved bottles of beer into the large refrigerator and restacked the rest of the beer crates around the store safe. She patted her face with a clean handkerchief to wipe away the perspiration from her fast walk to the store.

"Not yet." Sarah would most probably pretend she knew nothing about Helen's activities in the same way that she had pretended to know nothing about Harry's gambling.

"I'll need another place for Joe to pick me up tomorrow for the dinner."

"And an exit plan if the dinner goes amok."

"I'll work on that and talk to you later." She hung up as Harry opened the door and walked in, shrugging into a clean shirt as he did.

"You were a little late this morning," he said.

"Sarah and I got to talking about my social life." She smiled at him. "She worries, you know."

"For a girl with nobody out here but us when you came, you sure have gotten a lot of interest." He walked over to the window and tapped the Cinzano poster.

"I like those ponies, but the high-end product doesn't move for shit," he said. "That's like life, you know. You can like the crap out of something but in the end, nothing."

Helen waited, leaning back against the counter.

"On the other hand, you can think something is pretty low class, but it flies off the shelf."

"Like beer," she said.

He nodded. "Like people, too, I have learned."

"A life lesson from Harry," she said. The gentleness around the words surprised her.

He cleared his throat. "Ralph was here yesterday just after you left with that skinny broad. The jittery one," he added in case Helen did not remember leaving with Winona.

"He's wants to be sure you are okay. The skinny broad can be difficult, he said." He shrugged, his hands palm up.

"Two talks about my acquaintances in one morning?"

"Yeah, well. Ralph said he was going to keep an eye out for you."

Helen considered the possibilities. Ralph slugging Joe, Ralph shooting Schwinn, Ralph getting shot, Ralph messing up her plan.

"I've got his card someplace in my purse. I'll tell him 'no' myself," she said. She slid her handbag into the shelf under the register and sat on the three-stair stepstool they both used to reach the high display shelves.

"Maybe, but I don't think he'll listen."

Harry stood close enough to Helen that she could see the small patch of stubble he had missed in his morning shave and smell the sugar of the sweet roll from his breakfast on his breath. Her sitting position equalized their heights so he could stare squint-eyed into hers.

"I'm just saying what he said, Helen."

"You knew his brother in New Jersey. What kind of people are they?"

"People like you and me, who want to live comfortably with a little money."

"How are they about Jews, Harry?"

"Jews?" Harry whispered the word as if the empty store thronged with customers. "They are fine with Jews, Helen."

Helen pursed her lips and rubbed the side of her nose. Then she shook her head and laughed. Harry's mouth twitched up at the sides as well, followed by a snort.

"Okay. I get it. You and Ralph have some sort of pact that you are not going to level with me about him."

"Not just you. It's important to him and I'm a man of my word." Harry tilted his face as if his profile were about to appear on a coin.

"Yeah, fine. Just go and finish whatever you were doing in the storeroom."

The morning passed in its typical languorous way, with more than enough time to read the *Los Angeles Times*, dust the display shelves, and fill in gaps where customers had plucked bottles from the lineup. The fan made a soft snick-snick sound that made Helen want to put her head on her folded arms and take a nap. The usual before lunch customers came in for small-change purchases.

For lunch, Helen peeled an orange and broke it into sections. She bit off a small piece of the peel, letting the sharp tang tingle in her mouth, before eating the sweet, drippy pulp. The fruits and vegetables that Sarah brought into the house were still a wonder to her. Fresh oranges, the first cherries of the season, lettuce, zucchini, even pineapples from Hawaii; it really was a land of plenty in California. She sipped some Coca-Cola while looking out the window at the few pedestrians that walked by in the blue, pellucid day.

One of the walkers took three steps toward the building but quickened her step and hurried away as a car skidded up against the curb, facing the wrong way. Before the driver's door opened, Helen knew it was Winona, not just from the automobile's appearance but also from the entitled way it now sat, blocking half the crosswalk.

"Harry," she said, opening up the storeroom door, "I've got to go out and talk to 'that jittery dame.' We don't want her in here."

"She's back?"

"That's what I said."

Helen walked over to the door, flipped the sign to "Closed," shut the door behind her, and locked it. As she did that, Winona stood, one foot on the curb and one in the street, leaning against the open car door.

"Hey," Winona said. She waved her right hand like a windshield wiper, as if she were hard to see.

"I thought that was you," Helen said. Her voice was extra loud, friendly, and excited, suited for meeting elderly aunts who could leave something for you in their wills.

"Come on, I'm going down the street."

"Why?" Winona stepped onto the sidewalk. "Maybe I can drive us wherever you need to go."

Helen decided it was best to take Winona up on her offer to avoid an argument or worse.

"Great. I wanted a little fresh air, but never mind." Helen walked around to the passenger side and got in.

Winona sat back down in the driver's seat, closed the driver door, and slid the key into the ignition.

"Where to?"

"I just wanted to get out of the store for a few minutes."

"But you closed it up, which means you don't get any customers while you're gone."

For a dope-addled woman who let a man beat her buttocks, Winona appeared to have a decent sense of business. Maybe she'd gotten that from her mother.

"Harry was uhh, just finishing up in the—"

"Got it, I think," Winona said. "So when we get back I can buy a few bottles of beer there for dinner Sunday night."

She pulled out and made a U-turn. A mother with a toddler yanked his arm firmly to keep him at least a yard away from the crosswalk.

"Just tell me what you are thinking of and I'll bring it. My treat, a hostess gift."

"Are you trying to keep me out of the store? I just want to see what you do because you're my friend. I know I've never worked but Mother does. I mean I know what work is, just she won't let me do it."

Talking to Winona was full of land mines and odd turns.

"Why would I want to keep you out of the store? My work is so dull. There is just nothing interesting about it." The words came out in a quiet explosion of distress ignited by the need to keep Winona away and the truth of her description of the job.

Winona turned to look at her, leaving only her left hand on the steering wheel as a marker that she was driving the car.

"For God's sake, Winona, watch the traffic," Helen said.

"Bossy," Winona said, turning her head so her gaze confronted the front windshield and the car just ahead, slowing for the light. She hit the brake and smiled as Helen shot her left hand out to brace herself against the dashboard to prevent sliding off the front seat at the sudden stop.

Helen repositioned herself on the seat and began to rub her wrist. It throbbed from the impact.

Winona reached over and tapped Helen's thigh once in a bad imitation of sympathy. "I'm so sorry if your hand is hurt," she said.

A smile can have so many meanings, Helen considered. Winona's smile continued to play over her lips while they drove in silence for the next two blocks.

"I do want to bring a hostess present," Helen said to reopen the conversation. "Let me give you the beer. We carry Tornbergs and Kronenbrau from Germany. Should I bring some for you, Hermann, Joe, me, and George?"

At the mention of George, Winona's smile disappeared. She relaxed her two-handed clench of the steering wheel enough to push a lock of hair away from her forehead, and then re-gripped. She continued to stare forward as if she were playing the game "Statues," waiting for Helen to tag her.

Then she said, "He's not coming until later. We'll have most of the night to ourselves. I'll get out the Ouija board. It'll be so much fun."

"Oh, good," Helen said.

"I have some questions to ask it about you."

"I thought it only foretold the future."

"Not true."

Maybe it would be better to know what concerns Winona had about her so that she could develop whatever tale she needed to spin. Or should she just laugh that off?

"What do you want to ask that you can't just ask me?"

Winona rearranged the hair that fell again onto her face with an angry gesture.

"What color aura do you have, is one."

Helen stifled a laugh. This spiritualist stuff was serious business to Jessie and Winona, a need to feel connected to a higher plane that would justify any otherwise unjustifiable position. Murder, rape, pillage. Didn't bringers of mayhem always say they had the word from God?

"What does your mother say?"

"She says it's dark red. And she says mine is still green."

"Pull over here, Winona, if you would. We can get an ice cream in the Rexall drugstore. Look, they have a counter and they serve it homemade."

A teenage girl, three pimples on her cheek, face flushed from the heat of the grill, came over to take their orders. Helen wondered why she wasn't in high school.

Helen asked for chocolate fudge and Winona, vanilla with little chunks of frozen maraschino cherries. Each oversized scoop came in an ice-cold sundae cup along with a long handled spoon to dig out the last drops from the bottom. The fudge had the dense, almost bitter quality Helen loved. She ate five spoonfuls without talking.

Winona picked her cherries out with the tip of the spoon and pushed them onto the edge of the cup. Then she ate a small bite of the vanilla, followed by popping two of the cherry pieces into her mouth with her thumb and forefinger.

"A dark red aura means what?" Helen looked over at Winona.

"Strength. Courage. You know…"

"I don't know. But green sounds like a great color to have. Plants, earth, I mean that's what I think of."

"It's a crappy color to have. It's weak, jealous, oh yeah, and insecure."

"Really? You? That just does not match you at all." Helen put another spoonful of the ice cream in her mouth and considered ordering another scoop.

A tear trickled down the side of Winona's nose and she swiped it away with the side of her hand. Then she sniffled and put another piece of cherry in her mouth.

"Mother is very disappointed in my aura."

To Helen this sounded like a backdoor way Jessie chose to

criticize her daughter's obvious failings. It was quite a contrast to Sarah's direct assault.

"My sister," Sarah would say, "this 'B' on your spelling test means you are lazy and not studying. We will get up tomorrow at five and you will do the spelling for me for this week."

"I would never say that Jessie was wrong, but can these auras be interfered with?"

"You mean by an outside force? I never thought of that." Winona scooped a heap of vanilla ice cream into her mouth, her cheeks puffing up like a chipmunk. As the ice cream made its way past her mouth and down her throat, Winona tipped her head first to one side and then to the other in a parody of consideration.

"Who would want to harm me?" The thought seemed to have frightened her.

Helen had no idea who to point the finger at.

"Wow. I don't know. Is there anyone who maybe ..." Her voice trailed off leaving a path for Winona to travel down.

Winona twisted the wedding ring on her finger. "Not Norman. He's thrilled to be married to me and hobnob with Mother."

I'll bet, Helen thought.

"It's got to be Joe." Winona got off the stool, threw a dollar bill on the counter, and tugged at Helen's arm.

Helen slid off the stool and allowed Winona to walk her out of the store and back to the car. Winona could have focused on her, Jessie's newly anointed. Helen didn't doubt that Winona could and would try, at some point, to clamber into her mother's circle of confidants. And one way was to push the new girl out however she could.

"Joe has a very weak aura. Pastel, thready." Winona began talking as soon as she swung the car into traffic and was heading back toward Forester Liquor.

"I thought he was my friend. But I think he's used me to get close to Mother. He's bleeding out my aura. Hermann doesn't like him. You should have seen the look on his face when I told him Joe was joining us for dinner. He was disgusted. He only relented because you'll be there."

Winona nodded up and down, having convinced herself in her one-person argument. She was halfway toward chucking Joe out of her life; he'd be roadkill for her careening psyche by the end of the day.

"But your mother likes him."

There was a startled look on Winona's face, as if Raggedy Ann, sitting on the back seat, had suddenly spoken. She peered at Helen through squinted eyes.

"Mother does not like people. Where are my sunglasses?"

"Are they in your purse?"

"Yes." Winona began to angle over to grab her bag on the floor near Helen's foot.

"Here." Helen grabbed the purse, opened it, and felt for them. She handed the tortoise-shell rimmed pair, with their perfectly round, amber-tinted inserts, to Winona.

With a sigh, Winona perched them on her nose. "Squinting gives you wrinkles. Frowning, too."

"You don't have to worry. You have perfect skin."

Helen tried to drag the discussion away from Joe. She could not go to the dinner without him, she was certain, because of Winona's jealousy over Schwinn. And if she lost Joe, would he find out she was the cause of Winona turning against him?

"What beer did you want me to bring again?"

"Oh, the dinner. Yes, bring some great German beer."

"And Joe?" Helen's voice was quiet.

"Bring him too." Winona pushed the glasses higher on the ridge of her nose. "I should give him another chance. But just one more. Maybe you've improved his aura."

"If Joe was out, who would be the contact for the movie industry?" Helen hoped her voice was casual and just interested enough.

"Mother and Hermann have a few guys they are beginning to groom for that. Like I said, Hermann doesn't care for Joe."

Ralph, with his broken nose, his brief screen appearances, and his Screen Actors Guild membership might be one. She still didn't trust him, for all he had done for Harry, for whatever reason he had done it. All the more reason, Helen thought, to be sure Ralph didn't interfere with her plans, once she had them.

It was even possible that Jessie had told Ralph to keep an eye on her. Maybe what he'd said–that he'd given Jessie a good report on her—was a lie. Belief in the paranormal notwithstanding, Jessie did not live like a woman who took too many chances. Helen gnawed at the spot on her inner cheek that was already tender but invisible to the outside world.

"Why are you so interested, Helen?"

Helen hoped her nervous flush would be taken for embarrassment if Winona looked too hard. "Well, Joe...he's a nice enough guy and we've been dating." She let her voice fade off.

"You like him." Winona sounded as if Helen had just announced her impending marriage. Then she began to giggle, her head nodding up and down, and her eyes closed.

"Winona, please open your eyes because there are people crossing the street."

"Orders, orders." Winona opened her eyes and simultaneously reached over and smacked Helen's thigh. Her open hand made a loud clapping sound as it hit Helen's leg.

"Two virgins." She laughed again. "I wonder how much Hermann would pay to see that." The car came to a stop as Winona jammed her foot onto the brake.

"The store is just ahead. I'll slide out here, while the light is red, and walk. See you Sunday night."

Outside of the car, Helen braced herself for a moment against the light pole and watched Winona drive away. The air was mild, with a tang of car fumes. The sky was an unnerving, cloudless baby blue. Ralph was right. The skinny broad *was* difficult.

When she was twelve, Helen had been chased by a gang of five Catholic girls, identified by their St. Anne's blue-and-white-striped school uniforms, who were determined to beat up the only Christ-killer they had ever met. Rather than run into the alley and try to hide between the trash bins, Helen fled to the main street and into Roth's Deli, with "Kosher" and a Star of David painted on the window. There she had panted out an order for plain seltzer water and grabbed a nickel from her coat pocket. She sat at the counter and watched until each girl, bedraggled by the rain that began to fall, left the street.

What would be her Roth's Deli now?

Ralph's answering service seemed to be a one-woman operation. Helen was put on hold three times by the hoarse phlegmy voice saying, "Just a second, dear." She had a vision of an octopus, with a cigarette hanging out of its mouth, slipping tentacles in and out of phone slots. Still, the service took care to read back the message and ensure that the reply number was accurate.

The remainder of the afternoon at Forester Liquor drifted on, interrupted by the delivery of the *Herald Examiner* in the afternoon and then by a tall, heavy-set man, in a maroon plaid sports coat, accompanied by a woman easily a foot shorter than he was, but equally heavy-set, in a dress bought ten pounds ago, and gold hoop earrings that hung to her shoulders.

They were having a dinner party that night and argued with each other and then with Helen over whether the wine should be red or white and how much beer to have as a backup because "as my husband well knows, his friends do not like wine." The wife shook her head dolefully as her husband paid for the purchase and then she lugged what, to Helen, seemed like the heavier bag of liquor out the door.

Just after the couple left, the store phone rang. Helen waited to see if Harry had picked it up in the storeroom. When the phone kept ringing, she answered. It was Ralph.

"I'm just finishing up here, Helen. I'll come over and we can talk."

Before she could say "no" again, he'd hung up. , By the time he walked in, ten minutes later, Helen had stretched, shrugged her shoulders up and down seven times, and taken enough deep breaths to qualify for a place in a wind ensemble. Still, when she saw him silhouetted against the late afternoon sun streaming in as the door opened, she could feel her shoulders hunching up toward her ears as she took an inadvertent defensive step backward. Her head thunked against the wall.

Ralph stopped halfway into the store. "Jeez, Helen. I'm in my harmless mode right now. You want to frisk me to be sure?" He grinned and held his arms away from his body.

Helen could see the sweat rings on his blue cotton shirt. She let the corners of her mouth tweak into a semblance of a smile and slid her body around to the front of the counter, as if she was a cornered cat trying to assess the intentions of a large, not-yet-barking dog.

"Of course not."

"I'll stand behind this line, then." Ralph reached out and swept his arm a foot in front of his body.

"Okay. I need to ask you to stop saying you are going to follow me around. It's umm.." Helen stopped. "I don't like it, this feeling that you are…"

"Snooping around in your business." Ralph finished the sentence.

"Yes."

Helen had stepped away from the counter and toward him. She saw his brow furrow and his gaze drift over her shoulder. He shifted back and forth on his feet as if dancing a quick-step with an unseen partner. Then he quieted and looked at her again.

"Like I told Harry, Winona is a problem. Drinks too much and so on, if you haven't noticed. Drives loaded."

"Please…"

He nodded. "Okay. I'll consider your request. Is that all?"

"Yes."

Ralph cocked his head slightly to the right, then nodded, turned and walked out of the store. The screen door thudded twice against the doorstop as it swung closed.

Helen slipped onto the stool in back of the counter, her legs shaky and her hands cold. She crossed her arms, leaned forward and buried her face in them as if she were burrowing into her pillow. Her eyes closed, she breathed, her own smell acrid in her nostrils.

The door opened again, the bell chiming briskly.

Ralph walked up to the counter, leaned over it, and hissed, "Don't turn stupid on me. We're on the same fucking side. I told Harry not to tell you I'm Jewish because I didn't want you to do something and blow my cover. But you gotta let me watch you or you will be a very dead girl."

Ralph's nose was so close that Helen could see a thin, faded pink scar on the bridge.

"Okay," she said.

He turned and walked out, shutting the screen with a click as he left.

After a minute, she went to the cooler, got a Nehi, and took several gulps of the orange colored drink. Then she retrieved Jessie's telephone number from her purse and called.

"It's Helen," she said when the maid found Jessie and gave her the phone.

"My dear girl, what a pleasant surprise."

"I just thought I would call. I hate to bother you, but I wondered if I could ask a favor."

"Yes, yes." There was an eagerness in Jessie's voice, as if the asking of a favor and the granting of it would be a monumental achievement.

"I've been thinking a lot about my future. Of course I don't want to remain working in the liquor store."

"Absolutely."

"I think I want something quiet and stable. Something like office work, which I've done. You have a friend, George, who said he had a high administrative position someplace. I've forgotten where."

"George. Of course. The California Institute of Technology."

Helen paused. "Do you think that would be someplace suitable for me to apply to?"

"It's a fine university."

"Oh, is that what it is?" Helen said.

For her purposes, a naïve demeanor and lack of information could serve as a cloak of invisibility. Claude Raines, the Invisible Man, would have nothing on her, except that he wrapped himself in gauze bandages when he wanted to be seen and she would dress like a proper German young woman and hope to keep her intentions hidden.

Jessie's barking laugh burst through the receiver. "I forget that you haven't been here for long. Let me call George today."

"Will you tell him how to get in touch with me if he has something?"

"Yes. And, Helen, I'm so pleased that you asked me and that you are not chasing after this movie business thing, like so many silly young women."

"I want you to drive me out to that college," Helen said.

On the other end of the line, Sandy groaned. "Tell me why."

"Because I want to be able to tell George that I was out there, maybe looking for a job. I want him to think I'm interested."

"In him or in a job?"

"Maybe both. Whichever would work best. But I think it will go over better if I have some information about where he works."

There was a pause, the sound of something like a pencil tapping against a desk, and then Sandy said, "You're the girl and this is your area. I guess I didn't know that girls were so planful about interesting guys."

Helen flushed, part in anger and part in embarrassment. Making sure the heat of her cheeks didn't enter into her voice, she said, "The stakes are high."

"You are right, dear Helen."

Helen had not mistaken George's interest in her. Three hours later Sandy had commandeered a car and was driving her out to the Caltech campus in Pasadena so she could make the four o'clock appointment George had offered her.

"And you are doing this why?" he said.

"I may need reasons to seek him out Sunday night. Reasons that won't cause suspicion."

Sandy stuck his arm out to signal a right turn at Colorado Boulevard, which held two lanes of traffic going in each direction. It was as if every automobile and building had been put to a middle-class test before being allowed to exist in this area of Los Angeles County.

A few empty lots were jammed between new-looking Spanish Revival and Art Deco multi-storied buildings on the street. Those vacant spaces had "For Sale" signs announcing their suitability for retail development. The real estate agent's name and number was written in large lettering on each.

Automobiles were late models, clean, shiny, and often driven by women. Either their husbands took the bus or trolley to work or these were two-car families, an indulgence that was almost beyond Helen's ability to grasp.

"They had to widen this street about seven years ago to hold the traffic," Sandy said. "Rebuilt all of this." He waved his right hand back and forth. "I was out here just after they finished. A friend told me what a mess it was."

Helen stared out the window, unable to imagine disorder on the broad avenue where cars flowed smoothly in both directions.

"Do you know anything about Caltech?" he said.

"Only what you've told me and the little I could gather at the party."

"You've heard of MIT?"

"Yes."

"This is the next best thing to MIT. Phenomenal research in all the sciences and applied areas, like engineering, aerodynamics…"

"Bomb-making?"

"Possibly, but they'd keep that quiet. Well, until the bomb went off, I guess." Sandy smiled.

"George and the other men were talking about Jewish scientists there."

"Millikan—he's the president there—has a quota on Jews."

"What else is new?" Helen said.

"Zero is too many for him. He's on—are you ready for this—the Emergency Committee in Aid of Displaced Foreign Scholars." Sandy smiled, mocking each word.

"And they what?" Helen said.

"They are supposed to find safe academic havens for scholars and scientists fleeing Nazism."

Helen rolled down her window to let the fresh air in. The breeze ruffled her hair and she smoothed it back.

"The total number taken in by Caltech since the committee started in 1933 is three. And one left for Princeton," Sandy said.

She tried not to let Sandy's voice tug her toward him, tried not to have her left hand drift over toward his right, which rested on the seat between them until needed to shift the gears. Lifting her hand, she pointed out the window.

"Nice trees," she said.

Sandy turned his head to look at her. "And blue sky," he said. "The one who left was Albert Einstein, probably the smartest man who's ever lived. Theories about how stuff can become pure energy, I think. God knows I couldn't follow any idea of his much past him saying, 'I propose that....'"

"Did you try?" Helen had thought Sandy's interests were in drama and literature. Camus, Tolstoy, and O'Neil were names she remembered he had dropped, books he had loaned her, play lines he had rehearsed.

"Yep. I was out here and he was giving a public lecture so I thought I'd go since he was, and is, the preeminent Jewish refugee from Nazi Germany. The auditorium was packed, standing room only. I thought, 'How could a scientist get this kind of audience? I'd kill for a room full of people.'"

"And?"

"And he got a standing ovation before he started to talk and another one after."

"In between?"

"Like I said, I got the general idea, my friends assured me, but that was it."

"But he isn't there now," Helen said.

"No. We can probably rule him out as the object of their interest. It's something or someone else."

They turned onto California Avenue. Helen saw two thick, muscular-looking three story brick buildings that faced each other across a small courtyard. Someone she assumed was a student was sprawled out on the lawn, elbows propping up his naked upper torso as he read a book. A knapsack on one side and a shirt on the other marked his territory.

"I'm leaving you here," Sandy said. "It's a few minutes before four. I'll be back right here at five and I'll wait for ten minutes. If I don't see you, I'll assume you found another way home."

She shrugged and opened the car door.

The sunbathing undergrad stood up as she approached him, brushing fragments of grass off his slacks, and smelling of baby oil that reminded her of her niece. He pointed her down the courtyard toward the building that he thought housed administration. As she turned to walk away, he picked up his shirt and his knapsack, which bulged with the weight of unseen books.

"I'm going that way, so if I can, I'll walk with you," he said.

Sandy tooted the horn and Helen turned to see him grin and wave as he drove away.

"Is that your boyfriend?"

"I wish I knew."

Steve was a physics major who had gone to an undergraduate seminar Einstein had offered. He chatted about energy and matter with a delight Helen had seen attached to theater and art in New York and expressed admiration for Einstein that exceeded even the hero-worship the majority of Americans had for FDR. When he dropped her off in front of the building, she thanked him.

If Steve was an example, the few square blocks in Pasadena devoted to the campus were a different universe. There were no co-eds to be seen and therefore no flirtatious groupings on the steps of the buildings. Three young men walked down the stairs as she walked up, parting and snuggling up to the balustrade to let her pass. As they continued down, she heard them talking about something called field theory.

Helen tapped on the frosted glass window of Room 203, the

number George had given her. A woman's voice called out, "It's unlocked."

Helen entered a large room with four desks, each with a Remington typewriter, and, to the rear, a separate office. The room's perimeter was filled with five-drawer filing cabinets. A ceiling fan made desultory passes in an effort to move the air, which was thick, as if carrying the weight of all the paper, typewriter ink, and dust in the space.

The woman who had called out sat at the front desk. Her nameplate said "Anne O'Casey" and she had the look of an Irish immigrant, pale skin, blue eyes, and thick curly red hair. She didn't look much over her mid-thirties.

"May I help you," she asked with a slight Irish brogue.

"I'm here to meet with George."

At that the rear office door opened and George peered out. From where she stood, Helen could see rivulets of sweat on his thick neck. His bifocals looked as if they would slip off his nose with the slightest tilt of his head.

"Helen. Good. Right on time. Come on back."

Helen nodded to Anne and walked toward the rear. She sensed Anne turning in her chair to watch. Was her job on the line?

At George's wave, Helen perched on the edge of a folding chair tucked into the corner of the small room. He leaned against the edge of his desk, which had three compact, low piles of paper in stacks, a coffee cup stuffed with pencils, and a telephone. A narrow bookcase was packed with what looked like catalogs. Two five-drawer filing cabinets in gunmetal gray squeezed into the remaining space.

"I was delighted to hear from Jessie that you were inquiring about a job. It was timely."

Helen tilted her head and gazed up at him, waiting.

"My secretary, you met her on the way in, is a good Catholic woman. And therefore, she is …" His voice trailed off.

Helen raised an eyebrow. "She is in a family way?"

It was a source of amazement to her that men who dealt with finance, power, war, the fate of nations, could not ever bring themselves to discuss the normal biological nature of women. They could not utter the word "pregnant," would only refer to breasts and vaginas in contemptuous slang, and shuddered at the mere thought of menstruation, never mind having those twelve letters actually come out of their mouths.

"Yes. Much to be admired but still no pregnant woman should be working."

Helen refrained from asking if Anne's husband had a job or, worse, if Anne had a husband.

"When would the job be available?"

"Two weeks. I'd give her notice today. She expects it soon anyhow."

"I'd need more time than that. My brother-in-law relies on me and ..."

George looked at her with what Helen surmised was his attempt at solemn acceptance. He looked sad.

"Yes. Take a week or so."

Helen was concerned that she would be dismissed at that point. It would be reasonable since it had been a job interview of sorts. But she wanted to spend more time with him so that seeking him out again at Winona's house wouldn't seem so odd.

"I'd like to tell you about my credentials for the position or give you a resume at least. But I haven't brought one with me. It was so last minute, this interview. You're not the sort to buy a pig in a poke, are you?" She smiled.

"No, not at all."

"This is such an important position that you have. Overseeing supplies of such a large college."

"University."

"See how much I have to learn. What are some of the fields here?"

"That wouldn't be something you'd have to think about. We order material, just like you would for a department store."

"Surely not. I mean, you don't order hosiery or pajamas." She upped her smile to a grin.

George complied by laughing.

"No, paper, pencils, mimeograph ink, sometimes items that researchers need. You see we are just one branch of administration, the part that does supplies. Other areas are scattered around the campus. We've stayed here in the old building because it's easiest."

George had inflated his position during the discussion at Jessie's. Helen was not surprised but she was disappointed. Maybe George didn't know much about anything that was going on after all. The smile flickered off her face.

"The research orders are maybe the most interesting," he said. "I don't want you to think it's just pushing one form after another across the desk here. Some things we have to call all over for."

Procurement of research items was how George found out about new avenues these scientists were pursuing.

Helen smiled again. The act of willing it onto her face focused her back on George, who sat up straighter as she did so. "When I was in New York I worked in an office doing bookkeeping and typing."

"That's perfect."

"What kind of research?" Her voice was puffed up with awe.

"Mathematics, chemistry, aeronautics, that kind of stuff."

"So, you could order Bunsen burners, flasks, propellers. Golly." As she threw the last word in, she sighed and shook her head briefly back and forth. "And you think that I could learn how to order such important items?"

"Oh, indeed I do." He leaned over and took her hand. "You are just the sort of person we need."

"Could you show me some samples of what I would have to do? I wouldn't want to put you in a bad place if you hired me and

I was overwhelmed." Folding her fingers on her lap, Helen looked over at George's desk, with its short stacks of papers and its hidden secrets.

George reached over and grabbed a page, then pulled a three-inch-thick catalog from the second shelf of the bookcase.

"It's simple. Here we have ordered this chemical from this supplier." The catalog thudded onto the desk near Helen. George's thick thumb, with a slightly chewed cuticle, rested on the invoice. Upside down, Helen read "Guggenheim Aeronautical Laboratory."

"Most times we can just call because everyone knows Caltech. Sometimes, we have to write. The stuff comes in, we make sure the department that ordered it signs off that it is correct, and we pay the invoice."

"You were right. It is just like ordering hosiery," Helen said.

"Sometimes it's harder." George sounded wounded, like a boy who had been told he was just average.

"I only meant, George, that what you showed me made me feel much better, like I could do it."

"And I would be here to help you with the harder ones."

"Yes, of course. Could you give me an example? Like maybe some new thing you have to order for?"

"If I hire you, I'll train you in everything, Helen. And you can help me keep an eye on what goes on here in a way that would be helpful."

"To our mutual friends?" Helen said.

"I knew you would be the right person."

Anne knocked on the doorframe of George's tiny office.

"Mrs. Parsons is here again about the orders," she said.

"Tell her I'll be out in a minute." George patted Helen's thigh as if it were his pet dog's head. "I look forward to hearing from you soon," he said.

As Helen exited through the door, a slender woman in her

mid-twenties with brunette hair in a curly bob and a determined look on her face stood at the counter, drumming her fingers on it.

"Mrs. Parsons," Helen heard George say over her shoulder, "the material for the Guggenheim has been ordered."

"And when will it come?" Her voice had a low-pitched throb. "They've been waiting six weeks now."

"Mid-June at the latest."

"Maybe I should drive to the refinery and get it myself."

"Now, now," George said. "We take good care of our experimenters…"

Helen waited outside the office for the forceful-appearing, young Mrs. Parsons to come out. If she was another secretary, Helen wanted to chat with her about the relationship between the supplies and procurements that George handled and the high-end research going on. In Helen's experience, women, especially those close to her age, shared the details of their lives readily, and the more boring the details, the more readily they were shared. She glanced at her watch and calculated that she had ten minutes before Sandy would strand her in Pasadena.

"Mrs. Parsons, a word if I could," Helen said as the door banged shut and the woman emerged into the hall, beginning to take a long stride toward the stairs.

"I'm Helen." Mrs. Parsons held out her hand.

"How funny. I'm a Helen too."

"Come and walk with me, Helen. I'm heading back over to my husband to tell him the bad news. What he and the guys need won't be here until mid-June and that's a firm 'maybe.'"

"Thank you. I am thinking of applying for a position here," Helen said, matching Helen Parsons's pace. "Maybe you could tell me about the place."

"I don't know much outside of the area where my husband works."

"What does he do?"

"He's doing experiments."

"So he's a graduate student?"

"Nah. College dropout and self-taught genius." Helen Parsons grinned. "He's headed for great things, my Jack is."

"You have a lot of confidence in him."

"Indeed. So I don't mind working for the lab while he finishes here. At least that way he won't keep hocking my engagement ring to fund his projects. Or manufacturing nitro in the garage."

Helen looked. There was a speck of diamond flashing on the other Helen's left ring finger, just above a thin gold band.

"Then the sky's the limit."

"What is his research on?" Helen wondered about marriages to men who made explosives near their beloveds' bedrooms. Were they dangerous or thoughtless or both?

The other Helen grabbed the banister of the stairs as they headed down, taking two steps at a time. "Making sure the sky's no limit." She laughed. "Really, I can't say. I need to get back to the Guggenheim."

Helen Parsons waved her arm to dismiss the closed doors, neatly lettered signs, and wood paneling, and then strode down the hall toward the main doors.

Helen took three running steps to catch up, wanting more than just that brief exchange. Was this Helen working with her husband or just working to support him?

"One more question, please."

They both came to a stop on the lawn just outside the building.

"Which is?"

"What is the Guggenheim?"

"The aeronautical program. Funded by the Guggenheims. Jews, tons of money." She rubbed her fingers together, counting invisible cash. "They threw some of it here. Good for us."

"Thanks."

"Bye, Helen. Hope you get the job." Helen Parsons turned and ran across the lawn and between the two brick buildings opposite.

Helen slid into the car and turned to Sandy.

"It went well, I think," she said. "But I couldn't get any information about new research because he feels he has to train me in the job."

"So you will have to lurk in the shadows on Sunday?"

"Yes. The faster I get you this information, the faster I am free of being a spy, right? And I can—"

"You can cash in on Thalberg's promise to you, if that's what you mean."

"Partly. I have a hard time sleeping now. My sister is upset. This could all come down not just on me but on her."

14

HELEN FELT ANGER GROWING AT the Crayola colors of the yellow sun, blue sky, red and orange flowers, and green lawn. It was like opening up a children's book for a pleasant read and discovering demons, succubae, and golems romping on the pages. A dream turned inside out, that was California. She walked toward the liquor store on Saturday morning wondering if moving to the heart of the Dust Bowl would hide her.

No pedestrians were near the store and a single car was parked on the opposite side of the street. She'd seen two toddlers playing in their front yards, under the careful watch of their mothers, and one man, sleeves rolled up, washing his car with the garden hose in his driveway. Wherever the population of Glendale was, it was not outside.

Sarah had not talked to her since the exchange after she found the Aryan Bookstore pamphlet in her son's pudgy hand. Instead, she swept the children up into the bedroom or the backyard when Helen called out a greeting. They had been fed, bathed, and bedded before Helen could enter the kitchen in the evening.

Helen had tried to talk to her sister the night before without luck. She had no sooner said, "Sarah," than her sister had announced, seemingly to the ceiling overhead, "The children." Sarah had then risen from her kitchen chair and left, leaving Harry and Helen to chew on their Friday night chicken in silence.

There was justice in that. Sarah should have left her with her aunt and uncle in Poland and made her own way. Now she had children and what had Helen done? The fetid waves of Europe lapped against the walls of the bungalow in California and every time Helen walked out the front door, the waters threatened the Philco radio, the Bell telephone, the O'Keefe and Merritt stove, and the baby's changing table.

Inside Forester's, Helen locked the door behind her and walked over to the phone.

"It's Helen, Joe," she said when Joe answered the phone. His voice was muffled and she suspected someone else was in the bungalow with him and he did not want the conversation questioned.

"I need to tell you something about Winona. Is this a good time?"

"Are you at work?" The question came as a harsh whisper, more sinister than she suspected he meant.

"I am."

"I'll come over there a little later."

She did not want the store to become Grand Central Station for Nazi sympathizers and thugs, but it seemed to be going that direction anyhow.

"I'd rather not meet here. What if there are customers? It's not a good place to talk. Look, I'll shut the store for an early lunch, say eleven, and walk toward your aunt's store. You can meet me on the street. Saturday's a busy day so I've got maybe fifteen minutes."

"Fine." In the background, Helen heard a door slam shut on Joe's end. Someone there was making a point.

Helen did the bookkeeping for the week leaning against the counter, as wisps of clouds slid across the sky causing sunlight to drift in and out of the store through its windows. From the outside it would be difficult to see anyone inside, which was what she wanted. The "Closed" sign firmly faced the sidewalk. It was not yet 9:00 a.m.

The woman with the twenty-dollar racing bets peered in for a second. Helen shrank back. The woman looked at her watch, shook her head, and walked away.

Helen knew Harry would have opened the door to take the early bet on the Kentucky Derby, but he had decided to stay home with Sarah and the babies for the day.

"I don't like her upset," he had said to Helen on Friday night, nodding toward the hall where Sarah could be heard reading Ben *The Little Engine That Could*, with Ben's "Train, train," punctuating Sarah's murmur.

Helen sat in the living room, a *Life* magazine open and ignored on her lap. Harry stood by the radio, sipping a finger of Scotch.

"It's taken me a long time to convince her that she isn't damaged goods. That she made choices that she had to make for herself."

"And for me."

"Oh yes, Helen, always for you." He put the glass down precisely on a coaster.

"I didn't bring gangsters into her life." Helen defended herself.

"True. But you've brought a certain drama—men, modeling, movies. And she can't tell you what to do anymore. So she worries, grinds her teeth in her sleep. Did you hear her call out, 'Helen, no' the other night?"

Helen shook her head.

"Is that what she said was bothering her? Men, modeling, and movies? I'm going to simplify my life right after this weekend."

"She didn't say but I have eyes. Three men, fancy clothes, parties." Harry paused.

"I've tried to make a quiet life for her. Maybe Glendale isn't so hospitable to Jews, but what place is? This is a solid house." He leaned over and patted the wall for emphasis.

"I may not look like a wonderful guy. I haven't been a wonderful guy in the past. I may not act all…what….tender? But I know what is important to me. Do not screw my life over, Helen."

Helen thought of saying that when she had arrived, Sarah was upset about Dragna and Harry's illegal bookmaking. That, between the two of them, they had pulled Sarah and the babies into more muck. She was too tired to argue.

"All right, Harry. I'll try to fix it."

The bookkeeping finished, Helen paused at the telephone. Then she picked up the heavy black receiver and dialed again.

"Is Jessie there? Please tell her Helen is calling about Winona."

"Are you sure, Helen?" Jessie's voice sounded raspy with worry. Even Nazi-supporters whose children disappointed them grievously still loved them apparently.

"No. That's why I'm calling you."

"Drinking again?"

"Yes. Or maybe something else."

"Back to marijuana?"

"Do you know who might be giving it to her?" Helen had to do very little to make her voice tense. Jessie could interpret that as she wished.

"No."

"It could be someone you'd least expect. A close friend who can get to sources because of where they work or who they know."

The very limited contact that Helen had had with marijuana

users had suggested that both they and their suppliers were un-expected people, people who did not hang around street corners with lit reefers dangling from the corners of their mouths, but who worked in theater or were students at the college.

"Joe?"

"I don't think so."

"He does work in the motion picture industry," Jessie said.

"I really don't think it's him."

Jessie sighed. "I'll just have to keep better tabs on her. You'll have to help me."

"Of course." Helen paused, sighed loudly enough to be heard through the telephone, then said, "She is already...I don't know how to say this."

"Out with it." No wonder Jessie had such prominence in her world; her voice was the female version of Hitler's: imperious, self-assured, and frightening.

"She's jealous of my new relationship with you. And because she seems so good at just making things up, I am concerned she might come to you with some tale about me."

"Yes, that would be just like Winona. Don't worry. I don't act precipitously. And I have people to check out everything."

That did worry Helen. Check out everything, including Harry and Sarah, Forester Liquor, Helen's background? Did she have more than Ralph making reports to her?

"You won't say I told you if you talk to her?"

"Of course not. You've only done what I asked you to do and what I hope you will continue to do."

At eleven, Helen put out the "Closed" sign, locked the doors and walked slowly up the street toward the Woolworth two blocks away. Two blocks past the Woolworth was Joe's aunt's cleaning shop. Joe would have enough time to find her if she strolled.

In the entryway to a shoe repair shop, a man sat on the black and white tiled floor. He had a full beard and the musty smell of the unwashed. With a start, Helen realized he was the first homeless man she'd seen since she arrived in Glendale.

"Can you spare a dime, Miss?" he said.

Helen dug into her wallet and pulled out a quarter. She felt a peculiar sense of shame as she handed it over. The man carefully took the coin, not touching Helen in the process.

"Much appreciated."

At that, the door to the shop opened, a man several inches shorter than Helen, bearded and wrapped in a workman's apron, stepped out, and kicked sloppily at him.

"Get outta here before I call the beat cop," he said.

"Yes, sir." The man stood, his pants revealing brown patches sewn in with twine at the knees. "I'm gone."

"Trash has no business by my front entrance," the aproned man said to Helen. He stepped back into the shop and shut the door with a loud click.

A few yards away from the Woolworth entrance, Joe caught up to her. He was, as always, dressed impeccably, as if an unguarded sartorial error would be his undoing, the unmasking of a weakness he wanted well hidden.

"Joe, so good of you to meet me like this."

"Of course."

He matched his step to hers and they continued up the street. A middle-aged woman smiled at them as she exited from the Woolworth, clutching a loaded shopping bag. Helen smiled back and took Joe's hand.

"Winona came to see me."

Joe looked at her. "You and she are getting to be good friends."

"I wish that were the case. In fact, though, she came because she is upset with me and with you."

"With me?" Joe stopped walking and tugged at Helen's hand. "Whatever for?"

"Let's keep walking, Joe." Helen took a step out and he followed. "As near as I can make it, she doesn't like your aura. Or maybe it was Schwinn who didn't like it. I'm sorry, I was so upset when she was telling me that I didn't get it all."

Joe's face turned red, almost matching the fire hydrant next to him. He gripped her hand, grinding the bones of her fingers together. She tugged them loose and rubbed them.

"My aura." He voice gurgled as if he were speaking underwater.

"Yes. She said it was weak. You didn't take charge enough. Anyhow, Joe, I defended you."

Joe's eyes were fixed on a spot over Helen's left shoulder. The red had bleached away from his face leaving him with blotched cheeks and almost blue lips. He shook his head the way Helen had once seen a man do after he'd been punched in the stomach, slowly, as if doubting that it had happened to him.

"The dinner is still on." Helen took a step sideways so Joe's eyes lined up with her. "Maybe there'll be a time you can talk to her then."

"Not with Schwinn there." He'd caught his breath and his voice sounded almost normal. "After what she owes me, what I did as a friend to help her."

"Yes, well, this should be talked about face-to-face, right? Not on the phone." Helen kept her voice low and the tone, reasonable. "So, if not sometime tomorrow night, then another time.

"I have to get back to the store, Joe. But we can fix whatever the problem is, I'm sure." Helen leaned over and kissed him on the cheek. It was like kissing the side of a refrigerated peach, fuzzy, cold, and hard.

She turned and walked away.

Sarah and Harry sat on the couch listening to *Your Hit Parade.* Helen sat in the arm chair opposite them. Sarah hemmed a pair of pants for Ben and then darned one of Harry's socks, anything, it seemed to Helen, to avoid looking at her.

At the end of the show, Helen excused herself and went to her bedroom. As she was undressing to go to bed, there was a light tap on her door and a whispered, "My sister."

Helen wrapped her blouse around her, turned the door handle, and Sarah slid in to quietly sit on the bed. She patted the blanket and Helen, feeling like an obedient five-year-old, positioned herself next to her. Sarah smelled of baby powder and her shirt front was still damp in the aftermath of Benjamin's bath an hour before.

"He must have given you a drenching," Helen said, rubbing the hem of Sarah's shirt.

"A great storm in the bathtub and the boat went down."

"If he only knew," Helen said.

"May he never have to find out."

Helen folded her hands on her lap. Sarah reached out, palm down, and cradled them.

"I am worried for you," Sarah said.

Helen nodded, eyes down.

"I know."

"The whole time we are together in New York, you never made me so worried."

"Not even when I got into that fight in fifth grade?" Helen smiled, the memory of punching Theresa Walnitz still alive in her knuckles.

"No. I would worry if you were a little mouse, hiding in the corner of the school room. You were a bold girl. That was a good thing. So if you were alone you had this thing in you to be bold."

They sat, their breathing coordinated as if playing the same tune. To be brave in the face of loss was the legacy of Poland, where the ledger was written in blood.

"I started to do this for the wrong reasons," Helen said. "But now I think about Benjamin and Rachel, and what I want for them. No Nazis. I have to finish this, Sarah. We have no more oceans we can cross."

"Okay." Sarah squeezed Helen's hand and stood. "You keep them away from my children. You do not bring the trash into my home. Be careful, my sister."

As Sarah closed the door behind her, Helen began to rub her eyes in an effort to keep the tears off her cheeks. Then she dropped her blouse on the floor and kicked it into a corner before climbing into bed and pulling the covers over her head.

15

HELEN AWOKE BEFORE SIX, A miasma of a forgotten night-mare thickening her vision. Quietly she brushed her teeth and splashed cool water on her face. In the kitchen she filled the perco-lator with water and coffee and turned on the gas.

With a hot mug of coffee in her hands, she sat on the back step of the house, facing out to the empty clotheslines; the just-mowed grass, which kicked up a green smell that collided with the coffee's aroma; and the early morning sun in battle with a low mist. Her thoughts were running laps in her head, chased by dread.

Jessie and Joe were now focused on Winona, with Helen in their peripheral vision, she hoped. If Winona chose to tell her mother something negative about Helen, Jessie would ignore it as the tale of a drug-addled child. And, Joe would use the opportunity at Winona's to talk to her about his aura and its improving luster. She'd give them privacy and they'd give her time alone. It was the best she could think of.

The screen door banged twice against the door post behind Helen like a toy drum. Ben's warm weight and sleep-smelling breath fell against her back, pushing her forward because it was unexpected.

"Anni 'ennen," he said, his version of "Auntie Helen."

"Ben, my boy," she said, pulling him around and setting him on her legs. "Is Mommy up?"

He shook his head and smiled at her. She had never understood what writers meant by an impish grin until she'd met her nephew. When he smiled, it was never clear whether chaos or cuddles were in the offing.

"Hungry?"

He nodded. She rose up, took his hand, and re-entered the kitchen to make him breakfast.

The day warmed up slowly but definitively. By noon, Harry had turned on the fan in the living room, which began to move the air around in a pillowy breeze. Sarah put the children down for a nap after their early lunch and retired to the back step with the front section of the Sunday paper. In the kitchen, putting away the children's washed dishes, Helen could just catch the sound of Sarah's voice as she sounded out the hardest words aloud.

There was a quick triple knock at the front door.

"Sandy, come in," Helen heard Harry say.

The way men just intruded themselves into her life was annoying. Helen pushed a lock of hair up over her ear, draped the wet dish towel over the refrigerator handle to dry, and stepped into the living room, putting a careful smile on her face.

"We weren't expecting you," she said. Her voice was absent any emotion except slight puzzlement.

He stood two steps into the living room, wearing cream-colored slacks, a short-sleeved brown plaid shirt, and an exaggerated expression of delight she had last seen when he was rehearsing for a play. It would have projected all the way to the back of the theater, had they been in one.

"I just thought I'd drop by."

"Obviously."

She maintained her even tone and he continued his expression. Harry had stepped back, his gaze first on Sandy and then on Helen.

"Would you go for a little drive with me?"

"I haven't eaten lunch yet."

"We can stop for something."

"No."

She knew he wanted to find out more about her plan for the evening. But the more she tried to figure out how she was going to pull off getting the information from George, by joining his conversation with Schwinn, overhearing it, asking Schwinn later, the more tense she became. Never having spied before, she could only rely on her instincts with men and women. Instincts could not be pre-planned.

She was tired of the men in her life. Each one used her without a gesture to suggest that he concerned himself with her except as an afterthought in his grand plan. She ticked them off silently in her head as Sandy and Harry looked at each other as if searching for a clue as to what to do.

Joe, Nazi. Schwinn, Nazi and sadist. Harry, middle-class bookie. Sandy, spy and schemer. Ralph, spy and gangsters' friend. She had no luck with men and neither did her sister.

"No?" Sandy said it in the tone of a six-year-old deprived of dessert at dinner for no known reason.

Harry said, "Feel free to stay for lunch, Sandy. I know we have plenty."

Helen sighed, projecting as much weariness as she could. "Harry wants to be a gracious host, but it is just leftovers. If you stay, I'll have to eat cold cereal."

"Well, I wouldn't want that," Sandy said. His voice had a slight caustic sound, reminding Helen, in its way, of accidentally drinking water from a glass that still held a drop of dish soap.

Harry held up both palms in a "surrender" gesture. "I never argue with the women about food. Sorry, Sandy."

"It's okay. I'll call you tomorrow, Helen. But walk me to the car." His tone was firm.

"Sure." She stepped into the living room and out the front door, which Sandy carefully closed behind them.

"You know about Ralph," he said. She had backed up against his car, and he was leaning in as if they were two lovers. His voice was humming in her ear.

"Jessie has him picking up someone important to the Nazis today at the train station. It might be Fritz Kuhn. We lost track of him in New York."

"Kuhn?"

"Head of The Friends of New Germany and your friend, Schwinn's, boss. We last saw him at the big national meeting in March in Buffalo," he said.

She remembered Kuhn now from their earlier discussion. "How big could it be if it's Buffalo in winter?"

"You'd think small, but the hotel was teeming with them like lice. They march with the US flag and the Nazi salute…thousands of them."

She heard a catch in his voice and started to raise her hand to his cheek. Then he added, "Anyhow, if it is him, he likes to dress just like Hitler. So compliment him."

"A meeting between Kuhn and Schwinn?" she said.

"Could be." Sandy picked up her half-raised hand and kissed the palm. "Stay safe. I'm sending in a rescue team if I don't hear from you by eight tonight."

Helen nibbled on a chicken leg left over from Friday night's dinner, then dropped it in the garbage can, half-eaten. She went into her bedroom, which was the temperature of a warm bath, lifted the window for a little breeze, and curled up on the bed.

The clock read 3:57 when she opened her eyes. Joe would be picking her up outside Forester Liquor in about forty-five minutes. She had told him that coming to the house and ringing the bell would wake the children from their long Sunday naps. He didn't know anything about children and naps except, apparently, that waking children was a bad idea.

From her closet, she chose a linen spring dress that emphasized her bodice and her waist, without revealing a hint of flesh below the collar bone. The butterfly sleeves were modest. The dress's muted grass green and sky blue plaid reminded her of Easter egg pastels.

Overall, the impact was as far from the hard-edged chic of high-end fashion as she could take without being insufferably Frau-ish. When she had seen it in the heap of clothing from Kate Hepburn, she could not imagine Hepburn in it either. And the tags still on the dress confirmed that it had never been worn. What would it be like to spend forty-nine dollars on a dress and toss it aside unused?

Helen left her hair loose, tendrils curling on her shoulders and down her back. Her eyebrows were thicker than fashion called for, but it saved her from buying an eyebrow pencil. She brushed mascara on her lower eyelashes, and smoothed a light pink color onto her lips. Her ivory skin required nothing. Satisfied without looking in a mirror, she slipped on a pair of pastel sandals with a low heel, and walked out the door.

"You look lovely, Helen." Joe opened his car door for her and she slid in. He put the six-pack of Tornbergs that she had taken from the Forester's locker and put it in the back seat.

He was turned out in cream linen trousers and a short-sleeved taupe shirt, opened at the collar. In the back seat he had tossed a white tennis sweater. He was definitely calmer than he had been on Saturday, when she had told him about Winona and the aura.

"Do you think I should have brought a sweater, too?"

"Well, it's too late now. And if you're cold, maybe Winona has a shawl."

She sat, knees firmly together, midway between Joe and the door. He pulled out into the boulevard with grim caution. After they had driven a few blocks in silence, she sidled two inches closer to him.

"I'm enjoying being with you and your friends, Joe. I hope tonight goes well." He pursed his lips together, almost a prelude to a reprimand.

"My aunt is not happy that I am taking you to this dinner."

"Did I do something to upset Elsa, Joe?" She said it in the same tone she would have used to ask what he had eaten the night before, flat, neutral, and conversational. But her mouth went dry.

"She met your sister once, when she went to Forester's to buy beer, which she rarely drinks, but needed for a recipe. Your sister helped her."

Joe looked at her and Helen nodded, her face a mask of attentiveness.

"They spoke, not for a long time, mostly about the beer choices and cost."

The light ahead turned yellow and Joe pressed on the brake. Helen slid forward as the car stopped a second shy of the light turning red, then repositioned herself. Sarah would never have been rude to a customer or mentioned her origins to a complete stranger.

"My aunt states that Sarah, and so of course, you, are a mongrel breed. She could hear it in your sister's accent and how her poor grammar reflects that."

"A mongrel breed?" Helen squeezed her voice into a flat package, absent any emotion except slight incredulity. "You mean she thinks we're...Jewish?"

Joe winced and said nothing. His lips returned to a pursed position. Helen could imagine his aunt's lips in that same tight, disdainful pose.

So, his aunt suspected that Sarah's accent had Yiddish inflections, but she wasn't sure. How could she be, when Sarah was fluent in Polish and German, but the Polish and German of a constantly fluid border, the Polish and German of people who lived away from cities and inside despair? If his aunt had been sure, Joe wouldn't be having this conversation with her.

"We're not Jewish, Joe. The part of Germany we came from had Jews, sure, and Poles, and who knows what else. We didn't grow up speaking High German, like people in Berlin. But, we're not Jewish.

"Look, I spoke to Jessie yesterday," Helen said. "She actually had an investigator investigate us. She doesn't seem to have an issue with me. Nor does Hermann." She put her hand lightly on Joe's forearm, which was warm and smoothly tanned.

"I know. And I told her that. But my aunt has her opinions."

"And you, what is your opinion?"

"I'm loyal to the cause. Whatever promotes and secures Aryan superiority has my support."

"Well and good. But I asked for your opinion of me and my supposed 'mongrel' nature."

Helen left her hand where it was and looked at Joe's profile. His eyes were fixed on the street light, which turned green as she spoke. In the act of shifting gears, he shook her hand off and she placed it on the seat between them.

"As you say, Helen, Jessie and Hermann and even Winona have no problem with you. I told you because I thought you should know. Possibly even speak to Sarah about it, so she is aware."

"I can't fix her accent. There are some things about everyone that can't be changed." The words came out quietly but with an underlying current of tension.

Joe's grip on the steering wheel tightened so that his knuckles merged out of his clenched fingers with the skin stretched taut.

"I don't know what you mean. Almost everything about people can be changed as long as they have the will to do it. Only those races…" He removed one hand and flicked it toward the window as if people were flies.

"We are the master race, Joe. I know that. I will ask Sarah to work on her accent. She wouldn't want people to have the wrong idea."

They drove the rest of the way in silence. At the intersection of Wilshire and Santa Monica Boulevards, the red light was endless. Helen looked around, scanning the cars as they queued up at the light, the department stores, the sidewalks, the phone booth at the corner, and pedestrians. Los Angeles was its own motion picture, complete with Silver Shirts banging on the Forester cottage door.

Joe gripped the wheel at ten o'clock and two o'clock, looking to Helen as if he thought driving the car in the right way would change his feelings about men. The only sound they made together was winding down the windows as the outside temperature inched higher.

By the time Joe turned up the dirt road to Murphy Ranch, the sun was tilted over toward the Pacific, casting sloping shadows of trees and cliffside onto the car. He unlocked the gate with his key and pushed it back. The gate kicked up dust onto his pants and he slapped at his trouser legs.

Helen considered that he would only have to re-slap himself when he closed the gate. But she could understand the underlying turmoil that drove him. She had had to restrain herself from chewing on her inner lip for the entire ride. Why did tension cause minor acts of self-harm, as if people wanted to beat themselves up for having problems? Weren't the problems, themselves, enough?

The house door stood open. As soon as Joe parked the car, Helen opened up her door, got out, and started toward the steps. Somehow she felt that the first person to see Winona would have an advantage. Joe might have thought so as well, because he trotted up and then took the veranda steps two at a time, holding the Tornbergs beer.

Hermann Schwinn stood just inside the door, the glare of the sun and the shadows of the interior making him almost invisible. Joe almost stumbled into him, but caught himself.

"Hermann, how good to see you," he said, holding out his hand.

As Helen stepped further into the foyer, she saw Schwinn take Joe's hand for a half-second and drop it. Then he turned toward Helen and smiled.

Schwinn was wearing a pair of dark trousers, with sharp creases pressed military-fashion into the legs, and a white, short-sleeved shirt with a bronze iron cross hanging from a white-bordered black ribbon pinned to the pocket.

"Helen," he said.

"Hello."

He raised her hand to his lips and kissed it, clicking his heels together. She hoped her mild shudder was seen as a frisson of sexual tension as his warm, thin lips left a drop of saliva on her skin.

"Your ribbon interests me," she said.

Joe hovered next to her, so close that she could feel his body's heat on her back.

"This." He waved in a predictable effort at false modesty. "Yes, my troops insist that I wear it. It is fashioned after the German Great War medal, but I'm sure you know that."

"Yes. Germany sent my mother one after my father's death. We buried her with it." This untraceable lie was offered with a sad gaze.

"Which one?" That was Joe's voice, insistent over her shoulder.

"I was so young. I just remember the colors, which were blue and orange, I think. And my mother slapping my hand ever so lightly when I wanted to put it in my hair."

"Of course," Joe said.

"You were just a child," Schwinn said, picking up her hand again and beginning to raise it to his mouth.

The odor of roasting chicken was accompanied by a door slamming. Winona stepped into the living room and said, "Why are you all standing in the hall? Come in, come in." She wore an egg-yolk yellow dress with cap sleeves that hung on her like a sack that had been oddly tied in the middle with a slim green patent leather belt.

"Is that chicken?" Helen said. "If it is, it smells divine."

"Yes, yes. And Lupita or Fransuelo or whatever the maid-of-the-day's name is just left, so we have the place to ourselves!"

"It was probably Maria," Joe said. "Did Jessie send her over?"

"Nice to see you, Helen," Winona said. "And you, too, Joe." The latter was offered as if acknowledging Helen's pet dog, which was expected to stay on the porch. Joe winced.

"So if Maria is gone," Joe said, persisting in his effort to be seen, "who'll help you serve?"

"Why, I thought you would. Be a dear and make sure the bird isn't going to burn. And check on the corn while you're at it."

Winona was having no part of leaving Schwinn and Helen alone. She walked over and gently tugged on Helen's arm to move her into the living room. Helen felt almost grateful for her jealousy.

Joe walked through the living room, the dining room, and into what Helen assumed was the kitchen.

"Where are the beer mugs," he asked, calling through the open door.

"I don't know." Winona's tone suggested a woman who had never been in any kitchen, let alone her own.

Still, Helen thought, she must know where some things were, beer glasses being among them. She seemed to drink enough.

"Helen, go in and see if you can scrounge around in the cabinets and find them. I assume the beer is from you, and *danke*. The bottle opener is in the top drawer next to the fridge."

Winona knew where the vital kitchen equipment was.

"Now, Winona," Schwinn said, "Helen is your guest."

Helen smiled at Winona. "It's fine. I'll go find them."

For Helen to be alone with Schwinn at this point would irritate Winona's jealousy like a skin rash inflamed by heat. To bend to her whimsy was far better.

"See, Hermann darling, she's my friend."

Winona had decided to have dinner in the formal dining room at a table suitable for twelve. She sat at one end, put Schwinn at the other, and sat Helen and Joe facing each other in the lonely middle.

Joe had carefully plated the chicken, mounded the corn kernels in a bowl, and located, in the refrigerator, a fresh lettuce salad, which Maria had apparently made earlier for the dinner. An apricot pie sat on the counter. Helen spied a bowl of whipped cream next to the salad when she was in the kitchen.

Everything, except the pie and whipped cream, but including a large crystal pitcher of ice water, now sat on the table.

"What lovely settings," Helen said.

The fork tines were tarnished to a moldy black. The white damask table cloth had been tucked away in a linen closet for so long that it popped up like a series of small military tents along the fold lines.

The china, however, was the color of thick cream, with hand-painted gold and green fleur-de-lis on the edges. It had the appearance of something delicate but very strong. Helen had not worked in a fine department store without visiting all its floors for daydream shopping. The china was exquisite.

"From my wedding. It was Joe's first expedition with me, to help me with my registry."

Joe carried the platter of chicken over to Helen and she stabbed a thigh for her plate. He turned toward Winona.

Schwinn cleared his throat and the table fell silent.

"I was wondering, Helen, when you might have the opportunity to visit the Aryan Bookstore? My good friend, Theimlitz, is eager to have you come."

"My schedule is so tight. I usually only have Sundays free."

"I could have him open just for you."

"Hermann, what a grand idea. We can have our own private book party." Winona smiled, slid a breast onto her plate, then added corn from the bowl which sat in front of her.

Joe continued as waiter.

"I thought, my dear, that Norman was due back this week for an extended stay." Schwinn's voice had a cool solicitousness Helen associated with a doctor delivering moderately bad, but not life-threatening, news.

Helen took the opportunity to cut into the chicken. The juices oozed out of the golden roasted skin. The aroma was of rosemary, lemon, and spices she could not quite identify, but which carried an exotic, non-European flavor. The flesh was tender.

If a refugee knew anything, she knew to eat when food was there. She took a second bite and then a fork full of corn. The kernels were fresh, sweet, and coated in a butter sauce.

"The food is wonderful," Helen said.

Winona looked at her as if she could not, for a moment, remember who she was. Then she turned back to Schwinn.

"Yes, he's back on Tuesday."

"Then we could hardly have a small soirée without him, could we?"

Helen put down her fork. "I am tied up on Sundays for several weeks with my family. They come first for me. So please don't plan anything on my account."

The look on Winona's face was relief and pleasure; the look on Schwinn's the mirror opposite. Both looks faded quickly.

Joe began talking about *The Red Network*, which he had bought at the bookstore. He intoned a paragraph from memory as if giving a speech and added a biting comment about Jews and Communism. The conversation swung away from Norman's imminent return to the grand plans of Germany to save the world from Communism.

Whenever Schwinn's attention turned to Helen, she smiled and put another forkful of chicken in her mouth. The only word she said during dinner was "delicious."

Just as the apricot pie and whipped cream came to the table, the doorbell rang.

"I'll get it," Schwinn said.

He got up and walked into the foyer. A minute later he returned and said, "George is a little early. And, Winona, we're expecting your mother with a very special guest." He looked at his watch. "They should be here in about half an hour. You'll be excited when our guest comes. Do finish dessert without me."

Winona sighed. "Don't I get to know who it is?" Schwinn shook his head and smiled as if teasing a four year old about a treat.

"At least take some pie and coffee to George, then," Winona said, turning away, her voice sad.

"My dear, we will keep you company," Helen said. "And we'll work with the Ouija board after we clear the table."

The pie crust sat in Helen's stomach like buttered lead.

"I am so full from your dinner," she said. "I think I need a little walk before it gets dark."

"Do you want me to come?" Winona's voice was flat and disinterested.

"Not if you don't want to. Maybe Joe can give me one of those whiskery things for the snakes."

At that, Joe got up and followed her towards the front door. To their left, Helen glimpsed Schwinn and George sitting opposite each other, two dainty china cups for the coffee in front of them on the cocktail table.

"Really, Joe, I'm just trying to give you a chance to speak to Winona privately about the auras and stuff. That whole mess that we talked about. I couldn't bear a rift between you." Helen tucked her hand into Joe's as they walked to the swimming pool.

"I'll just stay outside for fifteen minutes or so. This is a good place to sit."

Joe watched her settle onto a chaise lounge. "If you see a coyote, wave your hands, stomp your feet, and throw something," he said. "Here's a switch." He plucked one from the container.

"A coyote?" She could handle a rat or two, but rattlesnakes and coyotes made her feel as if she'd been dropped in the middle of a Gene Autry western, with no gun and in sandals.

"Yes. They come down for water at the pool around this time. But I'm sure you'll be all right." Joe turned and walked back to the house, his long stride in contrast with his slumped shoulders.

The tinges of color representing Joe faded towards the house. Helen got up from the chair and slipped around the corner of the pool to the path towards the bolted, barred storage shed.

The front windows were shuttered. Walking around to the back, Helen saw a single small, dusty window covered with mesh about a foot above her eye level. To her left a pile of discarded pieces of lumber lay in the dirt like a giant's toy blocks. Helen brought over two pieces, holding their cobwebbed faces away from her dress.

As she stacked the second on top of the first, a splinter stabbed into her thumb causing a trickle of blood. She pulled the wood needle out with her teeth and licked her skin. Then she balanced on the blocks and grabbed at the thin window sill.

About a dozen crates were stacked on the floor. *Walther PPK, Deutschland* was stenciled on all but one, which read *Česka Zbrojovka vz. 30.* She recognized the languages as German and Czech, and neither contained beer, whose logos she would have recognized, but that was as far as she could go.

"Helen?" Joe shouted her name. "Commander Kuhn is here with Jessie. Where are you?"

She walked around to the front of the storage shed, smiling. "I got restless so I took a walk. They're here earlier than expected."

Joe closed the few yards between them, dirt kicking up at his heels. Helen tilted her head and continued her smile, face muscles frozen.

"How did the talk with Winona go? Are things patched up, I hope?"

Grabbing her arm, Joe pulled at her. She fell forwards, grabbing onto the back of his shirt for balance. Her chin collided with his.

"I don't believe you," he said in a hoarse whisper.

She pulled her head away and tugged sharply down on the fabric of his shirt. It rode up against his Adam's apple.

"Let me go."

Helen mimicked his whisper, aware that she did not want shouts to reach the house any more than he did. Pulling down on Joe's shirt again so his head snapped back, she kneed him in the groin as hard as she could. He released her arm and reached for the crotch of his pants with both hands, going down to one knee. She leaned down, picked up a handful of dirt, and threw it in his eyes. Then she turned and ran towards the house.

Ralph was standing on the veranda, one hand shading his eyes as he looked down the path. As Helen turned the curve, she saw him take two steps at a time and sprint towards her.

"What happened?" he said as he came up to her.

"Joe saw me at the shed." She panted out the words, looking towards the porch. Jessie was not in sight.

"You bitch." Joe's voice careened into her ears. He staggered up the path, one hand still cupping his balls. "Get her, Ralph. She's a—"

At the sound of Joe's voice, Ralph had moved down the path. Helen saw a massive fist plummet into Joe's chin with a sound like a meteor hitting the earth. Then Joe was on his back.

"Joe's been bitten by a coyote," Ralph said, heaving the unconscious Joe up. He staggered back towards the house, with Joe's feet dragging. "He's a heavy mother…"

Ralph reached the car and Helen opened the back door. As Joe slumped across the seat, Ralph said in her ear, "Tell them I'm taking him to the hospital. He'll either listen to reason or die of the bite."

"Reason?" She froze over Joe's leg and Ralph bent it into the car at the knee like a snapped twig and slammed the door.

"Go in the house, Helen. Jessie is watching us."

Jessie stood on the porch. As Helen looked over, she turned back towards the open door, her floral-patterned dress twirled up and settling back on her calves.

"I'm sure Ralph will take care of whatever Joe's problem is, Helen. It's good he heard Joe calling and went to help. I was just in time to see him pick Joe up off the ground. Ralph hurried so to get us here and isn't that lucky for Joe."

"Ralph, be back by eight." Jessie's voice was full of the languid assurance of the wealthy.

"Yes, ma'am," Ralph said.

Helen excused herself and went to the first floor guest bathroom. Once in the white-tiled space, she sat on the edge of the bathtub, her legs shaking and her fingers numb, washed her hands with French scented soap and warm water in the porcelain sink, giving special attention to her thumb, dusted off her dress, slapped her sandals together over the tub, and prepared her story.

"Gentlemen, I've interrupted your meeting with this little domestic drama. I apologize."

George, Schwinn, and Fritz Kuhn had stood when she entered the living room, trailed by Winona. Jessie remained seated on the leather sofa, a Martini glass in her hand.

"Commander Kuhn," Schwinn said, "let me introduce our Helen Rice."

Kuhn was thickly built, with the beginning of a double chin, and the receding hairline of a man in his forties. His watery blue eyes starred at Helen with long pauses between blinks. At the introduction he did not hold out his hand, but nodded peremptorily.

Helen decided to dip into a small curtsey, cued in her mind by some historical movie she had seen. At that, Kuhn smiled.

"Your uniform, Commander Kuhn, is so much like the one I've seen Der Führer wearing in newsreels. The German Cross, all the ribbons. So…." She let her voice fade away.

"So what, Fräulein?" Kuhn's English was stuffed inside a German accent.

"Powerful." Helen looked at the floor, as if afraid.

"Ah, but never to be used against our fine German women. Are you married, Helen?" Kuhn said.

"No." She lifted her head and looked at him directly.

"Pity," he said. "Hermann mentioned that you were orphaned after the Great War. Where exactly in the Fatherland were you born?"

"East of Breslau, Commander. So far east that we had riffraff of all sorts."

"Riffraff," Schwinn said. "A good lead-in. With your permission, Commander, I'd like to put the question to Helen. Her response will be helpful in understanding how our actions will be viewed, should they ever come to light."

Jessie sipped the last of her cocktail and put the glass on the table. "Gentlemen," she said, "do stop cluttering around Helen."

"Perhaps Helen would like a drink?" George had a shot of amber Scotch which he held out to her.

"I don't drink liquor."

"Joe's aura is pretty bad alright." Winona leaned in to speak in Helen's ear.

Helen said, "Mmmm."

George and Schwinn took posts around Kuhn.

"If your sister's neighbor had…say…mice," Schwinn paused, then continued, "and her cat chased them all into your sister's home, what would you tell your sister to do?"

Helen shrugged. "I cannot imagine telling my sister how to run her house. But, surely she would think to set traps and get her own cat."

Schwinn said, "I agree. Now excuse us, Helen and Winona, we have traps and cats to discuss."

The Ouija box, with its "Try Your Mystic Touch" slogan, sat on the now-cleared dining room table. The board itself, worn at the edges and scratched lightly all over the surface, was open near Winona's chair. The planchette rested near the "Yes," reminding Helen of a large, legless bug.

She had taken the first turn at Winona's insistence. According to Ouija, she was lying about her age and was really twenty-seven. At this, Helen shrugged and smiled.

"Who knows for sure? I go by what my sister put on our papers."

Winona was now working on the board. She had declined to tell Helen what her question was. But, gauging from her focus on the planchette's position, it was important to her.

"Is it my turn, now?" Helen said.

Winona shook her head as her hand began to float the planchette over the board again. At least fifteen minutes had passed since they had begun this ridiculous and deeply boring game.

"I need to go to the bathroom again, Winona, dear."

A soft, burping "Okay," came from Winona's mouth.

Helen walked into the foyer and pressed herself against the wall nearest the living room.

"An accident?" George's back was to Helen but she could hear him clearly.

"We'll tell you what to order. You arrange to switch it for the fuel Von Karman wants. Boom—all gone. No more rocket project at Caltech. Bye-bye Guggenheim money, Hungarian Jewish scientist, and pot-smoking assistants," Kuhn said.

"No more Helen Parsons to deal with," George said.

"Tell George what we plan for Einstein," Schwinn said.

"A biking accident. He is a very distracted bicyclist. A quiet Princeton street with no one around. Ahh, our motorist is so apologetic," Kuhn said.

"And James Franck?"

Schwinn was ticking off the names of Jewish scientists, Helen realized. Einstein had fled the Nazis for the United States. Von Karman had also. *The neighbor got a cat...*

"Neils Bohr, Otto Stern, Robert Oppenheimer. We have plans for them all," Kuhn said.

Helen took a deep breath and stepped into the living room. George saw her first.

"Helen," he said, standing. The two others followed suit.

"Gentlemen, I did not want to leave without saying *auf wiedersehen.* I have had an eventful day here and the great honor of meeting you, Commander Kuhn. But I have work tomorrow."

Kuhn bowed slightly from the waist. "The pleasure was all mine, Fräulein."

"Who will drive you home?" Schwinn had a vulpine smile on his face and George seemed poised to offer.

"My dear friend, Winona."

"And the job? Any decision?" George said.

"May I have until Tuesday to discuss it with my family?"

"Of course."

With just one hand on the wheel, Winona kneaded Helen's arm rhythmically in her imitation of sympathy. Only the need to shift gears stopped her, at which Helen moved as far as she could toward the passenger side door.

"I'm done with Joe," Winona said.

"I'm not surprised." Helen's voice reflected the indifference she felt.

"Ouija confirmed that it was Joe's bad aura affecting mine."

"Why don't you talk to your mother about it?" All Helen wanted was Winona's silence, a wish as unlikely to be filled as the wish to have Winona drive safely. Maybe raising her mother's Medusa-like image would freeze her into not talking.

There was a minute of silence before Winona said, "Would you talk to Mother?"

Helen rested her forehead on the window. They were just nearing the intersection of Wilshire and Santa Monica. She readied herself.

Winona reached over in her perilous way and grabbed Helen's thigh. Shaking it, she said, "Helen, speak to my mother."

"Okay."

Replacing her hand on the steering wheel, Winona smiled.

"It's probably too late to do it tonight," she said. "I'll pick you up first thing tomorrow morning at your house."

"No. And there's a red light!"

Winona slammed on the brake. Helen slid forward sharply banging her upper arm on the dashboard. The car stalled out, nose well into the crosswalk at the intersection of Santa Monica and Wilshire, as horns tooted around them.

"Say 'yes' or I won't take you home."

On Wilshire, a half-block up, Helen saw the well-lit telephone booth occupied by a small, short-haired, trousered woman.

"That's fine, Winona. I'll get out here." Helen grabbed her purse and pushed open the door. Slamming it behind her, she strode toward the Wilshire sidewalk, while the angry honking of car horns continued behind her.

Helen watched as Winona restarted the car and made a hesitant, sloppy U-turn. She waited until the car was a block away before proceeding to the now-empty phone booth.

"Hello, police? There's a woman driving very erratically on Santa Monica Boulevard just south of Wilshire. She might be drunk or something."

Helen offered Winona's license plate precisely, 3 B 23 89.

Even if Winona wasn't arrested, even if the police didn't find the reefer she kept in her purse, being stopped would put her off her game, would rattle her enough that she would just want to stay home tomorrow, under the covers with her pot and her Scotch. If people did have auras, Winona's would be exactly as described.

Helen reached into her coin purse for the next dime.

The phone rang at Murphy Ranch. "This is Mrs. Murphy" Jessie said.

Helen's teary voice offered up the account of a weaving, nausea-inducing roller coaster car ride from which she just had to exit out of fear for her life.

"Oh, Jessie, I tried but I just couldn't stop her from drinking. And now I'm afraid, because I saw a police car pull out and start to follow her."

"A night in jail might do her some good." Jessie was in full Teutonic mother form. "You get a cab and go home."

The third dime went into the slot. Helen turned her back away from the man who was standing with foot-tapping impatience next to the phone booth.

Sandy pulled up twenty minutes later.

16

OTHER THAN ASK IF SHE was really all right, Sandy drove without a word. Helen tried to talk to him, but he recommended that she focus on what she overheard instead.

Helen closed her eyes to focus on making the scene vivid again, like a movie reel she could replay. She was on the fourth round, tapping the pencil against her sore thumb, when the car stopped. The only thing she had written was *Česka Zbrojovka vz 30.*

They were in front of Leon Lewis' house, parked in the driveway. The front porch light was off and the house was dark.

Sandy motioned her up the driveway. He unlatched the wrought iron gate to the backyard, walked over to the backdoor and tapped so lightly on it that it blended with the rustle of the breeze.

The door opened and Leon let them both in. Silently, they walked through the kitchen down the hall and into a heavily draped bedroom lit by a single low watt lamp on a bridge table in the center of the room, with four uncomfortable looking bridge chairs at each side. The walls were draped with thick wool blankets.

Sitting on the floor was a machine of some sort that Helen had never seen before although it reminded her of a four-foot-tall modified movie projector. On its face were two large reels, one loaded with tape and the other empty, several switches and a microphone.

"It'll record everything you say. Our newest purchase." Leon patted it. "A Blattnerphone by that German industrial powerhouse, AG Farben. The tape is so sharp it'll slice your fingers."

Helen considered, briefly, that a woman who took short-hand was now out of a job. She sighed and sat down at the table. Leon turned on the tape recorder, and then he and Sandy sat also.

Helen went point by point over what she had seen in the shed and overheard at the Murphy Ranch, reconstructing the exact sentences, the pauses and the comments.

"Is that all?" A sheen of perspiration coated Leon's forehead as if worry was seeping out in small drops.

"It's enough, Leon," Sandy said. "A plot to kill the leading émigré scientists. Eleven or so cases of service pistols and one case of light machine guns."

"Is that what they were?" Helen felt light-headed and the apricot pie crust wanted to come back up.

"Yes. This is huge." Leon sighed and offered his pleased-uncle smile.

"Is it too late to call headquarters?" Sandy started towards the door.

"Never too late," Leon said. "You know where the phone is."

Sandy stepped into the hall and shut the door behind him. His absence felt like a hole pricked in a balloon. Helen sank back against the chair.

"Will the ADL be able to protect them?"

Leon nodded. "We will try. And we have allies. Now, my dear girl, what about you?"

Considering a possible threat to Sarah and the children made her hands tremble in a frigid sea wind only she could feel.

"I'm worried about Sarah and the children. Also, Harry and the store."

"Ralph will talk sense into Joe, I'm sure." Leon had a cold smile. "Some photos of young Joe with what appears to be a very, very close male companion have come our way. And Elsa, well, it turns out one of her grandmothers was Jewish. It's wonderful how Germans keep such accurate records of births and baptisms and such.

"It'll be enough to either scare them out of the Bund and away from Schwinn, or, even better, to flip them to our side. Since we could, of course, make no promise as to what a disappointed Nazi with a gun and a predilection for hurting others might do to a homosexual and a Jewish woman who'd ingratiated themselves into the movement. They might be spies. If not, well, coyotes have rabies."

Helen reached for Sandy's hand in the car as he drove her back to Sarah. He entwined his fingers in hers.

"You must come back to New York," he said.

Helen nodded. Removing herself from Sarah and the babies was the best option. Bookkeeping, store clerk, waitress. She didn't care.

"I'll talk to our connections tomorrow. We owe you for this. We'll get you a good job, one that pays well. Better than being a bookkeeper or a clerk."

Helen opened the door and slipped off her shoes before entering the house. It was just before one in the morning. As she pushed the latch closed, Sarah appeared in the hall, wrapping her bathrobe around her, its whiteness giving her a ghostly quality in the dark hall. She made the "shh" gesture with her finger and pointed to the living room.

Sinking onto the sofa, Helen looked around the room which was barely illuminated by the ambient, yellow light of the street lamp on the sidewalk just outside. The objects had an outsized feeling because she could make out their bulk, but not their color or detail. Radio, ottoman, club chair, clock…everything carefully chosen by her sister and her husband for their solidity and durability.

Sarah sat down next to her.

"Are you done with this now?" Sarah leaned over and whispered but in the quiet of the room, it sounded like a gunshot.

"I'm going back to New York, Sarah."

Sarah touched Helen's face softly with an open palm. "My sister…."

Helen left for the store, kissing her nephew and niece on the head as she walked out of the kitchen. The air was already warm and scented with jasmine as she stepped onto the sidewalk. As she walked she tried to re-pin a stray lock of hair, but dropped the bobby pin near the foot of the streetlight two doors down from Sarah and Harry's house. She leaned over to pick it up but almost dropped it again. The iron filigree work on the light's base was a swastika pattern.

The lights had been there for a few years, at least, she reminded herself. The city meant nothing sinister by the design. Still her heart was pounding and she looked around as if expecting a uniformed Nazi to appear. If she had needed anything to remind her that the country was at risk, that was it.

When Harry came into the store an hour later, she said, "I'm going back to New York."

"Not surprised." He stood next to her behind the counter.

"You should be okay here. Business, meaning the sale of liquor and cigarettes, seems to be picking up. I can't say about the ponies."

Harry smiled his snake-smile. "Your sister is worried about you."

"If I go back, it'll be better."

"It is never better between sisters, Helen. You should know that. But," he held up his hand, "you evened the score a little between the two of you. I know this even if she doesn't."

"I have a little extra money," Helen said, thinking of the Irving Thalberg supplement and the gambling money, now almost $150. "I thought I'd put it in a bank account for the babies. You could be the other signatory, Harry, in case you needed the money to keep them safe."

"From?" His voice sounded puzzled.

"From dangers, Harry. There are always dangers. Or you could be short one month or...." She trailed off.

"You are more like your sister than you know. She sees a threat in every shadow on the street. Look around you, Helen."

He waved his arm towards the street just beyond the store's windows. An older couple was out for a walk. A young mother, passing them, pushed her baby's stroller. Two cars waited for the red light to change to green.

"This is Glendale, California in the US of A."

"Okay, Harry."

A message left with the Murphy butler, a quick call to George, and her California life seemed rolled up like a carpet for storage. Sandy called to tell her he had booked her railway ride back to New York.

Helen sat in the train car with her valise tucked against her leg, an old *Motion Picture* magazine on her lap. The car was half-empty, a signal, she thought, of westward migration. The seat next to her was unoccupied.

A hand suddenly pressed on her shoulder. "It seems urgent business takes me back to New York," Sandy said.

Startled, she slid over and he sat down, dropping an envelope on her lap as he did so. The warmth from her shoulder seeped through her body.

"Look in the envelope, Helen, and let me know if you want to do this."

Join us on

June 13

for a Fund-raiser at the

Yorkville Casino

New York, New York

All proceeds to support the

New Friends of Germany

Commander Fritz Kuhn in attendance

She scanned the words quickly.

"Care to go with me?"

She nodded and turned her face towards his for a kiss.

Epilogue

JESSIE MURPHY IS LISTED AS the owner of Murphy Ranch in real estate papers. Whether she actually lived or was a shell for ownership is unknown. Winona and Norman were listed as residents of the ranch. What their actual relationship was to Jessie Murphy is unknown.

There are numerous reports, though none authoritative, that the Murphy Ranch was raided by the FBI in December, 1941. Captain Schmidt, a known spy, may have been taken into custody during that raid. The Murphy Ranch is now a graffiti-ridden ruin frequented by hikers.

In December, 1939, Fritz Kuhn was sent to prison for embezzlement. While he languished there, his citizenship was revoked and he was summarily returned to Germany upon his release.

Hermann Schwinn lost his citizenship in 1940, while in prison. He was a defendant in the Great Sedition Trial of 1944.

The Anti-Defamation League and other Jewish organizations were actively engaged in infiltrating pro-Nazi organizations. Leon Lewis was their representative in Los Angeles. The primary source of funding for the ADL in Southern California, the equivalent in today's dollars of $500,000 a year, came from movie moguls, like Louis B. Mayer and Irving Thalberg.

Acknowledgments

F IRST, I WANT TO THANK my husband, Stan Mishook, whose steadfast love and encouragement supported me throughout the writing of this novel. Robbi Nester, a fine poet and professor of poetics, served as the initial editor and her gentle insistence on making the characters more vivid was pivotal in their development. Matt Balson, my publisher at Berwick Court Publishing, worked with me tirelessly; no fact or grammatical construction was too minor to escape his keen notice.

Every historical novel has its roots in reality. I relied on the works of historians, journalists and authors to point me in the right direction in the world of 1936. *Swastika Nation: Fritz Kuhn and the Rise and Fall of the German-American Bund* by Arnie Bernstein (St. Martin's Press, 2013, NY), *Lion of Hollywood: The Life and Legend of Louis B. Mayer* by Scott Eyman (Simon and Schuster, 2005, NY), and *Hollywood and Hitler, 1933-1939* by Thomas Doherty (Columbia University Press, 2013, NY) proved invaluable.

California State University Northridge's digital library offered the entire exhibit of *In Our Own Backyard: Resisting Nazi Propaganda in Southern California 1933-1945,* complete with documents and photographs of places like the Deutsches Haus Tavern taken at the time. *Life* magazine's archives provided countless pictures and articles that helped set the stage, as did the archives of the *Los Angeles Times*. Laura Rosenzweig's intriguing article in the Jewish Review of Books on *Hollywood's Anti-Nazi Spies* (Winter 2014) gave further support to my own research into the ADL's spying efforts.

What would we do without the world wide web and the extraordinary availability of material of all sorts? Thanks to whoever put that charming Cary Grant movie, *The Gambling Ship* (1933), set off the coast of Los Angeles, on You Tube. And those who wrote articles about Murphy Ranch, Jessie Murphy and that entire group, thank you, too.